SHE HAD NOTHING TO FEAR...

Gently, he lowered her to the sand, his body easing down upon her. His mouth crushed down on hers.

"How I have dreamed of this moment, this time," he murmured, his lips barely touching hers.

They lay together, neither wanting the moment to end. The closeness, the wonder of it all, was too overwhelming for either to comprehend.

EXCEPT DEREK HIMSELF!

At last, Derek rolled to his side, still holding her tightly. His lips mere inches from hers, he murmured, "Love me, Julie. Love me for all time, because now that I've found you, I'll never let you go again."

And then the sweet passion was returning, dimmed for Julie only by the gnawing realization that he had demanded that she love him for all time. . . . but he had professed no vows of undying devotion . . . he was taking, not giving, and despite the ecstasy that flowed through her veins, her heart shuddered with an unfamiliar sadness.

SOULS AFLAME

PATRICIA HAGAN

AVON
PUBLISHERS OF BARD, CAMELOT AND DISCUS BOOKS

SOULS AFLAME is an original publication of Avon
Books. This work has never before appeared in book form.

AVON BOOKS
A division of
The Hearst Corporation
959 Eighth Avenue
New York, New York 10019

First Avon Printing, April, 1980

AVON TRADEMARK REG. U.S. PAT. OFF. AND IN
OTHER COUNTRIES, MARCA REGISTRADA, HECHO EN
U.S.A.

Printed in the U.S.A.

For my mother,
Lavinia Wright Hagan,
with love

A special thanks to my aunt,
Ramona Wright Scarboro,
for the use of her valuable
Civil War Library

✵ Chapter One ✵

JULIE stood at the ship's rail, oblivious to the chill of the December night as she stared pensively toward the moon-swept wilderness of the Georgia river bank. She was leaving behind everything familiar and dear to her to journey across the ocean to a distant land and marry a man she knew she could never love.

A shudder went through her slender young body. Marriage. She did not want to marry anyone, and certainly not someone for whom she felt only polite regard.

But she was not the only person driven to act against her will, she reflected. The war between the North and the South had brought upheaval and chaos to thousands of lives.

From above, twinkling stars reflected in the rolling black waters danced merrily and shattered into thousands of shards. The silence was broken only by the croaking of an army of frogs and the mournful hooting of unseen owls. Wind whispered through the gray moss that hung shroudlike from the trees lining the shore.

They had left the landing some hours ago, traveling to the ship on a ten-oared barge hewn of thick cypress logs. She, her mother, and Sara, their most devoted Negro servant, had been taken to the low, marshy flat that the Yankees had not yet discovered. Steam-powered cotton presses had been built there, and the blockade runners took on their cargoes from that point.

They had been met by sentries, who were posted on the wharves at all times to prevent Confederate deserters from getting on board and stowing away. And, of course, they kept a stern vigil for Yankee spies.

1

Before Julie's betrothed, Virgil Oates, had left weeks earlier to go to England and make preparations for their wedding, he had explained that the conformation of the Atlantic coast and the direction and force of the winds were both factors in the successful blockade running.

"If the wind blows *off* the coast, it drives the squadron to sea," he had said. "It enlarges the perimeter of the circle through which the blockade runner can swiftly and safely steam. If the wind blows *landward*, the squadron must haul off to a greater distance to escape the consequences of the heavy seas that are so violent along the coast."

He talked of the shoals lining the North Carolina coast, saying that they extended for miles into the sea, and were unsurpassed in danger for navigating when strong easterly winds met the ebb tide.

"It's an easy matter, however, for an experienced pilot who knows the coast to run a swift-steaming light-draft vessel out to sea or into port. The heavier and deeper draft vessels of the Federal blockade squadron are buffeted by the stormy winds and waves."

Julie remembered how Virgil embraced her as he told her that he had engaged the *Ariane*, one of the swiftest runners afloat. "I certainly would not take a chance with my future bride's safety," he said, "and I am told that Derek Arnhardt is one of the most skilled captains on the high seas."

He kissed her then, and she prayed he would not sense the negative feelings she fought to hide. She was grateful for the kindness he had shown both her and her mother, and she was well aware that if he did not use his "connections" to get Rose Hill cotton through the Yankee blockade, all would be lost.

She could not let that happen, and not merely for her own sake. She was thinking of her mother, who had struggled so desperately to keep the plantation going since her father's death only five years past. Then there was her twin brother, Myles. Oh, God, he had suffered and was still suffering, and she wanted a home waiting for him when and if he was able to return.

Her hands gripped the railing tightly as feverish determination rippled through her body. Virgil had asked her to marry him, and when she accepted, she knew he would use all his influence and power to save her family estate.

But it still made her sick to the depths of her soul to know she was marrying a man she would never love.

There had been so much misery to bear. She could trace her own heartache back to that balmy spring afternoon when she was only twelve years old and discovered the horrible secret about her father. Lord, she would never forget that fateful day.

She and Myles were going riding, and she had gone to the stable ahead of him. It was located down a long, curving path, behind the big house. Stepping inside the structure, she paused for her eyes to adjust to the semi-darkness—then froze at the sound of whispering voices.

"Adelia, darling, you shouldn't have come here . . ."

She recognized her father's voice, and before she could grasp what was happening, she heard her aunt Adelia's voice replying, "Jerome, it's been weeks. When I saw Elena's carriage pass this morning on the way into town, I knew I had to risk coming. You don't know how I've yearned for your touch, your kiss . . ."

Cold reality washed over Julie in waves as she leaned back against the rough wooden walls, her legs no longer able to support her. Her *father* . . . and her *aunt*! They were *lovers*!

She was not able to will herself to move, though she wanted so desperately to run, to escape the nightmare. Helpless, she was forced to stand there, hands knotted into tight fists pressed against her quivering lips as burning screams struggled to surface.

And never would she be able to erase from her memory the sounds of their frantic, feverish lovemaking in the hayloft overhead.

It was only when silence descended that she was able to come out of her shock, and she slipped quietly outside, the memory forever etched in her brain.

She had not told Myles, though she would have liked to confide her heartache. She did not want him to be torn up inside too.

It had been terrible to force herself to pretend she knew nothing, especially when her father was around. A jovial, affectionate man, she reasoned he was the most wonderful father a girl could wish for. She tried not to despise him, blaming Aunt Adelia instead. It was only natural, she reasoned, that he would give in to a woman who threw herself at him, with no thought of morals.

She knew also how crushed her mother would be to learn her brother's wife was cavorting with her husband, whom she loved with all her heart. Julie had always known this. So why had her father turned to another woman, betraying his wife and the mother of his children? She did not know, especially since her mother was much prettier than Aunt Adelia. Perhaps, she reasoned, physical beauty did not ensure eternal faithfulness and devotion between a husband and wife.

The times when Aunt Adelia was around were the worst, and every Sunday she and Uncle Nigel would bring their son, Thomas, to Rose Hill for a sumptuous dinner. Uncle Nigel was not a man of wealth. He was but a poor dirt farmer who barely coaxed a meager existence from his land, and she had heard the servants whispering that Sundays were probably the only time the Carrigans ever got a decent meal.

Myles noticed her sudden dislike for their aunt and questioned her about it, but she never answered him. Cousin Thomas was another matter. Until Julie discovered the "secret" they had been quite close. Afterwards he badgered her constantly about why she had cooled towards him, never accepted an invitation to visit him at his house, and avoided him when he came to hers. He was hurt and puzzled, but she knew all too well how it would destroy him if he knew the truth about his mother.

So she told no one, harboring the agony herself.

Then came the night that would haunt her forever. Rain was pouring down fiercely, and she was awakened by the loud pounding at the front door and the sound of a man's booming voice demanding to see her mother.

By the time one of the servants answered and hurried upstairs to tell her mother Sheriff Franklin wanted to see her, Julie and Myles had come out of their rooms and stood at the top of the curving stairs. They waited with a chill of foreboding for their mother to appear. When she did, she murmured that they should return to their rooms, but they paid no attention, watching as she hurried down the steps to where Sheriff Franklin waited, twisting his big hat around and around in his hands. Water dripped from his clothes onto the polished oak floors.

In a trembling voice, their mother demanded to know what brought him all the way out there in the dead of night during a storm.

Over their mother's shrieks of protest, they heard him tell her that their father was dead—murdered in cold blood. He had been on his way home from town, and someone shot him right off his horse.

There had been much confusion, with their mother fainting, and Julie and Myles screaming and crying. It was only later that Julie was able to sort out the pieces of the story that no one else would ever know about.

The sheriff and their neighbors could not understand the reason Nigel Carrigan had quarreled with his brother-in-law earlier that evening in a waterfront tavern. They had no idea why Nigel had threatened to kill him. But when Nigel had disappeared that same night, the night her father was killed, everyone suspected that he had waited in ambush to murder Jerome Marshal.

He was never heard from again.

Julie knew what had happened . . . and why. It was another secret she would have to bear in agony, alone.

She was not surprised that once her mother recovered from the initial shock, she was able to cope with her life, and tried to keep the plantation going. But in the night Julie would hear her sobbing in bed, and knew how she was suffering.

The times since her father's death had been difficult. They discovered he had borrowed heavily against his land to pay gambling losses. Her mother was determined that they would not lose their home, and worked day and night, struggling to surmount ever-increasing obstacles. Many were the times she worked side by side with the field hands, and Julie and Myles also learned what it was like to toil in the hot Georgia sun.

The gala parties on the lawn were no more. The house no longer rang with the laughter of merry guests, the sound of music. There was neither time nor money for such social frivolities. And they learned quickly that for some time the opulent air Jerome Marshal had presented to his neighbors was merely a front, one he could ill afford as he sank further and further into debt from his compulsive gambling.

Julie blinked back the tears from the past as she stared into the future. She would try to make Virgil a good wife. Was there any other path for her to walk in life? When she looked at her mother, saw the grief reflected in those green eyes, the same color as her own, she knew how her mother would wither and die if she knew the truth.

And there was another memory, the terrible blow that had struck them harshly, cruelly, bringing them to their knees in the epitome of despair. God, if only it had not happened . . .

Suddenly a voice spoke to her left, and Julie jumped, startled, then turned and strained to see who was standing there in the moonlight.

"Sorry I scared you," the man said gruffly, "but we're making ready to run the blockade, and the captain wants everyone below that ain't supposed to be on deck. No lights. No sound. You just follow me, now."

She could finally make him out in the dim light. He was of medium height, stocky, with a briny smell of the sea about him. Then she gasped as her gaze touched his face. Deep, ribbonlike slashes ran across his cheeks, with one long gash descending from his forehead to run crookedly across his left eye and on across his nose.

He smiled, but it looked like a grimace because of the cicatrices on his flesh. "Don't be embarrassed because you find me ugly, lassie. I've grown used to the stares. And you should see the way the little children run screaming to their mothers at the sight of me."

"I—I'm sorry," she stammered. "Forgive me. It . . . it's just that you took me by surprise."

"The name's Shad Harky. I'm a boatswain. I heard we was taking on passengers for Bermuda, but nobody told me you was so pretty. That must've been your mother that went below with the nigger wench. I take it the cotton in the hold belongs to your mother too."

Julie could only stand there speechless, stunned by his appearance and his candor.

"Well, let's get along now." He reached for her arm. "I'd best be getting you below. You ain't supposed to be up here, you know. Or didn't you hear how the captain don't allow lady passengers to leave their cabins. He don't like passengers anyhow, 'specially ladies. So you're going to be holed up down there for the two weeks or so it'll take us to get to Bermuda."

She turned her head to take one last look at the Georgia shore before letting him lead her away. "I'm not going to stay below all that time," she murmured absently. "And I won't get in anyone's way, I promise."

"Well, that ain't up to me. The captain makes the rules, and when he sees what a lovely thing you are, he'll probably post a guard at your door. The crew, you see, gets excited over women, 'specially pretty ones."

They reached the opening to the narrow steps leading below, and Julie suddenly halted. The thought of descending and not coming up for two weeks, even for a breath of fresh air, was not appealing. "I wish to speak to your captain," she said sharply.

To her surprise, Shad Harky threw back his head and began to laugh. Julie felt rather foolish, wondering what she had done to cause such a reaction. Then, still cackling with glee, he told her, "Oh, lassie, you've got a lot to learn, you have. The captain, he don't even mingle amongst the crew, much less with the passengers.

"You see," he went on, "he hands down his laws like God did to Moses, and nobody hardly ever sees him, 'ceptin' for his appointed few, like First Officer Edsel Garris, or Second Officer Grover Watson. Then there's the Third Officer, Floyd Justice.

"So let's just be on our way. Got to get you tucked away before the ship starts to sea."

He gave her a gentle nudge forward, but Julie stood her ground, more determined than ever to confront the mysterious Captain Arnhardt. Her curiosity was aroused, but she was also concerned about her mother. Lately she didn't have much color in her face, and she seemed wan, listless. If she were forced to stay in stuffy quarters for some time, it might not be good for her.

"I demand to see the captain *now*."

He sighed impatiently. "I told you. You don't see the Captain 'lessen *he* wants to see *you*. Captain Ironheart is a strange man. . . ."

"*Ironheart*?" She was puzzled. "I thought his name was *Arnhardt*."

"Oh, that's his real name," he chuckled, as though he were the possessor of some secret joke. "But we all call him Ironheart 'cause it seems to fit him. If the man *has* a heart, it's bound to be made of iron. See these scars you been trying not to stare at?" He touched a finger to his cheek.

She glanced away, abashed, wishing she had gone below with her mother earlier and not remained on deck to become lost in reverie.

"Ironheart did this to me."

Julie could feel anger emanating from his whole being as he ground out the story.

"Had me keelhauled, he did. My face got tore to bits by the barnacles. Barnacles is little shellfish that hook onto the hulls o' ships. They keep hooking on top of each other, and they're like sharp rocks."

Julie shuddered, and he rushed on in a torrent. "You don't know what keelhauling is, do you? They tie you up and drag you under the ship's keel, real slow, till you're almost dead from drowning. The bastards what dragged me pulled me as close to the keel as they could, so's I'd scrape the barnacles. It was a long time 'afore I thought I'd even have skin on my face again, and it grew back like this."

"And see this?" He snarled bitterly as he held up his left arm. Julie could see that it hung crookedly from his elbow.

"They broke my arm. It never healed right. And it was Ironheart who ordered them to do it to me. Remember that."

"I—I'm sorry," she whispered, waves of pain flowing through her as she imagined what agony the man must have experienced. "He sounds like a very cruel man. I won't look forward to meeting him."

"I'll never forgive him for what he did to me, and there are plenty of others in the crew that hate him too. If you ever do get back up on deck in the daylight, when the sun's beating down, watch when the men take off their shirts. You'll see plenty with the criss-cross scars on their backs from the lash."

They stood in silence for a few moments. Julie did not know what else to say, and she sensed that Shad Harky was caught up in painful memories. Finally she took a step forward and murmured that she would go below and talk to one of the other officers about deck privileges.

He took her arm. "The furnace force and the crew have been loading cordwood, so I imagine we'll be moving out just about any time. I'll see you to your cabin. Watch that fancy hoop skirt, now. It's a narrow stairway. If I was you, I'd put them things away for the duration."

Julie paused one last time to look at the Georgia river bank. A cloak of impenetrable yet lovely silence had closed about the ship. She saw a single riding light hung high at the stern. Somewhere a bird chirped drowsily as

the moon, high now, burnished the entire surface of the
cove, flinging great shadows from low bluffs and trees
across the shining river as it swept out of sight in a silvery,
misty cloud.

One lantern hung from a hook in the ceiling and cast a
yellowish glow in the hallway. Julie saw that there were
three doors on each side of the hall, and wondered which
led to her mother's cabin.

Shad gestured to the dusty oil paintings that hung on
the walls. "This used to be a fine ship before the captain
got hold of her and turned her into a runner. It used to
carry a lot of passengers, I'm told. Tomorrow, if I get a
chance, I'll slip out and show you around. Maybe I can
take you down to the boiler deck so's you can see what
makes her run."

"That would be nice," Julie murmured, trying to be
polite even though she was starting to feel unnerved by the
way the man was staring at her. His gaze kept shifting to
her bosom, slightly exposed in the yellow muslin dress she
wore. With a quick movement, she jerked her shawl tightly
around her, completely concealing the bodice.

He gave her a knowing smirk before reaching to open a
door to their left. "This is your cabin, I suppose. It ain't
much, but it's not like you plan on living here."

Anxious to move away from such a close encounter, she
stepped inside the tiny room and glanced about at the
sparse furnishings. There was a wooden chair and a small
desk on which sat a bowl and pitcher. The bed, nothing
more than a thin mattress upon a board, was held in place
along one wall by chains attached at each end. A round
window, which she knew was called a porthole, afforded
the only view to the outside world.

Shad, sensing her reaction, leered. "I reckon this just
churns the stomach of a fine lady like you, don't it? Well,
it's better'n what the rest of us got. We sleep on canvas
stretchers in a space so crowded and hot the gnats have
trouble breathing. I can look at you and tell you're used to
real nice things, like having oils and perfumes rubbed on
that lily white skin o' yours . . ."

Abashed, Julie could only stare silently at him as he
moved quickly back into the hall to extinguish the overhead lantern, plunging them into darkness. She stepped
backwards as she heard his footsteps approaching. For

some reason she did not yet understand, she was frightened of this man who had seemed so solicitous at first.

"We can't have no lights now," he was saying. "Maybe you'd be interested in knowing just how we'll slip through the Federal blockade. You see, this steamer is painted a light lead color. Makes us blend in with the horizon. We got the smoke pipe lowered, and we're using just a single mast.

"When we came in," he continued, "we took precise compass readings of their fleet at sunset. They don't change positions after dark, so all the captain has to do is steer by compass back out to the open sea."

Even though she found what he was saying to be interesting, Julie was filled with a sense of foreboding that made her dizzy. She felt her back pressing against the wall, and the boatswain was so close his warm breath touched her face.

"If you will excuse yourself, Mr. Harky, I would like to retire." She tried to keep her voice even, her apprehension hidden.

"Of course," he murmured. "You're scared, though, ain't you? No need. I'll look after you."

The hinges squeaked as the door opened, then slowly closed with a click. Julie groped her way across the tiny cabin and leaned against it, washed over with relief. At last he was gone. As much as she hated to admit it, she was afraid of him.

Still feeling her way, she found the bed and sat down. It was silly, her being afraid of the man. He meant her no harm. He probably sensed her uneasiness over the voyage and was only trying to be friendly. Since he was from a different background, it was easy for her to mistake his intentions. That was something she would have to get over.

It was no wonder, though, that she was unnerved in face of all that had happened. Everyone in Savannah had panicked when the Yankees moved their squadron of steam-propelled vessels to the entrance of the sound between the two Confederate forts on Hilton Head and Bay Point in early November. They had fired a continuous broadside onslaught, and caused the Rebels to abandon both fortifications. Just a few days later, Port Royal, on the mainland, had fallen. Everyone said that with the

Yankees in sight of Cockspur Island, they were making ready to strike at Fort Pulaski.

All of Savannah went into an uproar, and those who could afford it fled to the interior of the state. People were even wilder with fear when Tybee Island was abandoned.

Virgil said it was an excellent time for Julie and her mother to leave for England, and he made immediate arrangements for the transport of Rose Hill cotton as well. There was a strong rumor going around that the Yankees were getting ready to move on the eastern part of North Carolina. If they were successful, they would not only gain control of the sounds on the coastal plain, with their important navigable rivers, but they would also control over a third of that state. That would pose a serious threat to the Wilmington and Weldon Railroad, which was the main line running South from Richmond.

Yes, there was much to be concerned about. Not only the war, but the other, terrible thing. . . .

"Julie?"

She sprang to her feet at the sound of her mother's voice calling from outside.

"Julie, darling, are you in there?"

She opened the door, relieved as her mother's arms found her and they embraced in the darkness.

"I was so worried. I was escorted to my cabin and told to remain there until further word, and I didn't know whether or not you had ever come down. Are you all right?"

She felt her mother's cool hand touching her brow to push back the strands of dark curls that forever tumbled out of place.

"Yes, I'm fine," she told her, "but it's positively eerie being in the darkness like this. Maybe we should sit up together."

"Nonsense," came her mother's chuckling reply. "You don't need to be frightened, Julie. Remember what Virgil told us about Captain Arnhardt. He's one of the best blockade runners there is. We have nothing to fear."

She stiffened. "Julie, you're trembling. What's happened to unnerve you so? This isn't like you. . . ."

Julie quickly told her about Shad Harky.

"Oh, Julie, I've warned you about talking with men when you haven't been properly introduced to them," her mother scolded. "And I've heard about keelhauling. It's a punishment inflicted for very serious offenses. This Harky fellow deserved his fate, I'm sure. I want you to stay away from him."

Julie assured her she intended to do just that. "Besides, he says Captain Ironheart, as he calls him, makes passengers stay below during the entire voyage. He doesn't like them about, particularly women. I don't want to run into Shad Harky again, but I certainly don't have any intention of hiding in this hole of a room all the way to Bermuda."

"If the captain requests that we stay below, then we will abide by his wishes," her mother said in her usually obliging manner. "I'm sure he has his reasons. While I don't know much about ships and the sea, I do know that a captain's word is law. I've no intention of questioning Captain Arnhardt's rules, and I expect the same of you."

She kissed her daughter's cheek. "Besides, it won't be so terribly long until we're in Bermuda, and then we'll change to a really nice ship, one that has proper accommodations for passengers. Let's just be thankful Virgil was able to get us *and* Rose Hill cotton out of Savannah.

"Now, then. You go to bed and get some sleep, and when the sun comes up in the morning, we'll be well out to sea. I don't want you fretting."

"That isn't easy these days," Julie said with a touch of sadness.

"I know, dear." Her mother hugged her once more. "But life will be better. You'll see. Virgil will be so good to you. He adores you so."

"It isn't that, it's—"

Her mother spoke sharply. "I know what you're thinking about, and all we can do is pray for Myles's safety. The thing we both must do, child, is not look back. We have to look forward. Myles did what he had to do, just as we all must."

One last embrace, and her mother left the cabin.

Julie slowly slipped out of her dress, making a mental note to discard hoops and heavy petticoats for the duration of the voyage. There simply was not room to move about in such attire.

The sheets of the bed were scratchy and uncomfortable, but the blankets were warm. Despite the apprehension that still held her in its grip, exhaustion took over and she felt herself slipping away into sleep.

Yet thoughts of Myles and the horror of the past kept dancing through her mind. Where was he? How was he? Was he even alive?

She bit her lip to hold back the tears. Tears made wrinkles, her mother said. Tears were useless, her father had often told her. But thoughts of yesterday's anguish always made her weep, because in defending her honor, the brother she loved with all her heart had been forced to run away . . . a hunted man.

Oh, dear God, it wasn't fair. *It wasn't fair. . . .*

The silent hand of sleep waved over her body. For the moment, the tears did not flow.

🐚 Chapter Two 🐚

THE ship creaked and groaned as it stealthily glided through the Federal blockade, but Julie was oblivious to everything except the maddening nightmare that clutched her in its throes.

It was that August night again, and she was walking into the woods surrounding Rose Hill, the air permeated by the sweetness of night-blooming jasmine. The grass beneath her feet was thick as wool, and she stooped to unfasten her high-topped shoes. Wiggling her bare toes deliciously, she ran the rest of the way toward the gurgling brook hidden in the inviting green forest.

She wanted to forget the scene of moments before, when Myles left for another of his secret meetings with those who were not sympathetic to the Southern cause. His activities had been a great source of heartache and worry to both Julie and her mother, for they were dangerous. Threats had been made and rocks thrown through their windows by thundering night-riders. But Myles would not listen to their pleas.

"A man does what he must," he had said many times. "I haven't said I will fight with the North, but nothing will make me fight for the South and a cause I don't believe in."

And so he had left once again, probably not to return till midnight or later. Julie was trying to escape her fearful thoughts about his safety, and she lifted her skirts about her waist as she stepped into the cool water of the stream.

Frowning because the pantalets she wore were confining and warm, she stepped back into the bank and wriggled

14

out of the long, frilly drawers. Tossing them to hang on a nearby bush, she felt the need for freedom, to run and splash and kick her legs in childlike glee, hoping to forget her cares, if only for a little while.

Dancing about among the slippery rocks, she lifted her heart in song. Here, among the green and gold world of the quiet, peaceful forest, there was no misery, no war. Only serenity. She wished she could stay forever.

Her voice echoed softly through the woods, and soon she was lost in her music. The trees became an appreciate audience, and the rustle of leaves her applause. Everything else faded into oblivion.

Suddenly she tensed. A feeling of foreboding crept icily through her veins as she slowly turned around and around, glancing about. Something was not right. Had there been an unfamiliar sound? She was not sure just what it was, but she had a dreadful feeling that she was not alone. Something—or *someone*—was out there in the murky shadows ... watching ... listening. ...

Standing in the middle of the rushing stream, she began to inch her way slowly toward the bank, moving cautiously over the slippery, moss-covered rocks lest she lose her balance and fall. Glancing about, she strained to see in the gathering darkness.

There was an abrupt crackling, crunching sound of footsteps as the two men came out of their hiding place. Julie recognized them at once: Jabe Brogden and Wiley Lucas—local riffraff, troublemakers.

Fear was a cobweb in Julie's throat through which she struggled to push her words. "Why are you spying on me? What are you doing on Rose Hill? You—you're trespassing!" She had been holding her skirt above her waist, bare legs exposed, and she let it drop quickly.

They exchanged snickers, then Wiley squinted at her and snarled, "I reckon if'n you know what's good for you, you'll be telling us where that traitor brother of yours rode off to."

"I don't know," she replied, hoping she did not sound as frightened as she felt. "And don't you call him a traitor. He has a right to his views."

"Not in these times!" Jabe cried. Then he started toward her. "You tell us what you know and you won't get hurt. We're gonna fix him and the bastards he runs with."

She saw Wiley tip a bottle to his lips before tossing it

aside to follow Jabe. Her mind whirled dizzily as she fought the wave of panic that made her whole body quake. She must not show fear. They were drunk, and the best way to handle them was with indignation, not fear. But they were coming toward her, and she had to escape. There would be time to argue later, when she was not alone with them.

"We like them pretty legs." Wiley grinned, exposing yellowed, chipped teeth. "We want to see what else you got that's pretty. I'll just bet you're pretty all over. . . ."

"No!" she screamed in panic. "No! Leave me alone!" She turned in the direction of the opposite bank, her foot slipped on a rock, and she fought wildly to regain her balance, only to topple into the rolling creek. Splashing, arms flailing, she struggled to right herself, but continued to lose her footing as she tumbled over and over in the rushing waters.

Strong hands were groping, reaching for her, and she slapped out at them, screaming, fighting, but to no avail. She was yanked up and out of the water, carried to the other side and into the thick brush.

They tossed her roughly on the ground and ripped her clothes from her body. When she was naked before them, Jabe hissed that if she would tell them where Myles had gone, they might let her go.

She begged and pleaded with them to believe that she knew nothing.

"Well, no need in wasting such good stuff," Jabe laughed, falling on top of her, his hands grabbing her breasts and squeezing them painfully. "We'll just take care of your brother tomorrow. . . ."

With a sudden surge of strength she did not know she possessed, Julie raised her hands to stab her thumbs into his eyes just as she brought her knee smashing up into his groin. With a shriek of agony, he rolled to one side, clutching himself.

Julie struggled to her knees and was almost on her feet when Wiley, who had been standing by and watching, stunned, came alive. His arm snaked out and his hand wrapped about her ankle to jerk her backwards. She felt the bare flesh of her belly and breasts scrape painfully against the rough ground beneath her.

"I'm gonna teach her a lesson," Jabe yelled. "Hold her

right there. I'm gonna take her like the bitch-dog she is. . . ."

They were holding her, about to defile her, Julie feeling anguished and tortured, when the angry, protesting shout erupted in the night.

They ran away, scurrying to disappear into the thick woods as the servant who had been dispatched to search for Julie appeared just in time to save her.

She remembered only bits and pieces of what happened after that. She awakened in her own bed, with Sara seated in a chair beside her, sobbing and wailing. Her mother had been nearby, and Doc Perkins was there also, saying something about how she'd had a terrible shock, but there were no physical injuries. Then they saw she was awake, and Doc gave her something to make her sleep again.

Then Myles was there, shaking her against the protests of their mother, demanding to know who was responsible, and she had mumbled the names, terrified when his scream of rage shook the whole house as he left to avenge her honor. Their mother was sobbing, begging him not to go, saying he should let the law take care of it.

But he had gone. And they had not heard from him since.

Myles was now a hunted man . . . wanted for what the sheriff called cold-blooded murder.

Myles had gone to town, directly to the tavern where Jabe Brogden and Wiley Lucas hung out. Without a word, he walked inside and shot Wiley Lucas dead. Jabe Brogden escaped.

It didn't matter that they had tried to rape Julie. The sheriff called it murder.

Julie and her mother knew the real reason Sheriff Franklin was so quick to put an ax to Myles. He, like so many other fire-eating secessionists, were quick to judge and hate a man who did not share their views about the war.

Julie woke up crying and calling Myles's name.

It had been so real, the nightmare that kept returning. She could feel their hands upon her body. She could hear Myles's raging screams as he stormed from the house. Dear God, she shook herself in terror, would it never end? Would she ever stop reliving the horror over and over again?

It was like that other time in the woods when they were both only ten. It had been years before she could close her eyes without seeing that wild hog ripping out of the bushes, charging straight at them. Myles had picked her up and thrust her skyward, toward the low-hanging limb of a nearby tree, as he screamed at her to grab hold and hang on.

He had taken the charge of that hog himself, saving her life at the risk of his own. Fortunately, there were field hands not too far distant who heard her screams and came running to slay the deadly creature, whose tusks by that time had pierced Myles in his right hip. He lay bleeding on the ground, moaning with pain, and he and Julie realized that had the others not arrived, the hog would have kept right on charging until it killed him.

Myles lost much blood, and for several days, Doc Perkins didn't hold out much hope that he would live. As it was, the wound left him with a permanent limp.

"Every time you take a step and I see you walk that way, I'll remember you did it to save my life," Julie told him tearfully one day.

"Aw, I didn't do it for you," he quipped impishly. "I just wanted to see if you were smart enough to climb that tree. I wasn't even thinking about that dumb old hog."

But she knew better, and he realized it. Myles being Myles, Julie accepted the fact that he did not want her to gush over his heroism, so she never mentioned it again.

Still, it grieved her when other children teased Myles about his limp, calling him "gimp," and being cruel as only the young can be. She remembered that Jabe Brogden and Wiley Lucas had always been the ringleaders of those who provoked Myles, and she hated them for it. Once she even slapped Jabe for saying something about Myles when he was not around.

"I'll get you for that," he warned.

And, she recalled with a shudder, he almost had. Only it hadn't really been *her* that he and Wiley wanted that night. It was their way of hurting Myles for being what they considered a traitor.

"Myles will return one day," her mother had said, her lower lip quivering. "That's why we must work extra hard to insure that we don't lose Rose Hill. We want a home for him to come back to, don't we?"

Julie got out of the bed and padded to the porthole to

stare out at the black water and the purple sky. Yes, she wanted a home for Myles to return to. She also wanted her mother to keep what was rightfully hers, what Adelia Carrigan would gladly have taken along with her father if she'd been able to arrange it.

So Julie would marry Virgil Oates. She would be a good, dutiful wife. And the two people she loved the most in this world might one day be happy because she had done so. What more was there to life, anyway, she reasoned, than giving joy to those you love?

Lost in thought, she did not hear the first soft raps upon her door. She could not have been asleep for very long, and she surmised that it was probably her mother. Perhaps she had heard Julie calling Myles's name, knew that the nightmare had come again, and wanted to comfort her.

Eager for her company, Julie fumbled her way to the door, threw back the latch and opened it.

"Aha! So I was right. You couldn't sleep, could you?"

She froze at the sound of Shad Harky's voice, and before she could recover and slam the door, he pushed his way inside, speaking rapidly. "Talked the cook into fixing you up with a nice pot o' tea. I imagine you can use it, what with you being nervous about the voyage and all. We're through the blockade now, by the way. The worst is over, though we can't light no lanterns for awhile yet, just to be on the safe side."

She chewed her lip thoughtfully and wondered what to do. It *had* been kind of him to persuade the cook to make tea at such an ungodly hour, but still, she felt uneasy. Reaching for her robe, which she'd laid at the foot of her bed, she quickly put it on as she said, "It just isn't proper for you to be here, Mr. Harky, though I thank you for your kindness. I'm not in the habit of entertaining in my boudoir, especially men, and certainly not in the dark. So if you will take your leave . . ." She tried to make him out in the darkness but could not, and had to guess where he might be standing.

"I only want to be your friend." He brushed against her, and she flinched. He chuckled at her reaction. "Aw, come on, now. You're going to need a friend. It's like I told you, the captain isn't a friendly sort. Says it's bad luck to have women on his ship. I can fix it so's you can get out a bit. I'll look after you."

She heard the clatter as he set the tray down on the

desk, which he'd managed to locate. "Now, then. What
say we sit down and drink this tea, and I'll keep you
company for awhile."

"No!" She didn't mean to shout, and she quickly lowered her voice. "I want you to go. We can talk tomorrow."

"Oh, you're just scared. . . ."

"I am *not* scared." Now she was becoming angry, and
she did not want to be. The man was scarred and unattrac-
tive, and she didn't want him to think that was the reason
she was rejecting him. He had already shown he was sensi-
tive about his appearance. Trying to make herself sound
as pleasant as possible, she explained once again that they
could talk in the daylight hours.

"Be still. . . ." he whispered tersely, interrupting her.

And then she heard it: footsteps scraping on the stairs.

"No one must know I'm here," he said nervously.
"Don't make any noise."

Julie had not closed the door, and a faint glow of light
filled the opening. Then a man appeared, his face framed
in the halo of the small candle he held. She could see that
he was over six feet tall, for he looked as though he were
stooping to peer inside. Large framed, there was a military
set to his wide, broadcloth-covered shoulders. His expression and high forehead beneath curling dark hair gave an
impression of great intellectual possession, and she sensed
at once that he was a man of importance.

Was this the famed and feared Captain Ironheart?
There was a glint in his wide-set dark eyes that hinted he
would be quick to anger.

Lifting the candle higher so he could see better, he all
but growled, "Harky! What are you doing down here?
You have no business in Miss Marshal's cabin."

Shad snapped, "I brought her some tea. Thought it
might settle her down. It's bound to be unnerving to a lady
whilst we're running the blockade, knowing we could get
fired on any second. . . ."

"We're through the blockade. Get to your post at once."
His eyes glowing in the candlelight seemed to sparkle with
tiny red dots of rage. "This will be reported to the captain."

So, Julie realized with surprise, this was not Captain
Arnhardt. Then who was he? He certainly seemed to have
authority, because Shad quickly obeyed. He scurried past

them, out of the cabin, and she heard him moving quickly up the steps.

The tall man bowed slightly. "I am First Officer Edsel Garris, Miss Marshal. Allow me to welcome you aboard, and please accept my apology for Boatswain Harky's intrusion upon your privacy. He's aware of the captain's rules where female passengers are concerned. He will be punished, I assure you."

"Not on my account, please." Julie raised her hand in protest. "He was only trying to be nice, and the tea will be welcome. He did nothing to offend me. He was concerned that I would be frightened as we ran the blockade."

He laughed softly, a warm sound that put her at ease. "I don't think you have anything to fear. Captain Arnhardt is one of the best when it comes to navigating. Only once has the *Ariane* even been fired upon, and we were able to show our heels and make a rapid escape."

He glanced about. "Are your quarters comfortable?"

Julie followed his gaze. "I suppose. But Mr. Harky tells me my mother and I will not be allowed on deck."

"That's true. Our crew can be an unruly lot at times, and the presence of women as lovely as you and your mother could present problems."

She felt herself bristling. "We can handle ourselves. You can tell your Captain Ironheart we don't intend to spend the next few weeks staring out a porthole."

He raised an eyebrow. "Ironheart, did you say? It seems Mr. Harky has done a lot of talking."

"Your captain's reputation travels before him. I've already heard how the crew calls him that behind his back, and I've seen the scars on Mr. Harky's face from being keelhauled. That sounds quite barbaric to me."

"The crime he *committed* was barbaric." He stared at her thoughtfully, a muscle in his jaw twitching slightly. "I'm afraid you don't understand the law of the high seas, Miss Marshal. A captain is almost godlike in his powers. He can sentence a man to death if he so chooses. I won't go into details of Mr. Harky's crime, however, as a lady should not hear such.

"I would suggest," he continued, "that you obey the captain and show him the respect he deserves. By so doing, you will ensure that your voyage upon our ship will be quite pleasant."

She gave her long black hair an indignant toss. "I've no intention of being dictated to. I do happen to be a paying passenger. Now, if you'll excuse me, I would like to enjoy the tea Mr. Harky so thoughtfully brought to me."

She placed her hand on the door and waited. Edsel Garris stared at her intently, pursing his lips as though he wanted to say more but decided it was best to keep his silence.

"As you wish." He blew out the candle, and for a moment they were alone in the inky shroud of night. Then she heard him step outside, and she quickly pushed the door shut and threw the latch.

If he and his captain thought they would order her about, they were in for a surprise. As for Shad Harky, there might be something slightly ominous about his manner, but that could be the result of his scarred face and the mental anguish he must suffer. Whatever he had done in the past was just that—in the past—and as long as he behaved himself around her in a gentlemanly fashion, then she would be his friend.

She poured herself a cup of tea, grateful he had thought to provide lemon. She found the tea relaxing, and when her cup was drained, she did feel drowsy.

Getting back in her bed, she pulled the blanket up to her chin and lay there tensely, wanting to fall asleep so it would soon be morning. Maybe things would be better then. After all, she had never been on a ship, and it would be nice to gaze at the rolling ocean and taste the fresh salt air on her lips.

Closing her eyes, she thought of Myles, and wondered once again whether he was all right. If only she could have seen him before he left, but there had not been time. Had he been captured, he would have been lynched by an unruly mob.

It wasn't fair, she thought angrily. Myles had a right to his opinions about the war. He hated slavery, and he'd often told his mother how, if it were left up to him, he'd free every slave at Rose Hill.

Their mother had argued that the Negroes at Rose Hill were treated very well. She also pointed out that if they were freed and turned away, many would starve. They would have no home, nowhere to go. She had also told him that she would never ask him to think any way except that which his heart dictated, but she did ask that he keep his views to himself in such tense, tumultuous times.

But Myles had not kept silent, and he and those who shared his opinions had angered many people in Savannah. So perhaps it was best that he had gone away, for his own safety. She only wished that he were not wanted for murder. That was a heavy burden for a man to carry. Myles was gentle and kind, and he would never have hurt anyone unless he was provoked to the breaking point.

The attack upon her had been that breaking point.

Once more the sound of someone coming down the steps made her instantly alert. Julie sat straight up, hoping that Officer Garris was not returning. She wanted no more company this night. She knew it would not be Shad, for he was already in trouble because of his earlier visit.

The footsteps stopped outside her door. She waited for a knock, but there was no further sound. Why was he just standing there? Why didn't he move on down the hall?

Then a chill gripped her as she heard the doorknob turning. Thank goodness the door was bolted. She was about to demand to know who was there when she heard the hoarse, rasping breath, and she could only lie there in frightened silence.

After what seemed hours, shuffling sounds told her that whoever he was, he was leaving. She let out her breath with relief, hoping and praying that sleep would come soon, for this had to be the longest night of her life.

Pulling the blanket over her head, she vowed to lie there and not move, no matter what further sounds she heard.

✿ Chapter Three ✿

THE *Ariane* had been at sea only a few days, but already Julie was bored and restless. Each time she appeared on deck, First Officer Garris inevitably emerged also, seemingly out of nowhere, to remind her apologetically that she was not allowed topside. With careful politeness, he would escort her below.

She had a choice of remaining in her cabin or sitting in the officers' dining area. The latter was furnished comfortably, with magazines and books aplenty, and tea or coffee was offered all day long. Her mother seemed quite satisfied there, chiding Julie for refusing to settle down and make do with the situation.

"I'm sure it's for the best, dear, and the captain has his reasons for his orders," she pointed out. "Once we reach Bermuda, we'll change to a nicer and larger ship, better equipped for passengers. We're fortunate Virgil was able to get us through the blockade. There wasn't time to think about comfort."

She quickly added, "Besides, this ship is probably full of rowdies, and it's best you aren't around them."

"They can't all be bad," Julie argued, pacing restlessly up and down the room, pausing now and then to stare through a porthole at the rolling ocean. "Anyway, we are *paying* passengers, and we should be allowed to do as we wish."

Her mother sighed and turned her attention once again to the book she was reading, ignoring her daughter's impatient grumblings.

One evening Julie arrived for dinner wearing a ball

gown of champagne silk. The bodice dipped low, accentuating her generous bosom. There were no straps; the material was fashioned beneath her arms, with slip-on puff sleeves from the elbows to the wrists. The skirt hung in graceful scallops, each caught with a tiny rosette of red lace below the tight-fitting bodice which came to a point over her firm stomach. Julie had brushed her black hair till it shone, and let it flow softly about her shoulders, with only a bright crimson ribbon for adornment.

When she appeared in the doorway, Officer Garris gasped out loud as he jumped quickly to his feet and made her a slight bow. Second Officer Grover Smith and Third Officer Floyd Justice sprang from their chairs also, eyes wide with appreciative awe.

Julie took her seat next to her mother, who frowned and leaned over to whisper coolly, "Why did you wear that dress, dear? This is a ship, not a ballroom."

"I thought dressing up might buoy my spirits a little," she replied, blinking back tears and not bothering to whisper. "I just wanted to do something different, so I decided to dress for dinner. Is that so wrong? Being confined below night and day is going to drive me insane."

She didn't add that she had too much time alone, when she brooded and remembered the anguish of the past. She needed to be with people, keep busy, and dwell on the future. But who would understand if they did not share her secret pain?

Edsel Garris reached across the table and patted her hand in a gesture of sympathy. "Well, at least you've buoyed *our* spirits, Miss Marshal. It's seldom we have an opportunity to witness such beauty. I'm just sorry that your confinement is necessary."

Mr. Watson joined in. "We're merely following the orders of our captain. You don't realize how rough and crude some of our crewmen are. He doesn't want you exposed to them."

"Captain Arnhardt is a strict and forceful officer," Edsel continued. "He demands that his ship be run efficiently and in an orderly manner. He frowns on his crew members even having the usual drunken binge when we put into port merely to take on a cargo. They have to wait until we reach our destination. Even then, he doesn't tolerate revelry to an extreme."

"That's right." Mr. Justice nodded. "The result is that

the men work better, but their dispositions leave much to be desired. It's best you keep your distance from them. Take our word for it, please."

The cook's assistant appeared, and Julie held out her wineglass to him. When he had filled it from the bottle he held, she took a slow sip, then gave each of the three officers a glance before saying, "I met one of your men my first night on board. I believe his name was Harky . . . Shad· Harky. He brought me a nice pot of tea because he thought I might be nervous and unable to sleep, what with our running the blockade and all. He seemed quite polite, certainly not the ruffian you portray all your men to be."

The officers exchanged looks with raised eyebrows, then Edsel said, "Yes, Miss Marshal. I know about Harky going to your cabin and, if you'll recall, I told him to leave. I reported his actions to the captain, and Harky received five lashes—"

Julie set her glass down so quickly that its red contents sloshed over the rim and onto the white linen tablecloth. Her heart was racing furiously as she cried indignantly, "Do you mean to tell me you had him beaten? Merely because he was being a friend?"

Edsel squirmed uncomfortably, aware that all eyes were upon him, but only Julie's were blazing with fury. "I didn't give the order. I merely reported his action to the captain, which was my duty. The captain ordered him flogged. But if I *had* been in command, I can assure you I would've issued the same orders. This fellow Harky is a miscreant by nature, and it wouldn't take much provocation for the captain to have him hung."

"I've never heard of anything so sadistic and barbaric," Julie exploded. "My God! His face is a mass of scarred flesh now from being dragged beneath your ship while he was tied to a rope! I don't know why he puts up with such tyranny."

Her mother reached out to touch her hand, and Julie turned to her and quickly said, "I'm sorry, Mother. I don't mean to embarrass you by my behavior, but I'm shocked that such things go on. When we get to England, I'm going to talk to Virgil. I'm sure he has enough influence to have this 'Ironheart' removed from command." She was shaking with rage.

"Captain Arnhardt happens to *own* this ship, Miss Marshal." Officer Justice spoke, eyelids lowered to angry, narrow slits, his face reddening. His hands were gripping the table edge, knuckles white from the pressure. "He may do whatever he wishes, as is the law of the high seas. He would have full command of this ship even if he didn't own it. And it matters not who your fiancé is or how much influence, power, or money he possesses. He has no control over Captain Arnhardt, and I'm sure Captain Arnhardt doesn't stand in awe of him. I've never known him to be intimidated by any man."

He paused to take a breath, then rushed on. "As for your encounter with Boatswain Harky, you might be interested to know that he was keelhauled because he attempted to rape a female passenger while under the influence of rum. And the *only* reason the captain didn't hang him then was because he believes in giving a man a second chance once he's been punished for his crime. But he *does* believe in castigation, and metes it out generously."

Floyd Justice looked winded from his eruption.

Her mother was clutching her throat in horror. "Oh, Julie! And you let that horrid man into your cabin? Whatever were you thinking of?"

Julie ignored her, speaking directly to Officer Justice through gritted teeth. "Perhaps Mr. Harky would've preferred death over the torture Ironheart inflicted upon him. He told me how little children scream and run at the sight of his face. But tell me, was he even given a trial, or did your precious captain proclaim himself both judge and jury?"

Without waiting for a reply, she rushed on. "Now I think I understand why the captain stays hidden and refuses to show his face. He's either ashamed to mingle with decent folk or afraid that one of his men will put a well-deserved knife in his back!"

The three officers gasped in unison, and her mother could only stare at her in stunned silence.

Officer Garris was the first to react. "Miss Marshal, you don't understand." He forced his tone to be gentle, trying to calm her. "If Captain Arnhardt weren't the strong commander he is, the *Ariane* would not be one of the best ships on the high seas. The men in our crew come from all walks of life. Some have murdered. Some have raped, robbed, performed all sorts of heinous, unspeakable crimes. But they make good sailors when they are controlled. It requires a man with an iron will to keep them in line. Captain Arnhardt is just such a man. True, some of the crew may fear and hate him, but while they would die before they'd admit it, they *respect* him."

He paused, glanced about the table to make sure everyone had calmed down, then continued, "As for your not having met him, he does keep to himself. But believe me when I say that he is aware of everything that goes on aboard his ship, and while it may seem strange to you, there is actually no need for the two of you to meet. The captain never mingles with passengers."

Pulling himself erect, he gave a forced smile to everyone and murmured, "Let's try to make the rest of your voyage a pleasant experience. For now, we have a delicious meal waiting."

He snapped his fingers, and the cook's assistant disappeared through a swinging door to return almost immediately with a large tray. He placed bowls of stewed chicken, boiled potatoes, peas, and corn dumplings on the table. Then he left to bring back another tray, this one containing a kettle of savory-smelling mutton stew.

"This does look tempting," Julie's mother laughed a bit nervously. "And if I know your cook, he'll have something equally scrumptious for dessert, so I'll have to save room."

"Apple cobbler," the assistant murmured before scurrying out once again.

The bowls were passed, and Officer Justice commented that they were blessed with an extraordinary cook. Edsel Garris agreed. As Julie helped herself to a bowl of the mutton stew, her mother inquired how they had managed such a feat.

Julie paid no attention to what was said. She was still angry, and refused to accept any attempts on their parts to include her in their conversation. They were treating her like a child.

Damn Captain Ironheart anyway, she thought bitterly, chewing on the tender meat almost with a vengeance. This was her first experience at sea, and she wanted to enjoy it. She could remember standing on the banks of the Savannah River as a child, with Thomas and Myles beside her. The three of them would talk about what it must be like "out there," on the other side of the world. Childlike, they fantasized about their plans to run away one day. They would build a boat or a raft, just anything to keep them afloat, and they would sail off to the horizon and experience all the wonders of the world.

Thomas. As always, thoughts of him brought a lump to her throat. Had it not been for his mother's sins, they would probably have married. Everyone thought they were an ideal match. He'd been so hurt by her rejection, and she prayed he never knew why. She heard he had joined the Confederate Army and gone off to fight in the war, and she prayed he was safe and well.

Blinking back the tears that always came to her eyes when she thought of the past, she made herself think instead of Shad Harky, wondering if he were actually guilty of the crime for which he had been punished. He had seemed nice enough that first night, even though she had been a bit wary of being alone with him. That was only natural, she supposed. It *was* night, and they were in her cabin, unchaperoned. Since then, the few times she had managed to slip on deck, she had only glimpsed him from a distance, and while she could feel him looking at her, he always glanced away when she turned toward him, and never made any attempt to speak to her. Now she could understand why. Because of her, he'd had five cruel and painful lashes of the whip across his back. All over a friendly gesture—a pot of tea! He probably blamed her, and, by God, that wasn't fair.

The men were discussing news they had managed to pick up from a passing ship that afternoon. The *Ariane* had sent a small boat over to the other vessel to gather any information it might have collected while in port in Bermuda. Edsel was talking about the Federal general named Sherman, who was reportedly in charge of the permanent garrison that had landed on Tybee Island near Savannah. "Mark my words. Fort Pulaski will fall before long," he said gravely. "It's only a matter of time. Savannah and all her ports will be lost to the Yankees."

Julie turned to see her mother's face go pale as she cried, "Oh, to think they might march on Rose Hill. . . ."

The officers laughed, but not unkindly, and Officer Watson commented that she should not waste her time fretting over such a possibility. "The Yankees will have more important things on their minds than marching on plantations right away, Mrs. Marshal. They want Fort Pulaski, and that's their main objective and concern. Once they have control, they'll have a tight noose around the city. President Lincoln seems to think the way to win the war is to cut off the South from supplies, thereby starving the Confederacy into submission. That's why the Yankees have tried so hard to make their blockade successful. I'm afraid that when the fort does fall, it's going to be quite a blow to the South, both economically and psychologically."

Floyd Justice nodded. "Be glad you aren't in Savannah. From what we hear, the situation is utter chaos. People are hysterical."

"Oh, they were trying to flee the city while we were still there," Mrs. Marshal said worriedly. "Those who could afford to do so were moving inland."

"It's that officer named Lee who ordered the abandonment of Georgia's sea islands," Edsel Garris said to no one in particular. "He was a commissioned officer in the United States Army when war broke out, you know, and when Virginia seceded, he resigned his commission to join the Confederacy. He's a Brigadier General in eastern Florida as well. I heard it said that the battle of Port Royal Sound made him see that without adequate naval support, it's impossible to defend small forts and batteries on the sea coast that fall within range of the Federal fleet's powerful guns."

Mr. Justice nodded. "Right. He said it would be hopeless to prevent enemy landings on the beach islands unless *thousands* of troops were mobilized from other areas and ordered to garrison duty. These soldiers are badly needed in other theaters of war. So that's why he ordered the abandonment of the sea islands and had the guns removed from the batteries."

Mr. Justice drained the last of his wine, then picked up the little silver bell that sat on the table and gave it a shake. The cook's helper appeared at once to refill his empty glass. He took a sip, then said, "The abandonment of Tybee is sure to make Cockspur vulnerable."

"Not really." Mr. Garris pushed his plate aside and leaned back in his chair. Pulling out a corncob pipe, he proceeded to pack it with tobacco from the small leather pouch he withdrew from his coat pocket. The men were waiting anxiously for him to begin speaking once again, and Julie noticed her mother seemed to be hanging onto his every word. She wondered dismally if she had ever been so bored in her entire life.

When he finally had the pipe drawing, and bluish smoke curls surrounded his head, Edsel continued to expound his ideas. "It's expected that the fort can defend itself successfully against a naval attack, and it's also considered safe from land bombardment. Did you know that all side channels leading into the Savannah River above the fort have been barred by obstructions to keep open a line of communications and supplies? And these obstructions have been protected by floating mines which are activated by galvanic batteries."

Grover and Floyd exchanged incredulous looks, and Floyd cried, "I've never heard of such a thing. How do you come by such information?"

Edsel looked smug. "The captain and I talk at night, and he confides many things to me. He keeps himself quite well informed, you know. These mines, or 'infernal machines,' as they are sometimes called, are a new invention which the Confederates have sort of 'borrowed' from the Russians. But as for the blockade itself, the captain doesn't intend to try to run it through Savannah again. He says it's far too dangerous."

Julie pushed away the plate of mutton stew, which she had hardly touched. Standing, she faked a yawn and murmured, "Excuse me, but I'm a bit tired and feel a headache coming on. I think I'll retire for the night."

The three officers rose politely, clucking their sympathies, and her mother asked if she wanted her to join her, but Julie quickly urged her to stay and enjoy the company. "War talk bores me almost as much as this voyage, but I'm happy that you are able to enjoy both, Mother. At least you aren't miserable, too."

She hurried from the room. Standing outside in the narrow hallway, she closed the door and leaned against it to hear whether anyone was going to follow to make sure she did go straight to her cabin. She heard Mr. Watson say, "I do hope we weren't too harsh on your daughter, Mrs. Marshal."

"No, not at all," came here mother's quick reply. "I hope it did some good. It worries me because she's so restless. She's such a child, at times. . . ."

"I'd hardly call her a child," Mr. Justice laughed, and

the other men chuckled along with him. "She's quite a beautiful young woman, and I'm sure you're very proud of her."

Mr. Garris chimed in. "Indeed, but unfortunately she lacks knowledge of the harsher realities of life. Like so many of our other genteel southern ladies, I'm sure your daughter has been protected from unpleasantness."

Julie made a face. She could tell them a few things about "unpleasantness" like that night in the woods with those savages.

Her skirts swishing, she moved on down the hall, walked right by her cabin, and ascended the steps quickly. Reaching the deck, she smiled and stretched her arms high about her head, drinking in the cool, pungent salt air. Stepping cautiously over ropes and riggings, she moved to the railing and stood there, marveling at the sight of the shimmering water. A half-moon peered out from behind a silver-tinged cloud, making the rolling sea sparkle like thousands of tiny diamonds. Julie had grown used to the pitch and roll of the boat, the chugging motion as it jerked along, and now it seemed like a sweet sonata . . . fluid . . . melodic.

She thought of Myles, how happy they used to be, and whispered a prayer for his safety as she did each night. She would not let herself think about her impending marriage, except to remember that Virgil had promised her he would use his influence to make it possible for her brother to return home. How she hoped it would be so.

Then, lost in her world of beauty and tranquility of the moment, she forgot about the crewmen moving about silently in the darkness, performing their duties. She began to hum softly at first, and then the words came. Soon she was singing to the wind and the stars and the moon, her voice ringing out clearly and sweetly in the night. How she loved to sing; she had even harbored secret fantasies of one day actually being a professional. But that was part of another world, another time.

She did not notice that the men had slowly stopped what they were doing and begun to gather behind her. They exchanged silent glances and nods of approval and appreciation for such a lovely voice. Only when she fell silent and they broke into loud, enthusiastic applause, was she aware of their presence.

Whirling about, hands fastened behind her on the railing, she faced them and gasped, startled, "I'm sorry! I guess I forgot where I was. . . ." She was flustered, embarrassed. "The ocean, the beautiful night, it just made me want to sing. . . ."

A stocky man stepped forward, a grin on his craggy face. "Lassie, how about another?" he asked hopefully.

In the pale glow of moonlight which illumined the scene, he, like the others, seemed pleased over the break in their monotonous routine, and she felt they all seemed appreciative of her singing.

Glancing to her left, Julie recognized Shad Harky's grotesquely scarred face, and a wave of sadness washed over her as she remembered he had received five lashes merely because he had extended a kindness to her. She nodded in recognition, and his mouth spread in a smiling grimace.

He turned to the others and called out, "That was the prettiest thing we've heard in months, right, men? All we ever hear out here is the screamin' of sea gulls and the officers yelling their orders. So let's beg her to favor us with another."

They shouted encouragement, coaxing her to sing for them again. "Please," someone called out.

Beaming, happy, enjoying the moment after days and nights of unfamiliar confinement, Julie felt as though her very soul were smiling as she said demurely, "If you really want me to . . ."

"We do! We do!" another voice called.

"Lassie, we beg you. . . ."

"Lovely . . . just lovely . . ."

And while she stood there, stunned, drinking in their praise, someone appeared with a fiddle. Stationing himself next to her at the railing, he began to play the lilting music of "Sweet Evalina."

"I know that one," she cried joyfully, and with the fiddle, she began to sing once more. When she'd sung every verse, the fiddler went straight into "Juanita." Somewhere along the way, one of the sailors produced a flute and began playing along. Then there were two men with harmonicas as everyone joined in to sing "Bonnie Blue Flag."

After each song, the air rang with applause and shouts from the crew for more. Julie became lost in her music, thrilling to their appreciation and enjoyment, heady with excitement. The men who had instruments went from song to song, and she knew almost all of them. If the words escaped her, she hummed along.

The selections became livelier: "Arkansas Traveler" . . . "The Goose Hangs High." Then someone began to yell out the words to "Hell Broke Loose in Georgia." Some of the men paired off to dance, jiglike, while Julie laughed and clapped her hands in childlike glee. Not only was she enjoying herself, but the pulsating thought rippled through her that they *liked* her singing, seeming truly appreciative.

So entranced was she with the merriment surrounding her, Julie did not notice a forbidden jug of rum being passed about freely. The men were so caught up in the excitement that all thoughts that they were breaking ship rules were pushed from their minds. They danced to the fiddle and the flute and the harmonicas, and the sounds filled the night.

Backed against the railing, Julie began to feel slightly uncomfortable. The songs were changing to bawdy tunes she did not know or like, and finally she realized the men were drinking and the scene was getting out of hand. Deciding it best to take her leave, she began to step sideways, only to bump into something.

Lifting her eyes, she saw the leering gaze of Shad Harky.

"You are a pretty one," he murmured, his voice slurring as he reached out to clamp a beefy hand upon her bare shoulder. She cringed beneath his touch, and he chuckled. "Ahh, you have no cause to be frightened of me. I'm your friend. I know how lonely you've been, cooped up below. We'll take a walk in the moonlight, and I'll show you how friendly I can be to a lovely lady. . . ."

"No!" She cried sharply, shaking her head from side to side. "I'm going below. . . ."

"Don't be shy. I've seen the way you look at me when you think I don't see. You know a real man when you see one. And you miss a man, don't you? Out here at sea, away from fancy balls and such, you're craving some excitement —some lovin'—and old Shad Harky's the man who can give it to you. Ask any filly I've ever bedded, and—"

"No! Stop it!" Now she was truly frightened. Turning to run from the lurching, drunken man, she became confused as to her direction, and instead of making her way to the doorway that led below, she found her ankles tangled in riggings and ropes. She didn't know which way to turn, and was unable to move.

Shad followed her. "Now don't be shy, missy. No need to be. I can tell by looking at you that you're a real spitfire, just waitin' for what I've got to give you. . . ."

Julie knew she had gotten herself into a dangerous situation. With all the noise the men were making, no one would hear her screams, and the way Shad was looking at her, she knew he meant business. Striking out at him, she cried, "Leave me alone! Get away from me. . . ."

Reaching out to yank her from the entanglements around her ankles, he jerked her against his chest, and his mouth sought hers. She twisted her face from side to side, shaking with terror.

He clutched her breasts roughly and cried triumphantly, "You got some nice ones, you have. Now stop pretending you don't like what I'm doing. I don't want to hurt you none."

She clawed at his face, hysterical with anger. It would be like the other time, that horrid night in the woods, only this time there would be no rescue. "No . . . no," she beat at him with her hands knotted into tiny fists. "Leave me alone . . . stop it. . . ."

"Hey, ain't no woman gonna slap me!" Shad swung and clipped the side of her jaw and for a moment, she swayed dizzily, fighting to remain conscious.

With one quick jerk, he yanked the soft material of the bodice of her dress, opening it to the waist. Her breasts tumbled forth, naked in the moonlight. He paused to bend his head and suck one nipple roughly into his mouth, giving it a little stinging bite before he pushed her down on the deck.

Falling on top of her, he began to shove at her skirt and petticoats, twisting and squirming his body against hers, grinding his hips, as he promised it would be good for her. "You'll feel like a real woman 'cause you've got a real man," he said with a snarl. "You'll be wanting me to slip into your cabin every night and give it to you."

Julie was still reeling from his blow. The cool air from the ocean touched her bare flesh as he jerked up her skirts and ripped down her pantalets, exposing her legs. He forced his knee between them, struggling to spread her thighs as she tried with every bit of strength to push him away.

He fumbled at his pants, and then she felt the hot, throbbing flesh of his organ as he jabbed at her. "Now you just relax," he commanded, his breath hot and ragged on her face as he finally succeeded in yanking her legs wide apart. "It's gonna be good, I tell you. Don't make me hurt you. I know you've wanted this. . . ."

Terror gave her strength. "I *haven't* wanted this," she shrieked, giving him another shove, this one harder than the last, as she caught him off guard while he tried to enter her. Anger overcame her fear. "I only wanted to be your friend. I felt sorry for you. Your face . . ."

"My *face!*" he screamed, and she shriveled beneath him terrified at his maniacal expression, made even more eerie by the filtering moonlight. "You felt *sorry* for me, did you? Why, you snobby little bitch! I didn't ask for your pity. I even welcomed those lashes on my back if it meant being close to you. I thought you were something special, but you ain't. I'll show you how I want your pity. . . ."

And with a roar that pierced the night, like that of an animal gone mad, he dug his fingers into her buttocks, slamming them painfully against the rough deck, at the same time spreading her thighs more widely apart with a quick swing of his knees. She lay completely vulnerable beneath him . . . helpless.

With one hand, he held her arms above her head. Then he covered her mouth with his hot, seeking lips, stifling her screams as he used his free hand to maneuver himself to enter her.

Julie's cries melded into the sounds of the revelry beyond and disappeared on the night wind like a fragile bird caught in a gale.

❧ Chapter Four ❧

No one had noticed the man standing topside on the ship's bridge. Hidden by the shadows, he was watching the scene below with agitated interest.

So that was the beauteous Julie Marshal, he observed curiously. He found her every bit as lovely as his first officer had said she was. The moonlight brushed her ebony hair with silver dust, and her face was a delicate sculpture of loveliness in the light's heavenly glow.

Even from where Derek Arnhardt stood, he could see that the young woman was generously endowed. He stared at the rise and fall of her bosom as she lifted her voice in song. Exquisite breasts, he thought, opening and closing his fingers as though actually caressing the firm, tender flesh. It had been a long time since he had pleasured himself with a woman, and he felt as though his eyes were feasting on the most beautiful specimen he had ever seen.

Something caught his eye, and he realized suddenly that a jug was being passed around. He slammed his fist against the wooden railing. This was the reason he had wanted her kept below. A woman was bad luck on a ship, especially one such as his, and she did not realize how she was incensing his men.

He noticed that she appeared frightened and was moving sideways along the railing, away from the crowd of men. Good. Perhaps there would be no trouble. In a little while, he would send Garris and his men down there to break up the revelry. For the moment, he would allow the crew to carry on since they were going to be punished anyway for breaking the rules about drinking onboard.

He drew on his pipe thoughtfully, thinking how Julie's fright was probably teaching her a lesson. She would, no doubt, be glad to stay below for the remainder of the voyage.

The door behind him opened, and he turned to see Edsel Garris stepping up beside him. Scanning the scene, he sucked in his breath, shocked, then faced his captain to cry, "Sir, she left the dining room over an hour ago and said she was retiring for the night. I had no idea she'd slipped up on deck. And those men appear to be drinking—"

"They're drunk, most of them," Derek commented tonelessly. "Someone began passing the jug, and what started out as a quiet little song fest is now a bawdy party."

He had been facing Edsel, and now he turned his gaze back to the deck. Leaning forward, he cried, "Goddammit, she's struggling with someone. Get down there quick—"

But Edsel was already through the door, taking the thin plank steps two at a time. The first officer made his way down below, yelling for Watson and Justice to come quickly and bring their side arms. They answered his call, demanding to know what was happening, but he cried that there was no time to explain, and urged them to hurry.

The three crashed through the opening onto the deck, pistols drawn. The crewmen, drunk though they were, saw them and immediately the revelry ceased, as though a giant, unseen hand had passed and dropped a shroud of silence over them.

Then they could all hear it—the muffled cries and moans as Julie struggled in the darkness beyond with Shad. The sailors moved aside as the officers picked their way over the riggings and ropes, making their way toward the sounds.

Shad Harky was on top of Julie, about to force himself inside her. Edsel swore as he swung his booted foot to kick the side of the boatswain's head, sending him sprawling sideways with a startled cry of pain. Floyd reached to scoop Julie quickly to her feet, and she sagged gratefully against him as he wrapped his arms about her to hide her nakedness.

"Take her to her cabin," Edsel ordered. "Make sure she's all right. Watson, help me get this bastard below. We'll put him in chains. I've a feeling this time his neck will stretch, for sure."

Julie kept her face pressed against Floyd Justice's chest as he helped her away from the scene. "Would you like for me to carry you?" he asked worriedly.

She murmured feebly that she could walk. She felt so foolish, so embarrassed. A few more seconds and Shad would have succeeded in ravishing her. Only by struggling with every ounce of strength she could muster, twisting her hips from side to side as he tried to penetrate, had she been saved from his full assault. Shuddering, she thought how terrible it had been, and how much worse it would have been had the officers not arrived when they did. And it was so humiliating for everyone to have seen her that way—naked . . . exposed . . . vulnerable. . . .

Floyd felt her trembling and patted her awkwardly as they reached the steps leading below. "It's going to be all right," he tried to comfort her. "It's over. I just hope you aren't hurt."

Just as they were about to descend, the outraged bellow came, splitting the heavens with its vociferousness. They turned to see Shad struggling against Edsel and Grover as they held him between them.

"I'm gonna get you!" he screamed at Julie. "You wanted me! I know you did! You led me on, you little trollop. I'll fix you good. . . ."

And then he turned his face upward, in a direction beyond Julie's view, and he bellowed once again: "I'll get you, too, you sonofabitch. I'll see you dead! Goddamn you, Ironheart. . . ."

Then he slumped forward, making a grunting sound, and hung limply between the two officers. Julie knew one of them must have silenced his tirade. Her body quivering, she allowed Floyd to help her on down the steps, thankful to depart the scene.

Just as they reached the door to her cabin, the one opposite swung open. Her mother stood there, clutching her robe to her throat, mouth agape. "Oh, dear God!" she whispered, swaying, reaching out to steady herself against the door facing her. "Julie, what has happened? . . ."

Floyd helped Julie inside the cabin, where she slumped gratefully down to the bed. Her mother hovered nearby, demanding to know what was going on.

When he had covered Julie with a blanket, Floyd turned to her mother and told her as gently as possible about Shad's attack.

"I'm all right, Mother." Julie was surprised at the calmness with which she could speak. "He didn't succeed with what he was trying to do. The officers got there in time."

Her mother sat down and put her arms around Julie. "But what were you doing up on deck? You said you were going to bed a long while ago."

Wearily, she shook her head and sank back on the pillow. "It doesn't matter now. It's over. I just don't want to think about it anymore."

Closing her eyes, she tried to shut out the sounds of Mr. Justice telling her mother what little he knew of the incident, and that Shad Harky was being placed in chains. "There's no telling what the captain will do to him now. Mr. Garris says he'll probably hang."

Julie didn't want to think about that possibility, either. She just wished none of it had happened. And why did Shad Harky accuse her of leading him on? Because she had not turned away in horror and disgust when she first saw his scarred face? The man must be mad. But then, she never should have gone on deck. It had all seemed so harmless at first, so pleasant. The quiet of the night, the singing . . .

There was a soft rap on the door, and Floyd opened it and murmured, "Oh, Jenkins, it's you."

Julie opened one eye and saw a disheveled crewman standing just inside the cabin, looking quite uncomfortable as he explained to Officer Justice that Officer Garris had told him to come. "He says the captain insists on knowing if Miss Marshal is hurt."

"I'm all right," she murmured wearily, wishing they would all just go away and leave her alone. "I've got a few bruises, probably, and I'm a bit sore, but I'll be all right if all of you would just let me rest."

There was an awkward silence, and the crewman repeated apologetically that the captain wanted to be sure.

Julie had closed her eyes, but she sensed someone leaning over her, and she looked up to see Floyd's slightly flushed face as he whispered tensely, "I'm afraid Jenkins will have to examine you, Miss Marshal. He used to be a doctor—"

"*Used* to be?" she echoed, stunned. "Mr. Justice, I'm afraid I don't understand."

"He was run out of the town where he was practicing, because of his drinking," he hurriedly explained. "A pa-

tient died when he bungled the man's treatment because he
was drunk. The captain signed him on to have someone
around when we need a doctor. It's all right. He's perfectly
competent, since he's sober. He wasn't involved in the
drinking tonight. Now he must examine you. I'm sorry.
Your mother may remain with you, of course."

Julie gritted her teeth and agreed to the examination.
Anything, she thought, suppressing a scream of fury, anything to get it over with and have everyone just leave her
alone.

The doctor's examination was embarrassing and degrading, but at least, she thought with a sigh of relief when it
was over, he was fast. The whole ordeal took but a few
moments. Then he was saying that indeed, she seemed
fine. There was no bleeding, no danger of hemorrhage,
and she had few bruises.

"I told you he didn't actually *do* anything," Julie ground
out the words. "Now please, may I get some rest?"

"I'll ask Mr. Justice to have some brandy sent in to help
you relax," he murmured as he hurried out.

Her mother helped her get into a gown, admonishing
her all the while for disobeying orders. "I hope you've
learned a lesson, dear. Let's be thankful it wasn't worse."

Edsel Garris arrived with a bottle of brandy and insisted
that Julie have a drink. "The captain is quite concerned,
and I'm to report to him and assure him that you are all
right."

"Concerned!" Julie snorted with disdain. "So he sends
you. He isn't concerned enough to inquire personally. He
sends his lackey."

Her lids grew heavy as the brandy made her relaxed and
sleepy. She closed her eyes, the sounds of her mother's and
Edsel's conversation drifting further and further away . . .
finally disappearing completely as she dropped off into
blessed oblivion.

She awoke with a start.

The dim grayish-rose light peeking through the porthole
told her that night was almost over and dawn was breaking in the east. She had slept soundly, but what had awakened her? Trying to focus her eyes in the haziness, she sat
up, apprehension making her flesh tingle.

And then she saw the shadow of a man. He was leaning
against the little desk in the corner. Gasping with fright,

she clutched the blankets tightly to her chin and cried, "Who's there?" as a scream bubbled deep in her throat.

A husky, mellow voice answered, "I thought I should prove my concern by inquiring personally. I understand you stated your doubts to my first officer to the point of dubbing him my lackey." He sounded slightly mocking.

While Julie could not see his face, she could distinguish that he was a large man. The image of the captain she had conjured was of a withered, sour old creature who hated the world and everyone in it, including himself. The richly masculine voice that touched her ears did not sound like that of an old man, nor was he small and shriveled.

Propping herself up on the pillows, she took a deep breath and silently vowed not to let herself be intimidated. "I hardly call the middle of the night an appropriate time for a personal call, Captain."

"It's dawn, Miss Marshal. My ship comes alive at dawn, but of course you wouldn't know that since you sleep till mid-morning."

"And how would you know my sleeping habits?" she snapped. "You never come out of wherever it is that you hide."

He laughed. "I know everything that goes on around here. I know my men, too, particularly Harky, and perhaps now you understand why I didn't want you up on deck."

It was becoming lighter in the cabin, the sky turning a glowing watermelon pink. Julie could tell that the captain's arms were folded across his chest and his legs were slightly apart. His face remained hidden by the lingering shadows.

"All right. You've paid a personal visit. I thank you for your concern, but I'm quite all right, as you see." Then she asked what he planned to do with Shad Harky.

Again his tone was mocking, infuriating her as he asked, "What would you have me to do with him? You were his victim."

Flustered, she replied, "Well, my goodness, I don't know. He *was* drunk, and even though I'm angry and upset over what he tried to do, I don't want to see him dead. Mr. Justice said this time he would probably hang. Last time you scarred his face."

"I've always been a firm believer that a person must learn from his mistakes. If he's punished severely enough, he seldom repeats them. Shad Harky is a scummy rogue who'll never learn anything, no matter how many times he's beaten. He could just as easily have killed you last night. He's killed before, but that was before he signed on board *my* ship. Many of my men are guilty of heinous crimes, but I don't hold their past against them; I only consider their present actions." Grimly he added, "Harky's had too many second chances."

"Then you'll hang him."

"I should. If I don't, it will set a poor example for my men. They'll think they can break the rules over and over and get away with it. So I really don't have a choice, now, do I?"

Julie's mind was spinning. True, she was angry with Shad. She never wanted to see him again. But to see him die because of her? And yes, she would have to share the blame for what had happened. Too late, she realized how foolhardy it had been to go on deck and sing and mingle with the crew. Had she stayed below, none of it would have happened. "Can't you just throw him off your ship when you reach port?" she asked hopefully.

He was silent for a long time, and she saw that he was packing a pipe. He lit it, drew in the smoke, and exhaled. She found the aroma of the tobacco pleasant. And it suited him, somehow.

"I understand you have a very soft heart." He finally spoke. "That is commendable, but I've a ship to run. I can't tolerate last night's behavior. Every man who was drinking will receive three lashes. They all know I don't allow drinking on board my ship.

"Harky has been punished once for trying to rape a female passenger, and the punishment was quite severe," he acknowledged. "But I told him at the time that a repeated offense would mean his death. Obviously he didn't take me seriously, and my men *must* believe me when I speak."

"Oh, damn!" she cried in exasperation. "Why is it so important to you that the men fear you? Are you suffering from some feeling of inferiority that makes you want people to bow down to you as though you were God Himself? Does it give you a perverted delight to know they call you Ironheart behind your back, or perhaps you do indeed have a heart of iron, with no compassion for your fellow man!"

His tone did not change, and she knew she had failed in

her attempt to goad him. "I've a ship to run. I can't do so efficiently without the respect of my crew. And it's their *respect* I demand. If fear must accompany that respect, then so be it."

He hesitated, then continued. "Tell me, Miss Marshal. What if Harky had been successful in his assault, and you had been ravished? Would you still plead for his life, or would you be demanding his death?"

She shook her head, blinking back the hot tears of frustration. "I don't know. I just wish none of this had happened. Please, just leave me alone."

But he made no move to leave. She jerked the blankets all the way up over her head and lay very still. She could feel him staring at her. When he did speak, she was stunned.

"There's no denying you have a lovely body."

She threw back the blankets and stared incredulously at him. Then she realized it was dawn at last, and the cabin was light enough for her to see him and make out his features. She was startled to find him handsome. His hair was dark, the color of rich, warm coffee. Long, thick lashes fringed eyes as black as the murky swamp waters of the Savannah marshes.

He was quite muscular, with brawny arms and shoulders. The shirt he wore was open to the waist, and his chest was covered with thick, curly hair that trailed down to his waist and seemed to ripple with each breath he drew.

Her eyes moved downward to tight pants stretched across strong, hard thighs. She sensed something quite fascinating about him, his lips slanted in a mocking smile, the long, straight nose with nostrils that flared ominously, the penetrating gaze as though he could see to the very depths of her soul. He looked dangerous and feral, and despite her determination not to be intimidated by this man, she fought the impulse to wither beneath his almost impudent stare. He exuded strength, as though he could easily crush the breath of life from a man with his bare hands.

Finally she found her voice once again, and choked out her indignant reaction. "How dare you say such a thing?"

He smiled lazily. "From where I stood last night, even I could appreciate such a fine figure of a woman. And I understand Harky tore your clothes, exposing you for everyone else to see. . . ."

He moved quickly, like the sleek black panther she had once glimpsed in the swamps. He was beside her, and she shrank back into the mattress as he towered above her. "I knew you'd have green eyes," he murmured, "as green as the cold, dark currents of the deepest waters. But I see a fire in them, a warmth, and when your passion is aroused, I'll wager they blaze like the sea at sunrise."

She could only stare at him, her lips parting and closing in surprise.

He chuckled. "You think me some kind of monster, don't you? I have my men beaten, keelhauled, and I possess the power to take their lives. You find all this repugnant. That shows the stupidity of women. You've no knowledge of how brutal and dominant a captain must be to run his ship and keep his men under control."

"I . . . I don't find you anything," she said nervously, not liking his nearness, the way his eyes kept moving over her as though she were naked. "You're nothing to me. I wish you would just go away—"

"But what about Harky?"

There was that mocking smile once more. He drew on his pipe thoughtfully, then set it aside on the desk. He took a deep breath, and the hairs on his chest rippled once more. "I will tell you what I intend to do. I'll have him kept in chains till *you* decide his fate. Since you're the one who was attacked, and you seem to find my methods of punishment so harsh, then you will be judge and jury. Do you find that fair?"

"Fair?" She sputtered angrily, "I want no part of it. I only want to be left alone. I can assure you I won't go on deck again till we reach Bermuda, when I'll gladly take my leave of this ship. Until then, I want nothing to do with you or your men, and that includes your officers. I'll take my meals in my cabin, and—"

But he was not listening to her outburst. He moved closer, his arms wrapping about her to pull her against him, his lips crushing down upon hers.

For an instant she was so stunned by his movements that she could do nothing but lie there, frozen. His lips were warm, teasing, and his tongue thrust inside her mouth and moved about deliciously. Suddenly she came alive and began to beat upon his back with her fists, but she was no match for his strength.

A powerful hand moved to caress her breasts. She felt herself yielding despite her fury over his boldness. Her brain screamed that it was insane, yet she acknowledged he was awakening in her a hunger she had not known existed so intensely, so fiercely. She could feel a warmth in her loins, and fought wildly within herself to keep from melting against him and reveling in the pleasure that she felt in every pore of her skin.

Abruptly he released her, staring down with those ebony eyes. "You liked that, didn't you? You may not admit it to me, but you can't hide the truth from yourself. And that's certainly no way for a woman to behave when she's betrothed to another man."

"You—you savage!" She shoved at his chest with both hands but felt as though she were pushing against stone. "You had no right. . . ."

"You needed that," he said quietly, moving away. "You need a lot more. But you're lucky. When it comes to ladies, as strong as my needs are, I try to control myself."

"You *do* have a heart of iron," she screamed in rage. "Get out of my cabin . . . now!" She reached out for the first object she could fasten her hands about—the brandy bottle—and sent it sailing through the air. He ducked as the glass shattered against the wall just above his head.

"Perhaps you could melt my heart of iron." He cocked his head to one side, a smile playing on his lips as his dark eyes twinkled mischievously. But I will go now and let you rest. We'll meet again."

He paused at the door. "Remember. Shad Harky's fate is in your hands, not mine. Send me a message when you decide what that fate will be."

And then he was gone. Julie stared at the closed door, trembling. He *had* aroused her. There was no denying that fact, just as she could not deny that she found him quite handsome. Still, there was something about him that incensed her to the point of near-hysterical rage. It was best, she decided, that she remain secluded, for she would not relish another encounter with him.

Her mother heard the sound of the bottle shattering against the wall and hurried in from her own cabin. She burst into the room, looking over her shoulder with wide, curious eyes, then faced Julie and cried, "What's going on here? And who was that big man?" She saw the glass on the floor. "Did you have a fight with him? I'll send for Mr. Garris, and he'll see that the captain puts a stop to these intrusions. . . ."

"That *was* the captain," Julie murmured feebly, leaning back against the pillows. She felt so weak and light-headed and something warned her that it was not just from the captain's kiss. A hot fever seemed to be engulfing her, and her stomach began to knot and heave.

Her mother opened the door to take another look, but Derek Arnhardt had disappeared. "*That* was Captain Arnhardt? He's a fine figure of a man. I had no idea he was so handsome." She turned back to Julie. "But what happened between you two, dear? Did you have a fight?"

She was not about to tell her of the kiss that seemed to have ignited her body into one giant flame. "We had words," was the only explanation she would give. "Please, Mother, let me rest now. I don't feel at all well."

Her mother moved to touch her forehead with the back of her hand, then stepped back, aghast. "You have a fever. I'm going to send for that ship's doctor and let him look at you again."

Feeling dizzier with each passing moment, Julie held up a limp hand in protest, but her mother was already scurrying from the cabin.

Everything was whirling about, becoming coated in a veil of dim, multi-colored lights and swirling currents that dipped her body up and down, making her even more nauseous. She reached out to grip the sides of her bed but only flailed wildly at the air.

A chill began, slowly at first, then moved to rattle her bones as her body contorted with spasms of cold. Her teeth chattered, and she huddled beneath the blankets, jerking and twisting from head to toe as she struggled to focus her eyes in the ever-tightening cloak of oblivion wrapping itself around her.

She was only dimly aware of people entering the cabin, of the chatter of concerned voices. From far, far away, a man was saying, "Yes'm, she's got the fever. It hits sudden-like, and she's got it right smart bad. Not much we can do except keep her warm and try to keep broth going in her so she won't get too weak. . . ."

The sound faded. There was only a giant roaring in her

ears that grew louder, louder, pulling, suddenly snatching at her. The shivering stopped, and in its place came a wave of heat pressing down, smothering her, drawing the breath from her body. She was fighting to stay afloat on a sea of fire, dimly frightened, feeling that at any moment her flesh would erupt into crackling flames.

Out of the darkness an unseen hand was reaching to coax her away from her suffering . . . and Julie held out weak arms to grasp that hand . . . grateful for escape. . . .

❦ Chapter Five ❧

THE invisible mammoth fingers opened, releasing her from their grasp. Julie was free. She had returned. She opened her eyes wearily, with great effort. She had an intense feeling of being drained physically and emotionally, as though she had been on a long, long journey.

But where was she now?

It came back slowly, heavily. The ship . . . on the way to Bermuda . . . then on to England and marriage . . . her cabin . . . no, not her cabin. This one was a bit larger and furnished differently. The bed on which she lay was longer. There were two portholes instead of one. A bigger desk occupied one side of the room, and it was covered with stacks of papers. Straining to see, she realized the papers appeared to be charts or maps of some sort.

There was a table, two chairs, a lantern hanging from a hook in the ceiling. Austere, sparse, almost harsh in décor.

She pushed back the blankets, which were like a giant weight upon her, and sat up, swinging about to gingerly test her feet against the rough-hewn wood floor. The ship was moving; she could feel the chugging steamer cutting through the waters. They were not in port, but she had a sense of time having passed . . . a lot of time.

She noted with distaste that the muslin gown she wore was stained, and her hair felt limp and dirty.

She stood on wobbly legs, then slowly shuffled over to stare at her reflection in the mirror which hung on the opposite wall. Gaunt, shadowy eyes stared back, with deep, dark circles beneath them. Her complexion was pale

49

and sallow, her lips parched and swollen. She shuddered at the sight.

The door swung open. She spun around in surprise and started to topple forward from weakness. Derek Arnhardt stepped up quickly to grab her elbows and steady her.

He smiled, his eyes mirroring concern. "So you're awake at last. Here, let me help you back to bed. You're still weak, as you've probably discovered by now, and you've got no business being up and about."

She did not protest, but once he had tucked her snugly back into bed, she erupted with questions. "Where am I? This isn't my cabin. How long have I been asleep?"

He chuckled softly. "You've been more than asleep. You've had the fever, and quite a case, I'm afraid. You gave us all a fright. The good doctor Jenkins cared for you, along with your mother. Then the two of them were stricken. I decided it best to quarantine that deck, and since there was no one else I could risk having exposed in order to look after you, I had you brought here. This is my cabin."

He went on to quickly assure her that her mother had not been quite so sick and didn't need constant care. "When I tell her you're awake and the fever's finally broken, she'll be in to visit.

"We were worried for awhile there you might not make it." He winked. "What a pity 'twould have been to dump you overboard to feed the fishes, though I would've envied them such a delectable morsel."

It was all coming back to her—that night on deck when Shad Harky attacked her, the scene with Captain Arnhardt when he kissed her. She felt her face flaming with the memory of her aroused passion. But strangely, she felt no animosity toward him now. After all, she supposed he had saved her life.

"How long before we get to Bermuda?" she asked, reaching up self-consciously to push at her mussed hair. "I've caused so much trouble on your ship, I suppose you'll be glad to be rid of me."

"A few days yet. And yes, it will be a relief to have you and your mother delivered to your destination. By the way, that old Negress you brought on board with you was taken ill too. I hear she's slowly recovering."

Julie nodded. "Thank you for all your help . . . and concern."

"Under different circumstances, I'd be charmed by your company, but you've been a big responsibility. Now then, suppose I have the cook bring in some food. You're probably starving. I wasn't able to get much broth into you."

Julie murmured that she would like something to eat, and then she looked at him, *really* looked at him, and realized he was bare-chested. Never had she seen a man who exuded such strength. Despite her weakness, she had to restrain her desire to reach out and touch that massive, handsome chest.

A wave of guilt moved over her as she realized there was a warm tingling in her loins at his nearness.

He leaned over her, and for a moment she tensed, sure that he was about to kiss her again. Instead he touched his lips briefly to her forehead, then straightened and said, "Yes, I believe the fever is gone. That's the way my mother always checked to see if I had a fever when I was a child." He smiled slightly.

"Your mother . . ." Julie blurted out. "I've had such a vision of you, Captain, that I never pictured you as a child with a mother, only as a cruel, domineering man filled with bitterness and hate."

"Oh, I had a mother, Julie." He raised an eyebrow. "I hope you don't mind the familiarity of me calling you by your first name. After all, while you were delirious, we talked a lot, and whether you know it or not, we've become quite close."

He went on. "As I was saying . . . yes, I did have a mother, *and* a father. I grew up in Wilmington, North Carolina and had a happy, normal childhood as the only son of a fisherman. I suppose I had a lust for the sea from the time I could walk, and even when my father was lost at sea during a storm, I still knew what my future destiny would be: to have my own ship. My dream came true, and I had a nice fishing business going till the war came along. Now I find myself a blockade runner."

He paused to push her hair back from her face with a sudden display of tenderness. "I have a sister somewhere. She married young, shortly after my mother finally grieved herself to death over my father's tragic end. Selma and her husband moved west and settled there. I suppose she's written to me, but I haven't been home in quite a while."

"I have a brother," Julie said quickly. "His name is Myles, and—"

"I know all about Myles," the captain interrupted, watching as her eyes widened with surprise. Then he informed her that she had told him all about her brother. "I'm sorry to hear that he was forced to run away. You also told me about your father, how he died."

Julie was stunned, speechless. She opened and closed her parched lips, but no sound would come. How could she have divulged such deep, dark secrets? The fever must have made her insane, forcing out the things she kept locked deep inside.

"And if you're wondering whether or not you told me about the truth of your impending marriage to Virgil Oates," he continued, further shocking her, "you left nothing out, I can assure you."

Her cry was barely audible: "Oh, my God . . ."

He paused at the door and gave her a penetrating look with those smoldering eyes. "I took care of you as best I could, Julie. And by the way, what I heard was true. You *do* have a lovely body."

He was out the door and gone before she could vent her quick flash of anger. The nerve, she thought, regaining her strength as fury charged through her veins. He had the gall to make such a remark, to remind her of her feverish ramblings.

Oh, would they never get to Bermuda? she fumed. Would she never be out of the company of this man? Besides, she did not like the way her body betrayed her, the way he made her feel, all warm and glowing and tingling with emotions she did not quite understand.

He was every inch a man, and just being near him reminded her that she was a woman. She did not like the feelings he aroused . . . not at all.

A short while later, her mother came with a tray of cooked beans and potatoes that had been simmered into some kind of palatable stew. Julie ate ravenously and sipped at a mug of hot tea while her mother clucked over her anxiously, wanting to be reassured that she was indeed going to be all right.

"We were all so scared. You gave us such a fright." She repeated the earlier words of the captain. "And he was so good to you, dear. I didn't like it when you were moved in here, but I was so sick I couldn't care for you any longer. Mr. Garris said the captain didn't sleep a wink for several days and nights. He just hovered over you constantly, afraid to leave you alone for a second."

Afraid he would miss something I said in my feverish ravings, Julie thought with silent ire which overcame any appreciation she might have felt for his solicitude.

She noticed that her mother had not regained any color in her face. "Are you sure you're all right now?" she asked anxiously. "You don't look well, Mother."

The answering smile was wan, weak. "Yes, I'm all right. I suppose I'm tired of being on board ship. I might as well get used to it, though, hadn't I? We've quite a ways to go after we reach Bermuda."

"Maybe it wasn't such a good idea, our going to England. Maybe we should've just remained in Savannah. Virgil and I could have been married there."

"No, I agree that it's best we left. Maybe by spring the war will be over, and we can all go home—and Myles will be there."

Julie saw her mother's eyes glistening with tears. "Let's just hope and pray Virgil can use his influence to bring him home," she said wistfully. "The way things are now, we both know he wouldn't even get a fair trial."

Her mother nodded in agreement. "We both know that nigra working in the tavern told Lionel he saw the whole thing, that those men drew on Myles first, but could we have expected anything different than for the others to say Myles just shot them down in cold blood? They all hate him because his sympathies aren't with the South."

"He just wanted to stay out of the war." Julie patted her lovingly. "Let's don't think about it, Mother. Surely things will change once the war is over."

But Julie did not believe her own words. Their only source of faith would have to be Virgil's promise that he would do everything in his power to straighten the matter out. Until the war ended, there was not much use in his even trying, though he had assured them that he would do what he could.

When she had finished eating, Julie felt stronger, and welcomed her mother's suggestion that she take a hot bath.

A wooden tub was brought in, and two crewmen made repeated trips to the galley stove to bring in buckets of steaming water. Finally Julie was able to strip off her soiled gown and sit down in the relaxing bath.

"I feel so much better," she told her mother. "To think I was so sick, and now I feel as well as I ever did."

"That's exactly the way I felt when the fever finally broke. It happens that way sometimes. And just think. A few more days and we'll be in port." She grinned at her daughter and seemed to have a little of her color back as she glowed with happy expectation. "It makes me happy to know my little girl is going to marry well and never have to worry about anything ever again."

Julie used a sponge to dribble water over her back. A thoughtful look came over her face as she murmured, "I can see how you feel that way, Mother. I suppose I should be grateful Virgil asked me to marry him."

"*He* should be grateful you accepted his proposal," her mother said quickly. "You're a beautiful young woman, Julie, and any man would be proud to have you for his wife."

She moved toward the door, saying she would go and get Julie a clean dress. "You just sit there and soak and enjoy yourself."

Julie suddenly felt melancholy. Perhaps she was still weak from having been sick. But she had to admit that a disconsolate mood came on whenever she thought of her impending marriage. Still, it was for the best. She had come to terms with herself long ago on that point. Virgil would be a good husband. She would have liked to be marrying a man she loved, but she knew she had to be realistic.

Myles. Her mother. The two dearest people in her world. They had both suffered so much. Sometimes when her mother did not know she was watching her, she would see a shadow of pain in her eyes, and Julie wondered if perhaps, after all, she had known of her husband's infidelity. She prayed not.

Myles. He was devoted and adoring, and after Virgil arranged for his safe return home, her marriage would bring still more happiness to them all. Virgil would see to it that they did not lose Rose Hill. It was home. It was security. They could not lose it, because they had worked too hard, sacrificed so much, to keep it this long.

The ship had been jerking and heaving more than usual, and Julie noticed that it seemed to be getting worse as the water in the tub began to slosh over the rim and onto the floor. There was a distant rumble of thunder, and just as she glanced toward a porthole, the sky exploded in a blinding flash.

A storm at sea. She had heard they could be terrible.

Quickly, she rinsed the suds from her skin, thinking she would feel safer out of the water and dressed. She picked up a thick, thirsty towel, and did not hear the door open as she dried herself.

Derek Arnhardt stepped inside the cabin and stood watching her with interest.

The towel dropped to the floor as she stretched her arms lazily above her head, wishing her mother would return with her dress.

With a stab of panic, she realized she was not alone. Whirling about, she faced Derek and cried, "How dare you spy on me? How dare you walk in without knocking. . . ." She scrambled for the towel at her feet to cover her nakedness.

His lips curved insolently. "Habit, I guess. It's my cabin. I don't normally knock when I enter my own room." He was carrying her dress, which he tossed on the bed.

"Well . . . you have no right. . . ." she sputtered. "Now get out so I can get dressed."

He appraised her coolly. "You seem to forget I'm the one who bathed you while you were sick, trying to get your fever down. I've seen all of you, and I know every inch of your body. It's a shame to cover it, too. You should live on one of those South Sea islands, where I hear the natives romp naked—"

"You're despicable!" she responded, shocked by his candor. "I suppose all you did was stare at my body like some . . . some *pervert*, while I was helpless."

"You're beautiful," he admitted.

"You probably molested me."

At that precise moment, a crash of thunder reverberated, and she froze as he murmured, "You'd best get your clothes on, Julie. That's a bad storm about to bust loose. The crew is busy battening down the hatches, and I sent your mother to her cabin to settle in for the duration of the blow.

"She trusts me, you know," he added with an insolent grin. "More than you do."

"I don't trust you *at all*. If you'll get out of here, I will dress."

His black eyes flashed with rage. A muscle twitched ominously along the line of his hard-set jaw. She had succeeded in arousing his ire.

He scooped her dress from the bed and flung it at her. The movement caught her off guard and she dropped her towel to catch the garment. As his eyes raked boldly from her breasts to her mons veneris, her own gaze instinctively dropped downward, then rose quickly as her mouth flew open with a silent cry of surprise.

"Well, what did you expect?" he asked quietly. "I am a man, and there are some things I can't control—things I don't *wish* to control."

"I—I just want to get out here. . . ." she stammered, shaken by the sight of the swelling in his crotch. "I want to get to Bermuda and off this ship and never see you again."

There was no warning. Her dress was yanked from her, and he tossed it aside and wrapped arms of steel about her, drawing her tightly against his massive chest.

"You *want* to see me again, and you know it." She could feel his hot breath upon her face. "You want to do more than see me. You want to touch me . . . and you want me to touch you . . . like this. . . ."

His hand moved to her waist, down the curve of her belly, and finally slid easily downward to caress her intimately. Moaning softly, she could do nothing but yield to him as he bent her backwards in his arms and continued to use his fingers to dance between her thighs in a silent rhythm of passion, giving her unfamiliar pleasure. She could not control the spasms of delight that rippled through her beneath his touch.

His middle finger lowered slightly, then plunged inside her cadentially, again and again. Her legs were like boneless appendages, lifeless and limp. Suddenly they straightened as her back and toes arched simultaneously. A deep rumble of joy worked its way up from the depths of her being to erupt in a cry of rapture.

When her last shudder was over, he flung her down on the bed, and she could only stare up at him in wonder and awe.

"You're a damn liar if you say you didn't like that." He glared at her, as though daring her to attempt denial.

"You had no right," she choked the words out. "I've never been with a man—"

"And you didn't know it could feel so good?" He chuckled. "Think how much better it would be if I spread those golden thighs of yours and filled you with everything I possess."

He walked slowly to the porthole and looked out at the angry, foaming sea. Without turning around he asked, "Why are you marrying Virgil Oates? You don't love him. Besides, he's a fake. I know him well. He's not what he pretends to be."

"What do you mean?"

"He has no wealth, no influence. He bartered for your passage and your mother's with a portion of your cotton. He didn't have the money to pay for it. He's marrying you because he figures he can get your family's precious plantation, but why are *you* marrying *him*?"

"You—you lie," she sputtered. "Virgil is everything he represents himself to be. He'll continue to help my mother get Rose Hill cotton through the blockade. And he'll make it possible for my brother to come home."

She shook her head in disgust. "I don't know why I even bother trying to talk to you. I think I hate you more with each passing second."

Again he laughed, but the eyes he turned upon her matched the storm about to explode beyond. "He wants Rose Hill, you little fool. He also wants your beauty, and I can't fault him for that. But I do think you're very stupid to marry him for the sake of your mother, your brother, or your plantation. Nothing is worth a certain life of misery, and that's exactly what you're facing."

"It's no concern of yours." She began jerking on her dress.

"That's true." He nodded thoughtfully. "But you're a beautiful woman, Julie. It would be a waste for you to marry a liar and a fake like Virgil Oates. Especially when I know why you're doing it. You're a martyr."

"A martyr?" she echoed, stunned.

"Like I told you, you did a lot of talking when you were delirious. I know the whole story. While it's admirable that you're so loyal to your family, it's not right that you should sacrifice yourself for them, especially to a wretch like Oates."

His audacity was overwhelming. "You are mad! And you've done enough to insult me. Now will you take your leave, or haven't you finished tormenting me?"

"No, I haven't finished with you." He was beside her in two quick steps, and she cowered beneath him, helpless. "Damn you, woman, I want you, all of you."

Her hand cracked across his face, but it was like striking stone. Her lips parted to scream, but he covered them with his own.

Beneath the onslaught of his seeking mouth and hands, she felt the betrayal once more of her own body. Slowly her fingers began to dig into the rock-hard flesh of his back, pulling him even closer as he delighted and aroused her with his tongue and fingers.

He raised his head, and in the flashing glow of the storm venting its fury all about them, she could see him smiling down at her as he whispered, "Tell me you don't want this, you misty-eyed vixen. I challenge you to tell me you don't want me inside you. . . ."

The tip of his swollen, throbbing member teasingly probed between her thighs, sending sweet, hot spasms of fire darting into her belly.

"Damn you, Derek. . . ." she sobbed, hating herself, hating him. "I can't. God help me, but I do want you. . . ."

With one mighty thrust, he burst inside her, and the pain she felt was overshadowed by the glory of his possession.

As the loudest crack of thunder split the night, her own storm erupted, and he silenced her cries of wonder and joy with his lips, devouring her mouth hungrily.

His penetration was deep, rough, but she welcomed every thrust. Only when it was over and they lay side by side, panting with exhaustion, did she begin to cry against his broad, perspiration-slick shoulder. The realization of what she had done flooded over her, and she felt only revulsion for being so weak.

How easily she had given in to this man she was so sure she hated for his bold interference in her life. What must he think of her now? How he must be gloating. She shuddered and closed her eyes, unable to face him.

He began to stroke her hair, then moved gentle fingertips to caress her face. She felt like a child being soothed and calmed, and when her tears subsided, he whispered, "I know what you're thinking, Julie . . . how you're ashamed . . . but you have no reason to be. You're a woman answering a need. I knew, somehow, that this would happen. There was something between us, a spark like the lightning out there that splits the night. We were meant to be. I feel it, and so should you. . . ."

"No. It wasn't meant to be. It never should have happened, and it won't happen again."

She turned her face to the wall, washed over with misery. "I'm going to marry another man! God, what kind of woman am I? . . ."

"A warm, hot-blooded woman, alive, passionate. That's nothing to be ashamed of, nothing to regret. It's wrong only when you deny it, when you lie to yourself about who and what you really are. Then you become a hypocrite."

He cupped her chin in his hand, forcing her to meet his eyes. "You've got to be honest with yourself, Julie. Admit you care for me and desire me."

"I don't. You're wrong. . . ."

But her denial sounded weak even to her own ears.

Then she realized with a start that his hardness was pressing against her bare thigh. He was ready for her again, and she accepted him as he entered her. He rocked gently this time, slowly, teasingly, till she was clutching at his plunging buttocks with her fingertips, urging him on. Only then did he move harder, faster, taking her with almost a surge of violence, until they reached the pinnacle of pleasure in unison.

He held her for a long time afterward, and this time she did not cry. She wanted to savor the moment of tenderness, for she knew it could never happen again. It had been precious and wonderful, a time to be treasured, but it was now only a memory and nothing more. She could not let it be more, for it could only cause her pain.

Derek Arnhardt loved no woman. His harlot, his lover, was the sea—always and forever—but having him inside her, being as close as a man and woman can be, had made them a part of each other, if only for a little while. But now they were separate entities once again, which was the way it had to be.

The storm subsided as slowly as their passion, and finally all was calm once more. She dressed, and together, arm in arm, they went up on deck. The air tasted so sweet after the rain that Julie drank in big gulps of it, reveling at its clean sweetness.

The wind was cool and gentle, and blew her hair about her face. They paused at a railing in the shadows, and

Derek put his hands on her shoulders, turning her to face him. She could barely see him in the darkness, but she sensed he was not smiling.

"It doesn't have to end when we reach Bermuda, Julie." He spoke quietly, his voice firm and sure. "You don't have to go on to England and commit yourself to a life of loveless misery. You can be my woman. I'll find a place for you there, away from the turmoils of the war, and I'll see you as often as I can. We'll get to know each other, and when the war is over—"

"No!" She all but screamed the word, jerking from his grasp and turning quickly to clutch the railing with both hands. It couldn't work. It was not possible. She did not want to be his mistress. She wanted to go on to England and marry Virgil so they could return to Savannah. She couldn't walk out on her family, turn her back on them. And she and Derek did not love each other. What they felt was the desire between two animals, she reasoned, nothing more.

"I've never asked a woman to be mine before." He seemed to be struggling to control his anger once again. "If you refuse me after all you told me while you were in your feverish stupor, you're going to make me think what we shared means nothing to you and any man with the right touch could have you the way I did."

"That isn't fair," she responded tightly. "I wouldn't be like that. I know I wouldn't."

"You didn't think it was possible with me. Now it makes me wonder just what kind of woman you are. You plan to marry a man you don't love, for the sake of your family and your precious plantation, yet you turn into a bundle of squirming, screaming flesh in my arms. Perhaps I judged you wrong. Maybe you just put on a good act, and you really are willing to couple with any man."

"Derek, I hate you when you talk like that." She faced him once more. "The plain, simple truth is that I don't love you. So just leave me alone. It seems we bring out the worst in each other. Forget what happened, and I'll try to do the same."

He laughed then, an ugly, cruel sound. "I'll leave you alone once I've left you safely in Bermuda. Till then, you will obey me and come when I call you, or I'll see to it that Virgil Oates is informed that his bride-to-be isn't the virtuous lady he believes."

"You would do that, too, wouldn't you?" She stared at him with loathing. "After your tenderness of a short while ago, you'd blackmail me into submission. I don't know you at all, Derek. I don't think you even know yourself. You're mean and vicious and unscrupulous."

"No," he said simply. "I meant the tender words I spoke. I do feel we were meant to be together. It angers me that you refuse to acknowledge that fact. You're denying your heart, your womanhood, and you turn your back on an emotion that could easily lead to the real and deep love I know you'd like to share with a man.

"And yes," he went on bluntly, "I would be vengeful enough to tell Oates about us, to keep you from destroying yourself."

"You don't know what you're talking about." She turned away from him once again. Oh, would he never stop tormenting her? Would he not just leave her be? "You made me respond to you. I didn't ask you to make me feel that way. Why can't you understand that?"

She turned to face him, blinking against the darkness as she realized she was speaking only to the night wind. For silently, like an animal stalking its prey, he had slipped away. She was left alone, there beside the railing, the ocean waters still churning angrily below, Derek's threats echoing in her soul. Without a doubt, she knew he'd meant everything he said, and that he would again call her to his bed to fill his needs.

She had no choice but to answer that call. Derek Arnhardt was not a man to bluff. A shudder passed through her body as she remembered his kisses, still sweet upon her lips . . . and his caresses, the feel of him lunging powerfully inside her body, filling her with his manhood.

God forgive her, but for the time left, she would secretly welcome his call.

✺ Chapter Six ✺

EACH night Derek would slip silently into Julie's cabin. There was no set time, so she never knew exactly when he would appear. It could be any hour between midnight and dawn. Sometimes she would fall asleep, only to awaken to his warm, tender kisses and hungrily seeking hands. And always, no matter how hard she tried to be cold and unyielding, he could arouse her body to a fever pitch. She would answer his hunger with her own, and the two would entwine passionately, hotly. He would thrust himself inside her again and again until he was sure that she, too, was satisfied and fulfilled.

One night he waited till just before dawn to steal into her bed, and after they had made love, he held her against his powerful chest and stroked her hair lovingly for a long time without speaking. Then he whispered, "Soon we'll be in Bermuda, Julie. Do you really want to continue on to England? Haven't I proved to you by now that you want me every bit as much as I want you?"

She stiffened. He felt her rejection and stopped caressing her, waiting tensely for her reply. "I *am* going on to England, Derek. It would be hypocritical for me to say I haven't enjoyed these hours in your arms. I have. Very much. I've tried to fight it—"

"How well I know." He chuckled softly, rolling from his side to his back and folding his arms behind his head. "I keep waiting for the night when you stop pretending, and I'll find you waiting for me naked and eager, the way you really want to be."

She thought how desirable he looked, lying there in the

gray-rose light of dawn that filtered through the porthole, his muscles glistening with perspiration from their passionate lovemaking. Her fingers tingled with the desire to dance down that beautiful, massive chest, but she held back. "Derek, you are a wonderful lover, and shameless as I may be, I have enjoyed all we have meant to each other, but soon it's going to end. It has to. I can't be what you want me to be."

He raised an eyebrow, and she could tell by the flash in his eyes and the twitch in his jaw that he was getting angry. "Just what the hell do you think I want you to be?" he snapped.

"Your mistress," she said simply as she fumbled beneath the mussed blankets in search of the gown he had removed from her. She found it and pulled it over her head, shaking her hair loose about her shoulders and tying the bow of the gown beneath her chin. "I don't want to be any man's mistress, Derek."

He snorted contemptuously. "That's all you'll be as Virgil Oates's wife—his mistress. You won't have a marriage in the true sense of the word, and you know it."

"At least I'll be his wife. That will give me respectability, security, something I would never have with you."

He drew in his breath, then let it out in an annoyed rush. "Women! By any other name, they're all prostitutes, wanting something from a man, whether it's money or a husband. I'm not surprised to find that you're no different."

Momentarily she felt a ripple of anger move over her, but refused to let it take hold. Instead she kept her voice calm and even. "Someday you will fall in love, Derek, and then you'll want to give a woman what Virgil is giving me. Will you consider your wife a prostitute?"

He looked at her as though she had lost her mind. "I'll never marry, Julie. If I have a wife, it's the sea. I've known plenty of women, but I've never thought about marriage."

"But have you ever been in love?" she pressed on.

He looked thoughtful, then shook his head slowly. "No. I don't guess I have. But then, I have never stayed with the same woman for very long."

He lowered those thick, dusty lashes that she found so appealing and gave her a strange, thoughtful look that made her uncomfortable. Scrambling from the bed, she stood barefoot on the rough floor and murmured nervously that he'd best be on his way. "It will be completely light soon. You might be seen leaving. Others will be waking."

He continued to stare at her in that puzzled, searching way that made her feel so odd. Finally, almost reluctantly, he got up and began dressing. Julie walked over to the porthole and stared out at the rolling sea. A greenish mist clung to its surface, but she knew that would soon rise, giving way to the usual sparkling, azure waters. She loved the sea and found it strangely mysterious, as though a million secrets lay beneath its depths, forever hidden. She could stand for hours and dream of those secrets, wondering how many before her had done the same.

Suddenly something caught her eye—an object, far away, as best she could tell; but no, it was close by. The fog played tricks with her sense of distance. She could not make out what it was, but here, this far from land, the only thing it could be was a ship. "Derek," she whispered, a feeling of undefined terror making her heart beat faster. "Derek . . . I think there's a ship out there—"

"A ship?" he cried, forgetting to keep his voice low, forgetting that her mother slept just across the narrow hallway. He bolted to the porthole and roughly shoved her aside as he squinted to see through the thick mist that still clung to the ocean's surface. "Where? Show me. You must be seeing things."

"There. . . ." She squeezed next to him to point. "Wait a moment, till the fog rises a bit. There. Can you see it now? Doesn't it look like a ship? What else could it be? Or perhaps it's land. Maybe it's Bermuda, and we're arriving sooner than you thought—"

He pushed by her to scramble into his trousers, forgetting about his shirt and boots as he hurried toward the door. "Hell, no, that's not land," he yelled. "That's a goddamn ship, and I don't know what *kind* of ship. . . ."

He opened the door and slammed right into his first officer, who had been about to knock.

"Sir, we've been looking for you," Edsel Garris cried, feeling slightly embarrassed at finding him in Julie's quarters. "We've caught sight of a ship, and it's too far away to tell what flag she flies. I've ordered the men to their battle stations."

"Let's go. . . ." Derek shouted, and the two ran down the hallway as Julie's mother opened her cabin door. Her sleepy eyes were instantly wide awake, shocked at the sight of the captain coming out of her daughter's room, his chest and feet bare.

"What on earth . . ." she gasped.

Julie ignored her mother and scurried after Derek, forgetting that she wore only her dressing gown. "Derek, what's wrong? What's happening? We've passed ships before."

He whirled about at the bottom of the steps, his eyes narrowed grimly. "Julie, go to your cabin and stay there. I told you: we don't know what kind of ship it is. We may be fired on. Federal steamers are in these waters, and if they demand to board, we'd have a hell of a lot of questions to answer. If they find out the *Ariane* is a blockade runner, then we're all in danger. Now do as I say. I'll let you know when it's safe."

He saw her mother for the first time. "You too. Get in your cabin and stay there. If you hear any firing, lie down on the floor."

Then he disappeared up the steps. Julie turned and hurried back to her cabin, looking about for something to put on. She had no intention of being caught in her nightgown if the Yankees did board.

Her mother followed her. Instead of being frightened about the possibility that their ship might be attacked, she was overcome with rage because of the implication of Captain Arnhardt being in her daughter's cabin, especially the way the two had been dressed, and at such an early hour.

"I demand to know what has been going on here," she cried. Then she saw Derek's boots, carelessly tossed on the floor beside the bed, and his shirt lying nearby. In anguish she whispered, "Julie, no. Don't tell me you and the captain were . . ." She could not bring herself to speak the actual words.

Julie felt herself reddening as she groped in her trunk for a dress. What could she say? Denial was futile. Finally she croaked out an apology. "I'm sorry you had to know."

"I . . . I thought you loathed him," was all her mother could think of to say. "I never dreamed this was going on."

Julie finished dressing, then went to where her mother had sunk down on the edge of the bed. Kneeling before her, Julie reached up and clasped her mother's trembling hands. She attempted to explain herself. "Mother, I did loathe him at first, but he's so tender and loving. Oh, how can I tell you what's happened to me? I don't even understand it myself. I can't describe it. I know it's wrong, but I'm helpless."

"Dear Lord." Her mother swayed. "Julie, you aren't falling in love with him, are you? Oh, please say that you aren't."

It was a long time before Julie could answer. "I haven't thought about it." And it was true. She hadn't, not till now, when her heart began to pound tremulously at the idea. Did she love him? Was that the reason her body could not deny him and came awake so easily beneath his touch?

No. It wasn't possible. Especially when he'd made it clear she was merely a woman to take his pleasure with whenever he felt the need. He would never offer her more than the degrading status of being his mistress. He'd certainly given her no hint that she could ever possess his heart. What they shared was passion, lust, pleasure—nothing more. It would be foolish to think their coupling meant anything else.

Not wanting to discuss it further, Julie got to her feet. "I have to know what's going on out there." She ran out of the cabin, down the hall, and scurried up the steps. Her mother called to her frantically to return, warning her there might be danger, but she paid no heed. For not only was she running to find out whether there was going to be an attack, she was also running *away* from something she was not ready to face or think about.

The upper deck was in a state of confusion as crewmen scurried about loading guns and stacking ammunition. The air was tense, strained, and no one so much as glanced her way as she moved to where Derek and his three officers stood on the bridge. Derek peered through a long, cylindrical instrument with one eye; his other was squeezed shut. Julie assumed it must be a telescope, though she'd never seen one before.

He barked with authority to no one in particular, "Tell the firemen to keep stoking the furnaces. We've got to move faster. That's a Yankee ship, and she's gaining on us. Hell, why didn't someone spot the bastards before now?"

"The fog," Mr. Garris answered nervously. "The watchman sounded the alarm as soon as he spotted it. I roused the crew, but as I told you, sir, when you weren't in your cabin, I had to look for you."

"Don't worry about that now," Derek snapped, turning to give him a black look. Then he saw Julie clinging to the railing, her face ashen with fright. "What the hell are you doing up here, woman? I told you to stay below. Watson, get her out of here."

Grover Watson clamped a firm hand on her arm, but she pulled away. "No. I've a right to know what's going on."

Derek walked over and towered above her, glaring down. "That Yankee cruiser out there is about a mile away, and they've spotted us. They're coming after us at full steam. We have no way of knowing how many guns they've got, so we've got to try and outrun them. If they capture us, they're going to find the cotton stashed below and other cargo that will prove we're a blockade runner. That means we're captured, Julie. *If* they decide to capture us, that is. They could just blow us to bits and sink us. So I want you to go below. If shells start flying, I don't want you hurt." He sucked in his breath after his verbal explosion.

Garris had hurried down to the engine room to urge the firemen to stoke faster and thus build up more speed. The other officers, and a man someone called a "pilot," looked away uncomfortably. They all turned to stare toward the pursuing Yankee steamer.

Derek reached for Julie's hand, which was cold and stiff. His eyes searched hers deeply, as though he were trying to convey some silent message, but she could only look up at him in confusion. He said, "Julie, this isn't the time or the place, but perhaps somehow you'll understand when I say I care what happens to you. I *care*! Now please, go below and stay with your mother. I'll let you know when the danger is past. Be the brave, courageous woman I know you're capable of being. The time for shriveling, helpless femininity has passed. We're at war."

She turned and fled, hurrying down to her cabin, heart and mind jumbled, dazed. He *cared*. What did that mean? Did he care about her as a woman, or was it merely concern for a passenger in his charge?

She did not know, but even with the tension surrounding them, as though the fog itself had crept up to consume them in its midst, Julie had found herself aroused by his closeness, the huskiness of his voice. The strength and power he exuded had made her want to melt into his arms once again, where she knew she would feel comforted and protected.

Her mother was waiting for her, face white with panic. "Did you find out anything?"

Julie told her all she knew. There was nothing to do but wait, and while her mother kept stealing curious, probing glances at her, Julie was grateful she asked no more questions about her relationship with Derek.

Perhaps a half hour passed, though it seemed much longer, before there was a loud pounding on the door. Julie hurried to answer, and found herself facing a crewman she'd never seen before. He was leaning on a crudely fashioned crutch, his leg bandaged in a splint.

Doffing his cap, he explained that he'd been sent by the captain. "My name's Duffy, and Captain Arnhardt said I was to come down here and sit with you ladies and try to keep you from gettin' too upset. I ain't no good topside nohow, not with this busted leg I got a few days ago when I fell from some riggings." He smiled nervously.

Grateful for the company, Julie waved him inside, saying, "Maybe you can tell us what's happening up there. It's agony not knowing."

He glanced nervously toward the round window. "The Yankees are gaining at a rapid speed. From what I heard some of the men say, they're bearing down on us with sail *and* steam, and they're sailing from the north, so they're making fast time. We're almost into the Bay of Bermuda, so we're actually trapped. It don't look good. Not at all."

They heard the first shot, a whining sound, then an explosion. Julie and her mother screamed in unison, but Julie quickly recovered and cried, "Are we hit?"

"That one fell short. Now's the time for us to start firing back."

Another shot streaked through the sky. This one, Duffy said, fell about fifty feet short on the starboard side. The third, he figured, went straight over, close to the riggings. "They're shooting nine-inch shells from a Parrott gun, I'd say. Can't understand why the captain ain't shooting back."

More explosions, each one seemingly closer than the one before. Suddenly, with a lurch the ship began to slow its forward motion. Duffy swore and yelled, "I can't believe it. The captain must be hoisting a white flag. He ain't going to put up a fight."

He turned sharply to give Julie an accusing glare, his eyebrows knit tightly together. "There's a story going around about you and the captain . . . how you're sweet on each other. Must be on account o' you. He's scairt you'll get killed."

"I'm going up there." Julie started to rise, but Duffy swiftly swung his crutch in an arc and blocked her path.

"Naw, you ain't goin' nowhere. I'm obeying orders no matter what, so don't make me crack you 'cross your head, Miss Marshal. You just sit tight."

He continued to hold the crutch across her bosom, and from the look on his face, she knew he would stike her if she attempted to move. She could do nothing but sit down and wait, praying that by some miracle, they had not been captured.

There was the sound of hurried footsteps. As three pairs of frightened, anxious eyes turned toward the door, it swung open and Edsel Garris stood there, the hand twisted about the knob as white as his stricken face. "It's no use," he said in a rush. "We were taken by surprise. We couldn't outrun them, and they had bigger guns."

"You mean the captain just . . . *gave up?*" Julie blinked, stunned. As strong mentally as he was physically, Derek seemed like the type of man who would never back off from a fight.

"You haven't seen the size of that ship bearing down on us, Miss Marshal. We wouldn't have had a chance. The *Ariane* isn't a war ship. We've always been successful at navigating and slipping in and out of blockaded ports. We've always been able to outrun a suspicious ship at sea. This time, luck wasn't with us. We're better off taking our chances and letting them pull alongside and board. Maybe we can convince them we're merely a merchant ship. The men are dismantling the guns."

Duffy shifted his weight to his crutch and struggled to stand. He was beyond caring at the moment that he was out of line in arguing with his commanding officer. "You don't think they'll *search* this damned ship? They'll find the guns and the cargo."

Garris withered him with a look. "That's a decision for the captain to make, not you. He's in command. You just stay here and keep the ladies here. There may be trouble if the captain doesn't like the way things are going once the Yankees come on board."

He stepped back into the hall and Julie tried to rise, but instantly felt the pressure of Duffy's crutch. "Please," she called out desperately. "I must speak with you privately."

Frowning, Garris nodded to Duffy, who reluctantly allowed her to hurry outside. When the door closed behind them, she whispered anxiously, "It's because of us, isn't it? I mean, is the captain giving up because he's afraid my mother and me would be hurt if there's a battle?"

Edsel Garris's smile was mocking. "Miss Marshal, when it comes to saving the *Ariane*, the captain wouldn't care if his own mother were on board. He's doing what he thinks is best for his ship. It has nothing to do with you, however close the two of you may have become in recent nights. . . ." His voice trailed off meaningfully, and she was aware of the shadow of contempt that flashed across his face.

Duffy quickly slammed and locked the door when Julie was back inside the cabin. Her mother gasped as he pulled a pistol from inside his shirt. "Just relax," he snapped. "The captain told me to take care of you two, and if any Yankees come nosing around, I'll be ready."

He tucked the gun in his belt and hobbled over to a position where he could stand facing the door. Then he motioned for them to get up on the bed together, out of the line of fire.

The moments ticked by with agonizing slowness. They could hear distant voices, angry words, shouting. Then there was a shot, and another, and both Julie and her mother covered their ears as the sound of gunfire split the air and all hell seemed to be exploding above them.

There was nothing they could do but wait . . . trembling in terror as Duffy kept his eyes and gun trained directly upon the closed door.

After what seemed an eternity, heavy footsteps could be heard thudding downward. Julie and her mother clung together as they heard the doors being opened and closed up and down the hall.

"No one here," a man's voice snarled. "That man in chains said there were female passengers on board. They're bound to be in one of these cabins."

They watched as the doorknob turned slowly. A man in a dark blue uniform seemed to fill the doorway. Julie glimpsed his startled eyes for only a fraction of a second before Duffy fired his gun. The man screamed, clutched his stomach, and fell forward as blood poured between his fingers.

Another uniformed figure moved quickly to return the fire and Duffy slumped to the floor, his face blown away.

Julie's mother fainted, but her own terror was replaced by outrage. "You . . . you damned Yankee!" she screamed, struggling to push her mother's limp body away from her and scramble toward Duffy's gun upon the floor.

The man flung her backwards and pointed his still-smoking gun at her. "Don't try nothing, lady. I'd just as soon shoot you if I have to."

He stared at the body of his dead comrade, then walked over to where Duffy lay and turned him over on his back by kicking at him with his booted foot. Satisfied that the sailor was dead, he reached down and picked up his gun, stuck it inside the waist of his pants, then turned to give Julie a snaggle-toothed grin.

"Looks like you two wasted a whole lot of time and money getting your cotton through the blockade. We're confiscating the entire cargo."

"You have no right," Julie spat out angrily. "We're private citizens. I'm on my way to England to be married. You've no right to interfere."

"We got every right, seeing as how you ain't nothin' but blockade-runnin' Rebs. We done found the cargo, and we also found a man chained in a hold who told us the whole story. You're in big trouble, and the best thing for you to do is sit there and keep your mouth shut before *you* wind up in chains."

They had not noticed the man standing in the hallway, who had silently been taking in the conversation. When he stepped inside, the scowling sailor stiffened. By the man's dress, Julie took him to be an officer.

Expressionless, he looked at the two bodies lying in the slowly spreading pools of blood. Then he nodded to Julie and her mother with cool politeness. "I'm Captain Benjamin Guthrie. It seems we've experienced more unnecessary bloodshed."

"I have to know." Julie could contain herself no longer. "Captain Arnhardt . . . is he—"

"I told you to keep your mouth shut!"

Captain Guthrie gave the man a withering look, then snapped, "Will you put that thing away? I think you enjoy killing, McCredie."

"He shot Davis!" the other yelped defensively. "He would've shot me too."

The captain leaned over Julie's mother, eyebrows knit in concern. "She's just fainted, hasn't she?" Without waiting for a response from Julie, he turned to the crewman and told him to find some smelling salts. "And get some men down here to get rid of these bodies and clean up the mess."

To Julie he said, "In answer to your question, miss, Captain Arnhardt is very much alive. We've secured him, of course, but he was not one of the fatalities."

Julie offered a silent prayer of thanksgiving, then appraised the Yankee officer. His hair was the color of snow, and curled softly about his boyish-looking face. His eyes were the blue of the robin's egg. Though he looked quite effeminate almost to the point of being pretty, there was something in the shadowy eyes that told her he was not a man to be trusted—and not merely because he was the enemy.

The crewman returned with smelling salts, which Julie passed slowly beneath her mother's nose. Almost at once she raised her head, eyes fluttering open, body trembling.

Julie did not like the way she looked. "We have a servant traveling with us," she said to the officer. "Could she come and tend her, please? I'm worried about her. There's been so much stress. . . ."

Her mother responded weakly. "I'll be all right, dear. Don't be concerned about me."

"Of course you may have your servant." Captain Guthrie turned to the other man and told him to fetch her at once. Then he faced them and said, "Please accept my apologies. I'm sorry you're involved in all of this, but no doubt you were aware of the possible danger you were in when you left your home on a blockade runner."

"I must know if we'll be allowed to continue on our way," her mother said quickly. "We mean you no harm. We're en route to England, where my daughter, Julie, is to be married. And we were only trying to get our cotton out so it could be sold. We need the money to save our plantation. Please, surely you can understand our plight." She was furiously blinking her eyes to keep back tears.

The captain sighed, shaking his head. "Frankly, I don't know what to do with either of you. We must confiscate your cotton, of course, along with the entire cargo of this ship."

He started to say more, then glanced at the bodies and wrinkled his nose in distaste. "I don't think this is the proper place for ladies to be at the moment. Suppose we move to the officers' dining room? I'll have tea made, and we can talk there."

Julie wanted to go up on deck and find Derek, yet knew she would never be allowed to do so. She had no choice but to follow the Yankee officer and her mother.

Once they were seated at a table with steaming mugs of tea before them, Captain Guthrie explained that he knew all about them. "The man we found in chains—Harky, I believe his name is—was only too glad to tell us everything we wanted to know."

He smiled, almost insidiously, Julie thought, as he commented on how the Federal navy had been trying to catch Arnhardt. "And thanks to this fellow Harky, we're now aware of the routes the infamous Arnhardt used to slip in and out of our blockade. This is valuable information. We'll be taking immediate steps to reinforce these points.

"We also know," he continued, "that Arnhardt has been getting supplies into the Confederate ports: guns, ammunition, medical supplies. We know quite a bit, thanks to Harky. Needless to say, he'll be given his freedom in exchange for his cooperation. He quickly pledged allegiance to the North, and I think we have a very loyal seaman in our service."

Julie exploded, her fists pounding upon the table and making the mugs rattle. "The bastard! Derek left his fate up to me, and now I wish I'd had him killed. I'll never hold pity in my heart again. Every man who walks this earth has treachery in his bones. . . ."

Her mother reached out to pat her hand in understanding. "We can't help the past, dear, but don't condemn all men because of one. Remember your brother—and your father . . . they were good men."

"Myles still is," Julie said tightly, not liking to speak of her brother in the past tense. She had the fleeting thought that she was grateful her mother did not know that her father was also capable of treachery—of another kind.

Captain Guthrie ignored Julie's outburst as he commented that one of the ship's officers had been killed. "I don't know his name. It was foolish of Arnhardt to resist our boarding. Needless bloodshed." He made a clucking noise with his tongue.

Julie's next words were forced out through the rolling, heaving fear within her. "What will you do with Captain Arnhardt?"

"He and his officers may be hung from the yardarms."

"Oh, my God!" Her hand flew to her mouth as she began to tremble from head to toe. "Please, no . . ."

"Or they may be sent to prison," he said with a shrug, as though he really hadn't given the matter much thought and it was not important enough to dwell upon anyway. "I haven't decided. As I said, Arnhardt's been sought for some time. He's quite adept at running our blockades, and it was only through great diligence and perseverance that we were able to catch him unaware and capture him and his ship."

He sighed and patted his lips with a napkin. "It's most unfortunate you two ladies are on board, because I'm in a quandary as to how to deal with you."

"You'll let us go on our way to Bermuda." Julie's mother showed spark for the first time. "There are certain rules and codes of etiquette in war, I'm sure. Or have the Yankees stooped to capturing helpless women and sending them to prison? Maybe you plan to hang us from the yardarms as well."

Julie saw the flash of anger in Guthrie's eyes, and she reached beneath the table to squeeze her mother's arm in what she hoped her mother would understand as a silent message for her to calm down. Riling the man was not the answer to their dilemma.

Taking a deep breath, she faced the man. "We are private citizens, sir." She spoke quite calmly. "We're not soldiers for the Confederacy—or spies. I see no reason why you would object to our continuing on our way."

He drummed his fingertips on the table, his lower lip jutting out in a thoughtful pout. Then he surprised her by declaring with a smile, "You really are a beautiful woman, Miss Marshal. Or may I call you Julie? It would make the situation much more pleasant if we can all be friends."

"Friends?" she cried, aghast. "You are the enemy, sir, in case you've forgotten."

"Oh, why should we be enemies?" He cocked his head to one side, eyes sparkling with amusement. "You've nothing to fear from me. Of course you're distressed because you've lost your cotton, but you knew that was a possibility when you left Savannah. You could have been blown to bits when you ran the blockade."

He got to his feet, signaling that teatime was over. "I have business to attend to. I'm sure you understand. You ladies relax and try to not to worry. I'll decide what's to be done with you after I see to a few other matters."

Julie and her mother returned to their cabins. Once she was inside her own, Julie flung herself across the bed, shaking with frustration and worry, not only for herself but for Derek as well. True, she was engaged to another, but there was no denying she felt something in her heart for Derek. The closeness and passion they'd shared made warmth spread over her body like a cloak; then it disappeared and left her chilled with foreboding over what might come.

Suddenly remembering the tragedy that had taken place in the cabin earlier, she raised herself up and turned her head, almost afraid of what she might see.

The bodies had been removed, but there were still large splotches of blood on the floor. Would she have to spend hours staring at them? she wondered with resentment.

The day wore on. Her stomach rumbled with hunger, but she had only to glance at the crimson stains and her appetite was quelled. She thought about going to her mother's cabin, but decided the older woman might be sleeping, and Julie did not want to disturb her.

Her heart twisted with agony whenever she thought of Derek. Perhaps he'd already been hung. There was no way of knowing.

A look toward the porthole told her darkness would soon be falling. Maybe she could slip out, move about in the shadows undetected, and find out what was going on up on deck. It was risky, but what could they do to her, anyway, if she were discovered? Surely Captain Guthrie would keep his promise that no harm would come to her.

As a black drape descended in the sky, Julie decided that if she were going to prowl around the ship, she would have less chance of being spotted if she were wearing something darker. The dress she wore was a pale lemon color, so she changed to a gown of dark green muslin with a high neck and long sleeves.

She had almost finished dressing when a voice in a clipped northern accent startled her by calling through the door, "The captain invites you to dine with him."

"Thank the captain for his invitation," she responded with exaggerated politeness, "but I'm not hungry."

"As you wish," the voice answered.

She pressed her ear to the door and heard him call out the invitation to her mother, who accepted. Good. That would keep them occupied while she prowled about. If her mother found her gone from her cabin, she might sound an alarm because she would be so frightened. And if Julie told her in advance what she intended, her mother would try to stop her, saying it was too dangerous.

When she heard her mother leave to go to the dining room, Julie waited a few more minutes. Just as she was about to leave, there was an almost apologetic knock upon her door. Annoyed, she snapped, "I told you I wasn't hungry."

"It's me, Miss Marshal," a familiar voice replied. "Doc Jenkins. They sent me to scrub the floor."

Surprised, she yanked the door open and saw the doctor standing there with a mop and pail. He stepped inside, and as soon as she'd checked the hall to make sure no one was about who might eavesdrop, closed the door and turned on him, hungry for information.

"You must tell me what's going on. I don't know anything. Where's Captain Arnhardt? How many of his men were killed?"

He looked sad, withered, as he sloshed the mop in the bucket of water and began scrubbing at the blood stains on the floor. "They killed Officer Justice and four crewmen. We never had a chance. From what little I've been able to gather from the whisperings amongst the crew, Harky was behind the whole thing."

She stared at him incredulously. "Harky? But how? He was in chains—"

"Yeah, but he has a few friends on board, it seems— scoundrels though they be," he added sardonically. "They were hoping a Yankee ship would happen by, because Harky told them he had a chance if the Yankees took over the ship. Otherwise, he figured he would hang for sure. So they sabotaged the guns.

"Like I said," he murmured with a sad shake of his head, "we just never had a chance."

He told how Captain Arnhardt pretended to surrender when he realized the *Ariane* could not outrun the Yankee ship. Then, when the Yankees started to board, he ordered his men to put up a fight. "But we were outnumbered. Hell, they came on board with God only knows how many men—from all sides! It's a wonder we all didn't get slaughtered."

"Then what's to become of us?" she asked fearfully. "What do Yankees do when they capture a ship?"

He looked at her with despair. "Miss, they aren't regular Federal navy men. They're privateers. They just like to act as though they're the regular navy."

"And what are privateers?" She blinked at the unfamiliar term.

He explained as he scrubbed diligently at the blood stains, which had by then soaked into the wood and were difficult, if not impossible, to remove, "A privateer is a privately armed ship fitted out at the owner's expense. I doubt this Guthrie fellow is the owner. Anyway, they're commissioned by their government to capture the ships and goods of the enemy at sea, or even the ships of neutrals. Then they're dealing with enemy goods considered contraband."

"They sound like pirates!" Julie cried indignantly.

He nodded in agreement. "In a way, I guess they are, but legally so. A privateer has a commission to do what he's doing, while a pirate has no rights."

Jenkins wrung out his mop and tackled the stains once more, sighing wearily. "The policy of neutral nations in recognizing privateers as legitimate belligerent ships of war is in the interest of humanity and is founded on the effort to try and *prevent* piracy. If privateers *weren't* recognized by neutral nations, they *would* become pirates, and instead of making prisoners of the crew of captured vessels, they'd massacre them, confiscate the cargo, and sink the ships.

"But," he went on, "by being recognized, they're under the surveillance of the government that commissioned them, as well as the governments of all neutral nations. So they're responsible for their acts to both."

Jenkins told Julie that privateers were a great advantage to their commissioning government because they cost it nothing and were owned and equipped by private individuals. "They're a source of revenue as well, because they're obliged to give a percentage of what they capture to the government that commissions them, in exchange for their license."

"Then they *are* no better than licensed pirates!"

"Exactly. And you may be sure that your cotton will be sold and a percentage paid to the Federal government."

"But what happens to you and the others?" she wanted to know, the familiar knot of fear creeping once again into her throat.

Jenkins scrubbed at the floor viciously, angrily. "Probably the same thing we hear that has happened to others just like us. We'll be treated like common felons, paraded in chains through the streets of northern cities for the amused enemy to gaze at, then thrown in the wretched dungeons of some place they call the Tombs." He shuddered. "I hear it's full of filth and vermin, and the prisoners are tortured by being hauled out every so often to be humiliated and put on display as the worst kind of criminals."

"And Harky?" Julie snapped with fury. "What of him? I suppose the Yankees consider him a hero."

Jenkins snorted. "Of course."

She slapped her forehead with her hand. "It's all my fault. If it weren't for me, Derek would've executed him and this might not have happened. As least we would've had a fighting chance. But no, *I* had to be sympathetic and weak!"

In her fury, she rose and kicked a chair, stubbed her toe, and cried out with pain. As she hobbled back to the bed to sit down, Jenkins watched her curiously, then murmured, "You know, the captain and Garris and Watson are down in the hole, in chains. The rest of the men, like me, know if we make one move to help them, we'll be shot. But I'll bet the captain is so mad he's trying to chew through his chains. If he was loose, he'd find a way to take his ship back over. I know he would.

"He's a fighter," he said proudly. "I've seen him in fights before, and I'll tell you one thing—it would take half a dozen men to bring him down. Strong as an ox, he is. He didn't get that build of his by pushing a quill at a desk like most captains."

"Then why don't you and the others free him?" Julie all but screamed, gesturing wildly. "Why do you stand there mopping up blood and telling me how great he is? Can't you slip down there and release him?"

Jenkins shook his head slowly from side to side. She wondered for a moment if the gesture reflected his dejection over being unable to remove the stains on the floor or the plight they were in. Then he spoke. "Miss Marshal, don't none of us want to die. We'd rather take our chances in the Tombs. We aren't going to risk our lives. I'm sorry."

Once again she was on her feet, determination and fury pounding wildly through her veins and making her feel warm, shaky. "I've no such fear. They wouldn't shoot a woman. Tell me where they're keeping Derek, and by God, I'll try to free him. I won't sit back like the rest of you and do nothing!"

He wiped his brow, unmoved by her veiled charge that he and the other crew members were cowards. "They might not shoot you—you being a woman and all—but if I were you, I'd just lay low. There's a lot worse they can do to you, if you know what I mean."

She knew, and her cheeks flushed with the knowledge.

He went on, "I should tell you that I heard Harky arguing with that Yankee captain that he should let Harky have you as sort of a reward. Told him a tale about you leading him on, then making a scene and having him thrown in chains and almost getting him hung. He wants revenge. You get caught trying to free Arnhardt, and Guthrie just might pass you around amongst *all* his men. Then you'll wish you were dead." He looked at her to see the effect of his words.

Without a trace of fear, she demanded to be told where Derek was. "Leave the rest up to me."

He stared at her thoughtfully, then a slow smile spread across his face that made her feel uncomfortable. Was he mocking her? Was he about to laugh at her, regarding her as just a weak, foolish woman?

Finally he chuckled, "My, but you're a spunky one. Never knew a lady like you." He said he would check with the others and try to round up some help. "If you're willing to stick your neck out, then by God, there are a few men I know who might be prompted to do likewise. Can't let a woman outdo us, you know." He winked, attempting to put her at ease.

For the first time since the nightmare began, Julie was able to smile.

Jenkins left, saying he would do his best to slip back down to her cabin when things quieted down for the night. After he was gone, Julie paced nervously up and down the small room, feeling that somehow she had to find a way to free Derek. He would know what to do. He could get them out of this mess; she was sure of it.

At last she heard her mother returning from supper. She was talking nervously to someone in a tone that hinted she was close to anger but struggling to remain calm. Pressing her ear to the door, Julie recognized Captain Guthrie's voice as he said, "I can sympathize with your plight, madam, but you must understand the ship is now captured and under my command. It's foolish for you to even suggest I should allow you and your daughter to continue merrily on your way with the cargo."

"But what will you do with us?" Her mother was close to the breaking point, Julie knew, and wondered if that meant an angry explosion or tears. Her mother could go either way.

"I'll decide tomorrow." Guthrie sounded bored. "For now, I'm very tired. I'm about to return to my own ship for a good night's sleep. I'll ponder the situation, but at the moment my inclination is to take you and your daughter back to Georgia and turn you over to the Federal government."

Julie heard her mother open and close her cabin door. Good. She had not given that pirate the satisfaction of seeing her break down.

A few moments passed before Julie heard Guthrie walk away, and during that time she was afraid he was going to ask to speak with her. She was relieved that he did not.

Restlessly, she awaited Doc Jenkins's return. She had almost given up on him and was toying with the idea of prowling about the ship on her own when at last he slipped into the dark cabin.

"Miss Marshal, are you asleep?" he whispered nervously.

"How could I sleep?" she hissed. "And what took you so long? I was about to leave without you! We must move at once."

"I was afraid you'd take matters into your own hands, and that would have been foolhardy. You've got to have help, and it's taken time for me to pick out the men I can trust and who've got guts enough to carry out my plans."

He explained how he'd found three crewmen who were willing to help, and discussed the situation with them. After checking, they found there was only one guard at the entrance to the hole where the captain and his officers were being held. A few other heavily armed guards had been left posted about the ship. The others had returned to the Federal cruiser, confident that all was under control. Harky himself was roaming the ship, cocky because he'd been left in command.

"I don't mean to alarm you," Jenkins said worriedly, "but I overheard him and Guthrie arguing again. Harky wanted to come down here and claim you for his own. Guthrie said no. He's got his men watching Harky to make sure he doesn't try anything."

"Thank God for that, but is it possible for me to get up on deck and make my way to where Derek is? Perhaps, if you've found three men willing to help, the four of you can do the job without me. I don't want to risk running into Harky."

"No," he all but shouted, "because here's our plan." And he told her how she was to go to the guard near the hole and use her feminine charm to catch him unaware, using whatever means necessary to take his attention from his duty. "Get him completely engrossed in you. Our men will do the rest. You can't act the least bit nervous, or he might get suspicious."

He eyed her narrowly. "Do you think you can do it? If you've the slightest doubt, then it's best to abort the plan for now and try to come up with something else later. If we're caught tonight, we won't get a second chance. It could mean our lives if we fail."

In the glow of the candle Julie had lighted, Jenkins continued to gaze at her with a piercing, searching look. She was able to return his stare confidently, her chin jutting upward with firm resolution. "There isn't time to think of another way, and we must move tonight. Don't worry about me. You and your men do your job, and I assure you I'll do mine."

He patted her shoulder. "Good girl! I've got faith in you. I can tell by the gleam in your eye you mean business."

"I do." Her voice was firm, sure.

He told her where the hole was located and how she could get there, moving in the shadows so as not to be seen. All was quiet on the ship except for the sounds of Harky and a few of the guards who were swigging rum up in the captain's quarters. They were obviously confident that all was under control, sure that the *Ariane*'s crew was subdued. And why shouldn't they be? Arnhardt's men had no weapons. Their captain and officers were securely chained, so the crew was effectively leaderless. And the privateers certainly had no reason to think Julie would not be so easily subdued or prone to acquiesce.

Jenkins told Julie to wait a half hour, then make her way to the hole. By then, he and the others would be in position and waiting. Once Derek and the others were freed, they would take over, finding a way to overcome the guards and take their weapons from them.

He turned to go but paused for one last, searching look. "I know you're concerned about your mother and your family's cotton, and I suppose you're anxious to be on your way to Bermuda and on to London to meet your fiancé. But if I may say so, Miss Marshal, I can't help thinking you're a bit fond of our captain, even if you don't realize it yourself at the moment."

She could only stare at him, wondering exactly what she did feel deep inside. Then she smiled secretively and murmured, "Let's just say I don't believe he has a heart of iron, Doc. I think I've come to know him a bit better than the rest of you."

He nodded, then left quickly.

Julie wondered if perhaps she hadn't come to know herself a little bit better also, after the harrowing events of the day. For maybe the first time in her life, she had really become acquainted with her true self.

And she had a scary feeling that before dawn broke on a new day, she would come to terms with herself and whatever the future held . . . *if* there were to be a future in view of the danger she faced.

❧ Chapter Seven ❧

ALL was quiet and still on deck. A light drizzle fell from the stormy sky, and Julie breathed a sigh of relief that there would be no chance of moonlight to expose her. She had changed from the high-necked dress to one that dipped provocatively and exposed much cleavage. Its color was also dark, and she wore a shawl about her shoulders, wanting to be as inconspicuous as possible as she made her way to the hole where Derek was held prisoner.

Her heart was pounding, her body trembling, but she swallowed hard, took a deep breath, and began to tiptoe along slowly, picking her way through the riggings and ropes which lay tangled upon the deck. The ship had been anchored, so at least it was still. Peering into the darkness, Julie could make out the lines of the privateers' ship perhaps fifty yards off the starboard side.

Spotting a guard, Julie stooped quickly beneath the railing, wrapped her arms about her knees, and drew them tightly up against her chest, not daring to breathe as he passed within a few feet of her. For a moment, she feared he might take his post there. Then she would be trapped and eventually seen. Finally he moved on. Before she rose, she scanned the ship, peering to see as much as she could in the misty darkness. There was another man, further away, with his back to her. As best she could tell, these were the only two on the deck, though she was sure there would be others within shouting distance.

When she felt it was safe, Julie straightened and moved

83

on. At the rear of the ship, between two wooden structures which looked like storage bins, was the entrance to the hole. She could see the guard sitting down, a musket across his knees. He appeared to be dozing, chin resting on his chest. She moved closer, wondering where Doc Jenkins and his men were hiding. Could they see her? Would they act in time? Perhaps he hadn't been able to muster enough of the crewmen to be effective. Captain Arnhardt was not loved by his men, that was a fact, and if they were assured of their own safety in the hands of the Yankees, they probably would not concern themselves with the fate of their officers.

"Eh . . ." the seaman's head jerked up. "Who's there?"

Julie found herself staring down at the musket, which was pointed straight at her. For a moment she froze, then reminded herself she must have courage. She must be strong. Now was not the time to be afraid. She was surprised to hear the calmness of her voice as she spoke softly. "Hello, there. I hope I didn't frighten you. I'm a passenger on this ship, and I just had to get some fresh air."

Quickly he scrambled to his feet, embarrassed to be caught sleeping on duty. He stepped closer, gun still pointed at her, and snarled, "You ain't got no business wandering about, miss. You're just as good as a prisoner, you know. Now you best get down below before you get yourself in trouble."

Very slowly, Julie let the shawl drop from her shoulders. There was a small lantern burning nearby, and it gave enough illumination that she knew he could see her clearly, see the way her breasts poured teasingly out of the bodice of her dress. She heard the quick intake of his breath, and she forced herself to take a step forward to give him an even better view. "It's such a nice night," she said petulantly. "And it's so stuffy down there in that old cabin. You know, it's not a bit cold, even though we're supposed to be in the middle of winter. I suppose it's the tropical air, being so close to Bermuda. Don't you find it unusually warm? . . ." She moved even closer.

He lowered his rifle so that it was all but drooping limply at his side, and she could feel his gaze riveted on her bosom. She leaned over quickly, as though adjusting one of the tiny bows on her skirt, so that he could see more of her, and she smiled with satisfaction as she heard his soft moan, "Oh—my—God!"

She straightened, smiling brazenly in the soft glow of the light, and forced herself to behave calmly, though she wanted to hurry and get it over with. There was a chance a passing guard might see them, and that would never do. Doc Jenkins and his men might not be able to subdue *two* men with weapons.

"Do you mind if I sit a spell with you?" she cooed, lowering herself next to the spot where he'd been reclining, without waiting for his response. "A girl gets lonely, you know. Don't you get lonely? Not only out here tonight but other times as well. I mean, it must be *terribly* lonely to be a sailor and seldom get into port where you can find the company of a young lady. . . ."

For a moment, he just stood staring down at her. He pulled at his chin as though deep in thought. Finally, just when Julie began to feel the first waves of panic, thinking that he might reject her, he fell quickly to his knees, a wide grin on his face as he moved closer. "Yeah," he whispered huskily. "I do get lonesome. I reckon it's the same for women, ain't it? I mean, you're supposed to make like you don't want the company of a man, but I know you do. All women do. They just put on an act, that's all."

He laid down his gun and, as he slipped one arm across the back of her shoulders, carelessly draped his other across her legs. "I heard about you. . . ." She could feel his hot breath on her ear, smell the sour odor of rum. Good. He had been drinking. That would make it all so much easier.

"Yeah, I heard all about you. . . ." he repeated, his hand straying to her ankle. Slowly he began to inch his eager fingers upward. "You're the one that scar-face had a fight with Captain Guthrie over. Hot-blooded wench, he said you were. Said you needed taming and he was the man to do it. The captain, he said he'd take care of you hisself in his own good time. And look who winds up with the treasure? Ol' Ringo! When I tell the guys about this . . ."

A lump rose in Julie's throat, choking and constricting her, as she fought to quell the feeling that she was actually going to be sick to her stomach. Then she forced herself to turn sideways in his arms, and slid her hands up about his shoulders. Closing her eyes, not wanting to see his face, she whispered huskily, "Just kiss me . . . I have this need . . . and I'm so lonely and frightened. . . ."

Her head was tilted back, lips parted, and the seaman whispered, "Sure, baby, sure. I got what you need. I can take care of you. . . ." And then his mouth clamped down on hers, and she felt as though she were being devoured. He seemed to come alive, to be instantly aroused. His left hand moved boldly on up beneath her dress to clutch possessively at her crotch, while his right hand quickly scooped her breasts out of her bodice. He began to fondle and pinch them, making little moaning noises deep in his throat.

She began to slide downward, wanting to lie on the deck with him on top of her body, thereby making him more vulnerable to what she hoped was the impending attack by Doc Jenkins and the others. Surely to God they will come, she thought with panic. If they didn't, then she was helpless. There was no way out of this situation, because if she tried to push the sailor away, make him think she had only been teasing, he would be furious, and he would take her anyway—roughly and brutally. Then, in revenge, he would probably alert the other guards, and she would be passed around freely. She was in a very dangerous situation; where was Doc Jenkins? If he were about, he must see that now was the time to act!

"Ringo knows what the ladies want. . . ." the guard grunted, lifting his weight from her to fumble with his pants. "Never get any complaints, I don't. And I'm ready to go again in no time a-tall. I really please a woman—you'll see. . . ."

Involuntarily, Julie felt herself stiffen. She was not going to be able to last much longer without screaming in revulsion. He shoved up her skirts and yanked down her pantalets, and she could feel him jabbing at her with his swollen organ.

"Come on, now. . . ." he was urging her, his voice raspy and hoarse with eager desire. "Open up. I know you want it—you don't have to pretend with ol' Ringo. . . ."

She could hold back no longer. Jerking her thighs together and pushing against his chest with both hands, she moaned her protests through clenched teeth.

Instantly he tensed, lifting his head to glare down at her with angry surprise. "What the hell do you mean—no?

What kinda tricks you playing on ol' Ringo? You asked fer it plain as day, and you're gettin' it. . . ."

With rough, calloused hands he yanked her thighs wide apart, and she knew that any second she would feel the first, hard thrusts. It could not even be called *rape*, not when she had offered herself to him. She was helplessly trapped beneath him unless she made a fuss which could give away the whole scheme. There would not be a second chance—Captain Guthrie would see through it all.

Her brain whirled maddeningly as she tried to think her way out of the revolting and dangerous situation she had gotten herself into.

Suddenly she decided on a different ploy. Pulling her legs tightly together, she pushed at him once again, this time asking in a whining voice, "Must you be in such a hurry? I thought you said you pleased your women! I don't think I'm quite ready. You could kiss me some more, and . . ." She took a deep breath, stomach heaving with nausea once again. "I was enjoying your—your fondling. . . ."

"Eh?" He stopped jabbing at her and stared down at Julie in pleased awe. "You say I'm too fast, eh? I see. You like to play, don't you? Well, never let it be said that ol' Ringo is selfish. I always pleasure my women, and if you want to tussle some more, then tussle we will. I know lots of ways to get you fired up, I do. I'll have you begging for it, you teasing little wench. . . ."

Quickly he ducked his head, fastened his teeth around a nipple, and bit down gently, sucking it into his mouth while flicking his tongue all about.

Julie knew she could not have felt more defiled if he were actually entering her with his swollen, pulsating member.

Suddenly there was the sound of bone crunching, and he opened his mouth to gasp with pain, her breast falling free as his head slumped downward upon her chest.

Quickly he was kicked away from her, and she was yanked roughly to her feet. She made out the anxious face of Doc Jenkins in the dim glow of the lantern just before someone doused it and they were in total darkness. "Are you all right?" he whispered, his trembling hands clasping her shoulders nervously.

Fumbling to cover herself with her clothing, she snapped irritably, "Yes, but you sure took a long time getting here. A few more seconds and I'd have been a true whore!"

"I'm sorry. We got here as quick as we could," he said in a rush. "We were planning to be here ahead of you, in position, but we had to take care of the guards on deck, and there were more than we thought.

"Now if you're sure you're all right," he went on anxiously, "we've got to proceed at once. If an alarm is sounded, we'll all be thrown to the sharks, for sure."

Julie shivered at the thought, and reminded herself that the danger was not over merely because Jenkins and the others had showed up. "I'm fine," she assured him. "Just a bit nervous. Let's get on with it quickly."

One of the men unbolted the hatch door and held it while Doc Jenkins descended. Once he was at the bottom of the ladder, one of the other men helped Julie down the narrow rungs. She could hear others following, but knew one man would be left up on deck to stand watch.

Groping in the darkness, Doc called out to Captain Arnhardt while Julie hung back, afraid of stumbling and making noise. Just as someone lit a lantern, Derek answered Jenkins's call, and Julie could see him. Her heart constricted as she thought of the excruciating pain he must have experienced from his arms being stretched high above his head, wrists shackled with heavy chains. On either side of him, his officers, Edsel Garris and Grover Watson, were likewise restrained.

"How in the hell—" He spoke to Doc in a rasping voice.

Doc interrupted him. "No time to talk now. We've got to get you out of here. You can thank Julie for occupying the guard so we could slip up behind him."

Derek lifted weary, swollen eyes to her, a weak smile touching his lips.

She saw the blood oozing around the steel bracelets on his wrists, and ground her teeth.

Doc told one of the men to go up the ladder and search the guard for the keys to the shackles. While they waited he told Derek how they had bound and gagged some of the guards. "We had to slit the throats of three of them. We hid all the bodies, but there's no telling how long before they'll be missed. We have to move fast, and the rest is up to you, Captain. I've no plans or ideas."

Derek pulled at the chains, the muscles in his arms

flexing and straining. "Just get me out of these things and I'll think of something." He bit the words off angrily.

"Hold on." Doc was trying to examine Derek's bloody wrists. "You aren't doing a thing now but cutting your flesh to ribbons."

The crewman scurried down the ladder to tell them he had searched the guard thoroughly but found no keys. Derek swore, then snapped, "Get something to break the chains. There's a sledge hammer in that storage bin up there. Hurry."

His gaze turned to Julie, eyes narrowed as though deep in thought. Finally he ordered, "Get her back to her cabin. Put her mother in there with her. Post a man with them, and make sure he has a gun and plenty of ammunition. I don't want them harmed."

"I don't want to be locked in my cabin and not know what's going on," Julie protested. "I want to help. . . ."

Despite the tension surrounding them, all of the men laughed, which infuriated her. Derek chuckled, "You've done all you're capable of doing, pretty lady. You'd only be in the way now. There'll probably be a lot of shooting and killing before the sun rises on this day."

"Give me a gun and I'll use it." She gave her long hair a toss. "I'm tired of being treated like a child, and I refuse to go to my cabin."

Derek turned his attention away from her as someone returned with the sledge hammer. A few quick, hard blows and the chain on his right shackle snapped. He held out his arm to Julie and said in a quietly commanding tone, "Come here."

She obeyed and moved into the circle of his arm. He pulled her tightly against his chest and held her there while the men worked to free his other hand. Her head was tucked beneath his chin, and he leaned forward to nuzzle her thick, silky hair, his fingers moving up and down her back possessively.

As always, she marveled at his strength . . . the sheer beauty of his massive, glorious body.

When his left arm was released, he lifted her up so that their lips touched. The others looked away self-consciously, then turned to free the other officers.

Julie felt as though the very life were being squeezed from her body, and a tremor rippled through her with the realization that he could very easily kill her just by using his powerful strength to keep on hugging and squeezing her till there was no breath left in her body.

He placed one hand on her bottom, pressing her against him, and she felt the hardness, knew that even then, in the midst of danger and peril, he wanted her.

"Later," he whispered, raising his lips only slightly above hers, so she could feel them moving against her mouth as he spoke. "Later, little one, I'll be inside you, where you want me—where I want to be. For now, you're going to your cabin."

"No—" she struggled against him futilely.

"Julie, you're going to learn that when I tell you to do something, I expect you to do it." His eyes twinkled in the soft glow of the lantern. "You only waste your breath and try my patience when you argue."

He bent his head to press his lips against her ear so no one else could hear his whispers. "You know what it's like when I'm inside you? I feel like I'm wrapped in sweet, hot velvet. You're so tiny, but you take all of me, and one of these nights I'm going to stay inside you till the sun comes up. I've never known a woman like you, so passionate, so eager to please. But there's much you need to learn about a man, things I'm going to enjoy teaching you."

Astonished, she jerked her head back to stare up at him in wide-eyed wonder. Then he patted her bottom soundly and grinned, "Be off with you! And no arguing. I haven't time!"

With an insolent wink, he turned toward the others, releasing and dismissing her.

Someone touched her elbow hesitantly, but she jerked away and called out frostily to Derek, "Just how long do I stay in my cabin like a child? If it weren't for me, you'd still be here rotting in chains!"

Without so much as a glance in her direction, he snapped, "Keep your voice down, dammit. You'll stay in your cabin until you hear from me."

"And if I *don't* hear from you?" she cracked sarcastically. "How will I know when to come out?"

"Oh, Captain Guthrie or Shad Harky will show up if I don't," he replied matter-of-factly, and even though his back was turned, she knew he was smirking. "Don't worry, misty eyes, your bed won't stay cold for long."

Soft laughter echoed around her as she scurried up the

ladder, shaking with rage. Her escort had to hurry to keep up with her.

How could he—she thought with wild fury—*How could he humiliate her so?* And in front of the others! Oh, she was a fool to consider caring for him. He was conceited, arrogant, used to having his own way. He wanted to dominate her as he did his crew. He probably even wished he had the nerve to use the lash on her back! He was a savage!

Even though she had secretly dreaded marrying Virgil, she now looked forward to the respectability of being his wife so she would never again be susceptible to the likes of Derek Arnhardt. All she wanted was to get off the *Ariane* and never think of what had taken place aboard it.

"My name is Lymon Anastor," her escort told her as soon as they reached her cabin. "It's my job to defend you and your mother—to my death, if need be," he added, pride heavy in his voice.

She whipped about and stared at him in the lantern's glow, realizing with a start that he was hardly more than a boy—skinny, with a thatch of unruly strawberry-colored hair falling across his forehead.

He sensed her doubts about his capabilities as a bodyguard, and his adam's apple bobbed nervously as he shook his musket at her with one hand, using the other to open his coat and display a Colt Navy revolver which was tucked into his belt. "You've nothing to fear, Miss Marshal. I'll gladly give my life, if need be, if that's what my captain orders."

"Well, that's very noble," she murmured, unimpressed. "But tell me why you worship Ironheart so. He'd as soon slash your back to ribbons as he would anyone else's. He's cruel and vile and vicious and—"

"Don't be a-talking like that about him," the boy snarled, eyes bulging as he cocked his head to one side. "It's my duty to protect you, but that don't mean I got to stand here and listen to you run down a man that I respect more'n any other I've ever known in my whole life. He picked me up outta the gutter and gave me a job—a reason to live. If he was to beat me, I'd deserve it."

He paused to take a deep breath, then rushed on, "He's a fine man, and you ought to be proud he cares for you like he does. Thinks right smart of you, everyone says.

And you should be glad, 'cause he's never taken to a woman for long at a time. Sure, he'd have one on board for a few nights, 'cause every man's got a need, but—"

"Will you stop?" she cried incredulously, eyebrows raised, hands on her hips as she faced him, stunned. "I do not care to discuss Captain Arnhardt's 'needs,' and I don't have to listen to a lecture from you."

They faced each other, eyes blazing. Then Julie shook her head, and covered her brow with one hand as she murmured, "I'm sorry. I don't mean to quarrel with you. It's been a very unnerving night, and I'm sure you have good reason to revere the man. We're both facing danger, so let's try to be friends."

She held out her hand, and he took it without hesitation, grinning broadly. Then he said he'd go and awaken her mother. Julie was glad to leave that task to him.

A few moments later, hair falling loosely about her shoulders, her mother hurried into the cabin, wrapping a pink satin robe about her. Mammy Sara was right behind her, looking very frightened.

"Tell me what this is all about," her mother commanded, sinking into a chair as Lyman took his position next to the door.

Julie told her as briefly as possible, and Mammy Sara rolled her eyes and kept saying, "Oh, Lawdy . . . Oh, Lawdy . . ." over and over.

"I don't believe it." Her mother pushed her hair back from her face with trembling fingers. "You helped rescue the captain . . . there's going to be another fight. I wish now we had just stayed in Rose Hill and let the damn cotton rot! We may all die now!"

Julie stared at her in wonder. She had never heard her mother curse before.

"Oh, I'm sorry, dear," Mrs. Marshal said quickly. "It's just that this trip has become such an ordeal. I wish we could turn around and go home. Virgil would understand."

"Ma'am, don't you fret," Lyman spoke up confidently, and they all turned to look at him. "The captain is a smart man, and brave, too. He'll save us and the ship. You'll see. All we gotta do is sit tight. I'm going to block the door, shove the desk in front of it, and I'll do my best to keep all of you safe."

"I wonder how long we'll have to wait," her mother

murmured as they watched Lyman position the desk. "I suppose I should have dressed—"

"It's all right." Julie forced a tight smile, wondering how it could matter what they were wearing. Despite Lyman's faith in Derek, in reality they could all be dead by morning. There were many Yankees, but only a few of Derek's followers. He'd lost many to Harky.

Her mother perched on the edge of the bed and began to rock to and fro, hands locked about her knees. "We'll think of pleasant things, not about what is happening above us. We'll think of how soon we'll be in Bermuda, then on a nice ship bound for England. And when we get there, Virgil will be waiting, and you'll have a beautiful wedding. Then the war will end, and we'll all come back to Rose Hill, and Myles will come home too, and . . ."

On and on she went, and Julie fought the impulse to scream. If it made her mother feel better to ramble that way, then so be it, but she would have preferred to just sit in silence and pray for safe delivery from their present peril.

"Did you hear me, dear?"

Julie's head snapped up. She'd been lost in thought, thinking about Derek, about the way her body betrayed her whenever he was near.

"No, Mother. What did you say?"

"I know you're going to be happy as Virgil's wife, even though you might not think so."

"I suppose," Julie commented absently, not wanting to discuss it. Once the decision had been made, she'd found she did not want to talk about it. It was going to happen, and that was the way it was. There was no need to dwell upon it.

"Are you sure you aren't marrying him solely because you know he can save Rose Hill and make it possible for Myles to come home?" her mother persisted.

Without realizing it, Julie looked Sara in the eye, and saw the old Negress give her a piercing glare. This she found surprising, and it was with a feeling of guilt that she lied to her mother when she answered, "I—I think I'll be happy with Virgil. We can have a good marriage."

"But do you love him?"

Again Julie locked eyes with Sara, who pursed her lips and frowned.

"I suppose." The words almost choked her.

It was a lie. She knew it and Sara knew it.

Time dragged by slowly. Lyman extinguished the lantern, saying he was sure that the captain would want the ship in total darkness. So they waited, with only the sound of their harsh, anxious breathing to break the tense silence in the inky blackness that surrounded them.

The cracking sound of a shot split the stillness, then another followed. Julie's mother screamed, covering her ears as Lyman hissed for her to be quiet. Julie crouched down beneath the porthole, covering her own ears against the sudden rain of gunfire all about them. Men were shouting, cursing, feet pounding on the deck above as they ran. The ship quivered and shook.

Julie felt a movement. Something hard and cold was being pressed into her hand.

"If I'm killed, use this." Lyman's voice cracked as he handed her the knife. "Defend yourself as best you can. God be with you."

He was afraid. For all his brave talk about duty and dying, if need be, in following his captain's orders, the boy was scared, Julie knew. And in between the shouting and screaming and shooting, she could hear her mother crying.

How ironic, she thought, dazed, *that at such a time, I am the only one in control.* But then she allowed as to how she was probably only in a state of shock, for she could feel her body tremble, knew that deep inside she was terrified . . . for at any moment, death could come.

And then silence fell.

For a long time, no one spoke, then Lyman said tersely, "We'll know soon. Someone will come down here. Pray it's the captain."

The captain! Julie felt a hot flush surge through her body. That taunting smile on those handsome lips, the way his strong hands could perform magic upon her body—she had never known anyone like him. And she hoped she never encountered such a perplexing personage again. He had a mystifying hold on her; this she could not deny. Her body, her will, combined to betray her in his arms. And even if he did not possess such powerful, feral strength, he had other ways of making her helpless, she knew.

Suddenly the sound of hard, sure footsteps descending the steps made everyone turn fearful, anxious eyes toward the door. Her mother's fingertips went to her trembling lips as Lyman raised his musket, pointed, aimed, ready in the first rosy hues of dawn that streamed through the porthole.

Julie could only hold her breath, hands clenched tightly together. She could hear Sara murmuring a barely audible prayer.

"Let me in, Anastor. It's over!"

"Praise God!" Sara screamed.

Julie let her breath out, swaying slightly as Lyman laid his musket aside to hurriedly shove the desk from the door.

Derek's huge frame seemed to fill the open doorway, and he stood with legs apart, a triumphant grin on his sweaty, grimy face. "We took them," he said quietly, his eyes searching for Julie.

He opened his titan arms, exposing his bare, rock-ribbed chest. So relieved was she that the Yankees had been defeated, Julie forgot everything and everyone and flung herself against him, sobbing with relief as he folded her tightly in his embrace. Instantly she was washed over with waves of emotion, knowing that as long as he held her, she was safe from any harm.

He rubbed his hands up and down her back comfortingly, affectionately, as he attempted to answer Lyman's anxious questions. "We lost a lot of good men," he said reverently, quietly. "We took them by surprise, but they were a large number. If we hadn't had the advantage of catching them off guard, I'm sure the story would have had a different ending."

Pressing his lips against Julie's forehead, he whispered, "Are you sure you aren't disappointed that it wasn't Captain Guthrie at your door?"

"Derek, how dare you . . ." She jerked away from him, hating herself for losing control, as she always did in his arms. Then she saw it—the angry, bleeding slash across his chest. "My God, you're hurt!" she cried.

"It's not deep. Just a scratch. I'll have Jenkins take a look at it later." He turned to Lyman. "We slipped on board their ship and sabotaged their guns just as Harky's friends did ours. We had most of their men overpowered before an alarm was sounded."

"Captain Arnhardt . . ."

They all turned to see Julie's mother getting shakily to her feet. "Please spare us the gory details. Now that the battle is over and you've won, what we're interested in hearing is how long it will be before we can be on our way to Bermuda."

"We won't be putting into port at Bermuda," he replied matter-of-factly. "You see, word spreads, even at sea. The Yankees are going to be looking for us, because we *are* blockade runners. So now we've no choice but to turn back and head for port in Wilmington. I can get through there, and we can dock for awhile till things cool down. Then I'll decide which course the *Ariane* will take."

It took a moment for his words to register, and then Mrs. Marshal gasped, "Are you mad, sir? You were paid to deliver us and our cargo to Bermuda. We can't turn back. My daughter is to be married, and—"

"That's the way it's going to be," he snapped, rubbing at his wound with the back of his hand, smearing the blood as he winced with pain. "I'm the captain. I make the decisions. We'll sink the Federal ship, set the survivors adrift, then turn and head north at once." He told Lyman to go topside, as there was much work to be done.

Derek kissed Julie's cheek and turned to go, but her mother had a conniption. "Will you stop trifling with my daughter? I will ask you to respect her state of betrothment. She belongs to another."

He released her at once, stunned by the woman's outburst.

"I'll pay you anything you ask," she went on in a rush. "Anything! Do you understand? I'll divide the profit from the sale of my cotton. I'll give you anything you want, but you must take us on to Bermuda."

"Are you insane?" He was bewildered. "I'd be captured and hung. The Yankees would consider me a pirate now. I have to go into hiding for awhile. There'll be a price on my head. In Wilmington I'll be safe till I get both my crew and ship ready to sail once again."

"Virgil will be worrying himself sick." Mrs. Marshal turned to Julie. "We have to go on to Bermuda." Tears were streaming down her cheeks as she wrung her hands in despair. Mammy Sara stepped forward and placed a plump arm protectively around her shoulders.

Julie bit her lower lip. She didn't want to go to Wilmington. And she didn't want to return to Rose Hill. Not now, with Savannah blockaded soundly by the Yankees. To continue on to England would mean a reprieve from the ravages of war. She would worry over Myles, but for the moment, she could do nothing to help him, and he would want her safely away from the conflict and strife.

"Take Mrs. Marshal to her cabin," Derek was saying to Sara. "It's been a trying night for all of us. I'll send in some brandy."

"You just don't understand," the woman sobbed as she was led away. "We have to go on. . . ."

When they were alone, Derek turned to Julie, his eyes devouring her. "I think I should save you from yourself," he murmured.

Shaking her head, she replied, "I don't understand what you're talking about."

Roughly he yanked her against him once more, smearing her with his blood but not caring. "You don't love Virgil Oates, and you know it. And I've told you he's an impostor. You're a fool if you think he's got wealth and power. He's marrying you for what he thinks *you've* got, in addition to your beauty. I damn well can't fault him on *that* point."

She managed to speak over the tremulous pounding of her heart. "That is no concern of yours. What we had . . . did . . . was wrong. We must forget it ever happened."

"We can't, and we won't." His laugh was short, bitter. Then he gave her a gentle shake and commanded, "Tell me the real reason you promised to marry him. You bared your body to me. Now bare your soul."

She could only look at him, helpless.

"You can't tell me you love him."

She was weary from the agony of sleepless nights. Now her brain was trying to whirl, function, but she felt only exhaustion. "Please, I don't feel like discussing this. I just want to go on with my life."

He went on as though she had not spoken. "I know you don't love him, and I know why you're marrying him. You're trying to make up to your mother for the way your father betrayed her with his sister-in-law. You told me all about it in your feverish ramblings, Julie. But you must understand that it's not your place to do this."

"You don't know what you're talking about," she gasped.

He nodded grimly. "Oh, yes, I do. You've got this fierce, insane devotion to your mother because you feel guilty carrying the secret about your father's adultery. You're feeling the shame that was buried with him. That's crazy. It isn't your place to make anything up to your mother.

"And," he went on, eyes blazing like the morning sun streaming through the round window, "you've got this equally insane loyalty to your brother, and you don't realize that it's based on guilt. In this case, your own. You blame yourself for his being forced to run away. You were the one attacked by those men, and he was avenging your honor."

She tried to protest, but he would not allow her time to speak as he continued his tirade. "I'll tell you something else, too. You think that marriage to Virgil Oates will insure a trade relationship with buyers in Europe. You think all your problems will be solved. But you're wrong. They're just beginning. He can't work miracles."

"I'm not going to stand here and listen to this." She tried to pull away, but he continued to hold her tightly.

"You *are* going to listen, dammit. It's time you faced reality. You're throwing your life away for your mother, your brother, and your goddamn precious land." Then he flung her away from him, and she fell upon the bed.

"What's the use?" he yelled. "Why should I concern myself with you, anyway? Go on and marry the bastard, if that's what you want. Make a martyr of yourself if that's the only way you can be happy."

Julie was seething. "Then why don't you just shut up and leave me alone? You got what you wanted from me. I 'performed' for you satisfactorily. Now get out of my lfie and let me live it as I choose."

He opened and closed his fists, teeth grinding together as he stared down at her. "So be it, pretty lady."

He rubbed at his wound again. He knew it needed binding, for blood continued to ooze from the torn flesh. He had been slashed by a knife wielded by a dying man who lacked the strength, thank God, to plunge the blade deeper, or Derek might have fallen to eternal sleep alongside him.

He turned to leave, then stopped to give Julie one final

glare. "And by the way," he said evenly, "you didn't 'perform,' as you call it, all that well. And who ever said I got exactly what I wanted from you? You were a woman, and I felt a need. Nothing more."

He walked out and slammed the door behind him.

❦ Chapter Eight ❧

THE day passed slowly. While she yearned for a breath of fresh air, Julie decided not to go up on deck. She could hear sounds of much activity there, and even though her curiosity was roused, she knew the scene would be unpleasant after what had taken place during the night.

It was Lyman who brought her food. A bowl of gruel and a cup of tea was the only offering at mid-morning. Then, as the sun began to die, he returned with another tray. Julie wrinkled her nose at the sight of the boiled fish stew.

"I'm sorry," he said matter-of-factly. "There's just been so much to do today that no one's had time to see to the kitchen. The cook was put to work with a mop and pail, and all he had time to do was get this pot of stew together."

Earlier, when he had brought the gruel, Lyman had left so quickly that Julie didn't have time to question him about what was going on above. This time, before he could take his leave, she quickly positioned herself in front of the door and said, "It doesn't matter about the food. I'm not hungry. But you aren't leaving this room till you tell me what's happening."

"Happening?" He blinked with contrived confusion, then added nervously, "Oh, you mean topside."

"Yes, I mean topside. I want to know everything that is going on up there."

"We've had a lot of scrubbing to do. Blood, you know."

He made a face. "And the captain is busy repairing our guns."

"Has he set the Yankees adrift? Did he sink their ship?"

Shaking his head, he shrugged and murmured, "I can't say no more, ma'am. Captain, he wouldn't like it. Now I really can't stay no longer. It'll be dark soon, and there's still a lot of work. . . ."

He took a step sideways, but Julie moved also, blocking his path. She placed the tip of one finger on his chest as her eyes burned into his insistently. "You must tell me everything, Lyman. I've a right to know what my destiny is to be. Is the captain turning us about to head for Wilmington?"

He swallowed hard, glancing about uneasily as he said, "Miss Julie, I'm just about the lowest rank of crewman there is. I'm only sixteen, and the captain, he was good enough to take me on, even though I got into some trouble with the law back in Savannah. He made it perfectly clear I wa'n't gonna be no more'n a swabby till I learned about the seafaring life. So how would I know of his plans as to the course of his ship? He don't tell me nothing."

"But," he paused to grin slowly, "after I proved my loyalty last night, I bet he's gonna see me in a different light. He sees how I took a stand for him when so many of the older and more experienced crewmen were afraid."

Julie sighed, exasperated. "Lyman, I'm sure you know whether we're going to Bermuda or turning around to go north. I'm also sure you're aware of whether or not the Yankee ship has been sunk and the crew set adrift. So why won't you tell me this much? I've a right to know. I am a paying passenger on this ship."

He looked down at his bare feet, and she followed his gaze to see they were pink-tinged—probably, she surmised, from mopping the bloody deck.

"Did Captain Arnhardt instruct you not to answer any of my questions?"

Without raising his head, he nodded.

"All right. I suppose I'll just stay here and worry myself sick over what my fate is to be." Turning her back on him, she pressed her face against the rough wood of the door, pretending to shudder with sobs.

The effect was as she expected. Lyman shuffled his feet uncomfortably, took a few nervous breaths, then whispered, "Please don't cry. I can't stand to see a woman cry. I'll tell you what I do know, which ain't much."

And he told her that the Federal ship was still afloat, with the crew being held prisoner. "That's all I know. Honest. I don't know which way we're going to sail from here."

She pretended to dab at her eyes with the hem of her dress. Giving him a grateful smile, she thanked him.

He left after asking her to promise she would not tell anyone he had revealed even that much information. Disappointed that she had learned nothing really important, Julie assured him she wouldn't.

Her eyes stung with weariness. Despite the anxiety she felt about all that had taken place, she was eager to succumb to much-needed sleep. Taking off her dress to put on a gown, she was about to snuggle beneath the covers when there was a sharp, insistent rap upon her door.

With pounding heart, she opened it. When she saw her mother standing there, she had to admit to herself that it was actually Derek she had been hoping to see.

Trying to hide her disappointment, she hugged her mother and told her to come in. "What have you been doing with yourself all day?"

"Napping when I could." Mrs. Marshal sat down in a chair. "And you?"

"I couldn't sleep. I was too worried over what our fate is to be."

"Well, it took a bit of doing," her mother gave her a secret smile, "but I've persuaded the captain to take us on to Bermuda.

Julie stared at her, mouth gaping open in surprise.

"That's right," her mother said in triumph. "He's a stubborn one, but like most men, he's weak when it comes to money. Everyone has a price. His was half of your dowry."

"My dowry? I don't understand." Now she was baffled.

"Of course, you have a dowry. It's only right and proper that a bride go to her husband with a dowry. That is, in circles of refinement. Virgil tried to tell me it wasn't necessary, but he understood the propriety of the gesture."

"And just what was the gesture?" Julie demanded suspiciously.

"I deeded to him one-half of Rose Hill and five thousand dollars."

"One-half of Rose Hill?" she echoed, not believing what she was hearing. "Oh, Mother, you didn't."

"Well, of course," was the surprised reply. "It's where the two of you intend to make your home. It was the proper thing to do."

Mrs. Marshal hurried on. "As for the five thousand dollars, it's all the money I could raise, and I was taking it to him. I persuaded Captain Arnhardt to continue on to Bermuda by giving him half of that money. But I let him think that was *all* I had to give him."

Julie was stunned. She paced up and down for a moment, then faced her mother and shook her head in dismay. "Mother, that was wrong of you, not only to give half of Rose Hill to Virgil but to give half of your money to Derek. What if we had been killed on this voyage? Virgil would have half of your property. That wouldn't be fair to Myles."

"We'll get to England safely." She smiled with the confidence of a child who anticipates a visit from Santa Claus at Christmas. "And I'll explain to Virgil about what happened to half of his money. He'll probably find a way to get it back, because he's going to be terribly upset when he finds out I had to barter our way when he already paid for our passage."

Julie pressed her fingertips against her throbbing temples. "Mother, why didn't you talk to me about this first? You don't realize what you've done. You're dealing with a—a *pirate*. We still have no assurance Derek will keep his word. And I don't like the thought that Virgil already holds the deed to half of your property."

A booming voice made both women jump. "Get your things together!" someone commanded through the closed door. "You're being moved to the Federal ship."

Julie yanked the door open to find Officer Edsel Garris standing there, a tight, set look upon his face.

"You're to come with me," he said, then, seeing her mother, told her to get her things together also. "The two of you are being transferred to the Federal steamer for transport to Bermuda. We plan to hoist the sails at sunrise, so it's best we get you all settled in as quickly as possible. We don't want any delays."

Julie and her mother exchanged puzzled looks, then her mother cried, "I just don't understand this, Mr. Garris.

Captain Arnhardt never said anything about our traveling on that Yankee ship. I'd like to speak with him."

"That's impossible, Mrs. Marshal. He's busy. We all are. Now if you'll just cooperate, we can have you on board the other ship in no time and properly settled for the night."

"I suppose it really makes no difference which ship takes us," her mother said absently, moving toward the door and her own cabin. "Tell your captain we'll be ready in a little while."

Garris left, and Julie heard her mother saying to herself, "No wonder he wanted money in addition to the cotton. He had no intention of taking it to Bermuda and selling it any time soon."

Julie laughed bitterly. "Don't worry about Ironheart, Mother. He won't lose anything. Let's just hurry and get off his infernal ship and be rid of him for all time."

It took but a few moments to pack her trunk. Then she decided it would not be appropriate to make the move from one ship to another wearing a gown and robe. She stripped, then searched through her trunk for a simple dress she could don quickly.

"An artist could never capture such beauty on canvas!"

Whipping about, she found herself staring into the hungry eyes of Derek Arnhardt. His gaze was moving arrogantly over her body. Despite her annoyance over his bold and silent intrusion, she was once again mesmerized by his ruggedly handsome face, the animalism that exuded from his rock-muscled body.

His chest was bare, and she wondered dimly if he realized how the sight always aroused her. She felt her fingers tingle with the desire to dance once again through the dark, thick curling hairs on that beautiful chest, and she longed to press her cheek against its hardness to feel the strong beat of his heart against her face.

She gritted her teeth, angry for being so vulnerable. Snatching up the first garment she came to, she covered her body and snapped, "A gentleman always knocks upon a lady's door, sir, as I've told you before."

He laughed, that cocky, smug laugh. It made her even more furious. "I don't pretend to be a gentleman. And why do you pretend to be a lady? Remember, misty eyes, I know only too well how you abandon that cool façade when I take you in my arms."

She turned away, frustrated. Jerking the dress over her head, she fumbled with the stays at the back while he continued to enjoy her indignant anger.

"Here, allow me." He moved to fasten her dress and she pushed him away, only to realize after several more futile attempts that she would need his assistance. Lifting her long hair from her shoulders, she shivered at the touch of his warm fingers. When he was finished, he quickly slid his hands around and down to squeeze each breast, pulling her tightly back against him.

She could feel the rigid pulsation of his organ throbbing against the top of her buttocks. She tried to wriggle away, but he held her more firmly.

"Why do you fight me?" She could feel his warm breath against her cheek as he leaned closer. "You know you want it as much as I do. Enjoy. That's what a man and woman were meant to do with each other."

Lifting her foot high, she brought it down hard, smashing his right toe. Stunned, he loosened his hold upon her, and she was able to jerk free. Then, before he knew what was happening, she spun around and brought her knee upward and smashed it into his crotch.

With a yelp of pain, he clutched at himself and, doubling over, staggered backwards.

"Damn you! Stop treating me like an animal!" she cried. "You're a savage, Derek Arnhardt, and you look upon a woman as someone to use for your own selfish pleasures and nothing more. I'm not your slave, your mistress, or your whore!"

He lifted angry, pain-filled eyes and stared at her in wonder, stunned by this violent explosion.

"I know all about your making my mother give you part of my dowry, you—you pirate! And to think I risked my life to save yours. I should've let you rot in chains. I hope the Yankees do catch you, and hang you, and—"

He straightened, a tight, menacing look spreading across his face. Julie tilted her chin upward in a gesture she hoped made her appear unafraid. Actually, she was trembling inside over the way this big, ominous man towered above her . . . and over the realization of what she had just done to him, the things she had said.

One giant hand snaked out to clasp her throat tightly, but still she continued to face him defiantly. "Let me tell you something, you conceited wench. My men are taking quite a chance by bringing you to Bermuda. It's certainly worth something extra to cover the risk they face. Your mother was willing to pay to get you quickly on your way. And I think it's best. I hope you do marry Oates. You deserve each other."

His eyes raked over her again, this time with contempt. "You may be quite lovely, but you're just another body. Remember that. I'm not bewitched by you, rest assured. And I don't lie awake at night with desire burning in my loins. You're like every other woman I've ever laid with, and no doubt similar to the ones who await me in the future. You like to think you're being forced, raped, ravished, whatever you wish to call it, because you're too goddamned hypocritical to admit to yourself or anyone else that you crave mating your body with a man's just as strongly as he craves mating with a woman's!"

He released her, flinging her away so roughly she had to struggle to keep from falling.

"You saved your own neck when you saved mine, and you know it," he continued, still enraged. "At last I see you for what you are: selfish and spoiled. I pity Oates or any other man who is so damnably stupid as to take you for his wife."

He turned to leave, then whirled about to point a finger at her and say raspingly, "Get your things together at once. I want you off of my ship and out of my life."

"You can't want that any more than I do," she retorted acidly. "And now I can truly understand why your men call you Ironheart . . . if you even *have* a heart!"

His black eyes burned with red fires. His nostrils flaring, he rubbed his hands rapidly against his legs. Never had he wanted so badly to strike a woman, and he was fighting for control. "If you stripped naked before me now and lay down on that bed and parted your thighs, I wouldn't touch you! That's how desirable I find you, wench. You were just someone for me to empty myself into, like all the others. Now get the hell off my ship!"

Reaching out for the object nearest at hand, Julie grabbed the bowl of fish stew and sent it rushing through the air. It splashed upon his chest. "You bastard!" she screamed, tears of humiliation streaming down her flushed cheeks. "You damned arrogant bastard. I hope the Yankees do catch up with you. I hope they throw you to the sharks!"

Julie watched the captain leave the cabin without another word, slamming the door behind him hard enough to make the walls rattle.

She covered her face with her hands, furious with him and herself. To think she had found him attractive . . . how embarrassing to remember the hours she had reveled in his arms as he took her to heights of untold pleasures and ecstacy. Fool! She had been such a fool!

Thank God she would never see him again. For that much, she was grateful.

Derek took a deep breath, hesitating before he started up the steps. Damn her. He still hurt from the blow she had inflicted on his most vulnerable parts. It was a wonder he hadn't lost control and killed her before he realized what he was doing. She was a wild one, but she also stirred something within him despite his ire—a twinge of desire . . . a shadow of tenderness.

Hell, it was best she was getting out of his life. He'd known many women in his lifetime, but never the likes of Julie Marshal, no matter that he'd told her otherwise.

He continued upward, drinking in the sweet salt air as he stepped on deck. There was a flurry of activity around him, but he removed himself from the fuss and walked to the ship's railing. Tightly he gripped the worn, splintered wood and stared thoughtfully out at the rolling green sea. Julie had touched his life only briefly, and they would never meet again.

Damn!

He turned around and stared at his men scurrying about.

He was a fool. She was spoiled, willful, nothing but trouble. He had enjoyed her body, but that was all. There could be no more. He didn't want a woman around him constantly. His mistress was the sea, and he was ashamed of feeling even the most remote attachment for the girl with hair the color of midnight and eyes as green as the deepest waters.

Someone called to him, and he moved in the direction of the voice. He had to leave his feelings behind, he told himself. There was no time to be melancholy. And what reason did he have, anyway? She was just another body, as he'd told her only moments before. Perhaps she was more generously endowed than most, but she was still merely a woman—good for a few hours of passion and frolic in bed, then to be cast aside.

Officer Watson approached him. "Sir, we're ready to move the women to the other ship."

"Then do so," he replied tonelessly. "I'll be in my cabin. We'll go over the rest of the plans when you return."

Watson nodded, turned, then wheeled about suddenly to inquire, "Will you bid the ladies goodbye?"

"Hell, no!" Derek stunned the man with his explosion, then, realizing how he'd reacted, lowered his voice quickly and said, "No, I've said my goodbyes. Proceed at once."

Derek continued toward his cabin, ignoring the men who called out to him as he passed.

It was over. It had to be.

But a voice deep inside caused him much distress, for it seemed to be telling him that . . . goodbye was not forever.

❧ Chapter Nine ❧

WITH Officer Garris commanding a skeleton crew from the *Ariane*, the captured Federal ship arrived off the coast of St. George on the northeast tip of Bermuda just two days after leaving the other ship.

Garris paid only one visit to Julie and her mother, to explain how they would put into port.

"We'll anchor out in the harbor, and two of my men will take you to shore by rowboat," he said tonelessly. "Once there, you will take your leave at once. We've no idea of what will happen once Guthrie and his men are found adrift and they start screaming piracy. We don't intend to be around to find out. My orders are to set you on shore, then see to the safety of my crew. You'll be on your own."

While they made the short trip into the harbor, Julie marveled at the beauty surrounding her. Peering over the side of the bobbing wooden craft, she gasped out loud as she realized that the water was crystal-clear. She could see down into its blue-green depths and watch the slickly gliding fish dart and weave as they searched for food.

The air was sweetly cool, scented not with salt but with the delicate fragrance of flowers, which reminded Julie of rare imported perfumes. "I don't think I've ever seen such beauty," she commented in awe to her mother. "It's the way I picture heaven."

Lost in the ethereal world surrounding them, her mother and Mammy Sara could only nod silently.

They reached the beach, and once again Julie was struck by the splendor of her surroundings. Dazzlingly clear water lapped against sand the color of pink-tinted coral which had been ground powder-fine by the wind and the waves. As soon as her feet touched land, Julie stopped to touch the sugary substance, letting it slide through her fingertips and laughing with a child's delight. "It looks so much like sugar, it makes me want to taste it!" she cried.

Her mother had lost interest in the scenery and was arguing with one of the sailors. "What do you mean, you don't have all our luggage? Several of my daughter's valises are missing. This is ridiculous. That man took my cotton, my money. Is he so greedy that he steals women's clothing as well?"

"I'm sorry," the sailor mumbled as though he really didn't care. "We couldn't get everything in the rowboat."

Mrs. Marshal pressed her hands against her temples and shook her head in frustration. "This is terrible. All her lovely gowns! I can't believe it!"

Julie started picking up her mother's bags. "Let's just be on our way and glad that it's all over. We can buy a few things to last us till we reach England."

"Virgil is never going to stand for such effrontery," Mrs. Marshal told the sailor, who snickered insolently. "He'll see that your captain pays for his wickedness." She continued to grumble, but Julie was too captivated with the majestic surroundings to be concerned about the loss.

Bermuda gave the impression of being a gigantic, well-kept flower garden. Even though it was late December, masses of gorgeous blooms could be seen everywhere: fields of delicate white Easter lilies, mile-long hedges of oleander, hibiscus, bougainvillea, royal poinsettia, and myriad other flora.

Beginning to feel intoxicated from the sweet essence that surrounded her, Julie delighted at the houses that dotted the landscape. Appealing and colorful, she knew they were made of limestone coral rock. Derek had told her about them, how the rock, which was soft enough to be cut with a wood saw, was cut from the ground. Once exposed to the air, the coral hardened with age.

She marveled at the roofs made of overlapping coral shingles which measured about ten by fourteen inches and were an inch thick. She knew, too, that these were washed periodically with a coating of lime for cleanliness's sake, since each household was dependent for its drinking water on the rains that slid over the shingles and were funneled into a reserve tank below.

As the three women made their way along the sandy beach, Julie could see the "welcoming arms" steps of one house, which were wider at the bottom than at the top. The chimneys were all huge; the windows surprisingly small-paned, each trimmed with shutters hinged at the top and swinging up and out.

Gazing about, Julie surmised that there was probably nowhere on the island where one would be more than a mile from the ocean. Bermuda was a busy place. This did not surprise her, since she was well aware that it was the chief supply depot for the Confederacy, and the port to which most of the South's cotton was shipped. Its proximity to the ports of Wilmington and Charleston gave it a superior advantage. And while submerged reefs made navigating difficult, all of the light-draft blockade runners carried Bahamian bank pilots, who knew every channel along the islands. The Yankee cruisers, Derek said, had no bank pilots and, since they drew more water, were compelled to keep to the open sea.

Captain Guthrie, Julie knew, would've had great difficulty navigating his ship out of the harbor. It was one of Derek's men, a bank pilot, who had been able to guide them in safely past the treacherous hidden reefs and who would take the others back to where the *Ariane* waited.

She explained all this to her mother as they walked.

"How do you come by all this information?" Mrs. Marshal wanted to know.

Julie hesitated, but only momentarily, deciding there was no point in being elusive. "Derek told me about it." Then she rushed on as her mother gave her a sharp look, "All of the islands are surrounded by coral reefs and shoals, and the channels are quite intricate. I also know that before the war, the chief industries of the islands were the collection and exportation of sponges and corals."

"You and the captain became rather close, didn't you?" Her mother spoke quietly, pensively.

"At one time, I suppose we were," Julie replied thoughtfully, not without a small twinge of pain, "before I came to fully realize what a savage he is."

The older woman raised her chin determinedly. "We will try to put it all behind us. Whatever happened on board that ship is now in the past. Let's not speak of it again."

Julie understood what she meant. Her mother knew she was sleeping with Derek the morning they were attacked by the Yankees. She not only saw him rushing out of Julie's cabin only partially dressed, but had noted his boots beside her bed. Now no more would be said about it. They had to concentrate on the future.

Julie was grateful. Her mother had every right to condemn her behavior, and she was glad the older woman chose not to, particularly since she wasn't sure she could explain it. How could she? Julie herself could not answer the questions burning inside her as to how Derek was able to possess such a hold over her.

They left the beach area, moving through oleander bushes to a narrow road. It wasn't long before a buggy appeared, with an old man wearing baggy pants and a shirt, a straw hat perched on his head, driving a team of horses. Mrs. Marshal and Julie waved to him, and he doffed his hat after obligingly reining in his steeds, bringing them to a halt.

When he was told they wished to find a place where they could book passage to England, he informed them in a clipped British accent that Hamilton was the largest nearby town, and that he would be pleased to take them there.

He drove them to a building on the waterfront. Mrs. Marshal handed him a few coins and thanked him for the ride. Then she turned to three men standing nearby and asked where she could find a shipping agent for vessels bound for England.

One of them hooked a thumb in the direction of a glass-fronted office. "There's an agent in there who represents the *Lady Dawn*," he told her. "I understand she'll be sailing before too many days have passed."

"Would you know exactly when?"

He shook his head. "Sorry. The agent will have that information. I'm a cotton buyer. I'm not traveling about at the moment."

"I see." She gave him a wary look, then prodded, "Would you mind telling me the price of cotton here?"

The man frowned. "Frankly, lady, it's highway robbery. We hear cotton is being purchased in the Confederacy for eight cents a pound, but we're forced to pay six times that sum once it gets through the blockade and arrives here."

Mrs. Marshal turned to Julie with a sick expression on her face. "Dear Lord, do you realize how much money that dreadful man will make on our cotton?"

"We can't dwell on the past, remember?" Julie touched her mother's arm gently. "Let's go inside now, all right?"

Her mother nodded and followed her. Julie was glad to get away from the curious, staring strangers.

When the agent told them the *Lady Dawn* would sail in just three days, her mother fumbled in her purse and brought out the money to pay for three tickets. Then she asked, "Could you recommend a decent hotel where we could stay till it's time to board the ship? I imagine a town like this is full of rowdies."

"That it is," he laughed understandingly. "I have a sister, name of Janie Margaret Odom, who runs a boarding house not too far from here. I'm sure she can squeeze you in for a few days. It's best ladies such as you stay off the streets, especially after sundown." He gave them directions to Mrs. Odom's, they thanked him, and left.

The town was wide awake. It seemed to Julie that every nationality on earth was represented there, and it was becoming quite crowded. She supposed the high wages ashore and afloat tempted adventurers from all over. The monthly wages of a sailor on board a blockade runner were one hundred dollars in gold, and a fifty-dollar bounty was paid at the end of a successful trip. Derek had told her that the captains and pilots sometimes received as much as five thousand dollars in addition to perquisites.

All of the cotton shipped on behalf of the Confederate government was brought to land and transferred to a mercantile firm in Nassau, which received a commission for assuming its ownership. The cotton was then shipped to Europe under the British or another neutral flag. Derek also told Julie that the firm in Nassau made many thousands of dollars from these commissions.

Of course, he added, there were many private companies, such as the one her fiancé would have her believe he represented. She winced at the word fiancé, and Derek smiled knowingly. She remembered hating him for mocking her.

She and her mother had met Virgil Oates at a tea, where

he was introduced as a cotton buyer from England. Word spread that he was also a member of an influential and wealthy family in London, and when it was discovered he was a bachelor, every eligible young woman in Savannah was literally paraded before him.

But it had been Julie's favor he sought, and while she never felt even the slightest twinge of affection for him, her mother was quite pleased and encouraged the match. between the two.

And, she remembered soulfully, at the time her life had been so full of strife and turmoil that she allowed herself to be swept along, unresisting, not really caring any longer what happened to her . . . concerned only with the fate of Myles and her mother, the people dearest to her heart.

Looking back over her shoulder toward the main harbor, she could see the water crowded with lead-colored, short-masted, rakish-looking steamers. "I wonder if Captain Guthrie and his crew have been discovered yet," she murmured.

Julie's mother followed her gaze. "I don't know, but that's another reason we need to be on our way as soon as possible. I want all of this behind us and out of our lives forever. I don't want us to be involved should Captain Arnhardt and his men be arrested for piracy."

Mrs. Odom's house was situated on a main street in the middle of all the hustle and bustle. Both Julie and her mother expressed doubt that there would be enough peace and quiet for them to get a good night's sleep during their brief stay.

Julie rapped on the door, and almost instantly it was opened by a gray-haired woman who told them that yes, she did have a room, and it was upstairs in the front, overlooking the street. While she was quite sorry that noise was a bother to be reckoned with, all her other accommodations were taken. Nodding toward Mammy Sara, Mrs. Odom said she could sleep in the room with her cook.

Julie's mother paid in advance, then asked if it would be possible for their food to be brought to their room. "We don't want to venture out."

"Oh, there's no reason to be scared," Mrs. Odom was quick to reassure her. It's true some of the sailors get a bit rowdy at night, but they frequent the taverns up the street. It won't be dangerous for you to go out during the day."

"We'll be willing to pay extra. . . ."

"Have it your way." The old lady brushed by and led them upstairs.

A large fishnet separated the parlor from the narrow stairway leading up to the second floor. Julie was delighted by the different-shaped seashells tied into the netting. The entire house was quaint and cozy. From what she had seen of the island, she loved it. It was a paradise where she could easily feel at home.

Their room was small but adequate. Lace curtains billowed at the open windows. There were two wood-railed beds covered with bright patchwork quilts, a dresser with a porcelain bowl and pitcher on top, and two rickety chairs.

"I'll fetch something for you to eat," Mrs. Odom said as she scurried from the room.

Mrs. Marshal began to pace up and down between the beds, wringing her lace hanky in her hands and pausing now and then to stare out the window and down at the street. Julie frowned, hoping this was not the way the next three days would be spent.

Mrs. Odom returned with a tray. "I have leftover cassava pie. I think you'll like it."

Julie leaned over to examine it and take a sniff. "It smells good."

"It's made of pork and chicken, and the crust is made from the grated root of the cassava plant. I also brought fried bananas and salt cod."

Her mother picked at her serving, but Julie found it quite delicious and ate her fill.

The sun was high in the sky, and the room was stuffy and hot despite the slight breeze from the bay which found its way through the windows. Julie dragged a chair over to sit directly in front of the moving air, and occupied herself by watching the people moving about in the street below.

Suddenly she gasped and stiffened. Was it possible? Surely she was seeing things. . . .

"What is it?" Her mother, who was lying down on the bed, sat straight up and stared in alarm. "What do you see?"

"I thought I saw Mr. Garris just now," Julie whispered incredulously. "But it couldn't have been. He's probably well on his way out to sea by now, though this man looked just like him. He was staring up at this window, and when he saw me looking, he ducked into an alley and disappeared."

"You're just tired, dear," her mother sighed, lying back down. "Try to take a nap, and you'll feel better. Mr. Garris has no reason to be in Bermuda. His captain got everything he wanted."

Julie continued to watch the activities below while her mother slept. No matter how hard she tried to control them, her thoughts kept creeping back to Derek. He was a beast . . . but a *beautiful* beast. Her body flushed with warmth when she remembered the sight of him naked. Oh, what a magnificent body, perfectly formed, hard-muscled, sinewy, tantalizing. And he'd been a glorious lover. Right or wrong, she thought guiltily, she had to admit to herself that she had enjoyed his every kiss and caress.

He could be so gentle one moment, then almost painfully brutal the next, but she had thrilled to it all. Never had she known such a man, and she probably never would again. She wondered sadly if she would fantasize that it was actually Derek touching her every time Virgil took her in his arms. His brand had been left upon her body, her very soul, and never, no matter how hard she tried, would she be able to forget him.

I have to. She gritted her teeth, clenching her hands at her sides. *I meant nothing to him. I was just another woman, one of many. I'm a fool to keep thinking about him.*

And suppose he'd been right about Virgil? She felt a stab of fear. What if he was an impostor? But no. Derek didn't know what he was talking about. He was only trying to frighten her into changing her mind about marriage, make her want to become his mistress. He was wrong. He had to be.

Finally she assuaged her conscience by reaching the firm conclusion that any normal woman would be smitten with a man like Derek. She had no reason to be ashamed. A skilled lover with a magnificent body, he knew exactly how to use that body to make a woman writhe with pleasure and joy. He was also intriguingly handsome. What female could resist him? Julie owed no apology to herself over the fact that she had been unable to deny herself or him. Her guilt, she decided, lay in the knowledge that she could not now put him out of her mind.

When Mrs. Odom brought their supper tray, she remarked that their servant was enjoying herself immensely. "She gets along well with Demora, the island girl who's been with me for several years now. They're going marketing in the morning and wanted me to ask if you two would like to accompany them."

"Mother, let's do," Julie said, unable to contain her excitement over the prospect of looking around the island once again.

"Well . . ." Mrs. Marshal shook her head doubtfully. "I don't think so, dear. True, there would be four of us, but—"

"I don't have much to wear on board ship, since my luggage was left behind," Julie pointed out. "I'm sure Virgil wouldn't object to our spending some of my dowry to buy me some suitable clothes."

"I know a nice dress shop not too far from here," Mrs. Odom offered. "They work quickly on alterations, too."

So the next morning the four women set out. Mammy Sara went to the vegetable and fruit market with Demora, and Julie and her mother visited the dress shop Mrs. Odom directed them to.

Julie let her mother select for her, as she really was not enthused about buying clothes. What she really wanted was to explore the beautiful countryside.

"Do you like this?" Her mother held up a pale mauve dress with a lace overskirt. "And look at this lime velvet and the darling matching bonnet. Oh, they have so many lovely things here."

Julie nodded at everything, dutifully trying on the garments for alterations.

"You have such a beautiful figure, madame," the lady on her knees beside Julie talked around the pins she held in her mouth, "but you are such a tiny thing."

"Isn't she?" Her mother laughed admiringly. "Her waist is so tiny she's never needed stays. And even though she doesn't try to look provocative, her bosom pours from a normally designed bodice."

Julie felt embarrassed. "Can we just hurry this along? I'd like time to take a walk, and we haven't had lunch."

Her mother looked out the shop window doubtfully. "I don't know, dear. Even in the daylight hours, there's such a crowd of men milling about."

The dressmaker spoke up quickly. "Oh, it will be quite all right. There are certain sections where it might not be proper, where the *bawdy* houses are located, if you know what I mean." She lowered her voice meaningfully, as though hating to mention such a subject.

They left the shop, returned to Mrs. Odom's long enough to leave their purchases in their room, then set out on a walk through the narrow, cobbled streets. They were delighted to find a little sidewalk café where they were served rice cakes and fish.

It was while they were sipping tea after their meal that Julie glanced up and saw a man quickly duck his head behind a leafy hibiscus hedge. Her cup clattered noisily to her saucer. She looked again, but there was no movement around the green foliage.

"What is it, dear?" her mother asked, concerned.

Julie shook her head. "Nothing. Nothing at all." She had to be imagining things again, and there was no need to upset her mother.

Mammy Sara and Demora passed by on their way from the market, and her mother said they should be getting back. "I'd like to have time for a nap before the night noises begin. I'm afraid I didn't sleep very well last night."

"You go right along," Julie urged her. "We aren't that far, and I can walk around in this area quite safely."

"But it wouldn't be proper for you to walk alone. . . ."

"I insist, Mother. Please. I'd like to be alone for awhile."

And before Mrs. Marshal could protest further, Julie arose and hurried away, leaving the three women staring after her.

She felt like breaking into song right there on the street. Alone at last! She could hardly believe her good fortune. Alone with hours of peace and solitude stretching before her. It was wonderful.

She walked toward the beach, stopping finally at the top of a ridge. She could not suppress the gasp that escaped her lips at the sight of the breathtaking beauty sprawled below. The clouds had parted, and the aqua waters of the ocean sparkled and gleamed in the bright sunshine. White puffs floated across the satin cerulean skies. Sea gulls darted and swooped in the air, calling out to each other melodically. The ships in the harbor stood at attention, white sails puffed out with the tropical breezes. Palm trees bent gently, their graceful green fronds dancing in the wind to an unheard rhythm.

"Gorgeous . . ." Julie whispered, lowering herself to the

soft velvet grass beneath her. Even the Savannah River, with its graceful tree-lined banks and magical, murky waters, could not equal this ethereal sight. Here was another world, one which she felt she had entered only for a brief time. Still, she would be forever grateful for having been touched by such splendor.

There was no one about. Behind and beyond her, the island and docks teemed with life. But here on this gentle slope there was only tranquility. Julie could not remember ever having felt so relaxed.

Resting her chin on her knees, which she doubled up after tucking her billowing skirt about her ankles, she drank in everything before her. She had to remember this moment. Oh, if only she were an artist, she thought wistfully, and could capture this beauty for all time.

Her eyelids grew heavy. The serenity of the place was causing her to drift away. Lowering her body to the soft ground, she curled up and gave in to the tropical breezes and warm sun. Soon she was fast asleep.

The sound of distant laughter awoke her with a start. How long had she slept? Blinking against the shroud of purple darkness, she could make out below the lanterns burning on ships, docks, and along the wharves.

Behind her, in town, the merrymaking for the evening had begun. Her mother would be frantic. Julie leaped to her feet, not taking time to smoothe her skirt or brush away the damp grass that clung to it. She had but one thought: to hurry through those crowded streets and return to Mrs. Odom's as quickly as possible. It was not safe to be out on the streets alone at night.

Just as she was nearing the edge of the thick palmettos and palm strees through which she had passed earlier to make her way to the ridge, something caused her to stop short. Turning about in a circle, slowly, her eyes searched the darkness.

It had to be the night wind, she thought nervously. It whistled through the rattling palm fronds with a sound that only made her imagine someone was calling her name. She took a deep breath, then started walking once again, her steps quick.

She heard it again and froze in her tracks. It was not her imagination, she realized. A man's voice *had* whispered her name. She told herself not to be afraid. Her mother had probably found some men staying at the boarding house who had agreed to search for her. There was no need for hysteria.

Without looking to the left or right, she tried to keep her voice steady as she called, "Who's there? Who calls to me?"

"I do, Julie."

She whipped about at the sound, heart pounding as she strained to see his face in the darkness. She heard footsteps coming closer, moving slowly, deliberately, but from the direction whence she had just come. She felt frightened, and her heart was thumping. Frantically she wondered why he had been *behind* her.

"Who are you?" Julie demanded, trying to hide her bubbling hysteria as she took a few steps backwards. Could she break into a run and make it out of the shadows and into the streets where the people were, before he could catch up to her? Would anyone hear her if she screamed now? "Who are you, I say! Don't come any closer to me."

"You've no reason to be afraid, Julie. It's me, Edsel Garris."

He stepped into the halo of moonlight that filtered down from the purple sky. It touched his face, illuminating him with a ghostly silver glow.

"It *is* you!" Julie realized her legs had suddenly become as quivery as the palm fronds bending in the wind. She reached out to steady herself by placing her hand against a nearby tree. Her breathing was ragged, hoarse.

"Why are you here?" She forced the words past the apprehensive knot in her throat. "I thought you'd be on your way back to the *Ariane*. Isn't it dangerous for you to be here?"

"So many questions," he chuckled, moving to stand mere inches from her. "And there's no time to answer them now. You see, Captain Guthrie and his crew were picked up by a passing ship this afternoon and brought into port. They're combing the island for us now. We're anchored off a remote point with a small boat that we 'borrowed,' and we'll be leaving shortly. We set the Yankee steamer adrift, you see."

Julie was bewildered. "Well, why do you risk being captured to come and see me? And how did you know I'd be here?"

Her mind danced suspiciously. Something was not right.

Then she remembered the times she thought she had seen him and pointed an accusing finger. "It *was* you! You've been following me ever since we arrived here, and you were supposed to return at once to your own ship. You stayed—to follow me . . . and that's how you knew I was here."

The reality of her situation made her dizzy. "You watched while I slept, wanting darkness to come before I awoke. But why? What do you want from me?" She backed away, silently commanding her wobbly legs to move.

"It's not me who wants you. It's the captain. This was all planned before you ever left the ship. I've orders to take you back with me."

"Are you insane?" she exploded, stunned. "My mother and I are leaving for England the day after tomorrow. I'm not going anywhere with you."

He sighed impatiently. "Julie, I have explicit orders, so come along peacefully now. You won't be hurt, and I don't have time to stand here arguing."

He moved forward.

She whirled about, ready to make a desperate attempt to run for the crowded streets. Surely someone would hear her screams and come to her aid.

But she found herself bumping into another man waiting to grab her as someone quickly stretched a foul-smelling rag around her face, covering her mouth to stifle her cries.

Struggling, she managed to free one hand to push the gag away as she cried, "Please don't do this. I can't go with you. My mother is waiting, and she'll be worried sick. . . ."

Edsel Garris clamped an arm tightly about her waist. "We can dispense with the gag, Julie, if you promise not to scream."

"All right, all right," she answered frantically. "Just tell me what Derek wants with me."

"Everything is going to be all right." He began to lead her away from the direction she had been headed and toward the dense woods and brush that led to the beach below. "You know you'll be treated well. We wouldn't hurt you. I've got my orders, and I'll follow them.

"As for your mother," he continued, "a message will be delivered to her within the hour, and she'll know what's become of you. She isn't alone, you know. She has that old Negress with her."

Julie was trapped, and she knew it. Several more crewmen emerged from hiding places and walked along with them. She was surrounded. "Just tell me why you're doing this horrible thing," she pleaded.

Garris took a deep breath and let it out slowly. Damn, he hated having to be so blunt; but it was obvious the girl was going to keep badgering him until he gave her an explanation. There was nothing to do but be completely truthful. "I believe, Julie, that Captain Arnhardt said something about a ransom."

"A what?" she yelped, jerking to a stop only to be roughly yanked along. "He's crazy! He has to be out of his mind. This is a crime. . . ."

Her struggles were futile. "I might have known," she cried to the wind. "I might've known the greedy bastard would want more money. But he won't get it. My mother and Virgil will hire men to hunt him and all of you down. You can't get away with this—"

"Julie, I'm going to have to gag you," Edsel said quietly.

"No." She lifted her chin defiantly. "You won't. I'll go with you."

He raised an eyebrow suspiciously as he stared down at her in the moonlight. "Is this some sort of trick? As I said, we don't want to have to get rough and maybe hurt you."

"No, it's not a trick. But mark my words, sir. Ironheart will rue the day he chose to make me his prisoner." Her voice was frosty, ominous.

He chuckled. "Aye, I can surely believe that, Julie. I surely can." He seemed relieved that there would be no more need to struggle with her, at least while he was in charge.

ᗖ Chapter Ten ᗹ

DEREK sat at his desk, shoulders hunched wearily over the clutter of maps and charts. The lantern began to flicker. He wondered absently when it was last filled with oil. No matter. He didn't need light simply to ponder.

Outside the wind swooped and shrieked, reminding of sounds he'd once heard coming from one of those places where they put people who've gone mad. Such people howl more when there's a full moon, someone had said. Derek wondered why, then shook his head, admonishing himself for letting his mind wander to subjects that didn't matter. Nothing mattered except getting his ship through the blockade and safely into port at Wilmington. There was a hell of a lot of cotton in the hold. *Rose Hill* cotton, he thought with a smile of satisfaction.

He leaned back, throwing his long, trunklike legs up and propping his booted feet on the paper-strewn desk.

He thought of Virgil Oates. He hadn't liked the man from the first time they'd met. He was pompous, the sort to flaunt whatever power he felt he had, trying to make people think he had money to go along with it. Soon he was going to find out he'd been taken.

Derek chuckled out loud as he imagined how Oates would sputter and stew when he learned his beautiful bride-to-be had been kidnapped.

A quarter of a million in gold. It was a high price. When Garris had seen the amount scribbled on the ransom note, he'd accused Derek of not expecting, or actually wanting, the sum to be paid. He accused him of kidnapping Julie not to collect money but rather to have an excuse to keep her on board for his own pleasures.

Derek liked Garris. He was a trusted officer. But that accusation had almost brought the captain to violence. And Garris had sensed he'd aroused his ire to the danger point and had immediately become contrite.

Now Derek wondered why he'd let himself get so angry. Perhaps until that point he hadn't realized his true intention himself. Someone else had had to make him see it.

There was no denying he was captivated by Julie's rare and delicate beauty. He had studied her features as he would a maritime chart, remembering everything until he could close his eyes and still see her clearly in his mind— the sensual shape of her mouth, her misty green eyes, mysterious, beguiling.

And how well he remembered what it was like to touch her naked body, the skin creamy, silky . . . as though carved from the finest ivory—but not as cold and dead. Not Julie. She'd stopped playing games and pretending to be indignant over his possession of her body. She'd returned his kisses, his caresses, and he was aware that she wanted him physically in every way. They'd spent many enjoyable, passionate hours together.

He frowned and reached into the bottom desk drawer to remove a hidden flask of rum. He uncorked it, tilted it to his lips, and took a large swallow. Wiping his mouth with the back of his hand, he cursed himself for being so weak as to need a drink.

Outside the ocean's swells grew larger, making the boat roll and pitch higher and higher. Thunder could be heard in the distance, and now and then Derek could see a hot white zig-zag of lightning fork across the inky black sky. The storm that had been brewing for several days seemed to be gathering strength to unleash its full fury at last. When it hit, Derek would need all his wits about him. He couldn't have his crew thinking he sat in his cabin getting soused on rum.

But he knew why he had to have that one drink. He wanted her. Dammit, he wanted her as fiercely as he'd ever wanted a woman in his entire life. Perhaps more so. Yet she was just that, he reminded himself crossly—a woman. Nothing more. He'd never let her mean more to him than any other female had, since he'd discovered how good it felt to empty himself in their belly.

That's all she was. A receptacle. No matter how loving, warm, or willing.

God only knew how many women there *had* been. He never tried to keep count. But one thing was certain. He seldom saw the same one more than a few times. Oh, there was Opal, who ran that house of pleasure up in Richmond. Still, that was different. He paid her well, and it was her business to please him. She would never make noises about wanting him to marry her, or say she'd wait for him when he sailed with the sunrise. Not Opal. She knew what a woman was for, and she was good at it. And that's the way it should be, so far as he was concerned. The sea was his wife. No one would ever keep him from it; not for very long, anyway.

All the same, he was starting to wonder about that, his love of the seafaring life. Where was it all going to take him? One day he'd be too old for it all. His skin would be parched and wrinkled from the salt and sun and wind. His shoulders would bend and ache from the damp and chill. What then? He could go and sit on the rotten, smelly docks and watch the ships come and go, swapping sea tales with others just like him as they all waited to die.

Oh, hell.

He lowered his feet with a thud onto the floor that pitched and rolled beneath him. This wasn't the time to be thinking grim thoughts. It was the damn war that made him feel depressed. True, as a runner he was making more money than he'd ever dreamed possible. When it was over, no matter which side won, he'd have enough put away to buy the best boat that ever sailed the seas. He wouldn't be forced to sit and whittle and spin yarns in his sunset years. He'd hire someone to run his boat, and he'd travel the seas till he died. Eventually he'd be buried somewhere in their murky depths.

Until then, he thought caustically as he stood up, he'd take care of matters at hand. Julie Marshal was his prisoner, and she'd remain so till the ransom was paid, no matter how long it took. His crew could gossip and grumble all they wanted. He knew what he was doing. Not only would he make extra money; he was also doing her a favor. He was saving her from Virgil Oates!

A sudden rumble of thunder exploded dangerously nearby, and he glanced sharply at the porthole to see the sky split with yellow-white streaks. Julie would be frightened, he knew. It had been over a week since she was brought on board and locked in her cabin. He hadn't allowed her outside for even a moment. Her food had been taken to her, though he received reports she was hardly eating enough to stay alive. She'd probably lost a lot of weight, and she was only a tiny scrap to start with.

He tugged thoughtfully at the beard he'd grown. The polite thing to do would be to go and see about her in person. After all, he was the captain.

But he'd promised himself to stay away from her. He had only brought her back for the money and in the hopes that he could save her from a miserable destiny in England. If the ransom weren't paid, what then? He shook his head.

Another crash of thunder, louder this time. Lightning flashed on top of it. The storm was almost upon them.

Derek walked to the door of his cabin, opened it, and peered out. There was no one about, as best he could tell. The lanterns had long ago been blown out by the fierce wind.

He moved down the ladder and stepped onto the deck, bracing himself against the harsh gale. It had to be a fierce storm to make *him* sway and bend, he thought with alarm.

The ship was taking a beating. He'd ordered the men to batten down the hatches and secure everything. He knew some of them had probably shirked their duties in order to hide below, fearing they would be washed overboard.

As the sky ignited, he could see the frothy, whipping waves. Never had he seen the ocean so angry, as though the wrathful breath of God, Himself, was breathing down upon them in His most vengeful of furies.

Derek moved slowly, feeling his way and making sure he had hold of something before proceeding any further. He wanted to check and be sure everything was secured. In times such as this, he didn't even trust Garris and Watson to see that everything was taken care of.

"Sir!"

He turned his face into the wind; he was already wet and dripping with rain. It was Thurman Debnam, the ship's fireman, and he was soaking wet. His body was bent against the fierce gale, and he held his cap on his head with both hands as he made his way across the deck with great difficulty.

"Sir, it's a bad blow," he said when he got closer. "I've got the fires stoked. All the riggin's are lashed. There's nothing we can do but batten down and wait 'er out. Mr. Garris, he ordered the men below. It isn't safe to be on deck. Gardner almost blowed over, and they barely grabbed him in time. Got him by the ankles, they did, and it took a few minutes of struggling to hoist him back over the railing."

Derek was alarmed and worried, but years of experience had taught him never to show the slightest sign of fear in front of his crew. Standing perfectly straight, he towered above Debnam and stared down at him as though quietly contemplating the situation but certainly not upset by it. Finally he gave a quick, authoritative nod of his head and said, "Very well. Go below. We'll just have to ride her out, Debnam. We've done it before. We'll do it again."

"Aye, sir," the fireman shouted, and turned to make his way back. Derek watched him stumble on the slick deck, then fall on his face. Righting himself by grasping a hatch, Debnam struggled to his feet and went on his way.

The boat gave a sudden downward lurch, and Derek grabbed the railing to hold on as his feet began to slip from beneath him. It was dangerous to be on deck. That was for sure. He started back for his cabin, then hesitated. Julie would be frightened. He had forbidden any of the crew to engage in conversation with her, so in addition to being scared for her life, she was probably starved for companionship.

He decided it was only humane to check on her. Precariously he made his way below, soaked to the skin by the time he reached her cabin.

He unfastened the heavy bolt, started to enter, then hesitated as he decided to knock first. No sound came from within. He rapped harder, but when there was still no answer, he turned the knob and entered complete darkness.

"Julie?" he called softly.

He heard a quick intake of breath, then an accusing voice. "It's *you*. Oh, how dare you come here to gloat!"

He kicked the door shut with his foot. "Don't you have a lantern in here? I told them to make sure your lantern was working at all times."

"I don't need light," she said quietly, emotionlessly. "It's miserable enough being kept prisoner, without having to look at my drab surroundings."

The boat heaved again, so sharply that for an instant, Derek feared it would plunge straight to the ocean floor. Then, with an upward bob, it lurched to the side. He steadied himself by flinging his hands out blindly until he could touch the walls. "Dammit, Julie, light the lantern before I break my neck."

He heard her emit an exaggerated sigh, followed by noises that told him she was obeying. In a few moments the cabin was filled with a mellow light. The glow gave the place some semblance of security, despite the raging storm outside.

"That's better." His eyes raked over her, and, as he had feared, he saw that she was much thinner, and her complexion was pale, sallow. Irritably he snapped, "I've been told you aren't eating the food that's brought to you. From now on, you eat everything or I'll have you fed by force."

She lifted her face to his, eyes flashing. "Yes, I suppose you do want to keep me alive, don't you? After all, you could hardly collect ransom on a dead body, could you? But does it matter how barely alive I am? All you want is the money!"

She turned her face away in the direction of the porthole and the forked lightning that continued to split the black night and illuminate the sky with streaks of jagged silver and gold. Her eyes were burning with tears, and she did not want him to see that he'd made her cry. "You're despicable, Ironheart," she whispered in anguish, "and I wish you were dead."

He could not suppress a chuckle. She was even more lovely, if that were possible, when she was angry. "Do you think it's only the money I'm after? Come now, misty eyes. I think you know I find your company most enjoyable. Maybe I kidnapped you merely because I couldn't stand to let you leave me. Perhaps the money isn't important, after all."

"I know how much money you make," she said sharply. "I have heard how a blockade captain can earn up to five thousand dollars a trip. Even your chief officer stands to make twelve-hundred dollars. And no doubt you will make much on Rose Hill cotton, in addition to what my mother already paid you. I hate you and your kind, who want only to make a profit on the war."

"Why not?" She was sitting in a chair next to the table beneath the porthole, and he positioned himself on the edge of the bed, so close he could reach out and touch her if he wanted—and yes, he thought warmly, he did want to touch. But not yet. Perhaps not ever.

He took out his pipe, then his pouch of tobacco, and Julie watched him in angry silence as he packed the bowl, then lit it and drew on it. He exhaled the smoke, which floated upward in a blue-gray haze. "Why should I get myself killed on a battlefield? I can do so just as easily at sea, and perhaps I will have earned a great deal of money before departing this life.

"And," he continued, "you must realize that the blockade runners are the lifeblood of the Confederacy. Lincoln's closing the ports might starve our people if it weren't for the ships that manage to slip through with needed supplies. I hear that Savannah is now closed. Wilmington should be kept open, as it is an ideal haven for smugglers, since the Federal fleet cannot effectively block the mouth of the Cape Fear River. It's divided by an island and blocked by a shallow bar. With Wilmington just a few miles upriver and at the entrance, Fort Fisher is their protector, with big guns. The gray steamers of the runners can go in and out of that port and be invisible for more than a hundred yards away at night or in the fog. The Yankees can't hear our engines over the roar of breakers."

He paused to draw on his pipe again, satisfied that his running conversation had taken her mind off the storm. The ship still heaved and tossed like the stomach of a sailor hung over from drinking too much rum, but Julie did not look quite so unnerved as when he had first entered the cabin.

"Big British steamers loaded with arms and luxuries from Europe unload at Bermuda or Nassau and take on cotton for their return voyage," he explained. "The last miles, which involve slipping into Confederate ports, are covered by swift, lean light-draft ships like mine. You may have noticed the *Ariane* is painted black. I had that done when I heard about the impending blockade and knew what my course would be.

"We should be in Wilmington in another week, if the weather clears," he went on.

Suddenly Julie jumped to her feet, fists clenched at her sides. "Derek, I demand that I be returned to Savannah. You have committed a crime, you know. If you'll just see me safely home, I'll do everything in my power to see that you aren't punished for what you've done. If you don't release me, then I can't be responsible for the consequences. I have a brother, you know, who loves me very much. He won't sit back idly when he hears of my fate, even if it means risking his own life.

Derek's lips formed a crooked smile. "Julie, when the ransom is paid, you'll be returned. Not before. Why don't you use the time to map out a new course for your life? One that doesn't include marriage to a man you'll never love."

Hot tears of frustration sparkled in her eyes. "Why are you doing this? I know you're greedy for money, but this is insane! What if Virgil doesn't have the ransom you ask for? And what if my mother can't raise it? All we had is in the hold of this ship."

She whirled in a complete circle, throwing her hands up in the air. "It's madness! Dear God, what can you be thinking? I'm in the hands of a lunatic!"

"You've enjoyed being in my hands, and you know it."

"Oh, is that *all* you think of, you—you animal!" She faced him, trembling with fury. How she ached to slap his smug face. "Go ahead and be done with it. Take me. Have your fill of my body, then set me free."

Derek never liked to lose control, but her caustic accusations and her sniping were starting to seep beneath his hard exterior. His eyes narrowed. He wanted her, true. He'd spent many sleepless nights tossing and turning in his bed as he remembered their times together. But now . . . now with her standing before him with those flashing eyes, that arrogant smile upon her lips, he knew he couldn't have taken her had he been about to penetrate at that very moment.

"You give me no more pleasure than any other woman I've ever bedded," he lashed out at her, his body trembling with rage. "In fact, I've known much better, so don't puff up your silly female pride and think I brought you on board ship because I was panting with desire."

"Weren't you?" She continued to rankle him. "If you say you don't want me, you're lying."

She gave her long, silky hair a toss. "Go on! Take me! Have your fill. Take me again and again, and then set me free."

His nostrils flared as the muscles in his jaw and neck began to twitch.

"I don't know how much ransom you've demanded, but surely you can take some of it out in trade, can't you? I mean, you did go to a lot of trouble to have me kidnapped. You must have planned it all well in advance."

All the long days and nights locked in her cabin had taken their toll on her nerves. Julie felt she had reached the breaking point and could control her tears no longer.

She lifted shaking fingers that she fastened on the bodice of her dress. Then, with a rough jerk, she snatched it downward, exposing her breasts. She loosed the stays and stepped out of the garment, kicking it aside before struggling with her undergarments.

She stood before him completely naked, hands on her hips, legs spread apart. "Now," she hissed, thrusting her breasts upward, "take me, you bastard."

He made no move to touch her as his gaze moved slowly up and down her body.

"Well, isn't this what you wanted?" she taunted, her voice rising shrilly.

Derek bolted to his feet, and before he realized what he was doing, cracked his hand sharply across her face. She reeled slightly, then regained her balance and laughed while the tears streamed down her cheeks. "I'm not afraid of you, Ironheart. Do with me what you will—"

He grabbed her shoulders and shook her so violently that her head bobbed helplessly to and fro, her eyes mirroring the fright she was unable to conceal.

"Hell, yes, I want you," he cried. "A man would have to be a fool or a eunuch not to. But that doesn't mean I *have* to have you."

He released her so abruptly that she stumbled and fell to the floor. He made no move to assist her as he coldly said, "You don't mean a damn thing to me except a quarter of a million in gold, Julie. When I've got that, you'll be released."

She stared up at him in hatred and confusion. "You may not have raped my body, but you've raped my mind and soul and left me with nothing. Are you satisfied?"

Lifting herself up, she made her way to the bed, where she lay down and gave way to sobs that shook her body convulsively.

Derek stood quietly staring at her. God, she was beautiful. The firm roundness of her buttocks, the creamy skin . . . how he longed to stretch out on top of her and take her again and again.

But her tears moved him and erased both his anger and desire. "Julie, I'm sorry. I didn't mean to hurt you, but you provoked me and drove me to it. . . ."

She continued to cry.

Sitting down on the edge of the bed, he reached for the blanket that had been folded neatly at its foot and spread it over her. "I'm not completely mercenary. I actually did you a favor."

"A favor?" She raised herself up on her elbows and turned to stare at him in wonder. "Are you out of your mind? You think holding me for ransom is doing me a *favor*? And my mother is probably worried sick—"

"When the ransom is paid, you'll be set free, as I told you. As for your mother, she had her servant with her, so she wasn't left alone."

He smiled. "And the favor, milady, lies in giving you additional time to reconsider marriage to Virgil Oates."

Her long lashes swept her moist cheeks as she blinked in bewilderment. "If I mean no more to you than money, why do you concern yourself with my future?"

Raising up as she was, her breasts dangled free, barely brushing the bed. Derek felt his pulse quicken. Taking a deep, ragged breath, he turned his face away.

"Suppose I give you a portion of the ransom? That would give you a start on your own. You could go north and search for your brother yourself. Would that make up for some of the injustices you feel you've suffered at my hands?"

"If my mother somehow manages to raise the money herself, then it would be partly mine, anyway." She stared at him thoughtfully. "But what if you don't get the ransom? What will you do with me then?"

He shrugged. "We'll deal with that when the time comes. Till then, things would be a lot more pleasant if we could at least pretend to be friends."

"Friends? You're out of your mind." She laughed harshly.

"If we can reach some sort of understanding, I'll let you go topside for fresh air and sunshine. You could take your meals with my officers and have some companionship. I'm worried about you. You don't look well."

He pointed out that they might be together for some time. "In my ransom note, I gave the name of a contact in Wilmington, but there's no telling how long it will take for your mother to get in touch with him. As soon as we unload and take on a new cargo, we'll make another run. It might be a month before we return."

She pursed her lips, then nodded. "All right. We'll declare a truce. I may loathe you and despise you, but I'll put up a front if it means getting out of this cabin."

"That's a wise decision." Grinning, he slapped his knee and stood. "The storm's abating. Suppose you get dressed and we'll go topside. It'll do you good."

She padded over to where her clothes lay scattered on the floor, frowning as she realized she'd destroyed her dress in her angry outburst. No matter. She moved to her trunk, with its abundance of dresses. Long ago she'd realized the reason her baggage was not sent with her to Bermuda. Derek had known she would be returning once her mother was settled and his plan could be carried out.

As she dressed, she noticed Derek position himself so he could watch her. His behavior was puzzling. She had offered herself to him and been rejected. She had goaded him to such fury he had slapped her. Yet he had asked for a truce for the duration of the time they would be together. It was baffling.

Memories of their hours of passion danced through her mind, yet he could look at her naked body and not take her. What kind of man was he? A darting glance downward told her he wanted her.

Finally she smoothed back her hair and murmured, "I'm ready."

His eyes sparkled as he whispered, "You're lovely, Julie, as always."

He wrapped his fingers about her tiny hand, which she felt was lost in his grasp. Then he led her up on deck, where a light, misty rain was still falling. The distant sky still crackled with lightning.

They moved together to the railing, watching as the crew began to appear and clean up after the storm.

Suddenly Julie stiffened and squeezed Derek's hand. He followed her startled gaze and saw the strange light flickering high up on the masts. It danced along the spars like stark, cold flames, casting an eerie light as it outlined all that it touched. The air was filled with the smell of smoldering ozone.

Several men cried out in fright and backed away. Julie stood rigid, still holding tightly to Derek's hand. "It's beautiful," she whispered in awe. "Should I be afraid?"

He chuckled. She was so refreshingly honest at times that he found it amusing. "It's called Saint Elmo's fire," he explained. "It's a phenomenon often seen at sea during rough weather. I don't really understand it, but I've heard it's called Saint Elmo's fire after the patron saint of Mediterranean sailors. Seamen regard it as the visible sign of his guardianship over them."

"Its beauty is awesome."

And then it disappeared. Julie relaxed her grip on Derek's hand, quite suddenly, as though just realizing how tightly she had been holding onto him. He noticed and smiled to himself.

The storm was moving further out to sea, but the breeze was still stiff. Derek cupped his hands about his mouth and shouted to his men, "Hoist the sails. Let's take advantage of the wind. Everyone to his post. We can make good time in the wake of the storm!"

Julie watched as the sailors scurried about, each knowing exactly what he was supposed to do. Occasionally she could hear someone shout, and there was the sound of a sail snapping loudly against the wind, the creaking of the riggings, and water breaking on either side of the bow. The seas were still rough.

As her eyes scanned the darkness, she could make out

other objects besides the men. Her gaze fell on the spot by
the railing where she'd sung that night, then traveled on to
the place where Shad had tried to ravish her. With a
shiver, she asked, "Whatever happened to him?"

"Who?" Derek looked down at her, puzzled.

"Shad Harky." A wave of revulsion swept over her.

Derek did not answer. Instead he turned his face toward
the water, ignoring her.

"Derek," she persisted, tugging at his sleeve. "What
happened to him? Did you set him adrift with the Yankees? Did he join up with them?"

"No." He spoke so coldly that she felt a chill. "I guess
you could say he joined up with the sharks."

Nausea welled up in her throat. "You—you mean . . ."
and she shook with revulsion, unable to continue.

He nodded. "There's a lot you don't understand about
the sea, Julie. The man was a mutineer. I dealt with him
accordingly. Along with his friends. We forced them overboard. We saw sharks in the area. It was over quickly."

"Oh, my God, no . . ." She covered her mouth with
both hands and stumbled to the railing, stomach heaving
as the image marched in review through her shocked mind.

"It's the way of the sea." He placed a hand on her
shoulder. "You've got to understand that if there's disorder
and rebellion on board a ship, shipping cannot survive.

"I gave Harky a second chance," he pointed out, "and
he wanted me dead. I had no choice but to pass judgment
and have him and the others executed."

Swallowing hard, Julie struggled for composure. Finally
she was able to speak. "Perhaps what you say is true, but
it still seems cruel, barbaric."

"Life is cruel. Now come. I'll take you back to your
cabin, and tomorrow morning you'll join me for breakfast.
I'm going to make sure you start eating as you should. I
don't want you getting sick on me again."

She could not resist a waspish reply. "Heavens, no. If
something happened to me, you wouldn't be able to collect
your ransom, would you?"

He slid a powerful arm about her shoulders and turned
her toward the steps leading downward. "Julie, let's don't
spar with each other. We agreed on a truce."

"I suppose we did, but it's so easy to hate you when I
think how you've messed up my life and the way you've
probably caused my mother to worry herself sick."

"Ahh, but one day you'll thank me, little one." He grinned down at her.

When they reached her cabin, he told Julie he would not lock her door. "I see no need. Where would you go, anyway? We're miles from land, and I don't think you want to feed the sharks."

She chewed her lower lip thoughtfully. He was so handsome, illuminated as he was by the lantern's cozy glow. In his eyes she could recognize the desire for her that he refused to acknowledge. And she could feel a stirring in her own loins as she remembered the hunger he had awakened in her.

"Good night, Julie." He turned to leave, but suddenly she reached out and clutched his arm. With a raised eyebrow, he turned to look at her.

She could not put her feelings into words. She knew only that she had spent many lonely hours alone in her bed in the tiny cabin, and here stood a man who could answer all the needs he had taught her body to crave.

Slowly, deliberately, she reached to unfasten her stays, letting her dress fall to her waist. In seconds her breasts were once more exposed, and he feasted upon them with his eyes. Trancelike, silently, he reached out to press each nipple between his thumb and forefinger.

Closing her eyes, she moaned softly with the ecstatic rush that charged through her body. St. Elmo's Fire. She felt as though she were actually lightning dancing along the spars as her whole body ignited in sky-shattering explosions.

Her dress slipped to the floor, and she stepped from her pantalets with ease. He lifted her in his arms to take her inside the cabin, then kicked the door shut. He placed her tenderly upon the bed, then his hands seemed to travel everywhere at once. She writhed, moaning aloud with pleasure.

Then he was spread-eagling her, moving her thighs apart to probe with his swollen, seeking member, which he had released from his trousers. She gasped as she felt him enter, marveling that her small body could receive a man of such magnitude. In the beginning, when they first made love, she had felt some pain, but it had soon dimmed. Now she was able to take all of him with ease.

Sighing, she wrapped her legs around his narrow waist

and dug her heels into his buttocks, spurring him on as she wriggled her hips beneath him.

There was no world but this world. No pleasure but this.

And together, like the sails that unfurled against the never-ending sky, they soared to the winds . . . leaving everything else behind.

❧ Chapter Eleven ❧

IT was obvious to Captain Arnhardt that the man standing before him was quite angry.

"I asked you a question, sir." Edsel spoke coldly, evenly.
"How much longer do you plan to keep that woman on
this ship? And I'm not the only one who wants to know.
The crew is concerned as well. You know a lot of them
believe it is bad luck to have a woman on board."

Derek drew in his breath, an awesome sight, for he was
bare-chested, and his muscles rippled along his shoulders
and down his arms, making him appear even more formidable. His crewmen jokingly said he must exercise by
lifting the ship's cannons when no one was looking. A
powerful man, strength seemed to exude from every pore
of his skin.

"Garris, I don't give a damn what you or anyone else
thinks. You seem to forget this is my ship, and I'll run it
as I see fit. Now don't bother me with superstitious prattle.
We'll be in Bermuda by sunrise, and we've got a cargo to
unload."

He turned back to his pacing on the afterdeck and
peered ahead into the murk, worrying once again about
the wisdom of running ahead of the wind on such a dark
night. There were lookouts posted to watch for other ships'
running lights, but the danger of a collision was still a risk
to be reckoned with.

"Sir!"

Derek's head snapped about at the sharp tone. "I said I
wasn't discussing it. Now get to your post. I don't care
how good a bank pilot we've got working for us, navigat-

ing around the coral is always tricky. It's your job to help him. Now be on your way. You're trying my patience."

Edsel's face reddened as he exploded, "I don't give a damn whether *your* patience is tried or not, Captain, because *mine* is exhausted."

Derek's eyes widened. He was not accustomed to being addressed in such a manner by anyone, much less one of his men.

"Go ahead and get mad," Edsel rushed on. "It's time we got something settled. There's not going to be any ransom paid on her, and you know it. We've docked in Wilmington three times now, and there's been no money waiting."

He pounded his fist on the railing, his body heaving with rage. "Dammit, Captain, it's been over four months. If her people were going to pay that ransom, they would've done it. Maybe her mother died or something. Maybe she couldn't get the money."

He sucked in a deep breath. "So here we are, running blockades with a blasted female aboard. It isn't right, and the men are getting more and more indignant over it. I say leave her where you got her—in Bermuda. And let's get back to the business of sailing."

Derek turned his face back to the sea. The salt spray felt cool on his warm skin. He was mad. Hell, he was madder than he could remember being in a long, long time. And he was fighting for control. Early in life, he'd had to learn to keep a tight rein on his anger. Because of his size and strength, he could easily kill a man with his bare hands. So he had learned to intimidate with a look, or by flexing his enormous muscles. And it usually worked. But this time the man confronting him was hellbent on making his point. They'd been friends, as well as a shipping team for a long time. Derek wasn't about to hurt him, but dammit, he wished Edsel would back off while he still had those reins in check. . . . He was approaching the breaking point.

Through gritted teeth, without facing him, Derek ground out the words: "That's all, Garris. You're pushing."

The first officer started to speak, but there was no mistaking the fury boiling in Derek Arnhardt at that moment. Garris could see his face in the dim glow of the ship's running lights.

So with an exaggerated sigh, which, he decided, would have to take the place of a parting shot, he retreated, shaking his head from side to side in frustration. He had accomplished nothing. But at least Arnhardt knew his first officer and his crew were upset. That should give him something to think on, Edsel decided.

Derek's grip on the railing relaxed. He didn't need Garris to tell him about the crew's feelings. He'd seen it in their eyes, which were accusing and brooding. They didn't like Julie being on board, and it didn't make any difference that they were aware she was his mistress. They cared only that the ransom hadn't been paid and she seemed to have become a permanent fixture.

Frankly, he didn't know what to do with her. He had to admit, if only to himself, that it didn't look as though the ransom was going to be paid. And there had been time. Too much time.

He had thought of a hundred possibilities which might have prevented Mrs. Marshal from making the contact at Wilmington, but as time passed, all of his reasons grew weaker and weaker. Something had gone wrong. Either she'd died or didn't have the money. He knew Virgil Oates didn't have it.

He could have used that gold, too, at least what would've been left of it after he divided it with Julie as he promised. It was still profitable running the blockade, but not as much as before the Confederate government stepped in. It was smuggled luxuries that people wanted, items such as tea, coffee, sugar, and silks and satins. But the government had outlawed the importation of some luxuries entirely, stipulating that one-half of the space on every ship had to be reserved for government goods.

Derek didn't like it. There was more money to be made on luxury items, but he wanted no quarrel with the powers of the Confederacy, and conformed with the law.

He could've put his part of the ransom aside for use after the war, he thought with disappointment. More and more he was questioniong his life on the sea. True, he loved it, but now and then he had a strange desire to plant his feet on solid earth. Yet he would always hoist anchor and sail with the tide.

Julie was badgering him also, wanting to know what the future held. Though they enjoyed each other's bodies every night, and sometimes even in the balmy afternoons, they did not discuss a future. Theirs was a relationship existing solely to satisfy physical needs for the moment at hand, he reasoned. Tomorrow simply did not exist for them.

Derek had admitted to himself that if he allowed himself, he could fall in love with the misty-eyed beauty. But he kept himself in check. His heart would belong to no woman, no matter how lovely and enticing she might be.

He knew Garris was right. Something had to be done, and soon. It couldn't go on. And, though he didn't like to think about it, the fact remained that he was constantly putting Julie in a dangerous situation. Running the blockade was not something to be regarded lightly. Each man held his breath as they slipped through, knowing they could be spotted and fired upon at any second.

He decided the time had come to free her. Sure, he would miss her. No point in lying to himself about that. But reality had to be faced. No money was going to be paid, and he figured he had no right to endanger her life any longer. So . . . he'd just leave her in Bermuda and give her enough money to buy passage to England. And if she wanted to go home instead, she could find a way. It would all be up to her.

Sunrise. He squinted toward the east. Was the sky turning the least bit pink? He couldn't tell yet.

Soon it would be time to say goodbye and never see her again. The muscle in his jaw twitched. No, he wouldn't just say goodbye so abruptly. He'd do something he ordinarily didn't do. He'd send his crew ashore for leave. Usually they were in and out of port so fast there was no time for them to make merry and get drunk. This time, however, he'd make time, because the ship would be anchored in the harbor, and once he sent everyone in, he'd be alone with Julie.

He laughed aloud over his plans. Many times she had stared wistfully at the clear emerald waters surrounding the sandy pink beaches of Bermuda and murmured that she would like to go for a swim. Well, she was going to have her chance, he decided. For two golden days and nights, they were going to frolic on the ship and in the water. They would savor the delights of each other's bodies, tasting the fruits one last time before parting forever.

As though an unseen hand lifted a nonexistent curtain, the sky suddenly became pale pink, then shifted to a rosy hue, and a new day was born.

Almost simultaneously the cry of "Land, ho!" split the

reverent stillness of dawn, and Derek turned his gaze on the first sighting of the coast of Bermuda.

For the next few hours, the deck was alive with activity as men hurried back and forth to unload the cargo of cotton which had been brought through the blockade from Wilmington. Derek went onshore to take care of the paper work, pleased to learn he could pick up ammunition needed by the Confederacy, as well as medical supplies, and that there would still be room left in the hold for tea and sugar and fine silks. He'd make one hell of a profit off this run back through the Federal fleet.

By late afternoon, the ship's bowels were empty. Edsel reported to Derek's cabin to ask if they should wait till morning to begin taking on the new cargo.

"No," was his curt reply. "Have the men prepare to take the ship one mile out and drop anchor."

"What?" Edsel's eyes bulged. "What for—"

Derek slammed his hands down on his desk. "Dammit, why in hell do you keep questioning me? Now follow my orders at once."

"As you wish!" Garris ground out the words, turned on his heel, and stomped from the cabin.

Derek smiled, leaned back in his chair, and propped his feet on the desk. Soon he and Julie would be alone to romp like children, with no watchful eyes about. They would have complete freedom, no longer forced to be confined to a narrow bed in a cramped cabin.

All he had to do was wait. When the ship was secured, he walked out on the bridge after having the crew summoned. In clipped tones he informed them that, beginning immediately, they were on shore leave, and he would expect them back on board by sunrise of the third day. With all the cheering and shouts of jubilation, he doubted any of them had heard the termination date. No matter. He would inform Garris and Watson, and it would be their task to round up the crew. No doubt some of them would be in jail, and others hung over from too much rum and too many women. Loading the new cargo would be a problem, as he wouldn't get much work out of his crew till they got over their celebration—but it would all be worth it, he knew, to have the precious, private, final hours with Julie.

Edsel hurried to the bridge, his face tight with agitation. His mouth twisted in silent anger before he finally exploded, "Well, this came as quite a surprise, Captain. Since when have you stopped letting your first officer in on your plans?"

Derek ignored his question and ordered him to have the men take the rowboats to shore. "Miss Marshal and I will be staying onboard."

"Aha! So this is why you're giving the men leave. You plan to have a private holiday, just the two of you."

Derek withered him with a look.

Edsel's smile faded, then he dared to say what was burning inside him. "It looks to me like you're getting rather involved with her, Captain. I mean, you're taking several days off just to spend with her, sending the men ashore when you know some of them won't return or will wind up in trouble—"

"You won't have to worry about my involvement with her much longer. When we go back into port, she'll be staying behind."

"Thank God!" Edsel was beaming with joy and relief. "At last we'll be rid of her and can return to serious business."

He started to leave, then whipped back around to say, "I'm glad, Captain, really glad. I was starting to worry that you had finally met a woman who could take your mind off your ship, and with us in the middle of a war, now's not the time."

"Will you get out of here?" Derek snarled. "I've grown tired of all your prattling and needling, Garris. You're worse than the sea wives on the wharves in Wilmington."

He pushed by Garris to move swiftly from the bridge. Brushing by happy, noisy crewmen, he made his way through the throng to the steps that led to the lower deck. Reaching Julie's cabin, he flung the door open, not bothering to knock.

She lifted sea-green eyes to stare at him, marveling, as always, over the way he seemed to fill the doorway with his hugeness. She murmured a greeting from where she sat at the little table, brushing her long hair. Tossing the tresses back over her shoulder, she asked, "What was all that cheering about? Is something happening I don't know about?"

She saw the way he stared at her. The dressing gown she wore was lavender satin trimmed with delicate lace and tiny ribbons. While she was brushing her hair, she was bent over, and her breasts poured from the gown. Straightening, she lay the brush aside and rose. "Derek, why won't you answer me? What's wrong?"

She walked to where he stood. The top of her head barely reached beneath his chin. As she traced his lips gently with her fingertips, he stiffened, and she cried, "There *is* something wrong. I can feel it. Tell me, please."

"Nothing is wrong." He smiled warmly, then told her of his plans to send the crew ashore so they could be alone, adding, "You can have that swim you've been wanting, as we'll have the ship all to ourselves."

She threw her arms around him, standing on tiptoe as she tried to reach his lips, but as always, he had to lift her up for their kiss. As he set her back down, she laughed, "I think I'll get myself a stool and keep it close by so I can kiss you whenever I want."

"What is a little inconvenience," he responded with a soft chuckle, "when so much pleasure awaits us once the obstacle is overcome?"

And they clung together, each stirred by the deep, soul-searing embrace.

Finally the ship was a good distance from shore, and they were alone. They stood together on the afterdeck, staring toward the coastline of Bermuda.

The sky reminded Julie of the periwinkles that lined the streets of Savannah, and the clouds were shaded in silver and tinged with the reflection of the pink coral beneath the water's surface.

A balmy, tropical wind blew across their faces. Licking her lips, Julie said, "I can understand why you love the sea so much, Derek. After a time, it becomes a part of you."

"As you've become a part of me these past months," he whispered huskily, turning to fold his arms about her.

Coquettishly, she cocked her head, eyes dancing mischievously. "Oh, come now, Captain, sir. Don't tell me you've allowed yourself to be charmed and smitten by a woman. Weren't you the man who told me once that women serve only one purpose?"

"Yes, and you've served it well."

A shadow passed over her face, and the happy glow disappeared. Derek saw and gave her a squeeze. "Oh, come now, Julie. I wasn't trying to hurt your feelings. I want these two days to be special for us, so let's don't spoil it by talking of serious things. Let's just enjoy each other."

She took a deep breath, lifting her face away from him, toward the sea. She was a fool, she knew, to entertain notions of ever meaning anything to this man. He was right. They would enjoy each other, just as they always did. They would couple and experience passion, joy, everything that went with the act. And afterward there would be nothing between them except anticipation of the next encounter.

Julie was wearing a simple cotton dress of sunshine yellow. Her hair was caught at the back of her neck by a matching ribbon. Derek's eyes locked with hers as he reached to free her hair, touching the tresses lovingly with his fingers as they tumbled around her shoulders and face.

Moving his hands behind her back, he began to fumble with the stays. "I want you to take off all your clothes, Julie." He spoke with the tone he would use to his crew: authoritative and final. "I plan to keep you naked for the time we're out here."

"Will you join me?" she asked suddenly. He gave her a look of surprise, but she couldn't put her thoughts into words. It made her feel absolutely wicked to admit it, even to herself, but she adored seeing his naked body. She never ceased being thrilled by the magnificence of his physique, the sheer beauty of his manliness.

As he unfastened her clothes, she unbuttoned his shirt with busy, deft fingers, loving the touch of the thickly curling hairs upon his chest. Pressing her cheek against the down, she could not suppress the delicious sigh that escaped her lips.

When they were both naked, he led her to one of the covered hatches and spread an empty burlap bag across its top. "I've thought of taking you here, misty eyes, right in the open, with the breeze kissing our bodies."

He lifted her easily, and she lay back, opening her arms and legs to receive him.

There was no need for foreplay. Disrobing each other had aroused them to a fever pitch. Quickly he positioned himself to stand between her parted thighs, plunging up and in as she gasped with delight while he filled her. With his feet firmly planted on deck, he had the necessary leverage to thrust to and fro more firmly and surely than ever before.

Her senses screamed, and she raked her nails down his broad back. If he felt pain, he didn't show it.

Somewhere overhead a sea gull screeched, shocked, perhaps, by the sight of the man and woman copulating on the ship's deck. With a great flapping of wings, it soared higher, then dipped, swirled, and disappeared from sight.

Julie opened her eyes momentarily and saw the gull. She felt the quickening in her loins, and, like the graceful white bird, she, too, was soon soaring higher and higher, screaming with her own delight. Derek moved faster, harder, and soon he joined her in her celestial flight.

He held her for a long time. Neither of them spoke, lost in thought over the awesome glory of the moment shared.

Finally Derek released her and suggested they go for a swim. He seemed delighted by her prowess in the water, and they played and splashed like children in the clear, cool waters.

Julie felt a happy glow she had never experienced with him before. It was as though she had never really known him; now there was no pretense. She found she liked him more and more as he seemed to relax and let himself go.

Derek teased her about her cooking that night, saying he'd probably die of poisoning before the ship's cook returned.

"Well, the galley is almost empty," she replied in defense. "Besides, I thought this was supposed to be a holiday, and you're making me a slave."

"You can be both slave and mistress," he cajoled her. "Right now, I want you to be my mistress."

Shoving his plate of food to one side, he grabbed her about the waist, pulling her down onto the long table. And he took her then and there.

On the last afternoon, Julie stood on the afterbridge once again, this time staring toward the shoreline with a thoughtful expression. When Derek asked why she was so quiet, she did not answer but instead murmured, "I suppose they'll be coming in the morning."

He was silent for so long that she turned to stare at him. "Derek, the crew will be coming in the morning, won't they?"

"They were told to report at dawn," he snapped in reply, his face tight. "Then we'll go into port to take on new cargo."

Reaching out to slip her hand into his, she asked, "Is that why you're annoyed? Because it's time to discuss what to do with *me*? We haven't talked about it lately, and I can feel the resentment of the others."

He did not speak.

She squeezed his hand. "Derek, we can't go on like this. . . ."

He glanced at her, sighed, then turned his gaze back to the gently rolling waters. "No, Julie," he said finally. "We can't."

"Then what's to become of me?" she cried, suddenly bristling with anger and also embarrassed to be naked before him, even though they'd frolicked together that way for the past two days. She reached out and snatched up a burlap bag that was nearby, draping it around her body and holding it in place with shaking hands. "Do you plan to just set me adrift?"

"I can leave you in Bermuda," was his quiet response. "I'll make sure you have the necessary money for whatever you plan to do. You can go on to England or make your way back to Savannah. It's up to you."

She felt like crying and could not understand why. After all, she reasoned, freedom was near at last, and this knowledge should have made her happy, not sad.

"Just leave me in Bermuda." She blinked furiously, fighting to hold back the tears. "And don't worry. I can take care of myself. If I find myself starving, I can always go to work in some bawdy house. After all, you've taught me well. . . ."

"*I've* taught you?" He lifted an eyebrow. "Julie, what are you trying to say?"

Her green eyes snapped with the fires of hell. "What man would want me after you kept me on board your ship all this time? Everyone will know you forced me to share your bed—"

"*Forced* you?" he bellowed. "Now where do you come by that idea? Julie, don't you start yelling rape. I never had to force you, and you know it. I might've persuaded you and taken unfair advantage of you. Maybe it's fair to say I seduced you, but dammit, I never really made you do anything you didn't want to do."

"That's not fair!"

"*You* aren't being fair. And what are you so mad about,

anyway? I told you I'm giving you your freedom. What more do you want?"

"Something you can't give me, because you've taken it away!" she shouted, her black hair falling wildly about her face. *"Decency!"*

"Decency?" he echoed, bewildered.

"That's something you seem to find difficult to credit a woman with."

She whirled away from him, hating herself for being so foolish. Why was she reacting in such a way—saying such things? All she wanted was her freedom, and he was giving her that. There was no reason for her to be angry, except over having been kidnapped in the first place.

"I suppose you think I should marry you." His voice was frosty.

"Marry me?" She turned slowly to face him incredulously. "You—you think I *want* to marry you?"

"That's the impression you give me. You talk about decency, and in your mind, I imagine that's the only way you'd ever feel your virtue was restored, by becoming my wife. I've told you, Julie, my wife is the sea. Now if you want me to find a place for you in Bermuda, I'll take care of you, and—"

"And you'll let me be your mistress!" She felt as though her heart were breaking into bits and pieces, dissolving as quickly as the white-foamed breakers smashing against the sandy shore. But she wouldn't let him know it. Oh, no, he was far too cocky as it was.

"I wouldn't be your mistress or your wife. I want to be free of you, and as for what we've shared, I'll just look back on it as a time in my life when I stooped as low as a mating animal—just to experience what it's like to grovel in filth so I can appreciate being a respectable woman. . . ."

"Julie, you come back here. . . ."

Ignoring his call, she walked with chin held high, looking neither right nor left as she moved ahead to the steps. Only when she was in her cabin with the door locked and bolted behind her did she give way to the stinging, burning tears that demanded to be released.

She was a fool—a complete, utter fool. Why had she given in to him? she asked her tormented brain. He'd made it clear from the first he only wanted the pleasures her body could bring him . . . and she had given herself to him freely.

True, there was nothing he could do but let her go now that it was apparent no ransom was going to be paid, but at least, she reasoned, he might have behaved as though he cared—if only a little. That would have salvaged some of her pride. He didn't have to behave as though she were just some river trollop he'd picked up for a few nights of debauchery.

She had felt all along that her mother would never be able to raise the amount Derek demanded, but in the back of her mind had believed Virgil would. Could it be possible Derek had told the truth when he said the man was a fake—that he wasn't wealthy as he claimed?

So now she was faced with the decision of what to do with her life. Would her mother have returned to Savannah? Julie had no way of knowing.

She tried to sort out her thoughts, but it was difficult to think with her head aching from all the tears she had shed. Turning over on her back, she closed her eyes, trying to blot everything from her mind. If she could relax, the throbbing pain would go away, and she could think about what she must do. . . .

When she opened her eyes, Julie was staring into darkness. How long had she slept? Silence surrounded her with the oppressive cloak of night.

She sat up and swung around so that her bare feet touched the rough wooden floor.

Where was Derek? He was probably still angry over their argument, or, she reasoned, he would have been down to make amends. But maybe he didn't want to make peace. Why should he? After all, he'd be leaving her behind, never to see her again. He probably wasn't at all concerned over whether their parting was amiable.

Her stomach gave a hungry lurch. With a sigh, she decided there was nothing to do for the moment but go to the galley and find something to eat. Tomorrow she would leave the ship. There was no point in worrying until then.

But still, there was a pain in her heart she found disturbing. Surely she did not actually feel something for the man. With a toss of her head, she told herself she was being silly. It was over. It must be forgotten. All of it.

Leaving her cabin, she turned toward the galley, then decided it was only polite to ask Derek if he'd like something to eat also. She told herself she really didn't care whether or not he was hungry—it was that stove. She hadn't mastered it and didn't like using it when he wasn't around. She could forget about pride for the moment—at least until her screaming belly was fed.

Still, in the back of her mind, a little voice shouted, *You do care . . . you care whether he's hungry . . . and you care about him. . . .*

"That's absurd!" she said out loud, angrily, bitterly. The voice kept nagging her.

Looking up as she ascended the steps, she could see the night was clear, the sky a purple backdrop for the thousands of glittering stars that sprinkled the heavens.

It was difficult to see, but once her eyes became accustomed to the darkness, she could make out objects and shapes well enough that she wouldn't stumble and go sprawling upon the deck.

She called to Derek as soon as she reached the top step. "Derek, where are you?" Her tone was clipped, short— anything but friendly. "We can call another truce long enough to eat, if you'll help me with that confounded stove. . . ."

There was no answer.

A wave of apprehension swept over her. Then she told herself there was no need to be frightened. Derek was probably in his cabin, brooding over her caustic remarks or busying himself with charts and maps.

Or maybe, she thought suspiciously, he was deliberately not answering because he wanted to frighten her. All right, then, let him think he'd succeeded. She would go to the galley and rummage up whatever she could find to eat without using the old stove. *He* could go hungry.

A cool breeze whispered across her bare skin, and she realized she was still naked. Cursing herself, she started for her cabin to dress. It had become a habit all too quickly, she mused, this cavorting in the nude.

"Miss Marshal."

She froze, terror constricting her throat. *That was not Derek's voice.*

Someone was there, stepping out of the shadows, but she couldn't make out his face. Her legs were frozen, and she could not move . . . could not scream. Was it one of the crewmen returning early? He mustn't find her like this—without a stitch on.

Finally, after what seemed an eternity, she was able to

will her legs to move . . . but not soon enough. As she started to scurry down the steps, the man·grabbed her arm and held her tightly in his grip.

"Don't be afraid, Miss Marshal. I'm not going to hurt you."

"Captain Guthrie!"

Her brain was spinning dizzily as she recognized his voice. "I—I don't understand. What are you doing here?"

He chuckled with smug satisfaction. "I've been lurking about in these waters for months waiting for this opportunity. Arnhardt was a fool to think I'd let him get away with what he did to me and my crew. I would have searched for him the rest of my life, if necessary. And now I've found him—"

Abruptly he sucked in his breath, then cried, "My God, you aren't wearing any clothes!"

Her lips parted to speak, but what was there to say? She heard him snap his fingers and yell to someone to bring a blanket. Then she felt the rough material being draped about her shoulders, and she wrapped it closer about her.

"Now, then. Suppose you tell me why you are here? Of course, I knew you were on board—the two of you alone. My men have been watching from a distance with a telescope. Why weren't you left in Bermuda long ago? And where is your mother?"

So many questions, and she had many of her own. Not knowing where to start, she finally stammered, "I—I was held for ransom." She certainly didn't want him thinking she had stayed with Derek of her own volition. She managed to tell him the story about the ransom demand, how it had not been paid.

"That savage!" his voice boomed through the night, then he patted her shoulder in a gesture of sympathy. "You poor child. To think what you must have endured at the hands of that—that *barbarian*!"

He rushed on, "You aren't to fret a moment longer. I'll personally see that you are taken safely wherever you wish to go."

Then he told her Captain Arnhardt was securely bound in his cabin. "We took him by surprise. We waited till dark to board. We found him sitting on deck, and he was naked too. I wondered about that, but now I can see he's depraved."

Clearing his throat, he went on, "We won't discuss that,

as I'm sure it's distressing to be reminded of what you've been forced to endure. We thought it best to wait for you to come up on deck rather than search for you. We didn't want to frighten you."

"And what is to happen next?" she asked fearfully.

"Would you happen to know when the crew is to return? Arnhardt won't cooperate by answering our questions."

She stiffened. "I don't think I should tell you anything, either. After all, you are a Yankee . . . and the enemy."

"But I'm not *your* enemy," he said incredulously. "Really, Miss Marshal, I should think you would be grateful. After all, I've rescued you."

"He was going to let me go tomorrow—"

And then she realized she'd said too much, as he cried, "Ah, so it's tomorrow the crew returns. Well, they won't have a ship to return to."

She shook her head slowly, fearfully. "I don't understand."

He made it all sound so simple. "There won't be a ship because we're going to destroy it.

"Now, then," he continued, steering her toward the steps, "Suppose you get dressed and join me in the galley for tea. I imagine you're hungry. I'll have one of my men get something together for the two of us."

Bewildered, Julie dressed hurriedly, slipping on a dress and not bothering with petticoats. Her mind was whirling. What did the Yankees have in mind? Were they going to kill Derek?

That thought stabbed at her. Maybe she and Derek didn't share love, but they'd had many happy times together when they weren't sparring with each other. True, he was despicable and arrogant, and she found it quite easy to hate him . . . despite the rapture she had enjoyed in his arms. But that didn't mean she wanted to see him killed.

Perhaps there was still time to help, she thought with panic. What she could do, she didn't know, but at least she could try to sneak up to his cabin and talk with him, find out what was going on. What if Captain Guthrie were lying about letting her go? Why, her life might be at stake as well. She would never, ever trust a Yankee!

With these feverish thoughts swirling in her head, she

flung the door open to find the narrow hallway flooded with light. Someone had lit the lanterns that hung on the walls.

And then she found herself staring up into the smug face of a man in a dark-blue uniform. He was smirking, as though he knew what she planned to do.

"Miss Marshal, I'm to take you to Captain Guthrie. He's waiting with tea and food." He bowed slightly—insolently, she thought.

His hand fastened on her arm before she could protest, and she found herself being walked swiftly down the hallway. They entered the officers' dining room, and Benjamin Guthrie rose politely in greeting.

A mug of steaming tea sat on the table. Guthrie quickly pulled a chair out for her. "Now, then," he smiled when they were both seated. "Suppose we talk about what is to be done with you."

Staring down at the golden liquid in her mug, she murmured that she had no plans. "I've no idea where my mother is."

"There would've been difficulty had she tried to return to Savannah," he remarked. "For Pulaski has fallen, as I'm sure you have heard. The Savannah port is sealed off from the sea. I suppose it's possible she could have made it into Wilmington on a runner, then made her way home by land."

"We'd already booked passage for England, but she would have been quite upset when she heard of my being kidnapped. I just don't know what she might've done."

"It's logical to think she would've continued on her journey, possibly hoping your fiancé . . . what was his name—Oates? Yes, that's it. She would probably have gone to find him and asked for his help."

He patted her hand. "Don't fret, my dear. You're too beautiful to be so distressed. Finish your tea, and I'll have my men take you back to our ship. We'll be leaving soon to sail north. I must report to Washington for further orders now that I've settled my score with Arnhardt. I'll take you with me."

She pushed her chair back from the table and shrieked, "But I don't want to go north! I want to go home!"

"Nonsense." He waved a hand, as though dismissing such an absurd thought. "You're in the hands of a gentleman now, and if you'll just relax and leave everything to me, I assure you that you'll find I have only your best interests at heart."

Leaving her tea untouched, she arose, and he followed. Then he surprised her by bending to kiss her hand, a strange look on his face as he murmured, "I never forgot your beauty. It haunted me all these months. It's going to be a pleasure having you in my company. . . ."

She recoiled in horror, and he was quick to assure her he meant her no harm. "I won't be a rogue, my dear, but I must warn you I will be trying to win your heart—"

"I beg your pardon?" She stepped back.

He blinked his eyes several times. "I said I'd be trying to win your heart. Do you find that so unbelievable? I'm a man without a wife, and I would like to properly court you."

"I think you share the foolish optimism of your Yankee brethren," she responded icily.

"I don't understand. . . ."

It was Julie's turn to smile. "Like your fellow Yankees, you think you can win something from a Southerner. That is folly. You could never win my heart."

He bowed slightly. "I accept the challenge."

"There is no challenge," she snapped in exasperation. "Can't you understand—"

She fell silent at the sound of someone opening the door behind her. Turning, she saw a craggy-faced man appear and salute Guthrie, his eyes glittering excitedly. "Sir, we're ready. We've got Arnhardt on the plank."

"Very well. I'll be right up."

The sailor saluted again, then turned and quickly left. Captain Guthrie started to follow, but Julie felt a sense of terror and foreboding, and she reached out to clasp his arm. "What was he talking about?" she demanded.

"Don't burden yourself with unpleasantnesses. Finish your tea, and it won't be long till someone comes to escort you to my ship."

"I'm not going anywhere!" She picked up her mug and sent it crashing against the wall as fury soared through her. "I'm going up on deck and find out what's going on. I have a right to know what fiendish, barbaric torture you damn Yankees have planned for Derek."

"*Derek*, is it?" His eyes narrowed. "Perhaps I was hasty in bestowing sympathy upon you, Miss Marshal. It appears you've got a soft spot in your heart for your captor. Very well. I think maybe you should witness how I inflict retribution on my enemies. Come along."

He allowed her to move ahead of him, and when they reached the steps he moved to help her ascend, but she jerked away from him. She didn't want a Yankee to touch her. Maybe she didn't know all there was to know about the politics of the war, but one thing was for certain: to her mind the overbearing Yankees had started it by trying to force their will on the South, and she wanted no part of any of them—not now—not ever.

On deck, lanterns burned, and she could see perhaps twenty of the blue-clad sailors clustered at the bow of the ship. Beyond them, standing on a wooden board which extended out over the water, Derek stood, still nude, his hands bound behind him.

As she moved closer, his eyes fell on her, but only for a moment. Then he turned his gaze back to the sea. He didn't appear frightened. Actually, he looked quite annoyed about the whole matter.

"Arnhardt," Captain Guthrie shouted in a mocking tone, "do you have anything to say before we feed you to the sharks?"

Julie stepped back, horror-stricken with the realization of what they were about to do.

There *were* sharks about. Derek had seen them earlier in the day and said it wouldn't be possible to take another swim. And sharks had quickly taken care of Shad Harky and his fellow mutineers.

Now Derek would share the same fate.

No, she couldn't let it happen. She told her pounding heart she cared because he was a human being, not because he meant anything deeper to her. They were lovers, nothing more, not ever. . . .

No one was watching her as the men busied themselves and taunted Derek. Glancing about, Julie searched for a weapon, anything with which to try and stop this madness.

Her foot scraped against something as the unpleasant odor of fish filled her nostrils. This was the spot where Derek had scaled and cleaned the fish he'd caught for their breakfast that morning. He hadn't taken the time to wash away the mess, and now the stench was overwhelming.

Her foot touched the object again, and then she cursed herself for not thinking of it sooner. Stooping quickly,

hands groping in the darkness, she touched the knife
Derek had used on the fish and quickly hid it in the folds
of her skirt as she stood up.

Derek was looking coolly at Guthrie as he asked, "What
do you intend to do with her?" He nodded toward Julie.

"She'll be going to Washington with me," Guthrie replied. "But don't be concerned. You've made her miserable
for the last time. She's in good hands." He gestured impatiently. "Is that all you wish to say?"

"What about my ship?"

"Dynamite, Captain." Guthrie was unable to suppress
his glee and broke into happy chuckles, along with his
men. He hurried on. "You *have* heard of that marvelous
invention, have you not? It was invented by the Swedish
physicist, Alfred Nobel. You see, by mixing nitroglycerin
with a porous inert absorbent, Nobel has produced a solid
that is resistant to shock but readily detonable by heat or
percussion."

He waved his hand airily. "But what would *you* know
of such marvels—you, a common sea rat? Dynamite is
going to blow your ship into a million pieces, Arnhardt.
The *Ariane* will never run a blockade again."

Derek threw back his head and laughed tauntingly.
"You don't give a damn whether she runs a blockade or
not, you pompous bastard. You only want revenge because I made you look like the fool you are."

"Now is that any way for an officer to speak in front of
a lady?" Guthrie clucked, shaking his head. "Be grateful I
don't have you shot. I *am* giving you a sporting chance,
because you did leave my men and me afloat so we could
be found."

Derek laughed. "You call throwing a man overboard,
with his hands tied behind his back, giving him a sporting
chance? That's Yankee thinking, I suppose."

"Let's get on with it!" Guthrie snapped.

Julie could not contain herself any longer. Lunging forward, she screamed, "Wait! You must let me have a moment with him, please—"

Guthrie looked down at her reproachfully. "Well, I
think I was wrong about you, Miss Marshal. Now I find
your story about being held against your will quite hard
to believe. You must have enjoyed—"

"Oh, I don't care what you believe! Can't you grant me
one last moment to say goodbye to him?" she pleaded.

His face, in the lanterns' glow, was almost maniacal. "It probably *will* be goodbye." He sounded triumphant. "We've dumped quite a bit of raw, bloody meat into these waters to draw sharks. I'm sure they're waiting for their main course now." He laughed. "So go. Say your goodbyes. You've now lost your pride along with your virtue."

Undaunted by his insults, Julie pushed her way through the sneering, mumbling men, finally breaking through and stepping up on the plank beside Derek.

"Get down, Julie," he snapped, his face contorted with anger. "You could fall—"

Her arms went around him quickly, and she pressed the knife into his rope-bound hands. "Take it," she whispered anxiously. "Hurry!"

His eyes widened momentarily as he felt the cold steel, but he did not hesitate to wrap his fingers deftly about it. He stared down at her, caressing her with his eyes as he murmured, "Someday, after I've mastered the winds and the tides, I'll come for you, Julie, and conquer your love."

She stood on tiptoe, trying to touch his lips with her own, tears streaming down her cheeks. "I never got the stool, Derek. I—I still can't reach you. . . ."

"And I can't help you now, misty eyes." His husky voice sent chills racing through her. "But we'll meet again."

She clung to him and was shaken by the turmoil that raged within her. Why was she aching so? Why did she feel such pain and despair? She didn't love him. She couldn't possibly. . . .

"Enough!" Captain Guthrie bellowed impatiently. "Get her down. We must move quickly."

Someone yanked her away as she fought to keep her arms about him. Guthrie was drawing his sword, moving forward toward Derek. "No . . ." The cry came from deep inside, wrenched from her very soul. Struggling against the man who held her, she screamed, "You can't do this, you Yankee dogs! No . . ."

She kicked at the shins of the man who was holding her as Guthrie moved closer to Derek, sword pointed at his back. A sudden movement at the bow made her blood freeze. She stopped struggling and stared at Derek, who was inching his way toward the end of the plank, his back to the water so the Yankees could not see the knife he held behind him.

He turned to look at her one last time, the glow of the lanterns illuminating his face with an almost golden halo, making him appear ghostly. Was he smiling? She strained to see. A gasp escaped her as she realized that, dear God, he *was* smiling!

She swayed, her eyes scanning his strong muscular body. If he could cut the ropes binding his hands, then he had a chance, at least. He was a strong swimmer, and he could make it back to shore. But until he freed himself, he'd be struggling in an awkward position, hands behind his back, beneath the water, sharks all around. . . .

Yet he could still face death and smile so arrogantly, she marveled, awash with respect for the man she had been so sure she despised.

He stepped from the plank. Everyone held his breath as silence descended over the ship.

A loud splash broke the stillness, echoing sharply through the night. The men pushed and shoved against each other as they rushed to the bow to watch, all of them screaming with excitement.

Released and forgotten for the moment, Julie sank to her knees and gave way to hysteria.

"Hell, I can't see him," someone yelled.

Another cried, "He never came up."

They were holding lanterns in their hands, leaning over the bow, stretching as far as they dared. "Not enough light. Can't see nothing."

It was all too much. Julie felt in that moment death would have been welcome, compared to the unknown future that lay before her at the hands of Captain Guthrie. The tears came wildly, and she did not try to control them.

A heavy fog enshrouded her, and it was only dimly that she realized someone was nearby, speaking about *her*.

"You think she's gone tetched, Captain? She sure looks like a crazy woman, crying and moaning that way."

"Could be," came Guthrie's familiar voice, cold and condemning. "And to think I actually felt sorry for her. Why, she enjoyed living like a trollop on this ship. I was even considering courting her." He snorted with self-disgust. "It just goes to show how beauty can make a man think like a fool."

"Well, we gonna just let her lay there and cry like that?" the other man wanted to know.

"No. Take her to our ship. We've got to move quickly

and get out of this area. Once the *Ariane* blows, they'll be able to see the explosion from the coast. Blockade runners in port might seek retaliation, so we must be prepared to move with full steam ahead."

Julie felt strong hands being clamped around her shoulders. She was about to scream in protest when the captain's next words stabbed at her brain, telling her to stop—to think—for here was the possible key to her escape.

"We'll take her north with us, and then I'll have her sent to a hospital. Perhaps she has gone mad. She was probably never a stable sort anyway, or she wouldn't have allowed herself to acquire such low morals."

A hospital! They would let her go at once, and she could return home. Lord, it *was* the answer, she realized joyfully. It was hard to continue sobbing when she wanted to laugh with triumphant glee. But she had to continue to make them believe she had truly lost her mind. Otherwise, there was no telling what her fate might be.

She allowed herself to be lifted in the Yankee crewman's arms, gasping and crying and throwing her head wildly from side to side.

"Hey, what's wrong with her?" another crewman asked as she was being carried across the deck.

"Captain says she's gone mad," the man carrying her replied matter-of-factly. "I'm going to take her to our ship and lock her in a cabin. She's harmless enough right now, but who's to say what she might do? I'm scared of crazy folks."

She turned her face to his shoulder to hide the smile she could not contain. Yes, she thought happily, it was the answer—let them think her insane!

❧ Chapter Twelve ❧

JULIE sat huddled in a corner of the small room. It was
quite cold there on the hard clay floor, but she had no
wish to share the wooden benches with those sad, disheveled women.

This was the hospital Captain Guthrie had had her
taken to. On the outskirts of the Federal capital in Washington, it was drab and dreary, the patients herded about
like mindless sheep. Julie had protested in outrage, but the
attendants had shoved her along, believing that she was
truly demented.

When she refused to remove her dress to put on the
gray sacklike garment that was handed to her, a big, heavyset matron stepped forward to rip her clothes from her.
"Now you can walk around naked or put this on," she said
tonelessly. "It don't make no difference to me."

So Julie dressed in the loose-fitting garment. It fell to
her ankles, had long sleeves, and tied with a short string at
the back of her neck. For shoes, she was given cloth
booties.

All her combs and pins were taken from her, and she
had no idea what had become of her wardrobe trunks.

"I'm not crazy," she told the matron who watched her
carefully as she dressed. "I only pretended to be to get
away from those men. If you'll take me to a doctor, he'll
listen to me and I'll be discharged."

The woman gave her a rough shove as she barked,
"Get along with you. You sound like every other loony
that's been brought here. I know the story by heart. *You*

ain't crazy. *I'm* crazy. Me and everybody else in the world, right?" She threw back her head and laughed.

"You don't understand," Julie pleaded desperately, trying to keep her voice even so the woman would see that she was in complete control of herself. "I thought they were going to take me to a regular hospital, and that's why I went along with them. I had no idea they were bringing me to a place for insane people. I'm *not* insane. You have to believe me. Take me to a doctor, please. . . ."

She was shoved down a narrow, dimly lit corridor. When they reached a heavy door with a small window at the top, the matron pulled a ring of jingling keys from the pocket of her apron. Searching through them, she found the one she wanted, then inserted it in the hole below the doorknob. She gave it a tug, and the door squeaked open.

Julie gasped at the sight before her: dozens of women, all dressed in the same dress she wore, only theirs were soiled and filthy. Some sat in silence, heads bowed, while others shuffled around and around in a circle, babbling to themselves. Not a one had hair that was not stringy and matted.

"Oh, no!" She tried to back away. "You're not putting me in there. I refuse—"

The matron placed a beefy hand on her back, and with one quick shove, Julie was sent sprawling to the dirt floor.

The door clanged shut behind her.

Julie crawled to the corner, terrified. But the other women didn't seem to notice her. They were lost in their own private worlds, oblivious to everything around them.

I could become just like them, she thought wildly. *If I don't get out of here, I'm going to be just like they are.*

She realized she was not much better off than when she'd been in the hands of Captain Guthrie.

Locked in a small cabin on the Federal cruiser, food had been brought to her on a tray; she was left alone. She had not seen Captain Guthrie again, and she was glad, for she hated him—not only for what he had done to Derek, but for what he had done to the *Ariane* as well. She had only to close her eyes to conjure up the terrible sight of the ship as it was blown to bits by the dynamite. One second it was there, proud and regal with sails unfurled, as bands of lavender and purple blended and streaked the sky at dawn.

And then came the ear-shattering explosion, the blast of

white smoke that quickly turned red, then black, as pieces of the ship were hurled to the heavens, then fell to the sea like a rain of death. Flames shot upward from what was left of the *Ariane*—then it all sank slowly from view, gone forever.

Julie turned away from the porthole, sick at heart. Her one consolation was in knowing Derek had probably survived. Also, she believed she was on her way to a real hospital, where she would soon be released and could return to Savannah.

Suddenly a woman screamed and fell to the floor, kicking and screaming. Julie watched in horror as two of the others leaped upon her and began clawing and beating at her. Then several more joined in, and those who did not began to shriek and moan.

Julie pressed her hands against her ears to shut out the horrible sounds. It would not take long for her to go mad if she were forced to endure such an existence.

Suddenly she could stand it no longer. Running to the barred window in the door, she pressed her face against the cold steel and began yelling for someone to please come and help. "They're going to kill her! Please—someone—anyone—help us!"

A man was at the end of the corridor, carrying a mop and pail. He set them down and began walking toward her quite unhurriedly. She saw him and yelled louder. "Hurry. Please, please hurry."

As he came closer, fumbling in his pocket for a ring of keys, he looked at her with interest. "You're new here, aren't you?" he asked above the din.

"Yes, yes," she responded. "Hurry, please. They're going to kill that woman. They're all attacking her."

He opened the door and stepped inside. Julie jumped back out of his way as he moved forward and began kicking at the scrapping women. Immediately, as soon as they saw him, they began to shriek with terror, crawling on their hands and knees to get away from him.

The woman who had first screamed and fallen to the floor was crying brokenly, her face claw-marked and streaked with blood. Julie knelt down and tried to touch her, but the woman scrambled away from her, shrieking in terror. "She needs medical attention," Julie said as she got up. She turned to the man, who was watching, a bored expression on his craggy face. "Aren't you going to take her to a doctor?"

"Naw, I can't waste my time taking every loony that gets scratched up a little bit to a doctor." His eyes roamed over her, and a smile played on his lips. "You sure don't act crazy."

"I'm *not* crazy!" she replied in a firm, sure voice. Then she poured out her story to him, ending with the plea: "Can *you* help me? I'm going to *be* crazy if I don't get out of this place."

"I ain't got the authority to let you out." He licked his lips and ran long, bony fingers through his thick mat of dark hair. "I can make things easier for you, though. I can slip you decent food, see that you get a bath once in a while. Stuff like that."

"But why would you—" she started to inquire, but then she saw the look in his eyes and backed away quickly. "Oh, no. You can get that notion out of your head right now. I'm not about to bargain with my body for any favors from you or anyone else."

"So be it," he snickered. "It's up to you. I can get what I want from any of these daffies, any time I want. Besides, you'll come around sooner or later. I just thought it'd be nice to have you while you're still pretty—and clean. I hate it when they start stinkin' and get all covered with lice."

He slapped irritably at his arm. "I'm getting out of here. Every time I walk in this place, things start crawling on me."

He turned toward the door, and Julie cried, "Don't we ever get out of here? Even for a breath of fresh air, for God's sake?"

"Oh, once in awhile when the good ladies from some church drop by, we'll let you out in the fenced courtyard for a walk." He stepped outside and slammed the door. Peeking at her through the bars, he said, "You get fed three times a day. Once a month you get a clean gown. That's about it. I gotta go now."

"No, wait—" she screamed at his retreating back, but he did not turn. Her fingers clutched the bars, but rattled them only a little, for they were very secure. Then she moved around slowly, surveying the sight before her once again. They were all watching her now, and needles of fear began to stab into her spine. This wasn't safe, she knew. They might attack her if she did not quiet down.

Moving very cautiously, she picked her way back to the corner and slid down till she touched the hard, cold floor. Wrapping her arms about her knees, she dropped her head forward as though she were sleeping. After a time, the others forgot her and returned to the havens of their own demented worlds.

There was no way Julie could keep up with the passage of time. She lost track of the days as they blended together. With no windows to the outside, she never knew when it was light or dark, and could tell it was daytime only because the trays came then.

At first she'd refused the food, which consisted mainly of gruel and cold water. Finally she was forced to give in to the hungry rumblings of her stomach.

Her hair became matted and dirty like the others, and her gown was soon soiled. There were four buckets in the room for the twenty women to use for their personal needs, and the odor was nauseating. In hopelessness and despair, Julie wondered how much longer she could endure this bleak existence.

Then one day a very young girl of perhaps thirteen or fourteen years of age was brought in by the matron. She was still wearing her street clothes, and the matron yelled at her to start undressing, that she would bring her a gown.

The girl stared around the room with wide, frightened eyes. Her lips trembled but no sound came, and she backed against the wall and stood there, hands at her side, face white and frozen with terror.

Julie's heart went out to the girl, and she got to her feet and walked over to her. None of the others bothered even to look up. Holding out her hand, she whispered, "Hello. My name is Julie Marshal, and you've no need to be afraid of me. You may not believe me, but I'm not insane. I was brought here by mistake."

The girl reached out to her with the desperation of one who is drowning. "Oh, thank God," she cried, tears streaming down her pale cheeks. "I don't know whether to believe you or not, but at least you talk normal. I shouldn't be here. My stepmother did this to me, to punish me because . . ." She shook her head in shame, "I'm in the family way."

"But why would she have you sent here?" Julie asked, horrified. "Especially if you're going to have a baby."

The girl's eyes were the color of a robin's egg, and her hair as red as the lights of dawn. She was a pretty creature, Julie thought, her heart aching at the thought of what lay before her.

The girl told Julie that the young man responsible for her "condition" was a Union soldier, and she'd not had time to get word of her plight to him before her stepmother had her committed as insane. "My father's away fighting too, and she knows he'd never let her do this to me. She's going to tell him I ran away, and by putting me here, she says she won't have to bear the shame of my giving birth out of wedlock." She glanced about wildly. "Oh, God, I can't have my baby *here*. I—I'd rather be dead!"

Suddenly she clutched Julie's shoulders. "They're going to take my clothes. They already took my combs and jewelry out there. But they didn't get this." She reached inside the bodice of her dress and brought out a diamond brooch. "It was given to me by my father. It belonged to my real mother, who died having me. My stepmother will be wild with anger when she discovers I managed to sneak it out with me. She'll come here looking for it. Hide it for me, please."

Julie took the brooch and stared at it as she wondered where she could put it. They were allowed no undergarments, and she certainly couldn't pin it to her gown. Finally she stooped and slid it inside her bootie just as the matron's footsteps were heard outside the door.

"My name is Pauline Brummett," the girl told Julie once she'd been stripped, put on her gown, and the matron had departed. "I just don't know what I'm going to do. I just don't know. . . ."

She succumbed to tears, and Julie tried to comfort her, but the girl kept on sobbing. Soon, Julie hoped, Pauline would get some control of herself, but as time passed, she realized this was not going to happen.

Pauline would not eat, and after what must have been several days, she stopped talking altogether. Julie tried to coax her to take nourishment, if only for the sake of her baby, but she refused. She sat in the corner, face to the wall, the look in her eyes becoming more blank and empty with each day.

The squeaking of the door awoke Julie one morning,

and she stretched as the breakfast trays of gruel were brought in. Reaching beside her to touch Pauline's shoulder, she told her to wake up. "Maybe you can eat today," she said hopefully.

The young girl did not stir. Julie rolled her over on her back, then screamed at the sight of the unseeing eyes, the feel of her cold, marblelike skin. Pauline was dead.

The two matrons who'd brought the trays looked up sharply at the sound of Julie's cries, and, realizing there had been a death, they dropped the food with a clatter. The other women crawled forward on hands and knees to eat it from the floor, cackling with eagerness.

The scene was bedlam. "How'd she die?" one of the matrons demanded of Julie, then, not waiting for an answer, ordered the other one to go fetch an attendant. "We must get her out of here at once. Today's the day some of the church ladies are coming, and we've got to clean everyone up and get them out in the yard."

Julie was so saddened by the death of her only friend that several moments passed before she realized that here was her opportunity to escape. The door to the cell was standing open. The other patients were fighting with each other over the mess of food spilled on the floor. One matron had left hurriedly, and the other was still bent over Pauline, her back to Julie.

Quickly, quietly, Julie made her move, inching her way across the floor to the open door. Breathing a sigh of relief to find the corridor empty, she saw a passageway leading to the left. There was no telling where it led, but she could not risk going straight down the hall, for the main entrance was that way. The attendant would probably come from that direction.

There was a door at the other end of the corridor, but it was bolted. Behind her, Julie could hear excited voices. The other matron had brought help to remove poor Pauline's body. Desperately Julie tugged at the bolt, but it would not budge. She slipped down to the floor, lest she be seen standing, and wondered frantically how long it would be till she was missed.

She watched with agony as they carried out Pauline's body wrapped in a dirty blanket. Then, when the cell door clanged shut and the footsteps stopped echoing down the hall, she moved from where she had silently been crouched. Inch by inch she made her way toward the front of the building. Finally she could see the door. But just as she was about to spring forward and make a run for it, the sound of high-pitched female voices reached her ears. Trembling, she pressed herself against the wall and hid in the shadows as she watched the church ladies filing into the entrance foyer.

"Oh, we're so glad you could make it," she heard someone speak, then leaned her head forward just a bit and recognized the matron she'd first encountered—the one who'd stripped off her dress that memorable day. "Suppose we take a tour this way to begin with. Our patients haven't been up long. We let them sleep a bit late today. Had a little party for some of them last night, we did."

Julie made a face, wishing she could just leap forward and expose the old battle-ax for what she really was—a cruel and vicious liar. But there was no time, and who would believe her, anyway? They'd think she was insane. No, she had to take advantage of the situation. The staff was running behind schedule because of Pauline's death. They hadn't had time to clean up the patients and get them to the courtyard.

"We have coffee and crumpets waiting," the matron was saying. "Just follow me."

Once more Julie found herself alone. Taking a deep breath, she made ready to lunge for her freedom—only to be forced once again to press herself back against the wall as closely as possible, for the hallway seemed to be filled with matrons and attendants, all moving quickly toward the cells.

". . . have to hurry . . ." she heard one of them whisper nervously. "Miz Brandon said she couldn't keep them sipping coffee and nibbling crumpets for very long."

"We'll change their gowns and get them outside," another voice said quietly. "No time for a bath. We'll just make sure none of them ladies gets close to 'em. . . ."

As soon as they passed, Julie made her move. Hurrying to the foyer, she looked outside and felt a wave of panic at the sight of several carriages tied to the gate posts. They had obviously brought the visitors, but were there drivers waiting with the carriages? Of course, she reasoned, there would have to be. And they would see her in her soiled hospital gown and sound an alert! She'd be taken back to her cell and might never have another chance to escape! Her heart was pounding so loudly she was afraid everyone in the building would hear. She had to do something and do it quickly—but what? Then she spotted several of the drivers congregated around a water fountain. There was no way she could escape out the front door.

Glancing about wildly, she saw three other doorways. The visitors had gone through one of them. She hurried to another, opened it, and saw that it led to an office of some sort. It was not a good place to hide, she reasoned, because someone would surely be returning to it shortly.

That left the remaining door. When she opened it, a small shaft of light revealed steps leading downward. There was no other choice but to go down and hide until it was safe to go out the front door.

Carefully, cautiously, she took one step at a time, groping her way along by clinging to the damp walls on each side. Finally she reached the bottom, wrinkling her nose at the foul odors about her. It was so dark that the blackness seemed to reach out and gather her into it, and she quickly sank to the floor to wait, not daring to move about further.

As time passed, she clung to her sanity by filling her mind with thoughts of those she loved. Myles. Her mother. And yes, she thought of Derek too, praying he'd made it to safety. It seemed like years since he'd held her in those strong, wonderful arms of his, engulfing her with the awesome feeling that as long as he held her, no harm would befall her.

Myles. She could hear the voices of those taunting children as he limped along. "Here comes the gimp . . . look at the crip! Myles is a gimp-crip!"

He held his head high, those days when they were so young, pretending that the taunts didn't hurt. But Julie would never let them go unheeded. "You shut your hateful mouths!" she would scream. "He got hurt saving my life. I'll bet none of you ninnies would save anybody from a wild hog!"

Myles would tell her to be quiet, but she never paid any attention. They were hateful, cruel, all of them, and Myles was ten times the man they'd ever be—and she wanted them to know it.

She thought, too, of her mother, wondering *where* she was, *how* she was. Then it dawned on her, there in the smelly darkness, that the only person she didn't miss, the only one she never thought about, was the man who was

supposed to have been her husband—Virgil Oates. Well,
she sighed aloud, when she got back home, she'd just have
to tell her mother they must find another way to save Rose
Hill. She couldn't marry him. Not now. Not after Derek.
Did she love him? She didn't know. Her mind was so
confused, but she was sure of one thing: Derek had awakened a need in her—a need to be loved—and Virgil Oates
would never be able to fulfill it.

Julie's back and shoulders were aching from sitting in
one position for so long. Yet she dared not move, for she
had no way of knowing what was around her. She could
bump into something, make a noise loud enough to bring
the matrons and the attendants. And she'd come too far to
be discovered now.

Suddenly a thin shaft of light fell across the floor. At
the same time, she heard the door above squeaking open.
Someone was coming down the steps, and holding a lantern! She would be seen! Dear Lord, where could she
hide?

Then she saw the space under the steps, laced with
cobwebs, but she wasn't about to let a spider frighten her
now. Quickly she scurried into it. Something crawled
across her foot, but she stifled the scream in her throat as
she flicked the hairy creature away.

Through the slats of the steps, she could see their feet
coming down—a man and a woman.

"This has been a day I hope I never see repeated," the
man was saying. "First that crazy woman dies because she
starved herself to death. Then the church ladies come
a'calling, and to top it all off—"

"Someone escapes," the woman finished for him. "I'll
agree. It's been a rough one. And Miz Brandon is fit to be
tied. Nobody saw her leave, not even those drivers who
were outside most of the morning. But she got away."

He snorted. "Not for long. How long you think a loony
can run loose, wearin' a nightgown and booties and with
no money? Someone will pick her up and have her back
before morning. Just you wait and see."

"Miz Barnes is going to put her in chains, she says."
The woman sounded pleased over the idea. "She won't be
getting away again. Now if only we didn't have this dirty
task to perform."

"Miz Brummett told Miz Barnes there was a brooch
missing. She wants it found," he sighed with disgust. "Let's

search her body and be done with it. The undertaker will be here before long."

Bile rose in Julie's throat as she peered through the slats and saw Pauline's body lying on a table, not three feet from where she had been crouched for hours. Swaying, she caught herself, fighting back the scream of revulsion that was struggling to escape from her throat. Not now. No, she'd come too far to lose now.

She watched with repugnance as they yanked off the poor girl's gown. "How come we just now been told there's a brooch missing, and she's supposed to have it?" the woman demanded irritably.

"Seems Miz Brummett's been out of town visiting relatives. She only got to looking for it after Miz Barnes sent her the message the girl was dead."

"Here, you fool! Let me do that!" Julie saw the matron shove him aside just as she realized he was probing between Pauline's stiff legs. "I'll reach inside her to see if she hid it up there," she snapped. "You'd probably get your jollies from poking up there, even if she is dead."

His laugh had a nasty ring. "You like me poking in *you,* luv, and you'd probably still like it if *you* was dead."

"Oh, shut up. I want to hurry and get out of here. This place always gives me the creeps. Smells rotten 'cause of the vegetables stored that go bad." She shook her head and sounded disgusted as she murmured, "No, it ain't up there. All right, it's just gone, that's all. She probably never had it. She was stripped when she came in. Like all the others."

"Now we got to put her old clothes on her, the ones she had on when she first come. Miz Brandon said her step-mother didn't want her taken out in her hospital gown. Seems her father don't know she was in here."

The woman picked up the lantern, using its light to guide her to the bag she'd left on the bottom step. Julie recoiled from the illumination that fell across her, and jerked backwards into the huge web of a spider. Apparently babies had recently hatched, for she realized with horror that hundreds of the tiny, scurrying creatures were swarming across her face.

She wanted to shriek, to scream, to slap at her face and hair and run from the loathsome things. But she could do nothing without being discovered. She could only cringe and stiffen, willing herself not to move or make a sound, and let them crawl about.

Once the woman moved away with the lantern, Julie quickly stifled the retching in her throat as she silently, hurriedly wiped her hands across her face, trying to knock the scrambling spiders away.

It seemed to take forever to dress Pauline's corpse, but finally they stepped back. "That's it. Let's get the hell out of here. This place gives me the jeebies, too." It was the man who spoke.

They clumped up the steps together, leaving a curtain of darkness behind them.

Julie moved from beneath the steps, constantly swatting at her face and hair until she was sure she had rid herself of all the spiders. Still, she felt as though her flesh were crawling, there in the blackness with the sound of unseen things skittering about in the darkness—and the knowledge that a dead body was so close.

I'm being silly, she told herself. *I have to get my wits about me and get out of here.*

She decided she had no choice but to change clothes with Pauline. They were about the same size, and she'd have a better chance of getting away if she were not wearing the hospital gown.

She knew, too, that there was a good possibility she could buy her way out of the city with the diamond brooch still hidden in her bootie. Many times she'd tried to return it to Pauline, but the pitiful girl had been afraid her stepmother would discover it missing, and the matrons would come and search her and find it. Somehow, Julie knew Pauline would not mind if she used it to take herself to safety.

Moving cautiously through the inky blackness, she approached the spot where she remembered seeing the table. When she reached out, her fingertips touched cold marble —Pauline's face. Squeezing her eyes shut with revulsion, hands shaking as though with palsy, Julie began undressing her. She'd never touched a dead person before, and she kept telling herself over and over there was no reason to be afraid. But the skin felt clammy, unreal, as though it had never been warm or alive; yet she had the overwhelming sensation that at any moment the body would spring to life, and the cold, bony arms would reach out and grab her, enraged that she would rob it of its dress.

She tried to move quickly, but her fingers were clumsy with terror. Finally she had the dress off. For a moment she considered not taking the slips or pantalets, then decided it might be cold outside. It was certainly cold *here*. So she took everything, her flesh crawling as she removed her hospital gown and clothed herself with the garments of her dead friend.

With the brooch tucked safely inside her bodice, Julie turned to go. But something made her hesitate. Then, slowly, it came to her—even though it was dark, she could picture Pauline lying there naked. She could not leave her friend that way. Groping about on the floor, she retrieved the soiled gown she had just removed.

She felt a sense of satisfaction as she slipped it on the dead girl. Now there might be a chance that Pauline's father would discover where she had actually been. Her stepmother had given orders for her to be dressed, and she had no reason to think it would not be done. She would not say anything to the undertaker or ask any questions. He would bundle up the clothes she was wearing when he picked her up; they would be turned over to the family, probably to her father, who would settle the matter of the funeral with him. When her father saw the hospital gown, he would ask questions. And maybe, just maybe, Julie thought with her first smile in ages, the cruel stepmother would face retribution for what she'd done to Pauline.

As she made her way slowly up the stairs, she wondered suddenly what they would say had caused Pauline's death. Starvation, probably, and perhaps it was so, though she suspected the pitiful young thing had just died from a broken heart.

For long moments she stood outside the door, her ear pressed against the wood, listening for any sound that suggested movement. When she was reasonably certain the hallway would be empty, she slowly turned the knob, opened the door, and stepped out.

Quickly, holding her breath, Julie made her way to the front door. It was latched, but she easily slid back the bolt and stepped outside to freedom.

Once she reached the street, she broke into a run, and she did not slow her pace until she was several blocks from the asylum. She decided it must be quite late, because there was no one about. Since she had no idea where she was, she realized there was nothing to be done about getting out of the city until daylight. Creeping about in the shadows, she finally found an old vacant shed behind a stately-looking home, and there she slept until dawn.

By mid-morning she had found a kindly-looking old gentleman with a team of horses who listened to her tale of being stranded in Washington and having to go south at once. "All I have is this brooch with which to pay you," and she held out the diamond-encrusted pin.

His eyes widened as he lifted it anxiously from her outstretched palm. "Oh, miss, you must be really desperate to get home if you're willing to part with something this valuable."

"I am," she said firmly. "Will you help me?"

He thrust the pin back in her hand and shook his head. "No, I can't take that. It's worth much more than my services would cost."

Her voice cracked. "I don't care. I've got to get out of Washington. I must get home. Please."

Sighing, he took the brooch once again. "All right. If I don't take it, you'll meet up with someone who will. But let me tell you this, if the balls start flying when we get near the fighting, I'm turning my team around and coming back. I'm not about to get myself killed."

"I don't blame you for that," she said quickly. "All I want is for you to get as near as possible to the Confederate lines. Then I'll walk the rest of the way if I have to."

"If that happens, I'll see that you have the necessary funds to purchase a train ticket or rent another wagon," he assured her. "It's the least I can do, since you're parting with such a valuable piece of jewelry."

Several times along the way they were stopped by Federal pickets inquiring as to their destination. Julie told them in a mock-tearful voice that her father, a brave Union soldier, was being held prisoner by the Confederates in Richmond. The reaction she received was one of deep pity and concern, and they were waved on.

They reached Richmond safely, and the old man pulled out some money and pressed it into her hands. "I can't risk going further, ma'am. I hope you understand."

"Of course I do," she assured him with a smile. "And I thank you for bringing me this far. You be on your way, and if you're stopped, just reverse the story I used. Tell the Confederate pickets you're visiting your son in a Yankee prison."

"I just wish I weren't taking your brooch. . . ."

"Please, be on your way. You've done me a great favor." And with one final wave, she left him.

After asking directions, Julie found her way to the train station and purchased a ticket to Savannah, then went into the waiting room, where she spent the night. At least, she thought wearily, she would soon be home. Part of the nightmare was ending.

The trip took almost two days, but soon the train was rumbling into the marshy swamplands of Georgia. As she got closer to Savannah, her heart was thumping excitedly. Perhaps Myles would be there. Oh, God, it was good to be going home!

Her mind wandered once again to Derek. She whispered a silent prayer that he lived, her body trembling as she remembered his words that one day they would meet again.

In Savannah she had no problem finding a driver to take her to Rose Hill. Once she was settled in the carriage, Julie hesitantly asked him how things were going with the war.

"Bad," he said shortly. "With Fort Pulaski in the hands of them damned Yankees, we're havin' a terrible time gettin' supplies. Cotton rotted in the fields this year, most of it. Lots of the niggers run off to the North, so they ain't had the slaves to get the rice in. Lots of folk are goin' hungry."

As they approached Rose Hill, the landscape a burnished gold in the late autumn sunset, the driver remarked casually, "I reckon Missus Oates'll be glad to see you, since you say she's your mother. Talk in town has it that she's mighty sick, and what with the war and all, I don't imagine she's farin' any better than the rest of us."

Julie blinked. Something he had said . . . a mistake, no doubt. "You referred to my mother as Mrs. Oates. I think I misunderstood you."

"Oh no, ma'am." He shook his head positively. "You ain't heard? My, how families do drift apart in time of war. She's Missus Oates, all right. Married that man from England, the one what walked around full of airs, givin' folks the impression he had so much money. Well, if you'll pardon me for sayin' so, miss, folks are talking about how he ain't really got nothin', 'cept what he expects to get from your ma, and if the winds of war don't blow more favorable to the South, that ain't gonna be much."

He talked on, but there was a giant roaring in Julie's ears, and she clutched the sides of the carriage to steady herself as they bumped along the rutted dirt road. Mrs. Oates—Mrs. Oates—the name kept ringing in her brain like a thousand church bells. It could not be so. Why would her mother marry him? And the driver had said she was sick. Just what was going on at Rose Hill, she worried, a lump of fear constricting her throat.

The driver was still talking, but Julie leaned forward to tap his shoulder and say, "Could you pick up the horses' canter, please? I'm so anxious to get home."

He nodded and popped his buggy whip across the horses' backs.

Julie leaned back against the worn leather seat, shaking. Dear Lord, her heart was screaming, what awaited her at Rose Hill?

❦ Chapter Thirteen ❧

WHEN Sara opened the front doors to find Julie standing on the porch, she burst into hysterical tears, gathered her in her arms, and pulled her tightly against her big bosom. "Lawdy, Lawdy, it is you, Miss Julie. It is!" she cried. "Praise God for answerin' this tired nigger's prayers. You done come from providence's shores."

The two clung together emotionally, then Julie raised her head and looked over Sara's shoulder, stiffening at the sight of Virgil posed resplendently on the curving stairway. He wore an elegant red waistcoat, white silk cravat, and black and white striped pants tucked inside shiny ebony boots. One hand touched the bannister lightly; the other was placed on his hip.

Cocking his head to one side, he smiled slightly and said, "Well, this is a surprise. Welcome home, Julie."

Sara gasped and jerked away as though suddenly frightened. "I'll fix tea. . . ." she said nervously, scurrying from the room.

Virgil slowly descended the stairs, and Julie could only stand there, not knowing what to say. It was all so strange —as though she'd been asleep for a long, long time and awakened years later to find herself in a completely different world.

"I know it must have been a terrible ordeal for you," Virgil was saying, his lips brushing her cheek. "We'll talk about it all later, but for now, I'm afraid I have to greet you with distressing news. Your mother is quite ill and has taken to her bed. Do you mind terribly if we don't tell her of your homecoming just yet? I think the doctor should prepare her for such a shock."

"No, no, that's fine. I—" Julie shook her head to clear it. So many thoughts and questions racing through her brain. She tried to sort them out. "Mother," she said quickly. "I want to know her condition. What does the doctor say?"

"Dr. Perkins sees her every day. But come along. Let's not stand here in the foyer." He looked over her shoulder toward the open doors. "You have trunks? I'll get some-one—"

"No. No, I have nothing."

He raised an eyebrow. "You have only the clothes you're wearing?" he asked incredulously.

"It—it's a very long story, Virgil. I have questions of my own I want answered before we discuss me."

He led her into the parlor, and she glanced around and saw that everything was as she remembered. A fire was crackling in the grate to ward off the fall chill in the air. She walked over to warm her hands, then turned and faced him. Taking a deep breath, she cried, "All right, Virgil. I want to hear all of it. What is wrong with my mother? Why was my ransom not paid? And why are you now married to my mother?"

He raised both hands in a pleading gesture. "One question at a time, my dear. Now, don't be angry. You know it was you I wanted to marry, *you* that I loved—"

"*That* is the last question on my mind at the moment." Her voice cracked. "First of all, I want to know about my mother's condition."

"Her heart." He spoke so easily, so casually, that she knew her first suspicions had been correct. He did not love her mother.

"How bad?"

"The doctor says she's very weak. He can't say if she will ever get better."

Julie squeezed her eyes shut, her teeth grinding together. No, she whispered silently. No-no-no, she can't die. Not now. Not when we've both been through so much, and now that we're back together again . . .

Her head jerked up, eyes flashing open. "The ransom. Why wasn't it paid?"

"Because your mother didn't have it." His eyes narrowed. Julie had never thought him either attractive or ugly, just plain-looking. But with the expression on his face at the moment, she found him quite distasteful.

He rushed on defensively. "She gave her cotton crop and half your dowry to that bloody pirate. By the time she arrived in England, she was at the point of destitution. Did you actually think she could raise that kind of money?"

"I assumed she would seek your help," Julie said icily, pointedly, "since you were forever trying to impress us with your wealth and power. Yet despite the fact that you're obviously a fraud, as Captain Arnhardt tried to make me realize, you persuaded my mother to marry you. How did you accomplish such a feat?"

He smirked. "Now you're letting your jealousy show, my love. You mustn't do that. You will have to learn to control your emotions. Word of your attitude might reach your mother's ears, and she's in no condition to be unnecessarily worried." He reached out to her. "But don't fret. I still desire you as much as I always did. We'll find time—"

She knocked his hand away viciously. "Don't you touch me, and how dare you speak this way? I was a fool to even consider marrying you. You're nothing but a liar and a fake, and I want you to leave this house immediately." She was so angry she began to tremble.

He threw back his head and laughed, then turned a cold gaze upon her. "I'm master of this house now, Julie. Keep a civil tongue in your head and be respectful to me, or I will have to ask *you* to leave."

She could not believe this was actually happening.

"Your mother had no choice but to marry me," he continued matter-of-factly. "She was most vulnerable. When I couldn't have you, I reached for the next best thing. It got me what I ultimately wanted. . . ." He swept his hand through the air. "It got me Rose Hill."

"Well, you won't have it for long!" Julie's eyes flashed fire as she stormed from the room, almost knocking the tray of tea from Sara's hands as the old woman prepared to enter.

"Miss Julie, don't go up there, please. . . ." the old Negro whispered in anguish as Julie started up the stairs.

Julie turned to stare down at her. "Why? Is Mother really that ill, Sara? I think you know what's been going on around here, but now that I've returned, there will be a stop to all of it."

Sara's eyes were wide, beseeching. "Please, Miss Julie,

come on with me to the kitchen," she cried. "Let me and Lionel talk to you before you go runnin' off up there to fret your mama. Please . . ."

Virgil appeared in the doorway, thumbs hooked in his belt. He looked at the two of them, a smug expression on his face. "Yes, my love, you be a smart girl and do what Sara says. Hear her out before you go upsetting your mother. If you go up there now, I will hold you responsible for the consequences. She is quite ill, and if you don't believe me, Dr. Perkins can verify what I say when he arrrives."

Julie could bear to look at him no longer. She followed Sara to the kitchen, where Lionel was plucking a chicken on the back steps just outside the door. Sara told him to stop what he was doing and come inside. When he walked in, his eyes popped in surprise, then watered with tears of joy.

He gave her a quick hug. "Welcome home, missy. Praise the Lord you's safe."

"We got to tell her how it is," Sara said in a rush. "She done had a fuss with Mistah Virgil, and we gots to keep her from upsettin' her mama."

Julie sat down, glad to relieve her wobbling legs from supporting her. And she listened, shocked, as they told her how Virgil did, indeed, now run Rose Hill. It was also true that her mother had been in bed for some time. Dr. Perkins could give no explanation except to say that he suspected she had a weak heart. He held out little hope for her recovery.

"But you bein' home can change all that, missy," Sara told her in a desperate voice. "Her spirit's done gone, that's all what's wrong with your mama. She never was a strong woman nohow. And marryin' that man was the worst thing she could've done, though Lord knows she was so upset over you bein' gone on top of Mastah Myles, that she wa'n't in her right mind."

"Mistah Virgil, he's mean," Lionel interrupted. "He beat up on some of the field hands and they run off, and there weren't enough to get the rice in. And the cotton, it just rotted in the fields. Things ain't good. And yo' mama, she just kept on fadin' away, like she couldn't stand to see what was happenin' around here. Now that you's back, maybe she'll have somethin' to hope for, to live for."

"That's right." Sara nodded, lower lip jutting out. "You

can't go stressin' yo' mama. If'n we told her what-all goes on around here, she'd done been in her grave a long time ago. Maybe you can take a stand and not bend like a willow in a storm."

Julie chewed her lower lip thoughtfully, then asked anxiously if they had heard from Myles. Sadly they shook their heads. "I suppose it was too much to hope for," she sighed. "If only he were here—if we only knew how to contact him."

"He still can't come home," Sara pointed out hesitantly. "I mean, the sheriff, he comes around now and then, askin' questions. It's like he's got his mind made up he's gonna get Mastah Myles sooner or later."

Lionel snorted. "I'll bet if'n he did come back, Mistah Oates would run right to the sheriff to tell him about it. He don't want Mastah Myles around here. Naw suh."

"Myles would find a way to stop him," Julie said confidently, rubbing her fingertips against her throbbing forehead. It had all been too much, too soon. She took a deep breath, then let it out with disgust. "The very idea! Beating the servants and making them run away."

"And that man enjoys it, too," Lionel said excitedly. "His eyes was just a'shinin', every time he'd pick up that whip."

Sara snapped impatiently, "You get back to pluckin' that chicken. We don't need no more talk about beatin's. I gotta get Miss Julie fed so she'll feel like talkin' to the doctor and seein' her mama later."

Lionel lumbered out, and Julie gratefully took the tea Sara gave her. Then she was handed a plate of cold sweet potatoes and corn bread, which she ate ravenously. Lost in thought and worried about the future, she hadn't thought much about eating on the trip, just having a bite of something here and there to keep up her strength.

When she had finished and leaned back in her chair, Sara sat down opposite her, her brow furrowed. "Was it bad, Miss Julie? When the pirates kidnapped you off the island, was it bad?"

"They weren't pirates, Sara," she managed to laugh, despite the oppression that hung over the house like a shroud. She told Sara everything that had happened since they'd seen each other last, leaving out the intimate parts with Derek, of course.

Then she was blinking back tears of anguish as she told

about Derek stepping off the plank. Sara's eyes grew larger with each word, and then she clasped her hands across her big bosom and rocked to and fro, moaning, "Oh, Miss Julie, that's awful. That's plumb awful. Do you think he made it back?"

Julie lifted her eyes and gazed through the kitchen window at the brown and gold fields. Only the tall pines and magnolias lent any green to the landscape. "I like to think he did," she murmured in a faraway voice, remembering the hours of joy they had shared. "He wasn't really a bad sort, you know. He could be very kind, and he said he was actually doing it all for my sake, because he knew Virgil was a fraud."

"If anyone could make it to shore," she said finally, wistfully, "Derek Arnhardt could."

"Why, Miss Julie!" Sara slapped her knees jovially. "I do believe you went and fell in love!"

"What?" She couldn't believe her ears. "Sara, no! He was arrogant and bossy and headstrong, and once he even slapped me. Love him? Oh, no. I was fond of him because we spent some time together, but—"

Sara continued to laugh, brown eyes sparkling. "You don't get fond of somebody 'cause you spend time with 'em, missy, 'specially when they kidnap you. No suh. I knows what I see, and I see you lookin' all dreamy-eyed, and you ain't never looked like that when you was talkin' about other young men. It was like an angel was sprinklin' stardust in yo' eyes. You done went and fell in love—"

Suddenly Sara was struggling to her feet, hand flying to her gaping mouth in terror. Julie swung around to see what had frightened her so, and she saw that Virgil had stepped from behind the door that led to the front hallway.

"Well, how long have you been eavesdropping?" Julie demanded, standing to face him in a blaze of fury. "Did you hear anything of interest?"

"Oh, yes indeed." He rubbed his hands together gleefully. "So you were taken with Captain Arnhardt, were you? Well, from the sound of things, he's out of the way for good. That will save me the trouble—"

Julie laughed mockingly. "That's the funniest thing I ever heard. Derek could crush you with one hand, and I'm no more frightened of you than he would've been."

"Is that so?" His cheeks began to flush. "Well, then, suppose I just go up to your mother's room and tell her about all your escapades? You didn't tell what went on behind closed doors, but it doesn't take much imagination to fill in the details. She will be quite shocked to hear about how her precious daughter was ravished at will for months. It might even prove so disturbing she could have a fatal attack. . . ."

He turned to go, but Julie grabbed his arm. "You wouldn't do such a thing—"

"Oh, yes, I would!" He shoved her viciously away from him. "Let's get a few things straight right now, just so we understand each other. I don't give a damn whether she lives or dies. I've got what I want—this plantation!"

Julie felt herself losing control. "You won't have it for long." She rasped out the words. "I'll see that you're exposed for what you are: a conniving liar. . . ."

This time he laughed mockingly. "You? Why, in case you didn't realize it, my love, you're now considered white trash by decent folk."

"How dare you—" She raised her hand to strike him, but he caught her wrist and twisted her arm painfully downward.

"I wouldn't try that. And I speak the truth, you little fool. Did you really think you could return home and hold your head high when everyone knows you were kidnapped by pirates? Everyone knows you're soiled goods. Who would listen to the ravings of a trollop?"

Julie felt herself collapsing, and she stumbled backwards to the chair and sat down. She was stunned, and, for the moment, helpless. She did not know which way to turn or where to go for help.

Virgil turned his wrath upon Sara, who cringed before him, clutching the hem of her white apron all the way up to her nose. "As for you, you black wench," he screamed, "if I ever hear of you gossiping about anything that goes on in this house again, I'll beat the hide off your worthless back. Do you understand?"

"Yassuh, mastah, yassuh." Sara bowed, groveling before him, then turned and fled out the back door.

"Now, then." Virgil pulled at the front of his waistcoat, straightened his cravat, then pasted a stiffly triumphant smile on his lips. "I want you to go to your room and freshen yourself up. Dr. Perkins will be here soon, and once he prepares your dear mother for the shock, you will go to her and have your emotional reunion, then congratulate her on her good fortune in marrying me and tell her how you welcome me as a stepfather.'"

Julie said nothing. For the moment, until she talked with the doctor and learned her mother's exact condition, she must remain silent. Afterwards, she would deal with this hypocrite.

"My poor darling," her mother said over and over, her weak arms patting Julie's back as she held her against her frail body. "I thought I would never see you again. . . ."

She was unbelievably thin and frail. Julie tried to hide her concern. Lying there, propped on the pillows in the big canopied bed, her mother looked like a little doll, so tiny and fragile.

"Mother, you just get well. I'm home now, and everything is going to be just fine." Julie forced a smile to her quivering lips as she sat up, and nervously fluffed up the pillows.

"Yes, yes." Her mother's voice was weak. She closed her eyes for a moment, as though needing to rest before continuing. Julie glanced up sharply at the doctor. He nodded to let her know everything was all right.

Her mother was looking at her again. "Can you forgive me, Julie," she whispered, "for marrying Virgil? I knew it was you he loved and cared for, but when we couldn't raise the money, and we feared you'd been killed, we . . . we clung to each other for strength." Her chest rose and fell heavily, as though it were a struggle for her to utter each and every word. "We grew close. I . . . I needed him. Can you understand that—"

"Mother, it doesn't matter," Julie interrupted. "I just want you to get well and be happy." She leaned over and kissed her bony cheek. "Rest now. My return has been a shock, I know. Tomorrow I'll come and sit with you, and we'll have a long visit."

"Yes . . . a long visit. We'll talk about how it will be . . . when Myles comes home . . . and Rose Hill . . . in the spring . . . how lovely it will be . . ." She closed her eyes; this time her head lolled to one side.

Dr. Perkins stepped forward quickly and patted Julie's shoulder reassuringly. "Don't upset yourself. She's only sleeping. She's terribly weak, and she falls asleep quite easily, with no warning. Now, you've got to get hold of yourself. I can't have you going to pieces. We have to make her believe she's going to get well again."

Julie reeled, and reached out to clutch a bedpost to steady herself as she searched his face beyond the blur of her tears. "What do you mean?" she hissed. "She *is* going to get well—isn't she?"

His fingers gripped her arm, and he led her out in the hallway. The doctor cleared his throat and said, "Julie, you're a grown woman, and I think you should be told the truth. No, your mother isn't going to get well. She's going to die. It's her heart, and she's getting weaker every day. All I can do—all *anyone* can do—is try to make her comfortable."

With a sigh, he spread his hands in a helpless gesture. "Julie, it was the hand of God that brought you back here at this time. I think you'll be able to keep her alive awhile longer. Just do your best to make her happy. Don't let her get upset or worry about anything. Try not to discuss Myles, the war, or anything else that might put stress on her heart. I wish I could say something to give you hope, but I cannot."

There was a giant roaring in her ears, and she could not hear his words over its sound. She wanted only to be alone, to sort out the pieces, to absorb the harsh reality of the terrible blow she'd just received. Her mother was going to die! And there was nothing anyone could do about it!

Stumbling along, she made her way to her room and closed the door behind her. The doors to the portico were open, and a cool wind filtered through, making the delicate white curtains billow and float mysteriously about. Sara had turned the satin coverlet back to reveal crisp, clean sheets, but she did not want to lie down. Instead she moved outside, under the curtain of silver stars, to stare into the night and let the silent tears flow.

Fate had brought her home. Had she been delayed, she might have found her mother long dead, with Virgil in complete control of Rose Hill. No, she thought defiantly, clenching her fists, that wouldn't happen. She could not stop death from snatching her mother from this life, but she could prevent Virgil from taking what her mother had spent so many years building up. It was what her mother would want her to do, and by God, she vowed, she would find a way to stop him.

Standing there in the gentle breeze, wrapped in the

cloak of night, Julie lost track of time. She saw Dr. Perkins leave in his carriage and disappear from view. She was dimly aware that Sara and Lionel turned off the lamps downstairs and retired to the servants' quarters at the rear of the estate.

It was so hard to believe she was really here, in her own room, after so long a time. But why did it have to be this way? she thought bitterly, angrily. Why did she have to come home to find her mother on her deathbed?

Finally she turned and went inside, closing the doors behind her. The room was completely dark, and she saw no need to step behind the tapestry-covered dressing screen to remove her clothing. She stripped, moving from memory to where Sara would have laid out her nightgown.

She was about to slip the garment over her head when a hand clamped her left breast, and at the same time something covered her mouth, stifling her scream of terror. She was being wrestled backwards across the room, toward the bed, and she threw out her arms, clawing, scratching, kicking, struggling to fight and defend herself from the crazed attacker.

"Julie, stop it. . . ." A familiar voice hissed in her ear. It was Virgil! She stopped struggling, stiffening as he rushed on in hot little gasps: "Don't fight it, you little spitfire. I will make it as good for you as those pirates did. You'll see. Just relax, and I'll take my hand away from your mouth. Don't you dare scream. You mother might hear, and the shock would kill her. . . ."

When Julie made no move, he flung her down on the bed. She whispered harshly, angrily, "Have you lost your mind, you filthy beast? Just what do you think you're doing? How dare you come here and—"

He laughed, a deep, guttural sound. "I'm going to show you what it's like with a real man, my love. I'm going to make you moan and groan and beg and plead. I'll make it so good for you, my darling, that you'll want me in your bed every night."

He was making grunting sounds in anticipation, and she could tell by his fumbling movements that he was hurriedly getting out of his clothes. She rolled to one side and was on her feet, scrambling away from him in the darkness.

"Don't you play games with me, Julie." He spoke as

though addressing a child. "We must be quiet, you know. Now come over here. Don't make me search for you in the dark."

She did not reply. Instead she was taking tiny steps, silently moving toward her little desk which sat against the wall on the opposite side of the room. If Sara had not rearranged anything, the silver-handled letter opener would still be there, the tip as sharp as a knife and just as deadly.

"Julie, I'm warning you. If I have to raise my voice, I will. I'll tell your mother you coaxed me in here, that you still wanted me even though I married her. I'll say you were angry, jealous. She'll have an attack and die, and her blood will be on your hands. Now, I'm giving you a chance to cooperate and enjoy all that I want to give you."

She took a few more steps, slowly, cautiously. Reaching out, she groped for the desk but felt only air. It must be further away.

"Julie, I can order you to leave Rose Hill, you know." His voice grew louder and she tensed, fearing that her mother would hear, for she had always been a light sleeper. When he spoke again, she knew he was closer . . . coming after her.

"I'll tell people you went into a rage when you learned I married your mother, and I sent you away to keep you from causing trouble and upsetting her. And where will you go? Back to those savages of the sea? What can they give you except animal lust? I'll give you security, a roof over your head—"

Her fingertips touched the polished cherrywood, and frantically she ran her hands across the surface, groping for the letter opener. Where was it? Oh, God, please don't let Sara have moved it. She never rearranged things. But it had been so long. Perhaps Sara had put it in a drawer. . . .

And then she touched it, but her fingers were shaking, and instead of grasping the potential weapon, she knocked it to the floor. Dropping to her knees, she felt about, her fingertips fluttering, seeking, her whole body quivering with terror.

"Julie, I've had enough of this. I'm going to punish you. I'm going to take you to that bed and be very rough with you. I won't try to give you pleasure, but I will take mine. I'll spread your legs, and then I will—"

She tried to shut out the sound of the filthy, obscene descriptions. He was a madman! A fiend! And oh, what a front he had put on for them, pretending to be so aristocratic, such a polished, refined gentleman!

She touched the letter opener. Her fingers closed about the heavy, ornately designed handle. Squeezing it tightly against her bosom, she whispered as loud as she dared, "Don't come any closer, Virgil, or I'll kill you—"

"*Kill* me?" He laughed shortly. "Oh, Julie . . ."

She felt his hand groping for her in the darkness, and she slashed out, then felt the point of the letter opener strike flesh, puncture, stab. . . .

With a cry of anguish he leaped backwards, smashing into something. "You bitch! You dirty little bitch! I'll get you for this. You'll see! You'll pay—"

He stumbled across the room, groping for the door. Julie heard it open and close, then quickly yanked open a desk drawer, reaching inside for the sulphur matches. She struck one, then moved to the oil lamp on the desk. Soon the room was bathed in a warm, mellow glow.

She ran to put on her gown to cover her nakedness, then padded quickly to the door and flung it open, the letter opener still held menacingly in her hand. She was listening for any sound that might tell her that her mother had heard Virgil's cries and awakened.

The hall was dark, silent, with only a thin shaft of light coming from Julie's open doorway. She could hear no sound. But then she saw the blood . . . bright red droplets forming a path down the hall leading toward Virgil's room. Turning, she saw more stains on the rug in her room.

There was a lock on her door, but she knew it could be easily picked. As a child, Myles had done so many times in order to get into her room and mess up her toys and other possessions just to be pesky, as brothers can be. Quickly she dragged a heavy chair across the floor and placed it in front of the door. Should Virgil try to break in, she would hear him. And God forgive her, but next time she would send that letter opener straight into his evil heart.

She lay down on the bed, breathing raggedly. First thing in the morning, she thought quickly, she would have Sara get the bloodstains off the rugs before Dr. Perkins came.

Virgil would make up some story, she knew, to explain his wound.

Her mind was whirling. What if she had killed him? What explanation could she have given to her mother? It would kill her mother if she knew the truth. Julie had to protect herself against him, but she could not take his life—at least, not while her mother lived. And she really didn't want to kill anyone anyway, not if she could defend herself in some other way.

Squeezing her eyes shut, she gritted her teeth. Her weapon was tucked safely beneath her pillow. Visions of Myles floated before her, and she thought how he would know what to do. He would not allow her to be harmed. He would not let Virgil hurt her mother or take control of Rose Hill.

And then her thoughts drifted to Derek . . . his gentle kisses, bold caresses . . . his strength and warmth. It was his face she envisioned last, before sleep finally carried her away to peace.

❦ Chapter Fourteen ❧

JULIE spent her days sitting beside her mother's bed, ministering to her needs, reading to her, doing everything possible to make her comfortable. Her mother had bad days, however, when she would sleep almost constantly. Julie would awaken her periodically to patiently spoon Sara's special chicken broth through her lips, trying to keep her thin, frail body nourished.

Often she would ask Julie whether there was news of Myles. Tears would fill her eyes each time she was told there was none. And she wanted to know about the war, whether the South was winning. Julie told her only what she wanted to hear, never disclosing news of a battle or skirmish where the North had claimed victory.

One evening her mother seemed stronger than usual, and she asked to be propped up against her pillows into a sitting position. Julie thought it unwise but did not want to argue. Despite her illness, her mother still gave evidence of being stubborn. How Julie wished she could use some of that will to overcome her failing heart.

Her mother spoke in a hoarse, rasping voice, each word obviously an effort. "I . . . I'm so terribly sorry . . . I didn't have . . . the ransom . . . that you suffered so—"

Julie patted her hand, so white against the sheet that they almost blended into one lifeless color. "Mother, you mustn't dwell on that. It's over, and it wasn't so bad, really."

With a wan smile, her mother murmured, "Your Captain Ironheart, did you fall in love with him?"

Julie felt her cheeks flush. More and more, lately, as she

tossed and turned and tried to sleep, ever alert for any sound that might mean Virgil was trying to break into her room, her mind filled with thoughts of Derek and the moments they had shared. "No, I did not fall in love with Derek," she answered finally, turning away, not wanting her mother to see her face. "I don't even know if he's alive." And she told of his fate.

"That's terrible." Tears slipped down her mother's sunken cheeks. "I'm so sorry, dear. Maybe he did make it to shore. I pray he did."

"He treated me kindly, under the circumstances. But can we talk of other things?"

"No . . ." She was straining to speak once again. Raising a skeletal hand to clutch Julie's arm, she whispered, "I must tell you what . . . happened. Virgil was furious . . . said he would help me with the ransom if I married him . . . claimed it was me he loved all along . . . said he wouldn't have you after . . ."

Her voice broke. Julie hastened to tell her it wasn't necessary that she explain. "Let's don't talk about it, please."

"I must." She stared up at her daughter with beseeching eyes. "I have to tell you. He—he said he didn't want you . . . that he knew what they probably did to you. I had no choice but to marry him, Julie. I was desperate. I had . . . no one. Please understand—"

"Mother, I do understand, and I wish you wouldn't talk about it anymore. You should think only of regaining your strength and getting well so you can once again run Rose Hill. You'll make it as profitable and strong as it once was. I know you will."

"No . . . I'm not going to get well," she said matter-of-factly. "You know that . . . as well as I do. Virgil will take over. Don't . . . don't marry him, Julie. I know he'll ask you. He lied to me. He still wanted you . . . only married me to get my land. He was a fake. I found out he had lied . . . about everything . . . shortly after we married."

"Don't worry, Mother. You're going to get well, and besides, nothing could make me marry Virgil. And who knows? Once you're well and back on your feet, perhaps the two of you will be quite happy." The smile she forced to her lips was shaky. She hoped it looked real. She couldn't let her mother know what a real monster Virgil was. This was not the time to worry her with such matters.

Her mother turned her face to the side, pressing her cheek against the satin-covered pillow. "I was wrong . . . to ever want to marry him . . . even to save Rose Hill. What will Myles think when he hears?"

"He'll understand, as I do. He'll be back one day, and you can tell him yourself. But please rest now. You've talked more today than you have since I've come home. I can tell it's worn you out. Let me lower your head so you can take a nap before supper."

Her mother nodded, too tired to protest. Julie tucked the lace-edged coverlet under her chin. She was asleep at once.

Sara had been sitting quietly in a darkened corner of the room, and she followed Julie out into the hallway. "She just ain't gonna get no better, is she, missy?" she asked fearfully, knotting the hem of her apron in her hands. "She's gonna die. I just knows she is."

Julie swallowed hard, her throat tight with emotion. "Yes, Sara, she'll die, but we want her death to come as painlessly as possible. That's why we must do everything we can to make her comfortable and happy."

Sara glanced about suspiciously, as though she expected to see Virgil lurking about, eavesdropping. She spoke so low, Julie had to strain to hear her. "*He* don't do nothin' to make things easier fo' her. That's fo' certain. I hear him talk ugly to her lots of times. I think he wants her to go on and die so he can take over. I wish Mastah Myles was here. He'd put a stop to it. I knows he would. He'd fix him for botherin' you, too." Her chocolate eyes blazed angrily.

"He hasn't bothered me since that first night, Sara, except to whisper filthy words every chance he gets. Don't you worry about me. You just take care of Mother."

Sara shook her head fearfully. "He's gonna try again. I knows it, and you do, too. He's still mad about you stabbin' him. He ain't forgot it."

"I'm on my guard. Be sure of that." And she gave Sara what she hoped was a reassuring hug.

That night her mother was quite nauseated, and Julie sat with her till very late. Finally, when she felt her mother would rest and not awaken anytime soon, Julie returned to her own room, bone tired.

She pushed the chair in place in front of the door, but she did not bother to light her bedside lamp. She undressed, pulled on her gown, and lay down on the bed, glad that for once, sleep would probably come immediately, as she was exhausted.

Something awakened her. She sat straight up, darting frightened glances about in the darkness. Then she turned to reach for the letter opener which she kept beneath her pillow. But it was not there! Frantically her hands went under the sheets, the bedcovers, scrambling in search of the weapon.

Then her blood turned to ice as she heard the soft, evil laugh. Something smacked across her face before she had time to scream, and scream she would have, from the very depths of her soul, even forgetting about waking her mother. Julie was being forced back onto the bed, and realized dimly that one of the satin pillows was being mashed against her nose and mouth, muffling any sounds she made.

"There's no weapon for you tonight, my love," Virgil was grunting, tearing at her gown with one hand while he held the pillow in place with the other. "Tonight I'm going to take what I've been dreaming of for so very long. . . ."

She kicked out at him, but he was straddling her with his heavy thighs, weighting down her legs so she was unable to move. She felt his swollen organ thrusting at her, and then he penetrated, and she screamed against the pillow as the pain ripped all the way up and into her belly.

". . . told you I'd be rough if you resisted me," he panted, pushing himself in and out. "Oh, this is good, Julie . . . so good. It was worth waiting for. . . ."

The pain subsided as his strokes slowed. She forced herself to try to stop screaming, for blackness was beginning to inch its way into her consciousness, suffocating her as she struggled to breathe. Sensing her surrender, Virgil relaxed his hold on the pillow, allowing her to gulp in sweet, precious air.

"You make a sound and I'll smother you next time, you hot-blooded wench." He lowered his head, biting down on one nipple, and she clamped her teeth together to hold back her cry of agony. Suddenly he lifted his lips from her breast and made a whimpering noise, as though he, too, were fighting to hold back a scream. His movements turned to quick, pounding thuds, and then he was slumping over her, panting heavily.

He lay there for long moments, whispering how good it

had been, how much better it would be next time, because
he would not have to hold her down. "You know when
you're beaten, don't you? You know I'll take you anytime
I please! I would've been back before now, but there's a
black wench I've been taking my pleasure with every
night. Only she ran away, and I decided I'd kept you
waiting long enough . . . let you think you had the upper
hand. Only now, you know who owns you, don't you?"

He raised the pillow and released her, snapping, "And
don't scream now, or so help me, I'll gag you and beat you
within an inch of your life. One day, when I've got you off
somewhere alone, I'll make you pay for stabbing me. But
don't try my patience. I'd just as soon see your simpering
mother die anyway, so I can be rid of her."

Julie could only lie there, stunned, her body burning
with pain and humiliation. Never had she hated another
human being more. Never had she wished to take a life as
she did in that moment. But she was powerless to do
anything except lie before him, vulnerable and submissive.

Finally he moved off the bed, and though she could not
see his face, she knew he must be smiling in triumph.
"Tomorrow night and the night after, do not put a chair in
front of your door, for I'll be back, sweet Julie, to do with
you as I please. And remember, one word of protest, one
finger lifted in defense, and I'll see to it that your mother
knows all about us. The sooner I see her in her coffin, the
happier I'll be."

Venomously Julie spat out the words she could no
longer hold back: "One day, you contemptible savage,
you'll answer for this!"

Chuckling softly, he left her.

Julie lay there for a long time, crying until her head
ached as much as her abused body. There was nothing she
could do, not as long as her mother lived. She couldn't run
away and leave her at the mercy of that man. And she
would do nothing to hasten her mother's death, for then
Julie would not know another moment's peace. No, she
would have to endure Virgil's depravities and lust as long
as her mother drew a breath. But then, by God, if she had
to in order to escape, she would kill him!

Sara saw the bruises the next morning as she helped
Julie with her bath, and she covered her mouth with her
hands and wept out loud. "Lord, dear Lord. I knowed he
was gonna do it. I knowed it. He been stealin' down to

Sara Jane's at night, and he near 'bout killed her, and she run away. I should'a knowed he'd try again with you. . . ."

Julie winced with pain as she sank down into the tub of hot, soapy water. Virgil's long nails had scratched her in many places, and now the wounds were stinging. "Sara, I hate your having to know about this, and I wouldn't have let you see me this way, but I'm too weak to bathe myself. You mustn't say a word about this to anyone, do you understand? I'll deal with it myself."

"Oh, no'm. I wouldn't say nothin'. You knows that. But what you gonna do? If your mama finds out, it'll kill her. I knows it will."

"She isn't going to find out," Julie snapped.

Sara gently rubbed her back with a sponge. "How you gonna keep away from him? He'll be back every night."

"I could move into Mother's room, but he'd order me to come out, saying if I didn't, he'd make a scene. He's made it quite clear he hopes she'll hurry up and die, and he has no qualms about hastening her last breath. I suppose there's nothing I can do."

"But what you gonna do when she dies?" Sara cried. "You gonna let that man have Rose Hill?"

"The day my mother is buried," Julie replied quietly, "I'm leaving here. Virgil can have Rose Hill. If Mother knew the truth, that's what she would want me to do."

"But what about Mastah Myles?"

Julie squeezed her eyes shut as pain moved through her at the thought of her brother. "I don't know, Sara. I haven't made plans about that yet."

Sara was quiet for a long while, then, as she was drying Julie with a soft towel, she said, "Miss Julie, you gonna go off and leave that man with all your mama's nice things?"

"What things?" she replied absently, her mind burning with anger and fear over the suffering she would have to endure in the days and weeks to come . . . for as long as her mother lived.

"She's got a lot of silver. And what about her jewelry? She's got diamonds and gold. Them things is worth a lot. You gonna just leave them? You think she'd want *him* to have them?"

Julie sighed, thinking how that would be one more blow to suffer, leaving all the family heirlooms and her mother's expensive jewelry for Virgil. He'd be left with everything, and she would leave her home penniless and destitute. "I suppose I have no choice. When I leave, it will be quickly and quietly. I won't be packing trunks, Sara. He'd try to stop me if he caught me. He might even kill me."

Sara shuddered, then asked, "Why don't we start hidin' things?"

"What do you mean?"

"A little at a time. We'll sneak things out to Lionel, and he can dig a hole somewhere and bury them. That's what I hear folks is doin' all over Savannah—buryin' their valuables so if the Yankees come, they can't steal 'em. We'll do the same with all your mama's things. Then you can sneak back and dig 'em up. Won't be nothin' Mastah Oates can do, 'cause once he realizes they is gone, they'll be buried, and he won't know where."

Julie's heart began to pound with excitement. For the first time in so long she could not remember when, she felt a surge of hope. "Yes, Sara, that's what we'll do. But we'll have to be very careful and take only a few things at a time, so he won't notice anything missing. First of all, we'll start with Mother's jewelry and the small silver pieces." Julie hugged the older woman happily. "Oh, Sara, how blessed I am to have a friend like you."

Sara beamed. "Shucks, Miss Julie, I couldn't love you more if'n you was my own young'un, but they is something you better know—"

Julie raised an eyebrow. "What are you talking about?"

"When you go, me and Lionel is goin' too. We ain't staying with that man one day after yo' mama is buried."

"Sara, I'll give you your freedom today if you want it. That's the least I can do for all your devotion. I can persuade Mother to sign any papers necessary, and you can go on and leave."

"Oh, no," Sara said quickly. "I don't want to be free of you, and Lionel done said the same thing. We'd of run off a long time ago if it hadn't been for leavin' yo' mama alone with that man. And we felt like you and Mastah Myles would come back one day."

"I love you for this," Julie said fervently, and she felt a little better, despite her overwhelming fear of the horrors that surely awaited her.

Time dragged on slowly, and many were the nights when Julie found herself shamelessly praying for her mother's death as she lay beneath Virgil's panting, heavy body. He came to her almost every night. How much more can I endure? she thought wildly.

After the first few times, Virgil decided that just to ravish her was not enough. He forced her to perform all sorts of depraved actions upon his body, unspeakable things that she found utterly repugnant. Even Derek, for all his raw passion, had never made her feel so utterly defiled. She had enjoyed his touch, his caress, though she had hated to admit it.

Her mother continued to cling to life, and Dr. Perkins confided he had expected her to die long before. "If you hadn't returned, Julie," he said one night, "she wouldn't have lasted this long."

Julie prayed that her guilt over wishing her mother dead did not show on her face. If she could get well, it would be different, and Julie would endure anything to save her life. But it was all hopeless, and more and more, lately, she found herself wishing she could crawl into her own casket and die—for death seemed the only way to escape the hell she was forced to endure.

Her only respite was the nights Virgil stayed in town to gamble. Lionel reported on his activities in Savannah from time to time, when he went in for supplies. The Negroes would gather down by the waterfront and exchange gossip, and it was common knowledge that Virgil Oates was becoming a heavy gambler.

On one such night, he got up from the supper table, walked to where Julie was sitting, and planted a moist kiss on her cheek. She shuddered with revulsion, but he merely laughed and said, "I hate leaving you alone, my love, but don't worry. I'll make up for it tomorrow night. You can bed your mother down early, and we'll have the whole evening together."

After he left, she sat in her chair, fighting back tears of frustration and hopelessness. Soon she would have to go in to her mother to coax her to eat, just as she did each night. Julie would be relieved if she could get only half a bowl of broth into her, but of late, her mother would often shake her head wearily and say she had no appetite and could eat nothing.

Julie could not let her see that she was upset. On two occasions, her mother had noticed and become quite distraught. Once her mother had even broken into uncontrollable sobs, crying, "It's all my fault. I cause you so much misery, Julie. Why can't I just go ahead and die?"

Sara walked in, took one look at Julie's plate and cried, "You gonna waste away just like your mama if you don't start eatin', child. Look at that. You ain't touched that chicken, and you always loved my fried chicken—"

"I can't eat with that horrible man leering at me, Sara. He makes me sick." Julie shook her head in despair. "One of these days I know something inside of me is going to snap, and I'll throw my plate right in his face, and then hell and be damned if Mother hears and learns the truth. God help me, but I don't know how much more I can stand."

Sara put a plump arm around the girl's trembling shoulders. "Now you listen to me. I knows it's hard. I knows you feel like you can't stand it one mo' hour, but you got to remember that the good Lord don't put no mo' on his chillun than they can bear. You got to hold yo' head up and have faith."

"I think God may have misjudged my capacity for carrying a load," Julie sighed. "Even Myles used to tell me I was a weakling."

"Oh, he'd be right smart proud of the way you've kept from breakin' down. I know he would."

Julie pursed her lips. "Maybe. I look back on when I was Derek's prisoner, and even when he made me so mad that at times I could have screamed, I think I could have endured it for a lifetime. I never thought of breaking down."

"Why, Miss Julie," Sara chuckled, starting to clear the plates from the table. "Now I believe you loved that man, for sure. You get a dreamy, misty look in your eyes whenever you talks about him."

Misty Eyes—that was what Derek had called her. And even when he was angry he would call her that, and his voice, though cold and biting, sounded strange, somehow, when he said those words.

She shook herself and looked at Sara, who was chuckling to herself as though she knew some deep, dark secret. "I didn't love him," she snapped. "And no matter if I did. I'll never see him again. He's probably on another ship, running that infernal Yankee blockade and keeping a woman in every port."

"I'll bet you wish he'd walk in that door right now."

Julie let out her breath in disgust. "Can't we discuss something else?"

"Yes'm," Sara said with a smirk, then started rattling on about how she'd seen Adelia Carrigan in town that morning. Julie bit her tongue to keep from saying she didn't want to discuss that trollop, either.

"She says Mastah Thomas is fine and dandy. He's one of the officers at that Yankee prison camp up in Richmond. She said she'd written him you'd come home."

Julie stood and smoothed her skirt. "If you'll prepare Mother's tray. I'll take it in to her."

"She's yo' kinfolk, but she never comes to visit," Sara prattled on. "She knows yo' mama's sick and she always asks about her, but she never comes to call. Why, I can't remember the last time she set foot in th' do'."

Julie tugged at the high neckline of her dress. It was scratchy and uncomfortable, but she never wore low necklines anymore, not around Virgil. She didn't want to do anything to entice him. Surely by summer the situation would change. Otherwise she knew she would have long since been driven truly insane.

She went into her mother and coaxed her to drink some tea and eat a few bits of rice mixed with hot milk and sugar. Then Julie freshened her bed, sponged the invalid's emaciated body, and tucked the covers up about her neck. Sitting down, she began to read to her, but after only a few lines, glanced up to see that her mother was already fast asleep.

Sara came in and said it was a good time to sneak more things out of the house for Lionel to bury. "You can get some of yo' mama's jewelry, and I'll get some of her silver pieces she kept put back fo' special times. Mastah Virgil won't miss them."

"He's going to start to sooner or later," Julie said worriedly.

"I know. Let's just hope it ain't long. . . ." and her voice trailed off apologetically, shamefully.

Julie knew what she had been about to say: that perhaps it wouldn't be long before her mother died, and then they could leave. "I understand, Sara," she whispered. "Don't feel guilty. I've had the same thoughts."

Returning to her mother's room, she went to the jewelry box and took out a diamond and ruby necklace with matching earrings, then brought them to Sara. Along with the jewels, they carried a set of heavy silver candelabra and several trays out to where Lionel was waiting behind the house. He put all the items in a large burlap sack, slung it over his shoulder, and, pick in hand, set out for the woods in the far distance.

He had told Julie exactly where he was burying everything: in a spot at the edge of the Marshal family cemetery, not far from her father's grave. Lionel kept leaves and pine straw raked over the diggings, so no one who ventured there would notice and ask questions.

Julie said goodnight to Sara, then retired for the night, relieved that she would not have to put up with Virgil's filth. And that's all she could call it—filth. It was certainly nothing like what she had shared with Derek. There was no warmth or tenderness . . . only Virgil's lust, and his humiliation and degradation of her soul and body.

The fire in the grate had burned down to grayish-red ashes. Julie lay on her side and stared dreamily at it, almost seeing faces and images among the glowing embers. Her eyes grew heavy and she snuggled deeper beneath the quilts, trying to shut out all unpleasant thoughts. She would think of happier days, a brighter tomorrow—when all this sadness and misery would be behind her.

A strange sound brought her out of her somnolence. Her eyes flew open. The fire still glowed with lazy flashes of reds, oranges, blues, and yellows. Please God, she prayed, not tonight. Don't let Virgil have returned from town early. Give me this one night of respite, please. . . .

She heard it again, and realized it sounded like a pebble being thrown against the doors to the portico. She stiffened and clutched the covers tightly to her chin. Virgil wouldn't stand outside and throw rocks at her window. He would just charge right in and demand that she succumb to his lust. But who—?

The sound was louder, and this time she feared the glass would shatter. Forcing her trembling body to move, she eased herself up and reached for her flannel wrapper which lay at the foot of the bed. As she searched for her slippers, another stone hit the window. Padding quickly across the floor, she opened the door and stepped onto the balcony just as another pebble came zinging through the air, barely missing her.

A brisk wind was blowing, and it whipped her wrapper and gown up about her knees. Trying to hold her garments down, Julie crept toward the railing. Then, taking a deep breath and mustering all her courage, she leaned over a little ways and called softly: "Who's there? Who's there, I say!"

"Julie . . . oh, God . . . Julie!"

It was a dream. It could not be real. She had fallen asleep and was only dreaming that Myles's voice was actually floating to her on the night breeze. It could not be.

"Julie . . . it's me—Myles . . . can you hear me?"

"Myles, yes, yes . . ." Tears filled her eyes and she was momentarily overcome by shock. Her hands gripped the railing to support her watery knees. "It's you. It really is you—"

"Yes, it's me," he laughed nervously. "And I'm cold and hungry. Is anyone about? Can you let me in?"

"Wait there." She was giggling with near hysteria. "I'll be down. Oh, Myles, don't move, please—"

Laughing and crying all at once, she hurried back inside and through her room, making her way as quickly and quietly as possible down the stairs to the first floor. The house was dark except for the light left burning in the foyer.

Her heart racing, she was about to fling the front doors wide open when the sound of footsteps made her freeze in sudden terror. Whipping about, she gasped with relief to see Sara emerging from the shadows of the back hallway, a softly burning candle in her hand.

"Thank God it's only you!" she cried, her bosom heaving with the reminder of her panic.

"Miss Julie, what you doin' up this time o' night? I come to check on yo' mama, and I heard you runnin' down the stairs."

Julie ran to clutch Sara's shoulders, unable to contain her joy any longer. "It's Myles, Sara! Myles!"

Sara swayed slightly, her eyes widening. "What you talkin' about?"

Julie did not take time to explain. Instead she ran to the doors, flung them open, and stepped out onto the terrace. "Myles, hurry. It's all right," she called into the night as loudly as she dared.

And he stepped out of the blackness to fold her in his arms, his sobs mingling with hers as they clung together.

Finally they were able to break apart, and Sara stepped up to give him a weepy hug, then said gruffly, "Well, you

two young'uns step in out of that night air 'fore you catch
a cold. Get on back to my kitchen and let me fix this boy a
bite to eat. My, you ain't got 'nuff meat on yo' bones fo'
the buzzards to pick."

The old Negress led the way through the dark house,
holding her candle high, and Julie and Myles followed,
arms about each other. Julie felt she had to keep touching
him to make sure he was really there and not just a dream.
She caressed his tousled hair, then his face, so lean and
pale. "It *is* you," she whispered tremulously. "Oh, Myles,
it's really *you*!"

He gave her a fierce hug, then sat down at the long
wooden table in the kitchen and attempted to tell her what
had happened to him since he had left almost eighteen
months ago. "I didn't join the Union army. I just couldn't.
True, I don't hold to enslaving a man, but I'm still a
southerner, and I found I just couldn't take up arms
against my people. Not yet."

"I understand," Julie murmured, wiping at her eyes with
the back of her hand. "But some of them were certainly
anxious to take up arms against *you* and still would, for
that matter. Sheriff Franklin still stops by from time to
time to ask questions. You'll have to stay hidden."

Myles sighed, shoulders drooping with resignation. "I
know. I don't plan to stay long anyway, Julie. I want to go
west, make a new life for myself out there. I can never live
here again."

Sara set a plate of leftover fried chicken in front him,
and he picked up a drumstick and began to eat ravenously.
Exchanging a glance with Julie, Sara said, "I reckon yo'
sister ought to tell you a few things, Mastah Myles. They's
a whole lot done gone on since you left. And Miss Julie,
you needn't be a-makin' faces at me to hush up, 'cause we
both knows we gots to get him fed and outta here before
Mistah Oates comes home."

"Virgil Oates?" Myles raised an eyebrow. "Is he still
hanging around here? What's she talking about, Julie? I
noticed the place looks kind of run down. I've been hiding
in the woods since before sundown, waiting for night, so
things would quiet down before I slipped in." He looked at
her grimly. "Suppose you tell me everything."

She took a deep breath, then told him all of it as quickly
as possible. "Virgil only wanted to marry me to get Rose
Hill and now he's got it, because—" She lowered her

voice, choking on a sob, hating to continue but knowing she must. "Mother is dying, Myles. The doctor says she can't last much longer. He is surprised she's lived this long."

Myles was silent for a long time. His face became redder by the minute. Angrily he bent the fork he held in his hand. It finally snapped as he roared, "I won't have it! By God, I'll run him off. Where is he?"

He leaped to his feet, and the contents of his plate spilled to the floor. Julie rose also. Catching his arm, she cried, "Myles, no! You can't do or say anything. He'd turn you in to the sheriff. Don't you see? There's nothing you or anyone else can do."

She told him quickly how she and Sara and Lionel were planning to leave when her mother died, how they had been slipping out valuables and burying them. "Other than that, there's nothing we can do. And you must stay hidden."

He yanked his arm from her grasp and strode briskly to the back door. Jerking it open, he stared out at the night, breathing in deeply of the chilly night air. Fists clenched at his sides, he swore, "Dammit, this is our land, our home. I won't see a vulture just walk in and take over. There's got to be a way to stop him!"

"There isn't." Julie rushed to his side, pressing her head against his back as her arms encircled his waist. "Myles, I've prayed nightly for your return, and now that you're here, I can't let anything happen to you. Stay hidden, please, and when Mother dies, we'll leave. We'll go west—"

He turned and gazed into her eyes. "I want to see Mother, Julie, before she dies. Later I'll worry about how to deal with Virgil Oates. But I have to see her."

She nodded. "Give me time to arrange it. She couldn't stand the shock of seeing you without being prepared for it. And I'll have to make her see that she can't let Virgil know about it, either. Till then, will you stay out of sight?"

Myles nodded, but she could feel the tension rippling through him.

Julie clung to him, wishing she could pour out her heart and tell him how the days were filled with anguish because she knew night would follow and she would be forced to submit to Virgil. And she longed to tell him about Derek, also, and the confused dreams she had almost nightly, when his face would swim before her, in the murky blue-green waters off the pink-tinged sands of Bermuda.

But she couldn't share these thoughts, or her tumultuous world. Myles would kill Virgil, even at the risk of being hung, and he would never understand her feelings for Derek after he had kidnapped her. No, she had to keep these things inside. This was her own private hell. When her mother died, they would go away, and no matter how it haunted her, she would have no choice but to put Derek from her mind . . . and her heart.

The two clung together—brother and sister—alone against the world. Sara stood silently watching in the shadows. She could not be sure what Myles was thinking, but she could imagine what was going on in Julie's head and heart. Sara wanted to tell him all of it, but she did not dare.

"We'll make it," Myles whispered finally, patting Julie reassuringly and trying to give her a brave smile. "You'll see, little sister. We'll make it."

I pray to God you do, Sara thought, tears streaming down her black cheeks. I pray to God that *both* of you make it. . . .

ᙙ Chapter Fifteen ᙚ

"WE gonna be ready to go the day yo' mama is laid to rest," Sara said one afternoon. "All we gotta do is get our clothes together, which won't take long for me and Lionel. We ain't got that much."

"Or me," Julie said as she took a few more pieces of silver service from a velvet-lined chest. She watched Sara conceal them in the folds of her apron. "I'll be glad when I can stop worrying about Myles, too."

"Did I hear the name of that murdering brother of yours mentioned?"

They spun around, startled. Virgil stood in the arched doorway of the dining room, an insidious smile upon his lips. As always, he was dandily dressed, this time in a ruffled shirt and bright embroidered vest. His fingers toyed with the gold chain that stretched from his watch pocket. "Well," he said, quite annoyed, "did I?"

Julie fought for composure, darting a warning look at Sara for her to do the same. To Virgil she said, in what she hoped was a calm voice, "Yes, we were talking about Myles. We were saying we hope he comes home soon, so we can stop worrying about him."

"I don't want his name mentioned in my house!" he bellowed. "He's a criminal—"

"He is not a criminal!" Her ire matched his. "And I would like to remind you that this is *my* home, not yours, and you've no say-so about who comes here, certainly not my brother!"

He reached out to seize her shoulders and give her a violent shake. "It is *my* house, you ungrateful little wench, and if Myles ever shows his face here, I'll see that he's hung, as he should be. As for you, I'll not tolerate your insolence. Do you understand me?"

Julie knew she should not provoke him further, but she had been on the brink of losing all control for so very long that Virgil's verbal attack upon Myles pushed her over the edge. With all the strength she could muster, she raised her hand and slapped him. "Don't you ever speak of Myles in such a way again. I just wish my mother could know what a lecherous, conniving rogue you really are—"

He grabbed her wrist and tugged her roughly forward. "Then let's not wait any longer to tell her, my love. We'll go together, right now, to her bedside. You can tell her what a reprobate I am. You say this isn't my house, and you dare to strike me! Well, I think it's time we tell your mother the truth. So come along—"

"No! You can't!" Julie yanked out of his grasp and backed toward Sara. "You know it would kill her."

"So?" He cocked his head to one side, grinning. "I'm ready for her to die. She never satisfied me or brought me the pleasure that her daughter does. She should go on and die and get out of the way. If you behave yourself and show me some respect, I'll make you the mistress of Rose Hill."

"I would rather die. I hate you, Virgil. I wish you were dead. I wish I had a gun; I'd kill you here and now myself!" With such fury rushing through her veins, Julie knew at that moment that she was capable of murdering him without a second thought.

"I'll not have you speak to me that way," he cried, leaping forward to wrestle her arms behind her back and push her toward the floor. "We're going up to your mother's room right now and tell her everything, how we spend the nights in each other's arms, loving passionately, warmly. We'll tell her all the things we do to each other to make our union even sweeter—"

Julie was struggling, knowing her mother was probably awake at this hour, and if the yelling and screaming continued, she was sure to hear. "Let me go," she hissed, kicking out at his shins. "Let me go, Virgil. Stop this madness!"

Sara backed away, her hands pressed to her lips as she fought to keep from screaming. Terrified, she could only stand there and watch the horrible scene before her.

Virgil flung Julie to the floor. As she fell, she slid into a chair, sending it toppling with a loud crash. She scrambled to escape him, and he glanced about for some weapon with which to punish Julie. Spying the heavy braided bell rope which hung from the ceiling, he reached up and snatched it down.

Suddenly Sara came out of her horrified trance. Intending to shield her mistress, she sprang forward, forgetting about the silver she had hidden in her apron. It clattered to the floor like hail striking a rooftop.

Virgil turned, eyed the silver suspiciously, then shifted his gaze to Sara's petrified face. He shrieked, "You were stealing, you worthless black wench! I'll have your flesh stripped to the bone—"

"No, she wasn't stealing anything!" Julie scrambled to her feet as Sara ran from the room. "She was going to clean the silver, and she was carrying it in her apron to keep from making so many trips to the chest. You can't punish her for that."

Silently he stared after Sara, and when she had disappeared, he looked at Julie, his eyes glittering. "I'll deal with her later. You are the one who needs chastising at the moment. On your knees."

When she did not move, he whispered ominously, "You will obey me, or we'll go to your mother's room and tell her the truth."

Julie had already suffered too much in the past for it to have been in vain. Her mother would die, but not with a broken heart. Having no other choice, she obeyed.

"I'm going to take you here, on the floor, like the bitch you are," Virgil panted in eager anticipation as he pushed up her dress and yanked down her pantalets. Then he spread her legs and positioned himself between them. "Now, my love, take a deep breath and receive me," he commanded.

And with a hard, jolting thrust, he entered, grunting with pleasure. Mercifully it was over quickly, and he left her lying on the floor and walked out of the room.

Sara, who had been watching from her hiding place behind the door, rushed in, tears streaming down her cheeks. "That man's got to die," she sobbed, gathering Julie in her plump arms. "A man that evil, he don't deserve to live. Tell Mastah Myles. Let him do what has to be done—"

"No, we can't." Julie choked out the words. "He has to remain hidden. They would hang him if he's caught. We have to go on with our plans as they are. This doesn't change anything."

Sara helped Julie to the kitchen. She bathed her with water from a kettle on the stove. "Now you go lie down fo' awhile," she told her. "You can't let yo' mama or yo' brother see you till you calm down. I'll look after things. You just rest."

"I can't. Mother might have heard all the yelling. She might be upset. I need to go to her."

"I'll take care of her. I'll tell her you fell and hurt your ankle or somethin'. You got to get to bed."

Julie felt too bad to protest. Sara half-carried her up the stairs, and when they reached the top, they found Virgil leaning against the bannister, smiling insidiously. "What ever is wrong, Julie?" he asked with mock concern. "Aren't you feeling well? That's a pity."

Sara tensed, and Julie fought the impulse to lash out at him. They moved on by, and once in her room, she fell across the satin comforter and gave way to tears of frustration.

Her eyes were heavy, but she fought against sleep, wanting to think, to plan. This could not go on. Sooner or later her mother was going to find out, or else Julie would kill Virgil in a fit of rage. And she knew that it was only a matter of time before Myles was discovered. The situation grew more desperate with each passing day.

Could she go on and leave before her mother died? she wondered in sudden desperation. Did she dare? Which would be worse—to disappear or remain till something more terrible happened? Dear God, she did not know the answer.

Suddenly Sara was shaking her gently, and she realized that sleep had won and wrapped her gently in its shadowy cloak. "You got to wake up, Miss Julie," Sara was whispering frantically. "You got to get up."

A glance at the windows told her she had slept far too long, for the veil of gray creeping across the sky would soon give way to the darkness of night. "How is Mother?" she asked, needles of apprehension stabbing at her.

"She ain't had a good day. The doctor, he's in with her now. I peeked in on my way up here and saw him using that little silver thing with the rubber strings coming out of it."

"His stethoscope. He uses that to check the strength and regularity of Mother's heartbeat. He does that every time he comes, so why should that alarm you?"

"He was listenin' and shakin' his head. Mastah Oates was in there, too, and he saw me lookin' and grinned, like he's a-hopin' it means she's worse." Her eyes grew bigger. "But it ain't yo' mama I'm worried about. It's Mastah Myles. He sent Lionel to the house to get word to you that he wants to see his mama and be on his way. He seen some lawmen nosin' around in the woods, and he's scared they got wind he's back. He says it's too risky, and he's gonna leave tonight at midnight."

Julie knew he was right. Their mother was going to die. There was nothing she could do but leave in order to escape further abuse from Virgil. She could not save her mother's life, and if she stayed to try and make things easier for her, sooner or later, someone was going to get hurt, perhaps killed.

She was washed over with waves of desolation wishing there were some way she could convey all her feelings to her mother without causing her untold anguish. How she hated to disappear, knowing she would never see her mother again, and have her mother think she had just deserted her. But perhaps God, in His infinite wisdom, would let her mother know how desperate Julie had been, and that she did truly love her.

Julie quickly changed to a mauve-colored dress of heavy cotton with a high neck and long sleeves. Then she twisted her long black hair back into a haphazard bun at the nape of her neck to get it out of her way. No longer did she concern herself with her looks. Under the conditions she had been forced to endure, it was easy enough to stop caring about anything.

She told Sara to go to Lionel and have him tell Myles that it was going to be impossible for him to see his mother before he left. "Explain how she's too weak, and there isn't enough time to prepare her. Have Lionel tell him to wait for the three of us in the cemetery. We're all leaving together at midnight."

"Praise God!" Sara lifted her eyes upward, then said in a rush, "I knows you hate to leave yo' mama, but it's the only thing you can do."

"I know that, Sara," Julie whispered painfully. "Now go. I'll sit with Mother one last time, and you pack as much food and supplies as you can. Make sure Virgil doesn't get suspicious. When we go, we're going to have to move fast, because he'll no doubt have the law on our trail."

"He's been nosin' around. He's been checkin' on the silver and other stuff. I 'magine he's been snoopin' in yo' mama's jewelry chest, too. And Lionel says he saw him pokin' around in the yard, like he was maybe lookin' for somethin'."

"It's just too dangerous to stay. Now hurry."

Sara turned to go, but then Julie called to her once more and said she should inform the servants, whom they could trust, of their plans. "I want Mother cared for after I'm gone, and I can't depend on Virgil to do it. Surely there are others we can rely on."

"Yes'm. Don't you fret." And she hurried out.

Julie got to her mother's room just in time to see Dr. Perkins coming out. Seeing her, he frowned and closed the door behind him. "She hasn't got long, Julie," he said in a voice filled with sorrow. "I barely heard her heartbeat. And there are other signs, as well. The color of her skin, the way her breathing becomes more labored. And her feet and hands are turning unusually cold as the circulation of her blood slows. She's failing fast. I doubt she'll last the night."

"I—I'll go and sit with her," Julie murmured tremulously, shaken by his gloomy prediction. "I suppose there's nothing more we can do."

He placed a hand on her shoulder. "I'd stay with you, but I have a patient about to deliver who has had a great deal of difficulty in the past and lost several babies. I feel it's my place to help bring a new life into the world, rather than see one leave it, when I can do nothing to prevent it."

"Of course. You go along. I'll send word to you when . . ." her voice trailed off. She could not put the death of her mother into words, and she felt guilty to think she would not be there when it did happen. Dr. Perkins, like so many people, would wonder why she had disappeared so suddenly in the last hours of her mother's life, but she could not be concerned with their speculations and opinions. There was too much to be faced in the coming hours.

Moving into the room, she went to the side of the bed and stared down at her mother's still form. Her chest barely moved as she struggled to breathe. Julie touched her hand and found it frighteningly cold. Hurrying to the cedar chest in the corner, she took out another quilt and tucked it about her.

The hours moved by with agonizing slowness. Sara slipped in to tell her things were moving along as planned. She brought Julie a cup of broth, which she did not want but drank anyway, knowing she would need every bit of her strength for the journey that lay ahead. She had no idea where they were going. Myles had said something about heading west till the war was over, returning one day to claim Rose Hill. But they both knew that would not happen. No, they would not come back. Life as they had known it was gone forevermore.

Around eight o'clock, Virgil swaggered into the room, took one look at his wife, and chuckled out loud. "Well, it won't be long. I've seen death hovering before. According to Dr. Perkins's good news, she may not last till morning. What a relief!"

Julie gripped the arms of the chair in which she was sitting, her heart pounding with loathing and rage. "Get out of here, you despicable creature." She shook as she spoke. "Have you no respect in that evil heart of yours? Can't you let her die in peace?"

"Oh, quite, my love. In fact, I'm going to give you both peace to share your final hours together. I'm going into town for a game of cards. And when I return in the morning, I hope to find a wreath on the door, the hands of the clocks still, the mirrors covered with sheets . . . the usual procedure when death visits."

He walked to where she sat and leaned forward to kiss her cheek as she shuddered with revulsion. Laughing, he murmured, "Now is that any way for a prospective bride to react to her future husband?"

Whipping her head about, she stared at him in shock. "What did you say?" she gasped.

"Don't act so surprised. You will marry me and become mistress of Rose Hill."

"And you're out of your damned mind." She spoke as loudly as she dared. "I'd sooner die than feel you touch me again, Virgil and heed me well: if you ever do touch me again, I *will* kill you, somehow, someway. This I promise you!"

The smile on his lips quickly disappeared, and his eyes, which had been gleaming with enjoyment over his taunts, turned cold. "Well, then, suppose we rouse your mother and tell her of our plans? Suppose we just give her a parting gift by letting her know how we've enjoyed the fruits of our passion while she lay on her death bed?"

Turning about, he leaned over, clutched her mother's shoulders, and began shaking her roughly. Julie watched in horror, stricken, as the frail body bounced up and down on the mattress beneath Virgil's strong hands. But her mother's eyes remained closed, and her head lolled to one side. Her mouth suddenly gaped open . . . as though silently screaming.

"Oh, you devil, leave her alone—" Julie leaped up and shoved him to one side, placing herself as a shield in front of her mother's bed. "Get out of here, Virgil, or I'll send someone for Sheriff Franklin. I won't have you torturing her in her final hours. You are evil! A spawn of Satan himself!"

"Am I now? Well, you know you'll be punished for such talk. A wife must respect her husband. I'll remember you're due a lesson in obedience."

She placed both hands against his chest and gave him a shove so sudden that he almost tripped and fell as he struggled to steady himself. Reaching for the first thing she could get her hands on—the china water pitcher by the bed—she held it threateningly above her head. "Get out of here, Virgil! I'm warning you! Get out of this room and out of this house."

He brushed at an imaginary fleck on his waistcoat. "Very well, Julie. I suppose it's only proper that you sit with the dying instead of satiating the hunger I know you feel for me. It will keep. But remember, you'll be punished —and severely."

She shook the pitcher at him. "Out! Take your filthy, depraved mind and body out of this room at once."

He backed toward the door, smiling. "Very well. I'm leaving. But remember. Rose Hill is mine now, and you would be wise to come to terms with yourself regarding your insolence. I can throw you out of here any time I choose—"

How Julie longed to tell him this was the last time she would be subjected to his nauseating company. Instead she turned her back on him, focusing all her attention upon her mother. It was not long before she heard the sound of the door opening and closing and knew he was gone. A wave of relief washed over her.

Her mother continued to sleep deeply, her breathing becoming even more labored. Sara came in, and together they raised her head by putting more pillows behind it. This helped some; her chest looked a wee bit stronger as she struggled to breathe. But she did not open her eyes. If anything her slumber seemed even deeper with each passing moment.

Sara told Julie that Lionel and Myles had everything ready. They were taking a wagon and two mules. All provisions were loaded, and she had packed a small trunk for Julie.

"I even got some more silver out to 'em, and they're buryin' that now," she said proudly. "I'm gonna get a few more pieces of yo' mama's jewels. We're gonna be in the cemetery waitin' on you, honey. And whenever you gets there, we'll go.

"Praise the Lord that mean man went to town," she added.

Julie murmured, "Yes, yes. I'll be along, Sara. It's just that I hate to leave her. I wish—" she swallowed, choked on a sob, reached out to touch her mother's still face lovingly, "—I wish she would go on and die before I leave. The thought of leaving her here with Virgil is more than I can bear. She won't understand why I left her."

"She ain't gonna know you did." Sara shook her head with sad finality. "Miz Julie, I seen lots of folks die, and I knows the signs. She gonna lay just like that till the angels come to carry her home. Ain't nothin' fo' you to do but leave. And if she knew the truth, she'd tell you to go on. I knows she would."

Julie was silent for a long time before she whispered, "Yes, I know you're right, Sara. But please. Let me stay just a little while longer."

With a sigh, Sara walked out of the room.

The clock on the mantel ticked away their remaining moments together. There was so much Julie wished she could say, but when she really thought about the words, she wondered what they would be. How do you tell someone goodbye forever? How do you give your own mother up to death?

The clock struck twelve, its sound echoing through the still room. Julie had been sitting in a chair pushed up very close to the bed. When she leaned over, she could barely see the rise and fall of her mother's chest. A tear trailed down her cheek as she pressed her lips against the cold, clammy skin.

She rose to stand on legs that trembled as a pine seedling quakes in the fierce winds of spring. Tucking the quilt about her mother's chin, she whirled and hurried from the room, not looking back. It was done. There was nothing left. She must go forward, plunging into the future as Derek had plunged into those shark-infested waters. Whatever tomorrow held, she would face it. All she asked was the same thing that Derek had probably requested in that split second between life and possible death: a chance —just a chance—to face the unknown . . . and conquer it.

Lanterns burned dimly in the hallway, but Julie kept her eyes straight ahead, not wanting to take one last look at the house where she had been born and raised.

The late December wind was bone-chilling as she stepped out the back door. Christmas had come and gone with little fanfare. A few neighbors had stopped by with cakes and pies, to pay their respects to her mother, who did not remember any of them coming. Perhaps next year, Julie thought feverishly as she hurried through the night, things would be different. They would rejoice on the holy day, and there would be singing and laughter, with no thoughts of the miseries of days past.

She moved past the barns and farrowing houses, down the dark path that led to the cemetery. It was a moonless night, and she had to feel her way along, trusting her memory. She had trod this way countless times, but now and then she would step off into brambles and brush and her dress would catch on something, wasting precious time as she paused to free herself.

Then she heard it—the sound of a whippoorwill. Myles! It was the signal they had used as children, when he was hiding to keep from being punished for something he'd done. She would answer with the same trill to let him know it was safe to come out. So she answered him now, then saw his shadowy figure step out from behind a tree.

He grabbed her hand and squeezed it, whispering, "It's okay, Julie. We're on our way. Everything is ready."

"Myles—" she said painfully, her heart twisting for him.

He had moved ahead, still holding her hand as he led the way, but he paused to say in anguish, "Don't say anything, please. I know you feel sorry for me because I didn't get to see Mother, but that's the way it has to be. It's too dangerous for me to hang around any longer. It could lead to bad trouble."

They reached the cemetery, the crooked tombstones standing white against the darkness like curious sentries of the dead. "The wagon is over there." He spoke so low she had to strain to hear. "I've had a time keeping Sara and Lionel from leaving without us. You know Negroes don't like to be around cemeteries, especially at night. They're very superstitious—" He stopped and looked about wildly, straining to see in the blackness of the night.

Julie was frightened. "Myles, what's wrong?" she cried. "I don't understand. I left them here, by this wrought-iron fence that surrounds Grandfather Marshal's grave. I told them not to move. We were going to walk the mules down the cemetery path and then get in the wagon and leave as fast as the mules could go. I was teasing about them leaving without us, but now I'm starting to worry."

They stumbled about in the darkness, with Myles calling first to Lionel, then to Sara. "Dammit," he swore, "I've been back there behind that tree for over an hour waiting for you. I never heard a thing, but it was a good ways off. Where the hell are they?" He stamped around in little circles, waving his arms in despair and fury.

Julie swallowed hard. The knot of fear was getting tighter in her throat. She began to tremble. Surely they wouldn't have gone off and left them. Sara and Lionel were too loyal. Something had happened . . . something terrible. She could feel it.

Reaching out to touch Myles's arm, she said hesitantly, "Maybe you should go back into hiding. I'll go stay with Mother. I've been thinking perhaps I shouldn't go off and leave her this way. It won't be long before she dies, and I can meet you somewhere later."

"No!" he responded in a fierce tone. "I don't want you in that house with Virgil Oates another night. Something's going on that I don't know about. I can feel it, and I don't like it."

His tone softened as he said, "Julie, I know it seems cruel, running off and leaving Mother to die alone, but Sara said she'd never know you were gone, that she probably wouldn't last the night."

Julie sucked in her breath, swallowed the knot of pain, and murmured, "All right, but we can't just keep standing here. Please go somewhere and hide till I can find out what happened to Sara and Lionel. Maybe they did get scared, and they're hiding."

He didn't move, and she threw her arms around him to give him a reassuring hug. "Myles, this is the only way. Now don't worry about me. Virgil has gone to town and won't be back tonight. We can try tomorrow."

He sighed, disgusted and disappointed, knowing there was nothing else to be done. "All right. Can you make it back all right?"

She assured him she could. "I'll send word to you tomorrow. Sara will probably come creeping in sometime tonight, and then I'll find out what happened to frighten her away."

Myles bent forward to kiss her cheek. Just then they heard it . . . the sound of a twig breaking in the stillness. Instantly Myles grabbed Julie and shoved her behind him, then faced the direction of the sound. "Don't move," he whispered, so low she could hardly hear him over her thundering heart.

And then men were coming at them from all directions, stepping out of the woods. Lanterns were being ignited. The cemetery took on an eerie glow, and the faces of the approaching men leered out at them like the ghouls in the stories Lionel had frightened Julie with as a child.

Julie screamed and pressed her face into Myles's back. She wanted to run, but there was no way out of the tightening circle. She turned her head slightly and saw Sheriff Franklin, his fleshy belly bouncing with glee as he walked toward her brother, a handgun pointed straight at him.

She could feel Myles tremble, knew that it was with great effort that he made his voice steady as he said, "All right, Sheriff. You have me. I won't put up a fight. . . ."

"Damned right you won't," someone yelled, and Julie heard the sound of wood splintering against flesh. She clung to Myles as his knees buckled, and they sprawled on the dirt upon their father's grave.

A beefy hand clamped down on Julie's arm and she was jerked to her feet, pulled away as she shrieked and fought to return to Myles's side.

"Now, you just calm down, little lady," Sheriff Franklin was saying. "I told you we'd get him sooner or later. It might have took me awhile, but he's a murderer, and he's got to face the law."

"You call this the law?" She kicked out at his shin, but he jumped back, still struggling to hold her. He twisted her arms painfully behind her back and forced her down to her knees.

And then she saw Virgil coming out of the shadows. "Oh, Julie, dear," he said solicitously, a concerned look pasted on his face. "I was hoping it wasn't true, that my suspicions would not be confirmed."

She hoped the hatred she felt showed in her eyes as she looked up at him in the glow of a lantern. "You filthy animal! You set us up, didn't you? You found out Myles had returned and that I was going to leave with him. So you went and got the sheriff."

His eyes danced with malicious fires, but he kept that pitiful, hurt look on his face. "Julie, I always knew this boy had a hold on you, that you worshipped him because he was your brother, but I had hoped he could not persuade you to desert your dear, dying mother. . . ."

"Don't start your lies in front of these people," she screeched, knowing she sounded like a madwoman but not caring.

Desperately she lifted her face to the sheriff. "Please, you have to believe me. He has raped me repeatedly. That is why I was running away with Myles. Myles never knew about it. He would have killed him if he had. You've got to let us go. Myles will never hurt anyone again. All we want is to go in peace—"

"Why, Julie, I'm surprised at you," the sheriff drawled. "Sayin' such terrible things about your stepdaddy, and him such a fine man. And you know I can't let your brother go. He's got to stand trial for what he did. That's the law. Now you calm down and let your stepdaddy take you back to the house. If your mama is as bad off as I hear tell she is, then you ought to be ashamed of yourself for tryin' to run off. You go back there and do what you can to make her last moments peaceful."

He started to help her to her feet, but she twisted away, crying out for Myles.

"Sheriff, let her go to him," Virgil said with mock compassion. "That boy isn't going anywhere. He's out cold. She'll calm down in a moment."

The sheriff released her, and she crawled through the dirt to clutch at Myles and sob and plead with him to wake up . . . let her know he was not really hurt.

"Now, Sheriff," Virgil went on, quite calmly. "These are unfortunate circumstances. I mean, we're at war, and the boy's mother is dying, and he only came home to try and see her one more time. True, he committed a crime, but you and I both know if you take him into Savannah, a mob will form and storm the jail, and he'll be hung by morning. To them he's not only a Union sympathizer who shot and killed men they considered friends and neighbors, but also one who ran away to join the North—"

"That's a lie!" Julie lifted her head to scream. "He ran away to keep from being lynched, but he never joined the Yankee army. He told me he didn't, and Myles would never lie to me!"

"Be quiet, Julie." Virgil shook his finger at her. "I'm trying to help your brother." Turning back to the sheriff, he said, "Now I should think the people around here would respect my position in the community, including you. Therefore, out of respect for my dear wife, who will soon depart this life, God rest her soul, I must ask that you not take Myles into Savannah."

The sheriff raised his eyebrows. "What in hell you talkin' about? You're the one who come to my office and told me where I could find him!"

"This is quite true; however, I have an alternate plan for his disposal, and I think you will agree with me that it will satisfy everyone. Take Myles to the Confederate Army and turn him in for what he is—a man who was disloyal to his countrymen and went north and joined the enemy. He is, in fact, an enemy of our great Confederacy, and deserves to be treated as such. He will be sent, no doubt, to Richmond, Virginia, and placed in Libby Prison."

Someone snickered, "Hell, from what I hear about the 'Black Hole,' he'd thank you for hangin' him instead of sendin' him there."

"Well . . ." the sheriff pulled thoughtfully at his chin. "I don't know. I should take him in, but like you say, he'd be punished, and he'd be out of the way. There's prisoner swaps goin' on, I hear, but the North wouldn't have him if he's a deserter. They'd rather swap for a decent soldier who got caught fighting for their side, rather than the likes of this traitor. And Libby Prison is a fate worse'n death for some, I'm told."

Virgil smiled. "I'm glad you are an intelligent man. You are wise to keep up good relations with Rose Hill."

The sheriff snapped his fingers and two men stepped forward. "Take the prisoner to the Rebs and turn him over."

"No!" Julie clutched Myles more tightly as the men approached. "No, you won't take him. I won't let you—"

Sobbing and shrieking, she was pulled from him and thrust into Virgil's arms. He jerked her roughly toward the house. "Shut up, you little spitfire," he hissed in her ear. "Shut up, I say, or I'll make you suffer the agonies of the damned."

She continued to fight him, and he threw her to the ground in disgust and whipped around to call out to the sheriff and his men, "Wait up there. I've changed my mind. I think we'll just let you take him on into town and let the mob have him. . . .'"

Julie crawled over to clutch Virgil's leg. "You can't. . . ." she pleaded desperately. "Oh, Virgil, don't, please—they'll kill him. . . ."

"Are you going to get up and go to that house and not give me any more trouble?" He leaned over, his breath hot and ragged on her tear-streaked face. "I can have him killed with the snap of a finger, you bitch. You're going to learn, one way or the other, that I am your master, and you will bend to my will forever!

"Well? What's it going to be?" He kicked at her, sending her sprawling, face down, in the dirt. "Hurry up. The men want to leave."

She reached out, her fingers clawing at the red clay, squeezing and mashing it. How she wished it were Virgil's soul, and she was tearing it from his evil body. To return with him meant submitting to him endlessly. Death would be sweeter. But at least she could try to escape later. For now, there was nothing to be done but save Myles's life at any cost.

"All right," she said finally, with cold resignation. Slowly

she stood, lifting her chin in defiance as she faced the man
she had come to hate with every drop of blood that flowed
in her veins. "All right, Virgil. Tell them to take him to the
prison in Richmond, and I will go with you and do as you
wish."

"Good!" He grinned, his face grotesquely yellow in the
glow of the lanterns behind them. He turned and gave his
orders, then grasped her about her waist and led her
toward the house. He squeezed her breasts painfully, but
she did not cry out.

Damn him, she thought, gritting her teeth, *damn him
to hell. He can kill me, but I'll never cry out to him
again.*

When they were out of sight of the others, he bent and
ran his hands up under her dress, probing between her
thighs with his grubby fingers. She stood rigid, like the
marble statues in the foyer of Rose Hill.

"Ah, I'll make you grovel and groan and beg for it," he
said hotly, and she could feel him trembling with eagerness. "As soon as we get inside, we'll go to my room, and
I'll take you in a new way I've thought of. Oh, it might
hurt you a bit, but you'll like it. I know you will. . . ."

They continued walking. When they reached the slaves'
quarters, Julie could see the dim glow of candles from
within the shacks. "Sara . . ." she said in a dull voice.
"What did you do with her? And Lionel?"

"Don't worry. They're all right. When they realized they
had been discovered, they were only too glad to get out of
there. I sent Lionel to his cabin and told Sara to get to the
house when she saw you leave, to stay with your mother."
He made a clucking sound of disapproval. "What would
people think? Leaving her alone when she's dying?"

"That's all you care about—what other people think. As
long as they don't find out the truth about what a devil
you are, you'll stoop to any depths to get what you want."

"Exactly," he laughed. "And you, my love, are going
to discover just how cruel I can really be. When I'm
through with you this night, you will creep to your bed
and rue the day you ever dared to cross me. And I suggest
you give very serious thought to the proposal of marriage
I've made to you, because I've no intention of seeing you
leave here. If you try, I'll use my influence to have your
brother killed."

They reached the porch, and just then the wide doors

were flung open. From within, the glowing lights illuminated Sara's large frame. She stood there, chest heaving and eyes wide, holding the doors open with arms outstretched above her head.

"What is wrong with you, Sara?" Virgil snapped. "Get back inside and calm yourself down, or I'll punish you severely for taking part in this little escapade tonight. . . ."

Sara was gasping for breath, her eyes brimming with tears as she met Julie's questioning gaze. "She's gone. Your mama is gone—" she cried.

Julie did not weep. Lifting her head high, she moved forward as Sara stepped back to let her enter. With quick, sure steps, she hurried to the curving stairs. Behind her, Virgil was snapping at Sara to stop her sniveling and make the necessary funeral preparations.

Julie reached the second level and continued straight to her mother's room. The door was partially open, and she gave it a quick shove, then stepped inside.

Her mother lay there looking just as peaceful as when Julie had left her earlier, except that her eyes were open, staring blankly upward. There was a great roaring in Julie's ears as she went to the bedside and stared down, her heart heavy. She should close the eyes. But how? She had to do something about those staring yet unseeing eyes. Shuddering, she reached out with trembling fingers to draw the covers up and over her mother's face.

Still she did not cry. Tears were for sorrow, and how could she be sorry that her mother would not suffer at the hands of Virgil Oates? The lifeless body beneath the covers was far better off than she.

For her misery had hardly begun.

❦ Chapter Sixteen ❧

SARA knew what to do to ready Julie's mother for burial. First she summoned Lionel to find the washing board, a piece of wood shaped like a table top, on which the body would be prepared for burial. "The board will be wherever the last death was," Sara told Lionel, for it was community property, used by a family as it was needed, then put away to await the next death.

"That'd be the Peele family, over by the swamp. Mistah Durwood, he passed on a few weeks ago. Ain't heard of nobody dyin' since."

"Well, go along and get it," Sara said wearily. "Knowin' your mother, she wouldn't like to be washed on a board what ever'body else gets washed on, but they ain't time to make another. I reckon she should'a thought o' that 'fore it was too late."

From the kitchen doorway, Julie spoke. "You are right, Sara. Mother would not want to be washed and dressed on a board used by just anyone. She was very prim about such things, you know."

Sara looked at the girl with the gray-shadowed eyes whose stringy hair hung wildly about her gaunt face. "Miz Julie, it don't matter, chile," she said compassionately, her heart going out to the girl. The good Lord was really heaping burdens on Julie's shoulders, and Sara wondered just how much more her mistress could carry. "You go lie down and get some sleep. Lionel's gonna stop by the church and ring the bell to let folks know. He done rung it out back. Ever'body'll start comin' at daylight. You gonna have to speak to 'em. I'll take care of yo' mama and have

221

her all ready by the time they starts gettin' here. And I'll get some bakin' done. I can manage. You run along now."

"No!" Julie said sharply, straightening. "I will help dress my mother, Sara." She looked at Lionel and snapped, "Go to the barn, or wherever you can find a door, and rip it down and set it up in my mother's room. She'll be prepared there."

Lionel looked at Sara, who nodded, conveying the message with her eyes that there was no point in arguing with the girl once her mind was made up.

"You heat some water, and I will go up and find something suitable to dress her in. We'll need help, of course. Get some of the women in to start on the baking. I want more than pies and cakes. I want hens dressed and roasted. I want a hog slaughtered and cooked over the pit. Lionel will ride into Savannah and get the finest coffin available from Mr. William Culpepper, the undertaker."

Sara sighed, her heart going out to the tiny young woman who was making such an effort to be strong. "Miz Julie, you sure you want all these fixin's? I mean, the way things are with Mistah Virgil and all . . . and Mastah Myles bein' captured . . . wouldn't it be best to just get it all over with as quick as we can?"

Julie slammed both palms on the kitchen table, her face reddening as she cried, "My mother made Rose Hill into the most prosperous plantation in all of Savannah, Sara. Before the damned war came to eat away at her success, she was a proud, refined woman. And that is the kind of funeral she will have, with all the respect given to her that she deserves."

"Yes'm. Whatever you say. I'll just bet if we'd 'a gotten away last night, Mistah Virgil, he'd of just dumped her in a hole in the ground without a word said over her by no man of God, even. Maybe it was meant to happen this way, so she'd get a decent buryin', but it sho is sad about Mastah Myles, and you havin' to stay here—"

"Oh, I'm not staying here," Julie looked at her incredulously, "and neither are you and Lionel. We will bury my mother tomorrow, after proper respects have been shown to her by the people of Savannah, and then we are leaving. Lionel will again load a wagon and hide it deeper in the woods this time, and no one will stop us from leaving."

Sara looked about fearfully, as though at any moment

she expected to see Virgil appear from wherever he was eavesdropping.

"You needn't look so scared, Sara. Virgil has gone to get the parson. He's playing the role of the bereaved husband."

"But how you gonna leave, Miz Julie?" the old Negress said worriedly. "He ain't gonna let you. . . ."

Let me, indeed! Julie fumed. Oh, she was sick of having other people and other influences dominate her life. She was going to plunge ahead and face whatever lay ahead. For the first time, she felt she knew the same emotion as Derek when he took that step from the plank into the shark-infested waters. She was not as strong as he—few men could even hold claim to *that*—but she could make up for lack of size with her womanly attributes. And while she was not plunging into dangerous seas with her hands tied behind her back, many perils lay ahead. If she were cunning enough, she could handle them, just as she was almost confident now that Derek had survived.

A smile touched her lips. She *felt* it. There was a stirring deep within that told her somehow, by God, Derek Arnhardt lived! Would he help her? He *had* to!

Sara asked hesitantly, "Miz Julie, you all right? You looks funny to me. . . ."

The smile spread into a wide grin. "Sara, I'm fine. You leave everything to me. Mother is dead now, and I don't have to take Virgil's abuse any longer. Perhaps I never should've, but at least Mother died in peace. She didn't drop dead of shock at finding out her husband was raping her daughter. And now I don't intend to remain in this house one night after she is in the ground. This," she said tremulously, "I swear on my mother's soul!"

"He ain't gonna let you leave," Sara exploded, fear etched on her face. "That's one mean man, and he ain't gonna let you go, I tells you. You see what he had done to Mastah Myles—had him sent off to that prison up in Virginny—"

"Follow my instructions, please, and don't argue. We'll bury Mother tomorrow afternoon. Tell Lionel to have the grave dug. I want her placed to the right of my father. That's a sunny spot, too. . . ."

Julie shook her head. Exhaustion was creeping into every bone, every pore. "I'm going to find something to dress her in."

"She's got buryin' clothes," Sara said quickly. Julie turned to look at her, puzzled, and the older woman hurried to explain. "You been kept from some of the sad parts of life, chile, and you may not know it, but folks keeps buryin' clothes put back—nice things they have made special to be buried in. I know where your mama's are. I'll fetch 'em after we get her washed."

Julie hurried through the still house, noticing that someone had gone around and stopped all the clocks to mark the hour of her mother's death. She frowned when she saw that the mirrors had been covered with sheets. This was a superstition she did not believe in: that the spirit of the departed still lurks about, and if it sees itself in a mirror, it will be hindered from going on to another life in the hereafter. Julie sighed. If others believed in such notions, and it made them feel better, so be it.

It was not long before Lionel brought a door he had removed from inside the barn and Sara came with a kettle of hot water. Julie watched as they lifted her mother, still covered by a sheet, from the bed and placed her cold, stiffening body upon the wooden slab. When Lionel left to see to the grave digging, they removed the sheet and began washing the body.

"I can't stand them eyes a-starin'," Sara said suddenly. "Get some coins."

"Coins?" Julie blinked. Sara nodded, and Julie went to her mother's jewelry chest, where a little money was always kept. She brought the coins to Sara, then watched as Sara closed the sightless eyes and placed the coins on top to keep them shut.

Sara found the burying dress, a severely styled garment of gray linen, void of ornaments, with a high neck and long cuffed sleeves. Together they struggled to put the clothing on the body, then Julie labored to brush her mother's hair and fashion it at the nape of her neck in a neatly braided bun.

There was a noise in the hall, then Lionel was calling up to say that Mr. Culpepper had arrived with the coffin. "We're ready," Julie said, a lump in her throat. So far she was handling herself well, keeping one thought burning in her mind through all the sorrow that mingled there: *keep moving—it will all be over soon.*

Mr. Culpepper entered, a tall, spindly man with a

hooked nose and beady eyes. He wrapped long, bony fingers together and spoke in a voice that sounded as though it were echoing in a tomb. "You have prepared the deceased?" he asked.

Julie nodded, then stepped back as he and Lionel carried in the plain wooden coffin and set it on the floor, then gingerly lifted her mother's body from the washing board and placed her in it.

Sara went to her mistress's wardrobe and brought back packets of crushed rose petals that had been used to make her lingerie smell sweet. These she placed along the sides of the casket. Mr. Culpepper folded Julie's mother's hands across her chest, then motioned to Lionel that he was ready to take her downstairs.

"I told Annie Bell to fix up the parlor," Sara said as she and Julie followed the procession down the stairs.

They entered the room, and Mr. Culpepper and Lionel took the coffin to the spot beneath the heavily-draped window, where two straight-back chairs waited to hold it. At each end of the coffin, Sara lit candles and placed them so their illumination would cast a peaceful glow on her dead mistress's face.

Lionel left to return to the grave digging, and Sara went to oversee the goings-on in the kitchen. Julie excused herself to go to her room and change into a proper dress. She was crossing the foyer when the front doors opened, and she found herself staring into Virgil's sparkling eyes. He had brought the parson, who quickly stepped forward to clasp her hand warmly and offer his sympathies.

Thanking him, Julie said she wanted the service that afternoon. "Of course," he murmured. "We will send runners to spread the word. Is three o'clock agreeable?"

She looked beyond him, through the long, narrow windows on either side of the doors. The sky was getting light. Soon it would be dawn. "Yes. Three will be fine. The servants have their instructions. Now, if you will excuse me—"

Virgil stepped forward. "Julie, I would like a word with you—"

She turned frosty eyes on him that made him stop in his tracks. "I have nothing to say to you, Virgil. This house is in mourning. Excuse me."

She was aware of the puzzled glance the parson gave

her, but she hurried on her way. Virgil Oates would not touch her again! This she had vowed, and nothing was going to prevent her from keeping her word, even if it meant *dying*.

By mid-morning, the circular drive in front of the mansion house was crowded with buggies and wagons. Grooms wandered about the lawn talking with each other, while their masters remained inside to pay their respects and attend the afternoon funeral services. It was a cold day, and the sky was gray and overcast, with a hint of rain. Julie peered out and wished she had set the time for the service even earlier, for darkness would come sooner than usual with the threatening weather bearing down upon them.

The house smelled of fresh-baked goods and hot vegetables. People had brought food in covered dishes, and the dining room table was laden with it. Sara and the other house servants were kept busy bringing tea and coffee and constantly washing dishes.

The atmosphere in the parlor was somber, and Julie gave Virgil a glance of contempt each time she entered the room. He sat in a chair next to the casket, playing the role of the bereaved husband. Once she nearly gagged when she heard him murmur to a solicitous neighbor, "If it weren't for Julie, I could not have made it through these weeks. She has been the light of my life. She's so much like her mother, God rest her soul. . . ."

But the atmosphere in the other rooms was quite different. There the men talked of the war. Some still exulted over the December thirteenth battle on the heights overlooking Fredericksburg, Virginia, when the Federal General Ambrose E. Burnside had ordered six grand assaults against General Robert E. Lee's entrenched army. The result was useless slaughter, and some said Burnside had wept over the killing and wounding of ten thousand of his men. Lee had lost less than half that many.

The damned war, Julie swore, as she moved through the crowd. Soon she would be out of all of it. She and Myles would go west and start a new life, and they could turn their backs forever on all this grief and suffering.

Glancing up, she saw Sara motioning to her from the rear hallway. She followed the servant to the little sunroom at the back of the house. As soon as the door closed behind them, Sara asked, "Miz Julie, you sure you gonna want to leave tonight? Lionel's scared Mistah Virgil gonna be suspectin' something. He done said we gonna get a beatin' for what we did last night, after all this is over with, and if'n he thinks we gonna try it again, he might just shoot us. . . ."

"He would be least suspicious tonight of all nights. He thinks I'm too grief-stricken over both Mother and Myles to make any plans to run away so soon. We must leave tonight. We have to get to Wilmington without delay."

Sara blinked. "Wilmin'ton? What for? I heard they took Mastah Myles to Richmond. You ain't goin' there an' try to see him, is you? Won't be no need, nohow. Thing fo' you to do is just run and get as far from that sinful man in there as you can, Miz Julie. Run from the devil hisself, that's what you do!"

"I'm going to Wilmington to find Captain Arnhardt—"

"Arnhardt?" Sara cried, stunned. "You tol' me—"

"I know what I told you, but I also know the man, Sara, and I have a feeling that he escaped. He's not like other men. He's strong, both in spirit and in body. Oh, you'd never understand. But we are going to Wilmington and somehow, we'll find him, and he'll help me."

"If'n he *is* alive, how do you know he'd help you?" Sara looked at her suspiciously. "You ain't got time to dig up none o' that silver and jewelry to pay him with. And he's after money. Ain't that why he held you for ransom?"

A warmth moved through Julie's body. She wondered if that were the real reason. Perhaps at first it had been, but after awhile, when it became obvious no ransom would be paid, he had not been anxious to be rid of her. "Let me worry about that, Sara. Now I must get back to our guests. If Virgil sees us talking this way, he *will* get suspicious."

She turned to go, but Sara called out to her worriedly. "They is somethin' else, Miz Julie. Me and Lionel, we afraid. If'n somethin' happened to you, folks'd say we run away. He's got a brother, a free man, what works on a farm up in a place called Pennsylvania. Lionel say he knows right where it is. If'n we could go there—"

"Of course, Sara," Julie said without hesitation. True, she would miss the two Negroes, who had been a part of her life for as long as she could remember, but she acknowledged that they too had a right to pursue happiness. "I'll sign papers stating that you are free, and you can make your way north. There should be no problem. Lionel is too old to worry about conscription once he crosses the Mason-Dixon line. And you're getting on in years. I doubt anyone would try to make a slave of you again."

Returning to the front of the house, Julie, nodding and saying the appropriate words, graciously accepted condolences from those who had just arrived. All the while, she was wishing time would pass quickly so she could escape.

"We really would have liked to wait longer to bury her," she heard Virgil saying in that mock mournful tone he had so quickly acquired. "It's a tragedy, but she wasted away. She was sick for so long, you know. Julie and I discussed it and decided it would be best to put her to rest as quickly as possible."

Julie glared at him to let him know she could hear his lies. *She* had made the decision to have the funeral as soon as possible, not he—and that was so she could be on her way. Only he did not know that yet, and, she hoped, would not till she was safely gone.

Now and then Julie would glance toward her mother's coffin, silently offering a prayer of thanksgiving that she had never known what a defiled spawn of Satan she had really married.

"It's such a shame about Myles,'" someone said. The voice came from the parlor, and Julie paused on her way to the kitchen to listen. "After coming all the way back to visit his mother, only to be captured. Did he get to see her before she died?"

"Unfortunately, no," Virgil answered, his voice oozing pity.

Pharisee! she wanted to scream out at him for everyone to hear and know what he really was.

"Myles is my stepson, you know," Virgil went on, "but he was wanted by the law, and I couldn't stand the thought of him being hunted for the rest of his life, perhaps being hung by vigilantes. I did what I felt was best for all concerned and informed the sheriff that I suspected he was lurking about."

His listener gushed, "Oh, that must have been a very difficult thing for you to do, sir. You are to be commended for having the courage."

She could see Virgil in her mind's eye, belly thrown out, head held high, probably with a cigar in one hand and a snifter of brandy in the other.

"Well, I did persuade the sheriff to turn him over to the Confederates. As high as the feelings in town have been against the boy, I knew he'd never make it to trial. Why, he'd be lying in a coffin next to his dear mother here."

"Possibly. The riffraff of the waterfront can be a surly lot, and I've heard they were still after Myles. I wonder what the Confederate authorities will do with him."

"Well, he did run from the South to fight for the North. Obviously he deserted the Yankee army. The Confederates will send him to Libby prison in Richmond, where he'll likely be for however long the war lasts. The Yankees won't want him in a prisoner exchange, not if he deserted them."

"Oh, but Libby prison, sir," the man gasped. "They call it the Black Hole. The tales I have heard about that place are atrocious. They say our soldiers despised Major General John Pope for his antagonistic attitudes toward Southern civilians, so they're determined to vent their hatred on prisoners from his army particularly—but every prisoner there suffers. As well they should, being Yankees. Do not misunderstand me. . . ."

Julie listened in horror as the man went on to describe what he had heard about the prison; and with each word, she knew she had to move as fast as she could to get Myles out of that place. He told how the prisoners arrived in cattle cars, packed in tightly and covered in manure by the time they arrived. Then they were marched through the streets, amidst jeers and taunts, on their way to the Tobacco Warehouse Prison. Deserters, idiots, lunatics, thieves, murderers—all were packed in together with barely space to lie down.

He described tales he'd heard of the floor being over an inch deep in greasy slime, and a horrible odor permeating the air from the open privy which was used by all. And the walls, he added, were smeared from the floors on up with the slops and excretions of the hundreds of other prisoners housed up there.

"Well, you can't expect better for a stinking Yankee." A third voice joined the conversation. "And with all due respect, sir, the boy's a traitor to the South!"

Julie could not bear to listen to such drivel any longer. She moved swiftly into the parlor, where the three men looked up at her in surprise. She did not have to ask who had spoken last, for when she recognized Thad Parkland, a deacon in the church who took it upon himself to sit in judgment on everyone, there was no doubt in her mind that he had made such a remark.

"I will ask you to leave this house," she said tightly, struggling to keep her voice low, her anger in check. "I will not have you speak of my brother in that manner, and I should think you would have some respect for the dead. Go now. This is a day of mourning."

Several people standing about overheard Julie's remarks and gasped with surprise. Virgil's eyes bulged as he cried, aghast, "Julie—what is the meaning of this?"

"If you do not leave," she continued to glare at Thad Parkland, "I will call a servant and have you thrown out. Now, do you wish to make a scene?"

"You have already made one, Miss Marshal," Parkland said curtly. Turning to Virgil, he bowed slightly and murmured, "My sympathies, sir."

Everyone in the parlor followed him to the front door, buzzing among themselves and glancing back nervously at Julie.

Virgil reached out and clutched her arm so tightly that Julie winced with pain. He had turned his back on the crowd, shielding them from the view of the others. "Julie, how could you do such a thing? Thad Parkland is one of the most prominent men in the community—"

"He's a sanctimonious pharisee, and I would've attempted to throw him out of this house myself had he not gone willingly. It's quite enough that *you* are here, for you're the most damnable hypocrite of the lot! To think what you have done to my mother, my brother, and to me." She jerked her arm away, taking him by surprise; freeing herself, she stepped back. "I wish it were *you* in that coffin, Virgil Oates! And if you ever try to touch me again, I will see you in your grave!"

A few people closest to the parlor heard and turned their heads to stare. Virgil's face colored as he gave them a nervous smile and murmured, "The girl is grief-stricken. Pay no heed, please." With lowered voice he whispered to Julie, "You go to your room at once and remain there

SOULS AFLAME231

until the hour of the funeral. And remember, how long that bastard brother of yours lives depends on how you behave."

It took every ounce of self-control for Julie to walk out of the room. How she wanted to strike him . . . cursing and screaming for everyone to hear. But this was not the time. No, there were long hours to be endured before she could leave, and if things were to go smoothly, she would have to force herself to remain calm.

Nervously she paced about in her room, anxious for time to pass so she could be on her way. And all the while, she was reminding herself that she must face the possibility that Derek might not be in Wilmington. Perhaps he was somewhere between the port and Bermuda. Though his ship had been destroyed, he might be on another. How could she hope to find him?

In any case, she refused to let herself think he was dead. No, he was alive. He *had* to be. She would find out more once she arrived in Wilmington. Surely there would be a headquarters of some kind where blockade runners would be listed, crewmen and officers. Maybe she could locate someone who had been on the *Ariane.*

Sara's voice brought her back to the agony of the present. "Miz Julie, the parson says it's time."

Quickly opening her door, Julie stepped into the hallway and whispered, "We must succeed tonight, Sara. Is everything ready for us to leave? We won't get a second chance."

"Yes'm. Everything was done just like you said to do it. Now you better get along downstairs, 'cause ever'body is waitin' fo' you."

Julie led the way nervously, her whole body trembling with the fear that ran through her veins. Pausing at the top of the stairs, she was stunned to see the swelling crowd below. Not only was the parlor filled to overflowing, but so were the other rooms and the hallway as well. She stiffened as Virgil hurried up the steps solicitously to take her arm and lead her to her place near the coffin.

As the parson read from the Bible, Julie kept her eyes on her mother's stark white face. To think she had devoted her life to making this place so prosperous, only to lose it to such an unscrupulous man as Virgil. Shaking her head and biting her lip, Julie fought once again for control in

order to keep from raging at the heavens above. It was not
fair. Dear God, none of it was fair.

The procession formed behind the wooden cart carrying
the coffin and made its way to the cemetery. Virgil kept
his hand clamped on Julie's arm, squeezing even tighter
when they reached the spot where Myles had been captured. She stared down at the earth covering her father's
grave and wondered if anyone else would notice that it
had been disturbed.

The casket bearing her mother's body was laid in the
gaping hole in the ground, and then the parson was murmuring words she did not hear, and people were singing
hymns that escaped her memory. She could only stand
there mutely, stiffly, thinking ahead to the hour when she
could leave.

It was over. People were departing. Virgil released her,
to accept more words of sympathy. Playing his role to the
hilt, she thought with disgust.

Suddenly she heard her name called out. Turning, she
found herself staring into the sad eyes of Adelia Carrigan.
Of course she would come to the funeral, but Julie had not
thought of the possibility, or prepared herself for the even-
tuality of their meeting. Now she found it difficult to keep
from turning and running. This was the last woman on
earth she wanted to see.

"I am so dreadfully sorry, dear," Adelia murmured in a
soft, gentle voice, her hand extended.

Julie had no choice but to touch fingers with her. No
point in making a scene. Not now. "Thank you, Aunt
Adelia. It was nice of you to come."

"Please, if there's anything I can do, or my children—" she began, but Julie interrupted.

"No, there's nothing anyone can do. Mother is out of
her misery now. She won't suffer any longer. Now if you'll
excuse me, it's been a trying day, and I'd like to lie
down." She did turn away then, unable to bear the woman's presence any longer. There was so much more she
wished she could say to her, but it was not her place to
judge. Julie had spent too many years feeling bitter as it
was.

"Julie, wait. There's something I'd like to say. I . . . I
heard about Myles—" She sounded nervous.

Julie turned back, surprised. "Yes, I suppose everyone
has heard by now."

"Well, I didn't know if you knew or not, but Thomas is one of the officers at Libby prison," she said anxiously, hands clasped together to stop their trembling. "I heard your stepfather asked that he be turned over to the Confederacy. I expect Libby is where he'll be sent. I just wanted you to know that I plan to write to Thomas, so he'll be aware of what's going on. He says the prison is terribly crowded, but if he knows Miles is there, I'm sure he'll look for him."

"That's nice of you. . . ."

"Now, I can't promise Thomas can treat him any differently from the other prisoners, but they are cousins, and I just wanted to let you know I'll get word to him right away."

Julie was finding it difficult to contain her excitement. Not only was it highly likely that Thomas could make life easier for Miles, but there was a good possibility that he could help her get him out of that horrid place.

"Thank you, Aunt Adelia," she said, lips trembling. "Thank you very much." And then she turned and hurried toward the house, lifting her skirts so that she could scurry quickly across the red Georgia clay. She still despised the woman for what she had done with her father, but this day Adelia had done her family a great service.

Julie found the kitchen empty. The servants had gone to the grave and were singing gospel songs while it was being covered and the guests were leaving.

Quickly she looked around and found what she was after: a short-bladed butcher knife that could be easily concealed. She had just slipped it inside her high-topped shoe when she heard footsteps coming across the back porch. She straightened, and was smoothing her skirt as the door opened and Virgil walked in, frowning.

"I saw you running this way and thought perhaps you were ill."

"No, I'm quite all right, but don't concern yourself with me," she snapped. "What I do is no business of yours."

His voice was like a whip in the silent house. "I challenge that statement. I'm the undisputed master of this household now, and I have supreme rule over all that goes on."

"Not with me, you don't."

He took a step forward, then hesitated. "You're going to marry me, Julie. I'll give you a decent period to grieve, but then we'll plan our wedding. No one will be surprised. They all knew it was you I was courting in the first place, so it's only natural we marry now. So do your mourning and then make ready for our wedding."

"Marry you?" Her eyes flicked over him contemptuously. "I'd sooner die!"

She ran from the kitchen as he yelled after her, "You'll be sorry you said that. You're going to learn to show me some respect around here. . . ."

The sound of his voice faded as she hurried through the house and made her way to her room, slamming the door behind her. Outside a light, cold drizzle had begun to fall. The gray shroud that was enveloping the land would make darkness come even earlier.

She changed from her black bombazine dress to a simple woolen garment that would be warm and comfortable for travel. Then she began to count the hours till her escape.

Sara brought Julie a supper tray of warmed-over stew, a fried potato pie, grits, and hot tea. She was so nervous and jittery that Julie gently chided her, saying she would give everything away if she did not get hold of herself. "Virgil shouldn't suspect anything tonight, of all nights. He thinks I'm too grief-stricken to make plans to leave just now. And the weather outside is turning raw, too. But if he sees you behaving as you are now, he's sure to figure out something is up."

"Yes'm. I'll try. I'm fixin' to give him his supper, even though he says he don't want nothin'. Some o' the folks wanted to stay, but he tol' 'em he just wanted to be left alone with his sorrow." She snorted. "The only thing he's sorry about is that she didn't die before now. And he's a-drinkin', too. Hard liquor. He's a-sittin' in the library guzzlin' it down and starin' at the fire and mumblin' to hisself. It's gonna seem like fo'ever till midnight, Miz Julie. I just knows it is."

"I know. Let's just hope he passes out drunk. Now you be sure you and Lionel are in that wagon and ready to leave the second I get there. We're going to have to travel hard and fast and put much distance between Rose Hill and us, no matter what kind of weather we run into. We can't fail now."

Alone again, she wandered about in the dark room until

she grew weary. Then she lay down on the bed to wait until the appointed hour. The clocks had been restarted, and each time the chimes tolled, she held her breath and counted.

There was an eeriness in the air that made her flesh crawl, as though the house were a living, breathing thing, waiting for something to erupt within its very soul.

She was tired. She had had no sleep the night before, and the day had been exhausting. It would be so easy to fall into slumber, but she could not allow herself. The hour of departure was too near.

Something made a clicking sound.

Sitting straight up, her spine rigid with fear, she stared into the darkness. Was it her imagination or had she really heard the doorknob turn?

Suddenly the door banged loudly against the wall, and her hands flew to her throat, stifling her scream of terror. Virgil was in the room. She could not see him, but she knew it was him.

"Don't you come near me—" she heard her voice warble, hating its frightened sound. She had to be brave. "I'm warning you, Virgil. Don't try to touch me again—"

"Ah, you beauteous bitch, you've been waiting for me." The words were slurred. He was drunk. "Are you naked, my love? Are you waiting for me with parted thighs and eager loins?"

Quickly she yanked up her dress, reaching for the knife she had tucked into her shoe. Her trembling fingers wrapped about the handle, she slid from the bed, backing toward the doors leading to the balcony. "I'm warning you, Virgil. Get out of here! Now!"

He laughed—an evil, maniacal sound. "I've come to take what's mine." He lunged for her in the darkness, and she was caught off balance by the sudden movement. The knife slipped from her grasp. He wrestled her to the floor as she groped frantically for the weapon. His lips were covering her face with wet, eager kisses as his hands fondled her wildly.

Twisting, turning, she struggled to keep her hands free and upon the floor. Where was the knife? Dear God, she could not suffer one more night in his arms!

"You're mine!" he shrieked, fighting to hold her beneath him. "All mine . . . forever . . ."

Her fingers touched the cold steel blade. She had the knife in her hand and brought it plunging downward, feeling the sickening thud as flesh parted. Virgil screamed in agony and lurched to one side. Quickly she scrambled to her feet. The knife was still imbedded in his body. Where, she did not know, and she could only hope he was wounded badly enough that he could not stop her from escaping now.

"You cut me!" he screamed, thrashing about wildly, hands reaching out for her in the blackness. "I'll kill you for this. I'll fix you so no man will ever want you. . . ."

She tripped and fell to the floor, then scrambled up again and felt her way along. He was groaning—but struggling, she knew, to come after her. Once she found the door, she groped along the walls, moving her legs as fast as she dared. Reaching the stairs, she clung to the bannister, heart pounding and brain thundering as she hurried down. Escape. She had to escape.

"Julie—" he was out of the room, fighting to make it down the hall. Then she heard him falling. He gave one last moan, then there was only silence.

Bolting through the house, she ran out the front door, across the lawn, and around to the rear. Icy rain pelted down, and she realized dimly that she wore no shawl. It was very cold. But no matter. She was on her way, thank God.

Tearing through the woods, she took a short cut to where the wagon waited. Bursting into the clearing, she began to laugh and cry all at once as she heard Lionel's voice. "Miz Julie, is he after you? Oh, Lordy, he's gonna kill us all—"

He could not make out her face in the darkness, but he could distinguish her figure. She felt his hands reaching for her, and she threw herself toward him. "Help me onto the wagon. I stabbed him. I don't know how badly he's hurt, but for the moment we're one step ahead of him. Hurry. . . ."

Sara wailed, and Lionel yelled for her to be quiet. He slung Julie up onto the wagon, not taking the time to be gentle. Then he leaped to the driver's seat and gave the mules full rein, popping the whip across their backs to urge them on.

Julie clung to Sara as they bounced and jostled in the wagon.

"Is we gonna make it?" the old Negro woman kept moaning. "Is we gonna get away?"

"With God's help, Sara," Julie whispered, breathing a bit easier with every passing second. "With God's help, we will."

✺ Chapter Seventeen ✺

JULIE's chin trembled as she lifted her head and fought to retain her composure while she moved through the throngs of jostling, drunken men. They seemed to be everywhere, swarming down upon the staid old town of Wilmington like crazed wasps without a home. She had been in the city only two days, having been forced to take shelter in a barn, along with Sara and Lionel. They had no money for a hotel room, even if one could be found, and the two faithful Negroes refused to leave her until she found someone to help her.

She prayed that someone would be Derek.

The old woman who had agreed to give them shelter had warned Julie of the terrible conditions that surrounded them. "The town has just turned topsy-turvy," Pearl Watson said with disdain. "Speculators from all parts of the South wait around to go to the weekly auctions of imported cargo, and the town is infested with rogues and desperadoes who make their living by robbing and killing."

She went on to say that it was not safe to go out at night anywhere, and there had even been shootings and knifings on the streets in the daytime. "Between the crews of the steamers in port and the soldiers stationed here, there's always something going on. There's been plenty of bodies found floating in the water around the docks, and the civil authorities can't, or won't, do anything to try and control the situation."

Julie also heard how many of the permanent residents of Wilmington had moved elsewhere, letting their houses

to those who could afford enormously inflated prices, usually the agents and employees of blockade-running companies. "Those who stay, like me," Pearl explained resent-
fully, "who can't afford to leave and ain't got no place to
go anyway, stay inside as much as possible. You seldom
see a lady on the streets, believe me."

The morning Julie set out for the Office of Orders and
Details, Pearl was aghast. "You just can't do it, child. You
can't go walking down to the waterfront."

"I have to," Julie tried to explain. "I talked with a
soldier passing by the house yesterday, and he told me that
the office was established to handle all orders and assign-
ments for pilots and signal officers. He said he had never
heard of a Captain Arnhardt, but that if his ship had been
destroyed, and he was an experienced pilot, he would be
registered with the Orders and Detail office. So that's
where I must go to locate him."

"But you said you didn't even know if he was alive,"
Pearl argued.

"I can't just sit here, can I? My purpose in coming to
Wilmington was to try and find the one person I felt had
the courage to help me. And if I find out he *is* dead, or he
says he won't help me, then I'll just have to find another
way, because I have to get my brother out of that
prison—" Her voice broke, and she glanced away quickly,
blinking back tears.

So she made her way through the streets, ignoring the
crude remarks and hungry leers. Once a drunk grabbed at
her skirt, ripping it as she twisted away frantically. She
began to walk even faster, wishing it had not been necessary to sell the wagon and mules when they arrived in
Wilmington. It would have been better had she not been
forced to walk, but with no money for food, they had had
no choice except to sell the animals.

Suddenly a fight erupted in a crowd through which Julie
was about to pass. Trying to avoid the melee, she turned
down a nearby alley, not knowing where it would take her,
but wanting to escape trouble, if possible.

"Well, well, what we got here?"

Terror gripped her as she saw two bedraggled men
struggling to their feet. They had been sitting in the shadows, drinking, and as soon as Julie saw them, she turned
to run back toward the street. But they were too fast for

her. One grabbed her, slinging her to the ground, and her screams only made them laugh as they fell together on top of her thrashing body.

". . . been wantin' some . . ." one of them said huskily, as he struggled to pin her arms beneath her. ". . . And here you come, just prissin' along like some fine lady."

"Hey, hurry and get her dress up," the other panted. "I know it's gonna be some sweet stuff. Ain't she a pretty thing, though?"

Julie did not see another man rising from the shadows further down the alley, nor could she see the long stick he carried with a sharp nail protruding from its end. He moved swiftly, knocking her first attacker from her with one swift blow to the back of his head, then smashing the other across the face. With blood streaming down, the second man ran toward the street. The other lay on the ground, not moving.

Julie shrank away, trembling with fright over what lay ahead. This man would rape her . . . she knew it. . . . He had beaten off his friends because he wanted her all to himself. And then he would kill her, and there would be no one left to give a damn what happened to Myles. Her scream was low and piercing, like that of a dying animal. . . .

"Please don't be frightened," he said suddenly, gently, kneeling beside her. "Are you all right? Don't worry. I'm not going to hurt you. My, you are a lovely thing. What ever are you doing back here in an alley?"

She stared at him in silent confusion, praying he was telling the truth, that he intended her no harm. Nonetheless she remained on her guard.

He laughed softly. "I see. You don't trust me, do you? Even after I saved you from those two rogues! Well, allow me to introduce myself. My name is Harley Beaumont, and I'm a soldier in the Confederate army. I'm on leave. Now, I know you don't think me much of a gentleman, sitting back in an alley and having a drink or two, but it does get rowdy in those saloons. I felt I was safer here. So!" He took a deep breath and gave her a warm smile. "Suppose you tell me *your* story now that I've told you mine. I assure you I mean you no harm."

She eyed him warily. He was perhaps the same age as she, and while not handsome, he could hardly be considered repulsive. He had dark eyes, a ruddy complexion, and thin, straight lips. Despite his friendly overture, there was something indefinably sinister about his facial expression, and she still did not wholly trust him.

She saw no harm in telling him her name, however, or her mission. He listened, nodding now and then, and finally he got to his feet and pulled her up. "Now, are you sure you're all right? You weren't injured when they threw you to the ground?"

"No. I may have a few bruises, but nothing compared to my eventual injuries had you not intervened." She forced a smile. "I do thank you, Mr. Beaumont. Now if you'll excuse me, I do have to be on my way."

"Call me Harley. I intend to call you Julie, if I may. And I would like to escort you to the Orders and Details office. I think by now you realize it just isn't safe to be on the street."

They stepped out of the alley. Julie saw that the fight she had fled from earlier had ended, but there were still mobs gathering about. She would have liked to take leave of her new-found acquaintance, but the idea of continuing on her way unescorted was not appealing. "Very well, Harley. I accept your kind offer, though I don't know why you should bother with me. You've done enough already, and I can never repay you—"

He tucked her hand in the crook of his arm and murmured, "Don't worry about that. I've been rather lonely here in Wilmington, and it's my good fate to meet so beautiful and charming a woman."

Apprehension rippled through her and she decided it best to discourage any interest he might have in her as a woman. "I think it fair to tell you that the man I'm looking for is . . ." she took a deep breath, then easily rolled the lie from her tongue, "my fiancé."

She felt him stiffen, but only slightly, and the smile did not leave his lips. "Well, that is his good fortune, Julie. I envy him. But that doesn't prevent me from still wanting to help you."

She breathed a sigh of relief.

When they arrived at the office, they found it crowded with soldiers and crewmen who gave Julie curious glances. She left Harley standing just inside the door and made her way toward the counter that divided the room in half. She had no choice but to stand in the haphazardly-formed line, and almost an hour passed before she was actually pressing herself against the wooden bar.

A bespectacled man glared at her and said in an impatient tone, "Yes, what is it? We're quite busy here, and I can't see where a woman's got any business—"

Ignoring his rudeness, she said in a rush, "I must find someone. His name is Derek Arnhardt. Several months ago his ship was blown up by the Yankees near Bermuda. He was a blockade-runner. I wish to know if he is registered here as being in service."

He sighed with exasperation and snapped, "I've more important things to do than help you find your beau. This office was not established to locate missing suitors. Now if you'll just step aside and let me help someone who has real business—"

"Wait a minute, Leland," a stern voice spoke behind Julie. She turned to see a heavyset man standing there, and he looked quite angry as he said, "It won't take you long to see if the man she's looking for is registered here. Seems to me I heard about a runner by the name of Ironheart, or something like that. And you can look at this young lady and see that she's no waterfront trollop out to track down her lover."

Several others nearby chimed in in agreement, and the man called Leland realized he had no choice but to cooperate. Muttering angrily to himself, he moved from the counter to a shelf behind him, where several thick ledgers were stacked. Leafing through them with obvious irritation, he finally turned and snapped out the words Julie had prayed she would one day hear: "Yeah, there's a pilot registered by the name of Arnhardt, assigned to the steamer *Pamlico*."

Julie felt dizzy, and she gripped the edge of the counter with her fingertips to steady herself. He was alive. Derek was really alive. He had made it, and with a maddening whirl that sent her heart skipping, she wondered momentarily if she was overjoyed at the news because it meant he might indeed help her rescue Myles, or if there might be another, deeper, reason.

But this was no time to ponder the feelings in her heart. "Is he in port now?" she cried exuberantly. "And if he isn't, when is he due in?"

Leland slammed the ledger shut angrily. "Look, lady, that's all the information you're getting out of me." He looked about the room at those listening and snapped, "What's the matter with you men? How do we know she isn't a spy for the Yankees? We've got a war going on, in case you forgot."

An awkward silence fell over the room, and then the men began to shuffle their feet, moving away from her with suspicious glances.

Pushing his way through the crowd, Harley wrapped his fingers tightly about her arm and whispered anxiously, "Let's get out of here, Julie. You've gotten all the information they're going to give you. I think I can find out whether or not the *Pamlico* is in port. Let's just get the hell out of here."

They walked several blocks in silence before he said, "I think his steamer may be in port. Seems like I heard that one mentioned in a bar the other night. But if she is, she's due to run the blockade out of here anytime."

Julie stopped walking and faced him excitedly. "Then let's go at once and try to find him. We can walk along the docks and read the names on the ships, and when we find the *Pamlico*, all we have to do is ask to see the pilot—"

"No!" His eyes narrowed, and once again she was overcome by an ominous feeling about this man. He stared at her thoughtfully, tugging at his beard, then said, "I'll slip down there and see what I can find out. It isn't safe for you. Now where is this place you're staying? I'll walk you there, and when I get the information, I'll come and tell you about it."

She wondered why he seemed so nervous. He knew her financial plight, and could not expect to be paid for his services, yet there was definitely something on his mind. Surely he did not expect to be rewarded in "other ways." Rather than chance his entertaining that sort of notion, she murmured, "I'll just handle it from here on, Harley. You've been most kind, but I won't impose on you any longer. You are on leave and supposed to be enjoying yourself, certainly not getting involved in *my* problems. So I thank you, and—"

To her surprise, he laughed, but it was not a pleasant sound. There was something insidious in the tone and the gleam in his eyes. "If you think I'm going to expect favors

from you, Julie, you can set your mind at ease. I assure
you I've got more important things on my mind just now.
So just do as I say, and we'll both wind up quite satisfied, I
assure you."

She was puzzled over his behavior but decided she was
in no position to argue. It would be quite dangerous to
venture to the waterfront and wander about looking for a
steamer called the *Pamlico*, forced to ask questions of
anyone she chanced to meet along the way. There was
nothing to be done except allow him to help.

They returned to Pearl Watson's, and then Harley left
her, saying he would be back as soon as possible. When
she went to the barn and told Sara about what she'd found
out, Sara shook her head and said, "He ain't gonna come
back. And you ain't got no business goin' down there
lookin' fo' that man, yo'self. Why don't we just go on up
to Virginny and you can see about Mastah Myles yo'self?"

"I can't do that," Julie said quickly. "Those people at
the prison aren't going to just let Myles go, Sara. We're
going to have to help him to escape. And I can't do it
alone. If Harley doesn't return tonight, there's nothing for
me to do but search for Derek myself, no matter how
dangerous it might be."

The day passed slowly, and Julie felt it would never end.
Sara and Lionel exchanged worried glances as she paced
the straw-covered floor nervously.

Julie wondered how she would feel when she actually
saw Derek again. Just being close to him, his strength, his
courage, his all-encompassing command of any situation
. . . these qualities would make her feel that she could face
whatever life had to offer.

She stood at the open door of the barn watching the
stars above, a thousand fireflies twinkling in a cloak of
black velvet. Soon, she rationalized, she would have to
face the reality that Harley Beaumont was not going to
return. He'd probably found his way to a saloon, started
drinking, and forgotten all about her. She couldn't blame
him. Why should he worry about her problems?

"Julie . . ."

She stepped from the barn, straining to see into the
darkness.

"Over here. Come quickly."

She moved into the thick foliage of the scuppernong

vines that enshrouded the old barn. "Harley?" she whispered anxiously. "Is that you?"

"Of course it's me," he said nervously, stepping away from the thick vines. "We must move quickly. I found the *Pamlico*, and she's being loaded. They may run the blockade before dawn."

"Then we've got to ask to see the pilot." Her breath came in excited gasps. "Let's be on our way."

As they hurried through the night, Harley explained that the ship was being loaded on the opposite side of the river from Wilmington, on a low, marshy flat, where the steam cotton presses had been erected. There were sentries, he said, posted on the wharves, and she and Harley would have to be very careful or they might be shot as spies.

"Spies?" She laughed nervously. "Harley, all we have to do is explain to the sentries that I wish to speak to the pilot, Derek Arnhardt. They will go and get him for me. It's all quite simple."

"Not as simple as you think," he almost snarled. "Now let's don't waste time talking. Let's move fast."

Julie was puzzled, but she quickened her pace to keep up with him. It was a long distance, and by the time they reached the waterfront and Harley paid the owner of a small boat to take them to the other side, her legs were aching.

The boat pushed ashore among brush and brambles, and by the time they waded through the marshes, Julie's dress was soaked almost to her waist. "I see no need for all this secrecy," she complained, a mixture of anger and annoyance in her voice. "Harley, Derek *knows* me. He'll see me, I'm sure—"

"Will you shut up?" he snarled, his fingers digging into the flesh of her arm till she winced with pain. "Do as I say and stop nagging me."

"You're hurting me," she cried, trying to jerk away from him, but he held her tightly, dragging her through the reeds and saw grass as she stumbled and struggled to stay on her feet. "I want you to just go, Harley. Leave me be. I can make it the rest of the way alone. I don't know what's wrong with you, but—"

Abruptly he stopped and turned around, grabbing her shoulders to shake her so hard her teeth were rattling.

"Listen to me, you little fool. You think I'm doing all this because I'm a gentleman out to help a woman in distress? Why do you think those sentries are posted? They are there to stop deserters from sneaking on board the ships being loaded. I happen to be a deserter, and I want to get on board the *Pamlico*. I'm sick of this stinking war. I'm not going to get my guts blown out by some Yankee ball. I'm going to stow away and make it to Bermuda or wherever the hell they go, and then I'm going to lie on some beach and relax till the blasted war is over. And you're going to help me do it, or I'll slit your goddamned throat here and now and throw you in the river for the crabs to eat. Do you understand me?"

She felt cold steel pressing against her neck, and she could only murmur "Yes . . ." as terror struck her in the pit of her stomach. "Yes . . . yes . . ."

"Now I'll tell you how we're going to work this out. I'm going to hide in the bushes, and you're going to get the sentry's attention. That shouldn't be hard to do. You're pretty, and the son of a bitch will be only too happy to talk to you, figuring he can line up a little lovin' later on. Just leave the rest to me."

She felt a slight sting as he pressed the blade harder against her skin, knew the flesh was broken. "One more thing. You give me away, and I'll see you dead before they can get me. You understand?"

She could hardly push the word from her lips: "Yes . . ."

"All right. Now here's what I'll do for you: I'll get you on board. We'll hide out, and when we reach wherever we're going, I'll turn you loose to go to your lover."

He gave her a rough shove. "Let's get this over with."

Terrified, she knew there was no hope of escape for the moment. He pushed her along until they reached the edge of the marsh. In the light of the torches burning along the dock, she could see the long, sleek ship. From her experience onboard the *Ariane*, she knew this steamer was preparing to run the blockade. The spars had been reduced to a light pair of lower masts without any yards across them. The only break in their sharp outline was the small crow's nest on the foremast to be used as a lookout point. The hull, showing about eight feet above water, was painted a dull gray color, to render the steamer as nearly invisible in the night as possible. The *Pamlico* was lowered square with the gunwales. The funnel, which would spew forth the exhaust from anthracite coal, used because it was smokeless, had been lowered close to the deck. The steam would be blown off under water so that no noise would be made.

Julie saw crates of chickens about to be loaded, and knew there would be no roosters among them, for fear that their crowing might give away the ship's whereabouts to the Yankee blockaders.

As Derek had also explained to Julie, the in-shore squadron off Wilmington consisted of about thirty vessels which lay in the form of a crescent facing the entrance to the Cape Fear River, the center being just out of range of the heavy guns mounted on Fort Fisher. And these horns, as they were called, gradually approached the shore on each side, so that the whole line or curve covered about ten miles.

The hold of the *Pamlico* would be loaded by expert stevedores, the cotton bales so closely packed that it would be difficult for even a rat to find a hiding place. She wondered just where Harley planned to conceal the two of them.

Julie knew the hatches had been put on, and there was a tier of cotton bales fore and aft in every available spot on the deck, leaving openings and approaches only to the cabins, the engine room, and the men's forecastle. She could spot the somewhat thinner tier on the top, and with only its foremast up, the steamer, with its low funnel and gray-painted sides, looked like a huge bale of cotton with a stick placed upright at one end of it.

"They're ready to go," Harley said nervously. "I don't know what they're waiting on, except maybe to load those damn chickens. We've got to move fast."

There was one sentry, leaning against a crate, and his head nodded now and then as though he were fighting to stay awake. Harley instructed Julie to move as close as possible to the sentry and call to him.

"And what shall I say?" she asked, her whole body trembling with apprehension and fright. "He might shoot me...."

"Don't be a fool. He'll look up, see how pretty you are, and that's all it will take. Here, fix this—" With a deft movement he reached out and yanked at the bodice of her dress so that her breasts were almost completely exposed. "Make him think you've been raped or something. Ask him for help. You just get moving, Julie, or so help me . . ."

She winced as she saw the knife's blade gleaming in the starlight.

Julie began to move cautiously forward, and thoughts flashed through her mind—Myles . . . her mother in her grave . . . Lionel and Sara wondering frantically why she had never returned . . . Derek. . . .

Oh, God, she thought, feeling a nauseating wave of panic, *this can't be happening!*

"Halt!" The sentry snapped to alertness, the rifle he held pointing toward the saw grass. "Who's there?"

"Help me. . . ." she murmured faintly, stumbling forward. "I—I need help. . . ."

His eyes widened at the sight of her, dress torn, breasts all but pouring forth, hair disheveled. Dropping his weapon, he lunged forward. "What's wrong? Are you hurt? . . ."

Like a flash, Harley was out of the dense foliage and plunged his knife into the sentry's throat. Julie stuffed her fist in her mouth and fell to her knees, fighting the nausea, the hysteria, that threatened to erupt.

Harley was upon her, dragging her to her feet. "That man . . ." she whispered dizzily, sorrowfully.

"I've already dragged him into the bushes. Move quickly. They'll think he deserted. On board. Up the ramp. Fast. . . ."

A mist settled over her, and Julie allowed him to lead her. She felt as though she were walking in a fog, that none of this was real. She stooped and squatted when he told her, lay down flat when he ordered. It seemed forever, and then again, it could only have taken seconds, she reasoned. All sense of time and existence was dissolved.

Then she felt herself being shoved through a hole, deep into the bowels of the ship. It was hard to breathe, for the air was hot and close. Her skin was pressed against the rough burlap binding the cotton bales, and Harley pushed her back even further. "I can't get my breath!" she gasped, and he gave her another vicious shove.

"Shut up and save the air," he snapped. "No telling how long we're gonna have to hide here. We may be eating rats to keep from starving before it's over. But you better make up your mind whether you want to live or die, because I've come too damn far to let you mess me up now."

Finally they were presssed as far back into the tightly packed bales as they could get. There was no room to lie down, and for this, Julie was grateful. At least there was no chance of Harley forcing himself upon her.

Harley chuckled, sounding a bit nervous. "I wish I could see your Captain Ironheart when he finds out you helped a deserter kill one of his men."

A twinge of anger began to overshadow her fear and timidity. "When I tell him the truth, he'll hunt you down and kill you like the mad dog you are!" she hissed.

"You just shut your mouth, or I'll fix you so's you won't be able to talk. I'll slice your tongue out." He was silent for a moment, then went on in a rasping voice, "I've heard about him, how he's supposed to be so goddamned tough. If he ever comes up against me and my blade, there ain't nothing going to save his ass."

Not wanting to goad him further, Julie said nothing. Then she felt his hand groping beneath her skirt, and she opened her mouth to protest but froze, as did his seeking fingers, at the sound of voices drifting around the cargo.

"Where in the hell did Junius run off to?" someone was saying irritably. "Never took him for no deserter."

"Hell, maybe he had some 'pop skull' and got drunk and passed out in the saw grass. One thing's for sure—if Ironheart ever lays eyes on him again, he'll hang his ass. He hates a deserter. Here. Give me a hand with these chickens. We've got to get going."

There were sounds of movements, grunts, chickens cackling nervously as their crates were hurriedly stacked. Then the men's shuffling footsteps faded. Harley, thinking they were at last alone, began to explore Julie's trembling body once again.

Then more voices were heard, coming closer, and he whispered tersely, "Goddamn, I reckon we're gonna have these jackasses swarming around for a while. You stay quiet now, or I'll slit your throat."

It was difficult to raise her arm, as tightly squeezed in as they were, but she managed to do so, pressing her hand against her quivering lips. A sickening sight kept dancing before her eyes: the knife plunging into the unsuspecting sentry's throat, the sudden spurt of thick, hot blood, the way his eyes flickered but a second with surprise before glassing over as he slumped silently to the ground.

The ship began to move. They were under way. Crewmen wandered through the hold as they stacked and shoved and pushed the cargo about to better balance the load. Julie prayed for discovery, but Harley had pushed them so far back that their hiding place was not likely to be found.

After a time, they were alone. She realized Harley had fallen asleep, and she was tempted to give way to her own weariness. Her mind would not let her, remaining ablaze from all that had happened in the last few hours. She was so engrossed in thought that when the steamer slowed, she did not notice, but then she suddenly realized it had stopped all forward motion and was still.

Men were once again moving through the hold. Harley continued to sleep, and she prayed he would not awaken. Perhaps there was a chance they would be discovered.

An annoyed voice pierced the stillness. "It's stupid to take time to stop at Smithfield to look for stowaways. I wish we'd just go ahead and make the damn dash through the blockade and hit the Gulf Stream and be on our way."

"Yeah, I know what you mean," another voice drawled. "But they require all outward bound steamers to stop here and make one more check."

The first man continued to grumble. "Hell, we do a good job of checking when we're loading. We ain't never caught nobody."

"Well," the other voice laughed caustically, "I feel sorry for the poor wretch Ironheart ever does catch stowing away on his ship."

Ironheart! The sound of his name sent a thrilled shiver through Julie's cramped, tired body. Soon she would see him. She was warmed by the thought of being folded in those strong arms against that rock-hard chest. Once more she would experience the overwhelming feeling that nothing could hurt her as long as he held her in his embrace.

The men were coming closer.

The knife! Harley had tucked the knife inside his boot after killing the sentry. If he awakened, he would use it on these men, and he might kill her too, thinking she had alerted them. She had to get to the weapon before he woke up.

She tried to bend over but realized it was futile because she was so tightly wedged into position. Forcing her knees to twist slightly, she maneuvered herself downward, careful lest she jar Harley.

Her face rubbed painfully against the burlap. His right boot brushed her arm. Raising herself slightly, she touched the top rim of his shoe and carefully slid her fingertips inside.

She felt nothing!

Harley moved slightly, and Julie froze, holding her breath. The voices were getting closer. Any time now, he would hear them, wake up, and reach for his knife, and he would find her groping for it! Cautiously she moved her fingers out and down and across the top of his boot, inching her way to the left one. Once more reaching gingerly inside, her body tensed as she felt the knife handle. Carefully, slowly, she began to slide it upward.

She had it in her hand. Then, just as she started to move back, to struggle to an upright position, a loud voice slashed the air about them. "Let's look between these rows. Looks like these bales might be a little wider apart than the others. . . ."

Harley awoke with a start. Instantly he pushed his hand down, reaching for his knife, but instead of fastening his groping fingers about it, he found himself clutching a handful of thick black hair.

Startled, Julie dropped the weapon.

"What the hell?" He was too surprised to think about keeping his voice low. Twisting her hair so painfully she cried out, he snarled, "What're you doing? Where's my goddamn knife?"

"In there! Quick! Somebody's in there. Move these bales." The crewmen were working frantically.

Harley's fingers found their way to Julie's throat, pulling her roughly up beside him as he began to squeeze the breath from her. He yelled to the men: "Stay back or I'll kill her. So help me, I'll choke her to death. . . ."

The bales parted suddenly, and Harley had the necessary room to flex his arms and elbows outward to squeeze even tighter. The crewmen took in the sight with wide eyes, and one of them quickly yelled, "You think we give a damn? We'll blow you both apart where you stand—" He pointed a gun menacingly toward their faces.

Julie felt her life ebbing. If Harley did not kill her, then these two angry men, blurring before her swelling eyes, would.

And her last conscious thought, as the black shroud surrounded her, was of Myles, imprisoned beyond hope.

Then the image of his dear face faded, and in its place were ebony eyes burning with anger, shaded with desire. And as she succumbed to inevitable death, she felt only the pang of sorrow over never again knowing the sweet comfort of his arms. . . .

❧ Chapter Eighteen ❧

LEANING back against a small wooden table, arms folded casually across his massive chest, Derek stared down at Julie. She had been placed, unconscious, on his narrow bunk. And despite her haggard appearance, he thought once again, with a rush of desire, how she was still the most beautiful woman he had ever seen.

The doctor on board had examined her and said that she was unconscious because that man, whoever he was, had almost choked her to death. She would be all right, he promised, and could awaken any time. Derek told the doctor not to attempt to bring her around with smelling salts. He wanted her to sleep. They had to run the blockade, and there was no time for talk—and God knows, he had plenty of questions to ask. First of all, he wanted to know how she came to be on the ship, squeezed between tightly packed bales of cotton, with some rogue trying to kill her.

The crewmen who discovered them explained how one of the crew, quite adept with his knife, had sent a blade plunging into the man's leg. With a howl of pain, he'd released Julie. In the ensuing struggle he'd been killed, and his body unceremoniously dumped overboard for the sharks' supper. Julie had been brought to Derek.

Derek had not let on that he knew her, even though it had been extremely difficult to retain his composure and mask his concern. Often in the past months he had wondered about her fate, promising himself that once the blasted war ended, if he were still alive, he'd try to track her down.

And here she was, in all her glorious flesh. He only hoped that she remained in her present comatose state until they had slipped through the Federal blockade and were on the open seas.

He moved to tuck the blanket tighter under her chin, letting his hand brush her bosom. There was no denying the tightening in his loins. God, but she had been a warm, loving creature in his arms. He'd known the pleasure of hundreds of women's bodies, but never one that made him feel as though he were plunging into living, breathing velvet, so soft, yet so hot and eager to receive him. Chuckling to himself, he remembered how there had been times when she struggled to reject him, but he had been able to turn her into a writhing mass of begging ecstasy.

And he would know the joys again, he promised himself as he left his cabin. Whatever her reason and purpose for slipping aboard his ship, he would have his fill of her before letting her go.

Derek went topside, grateful for the moonless night. No matter how many times he ran the damned blockade, he always felt a knot of apprehension in the pit of his stomach until they had actually gotten through it.

He knew that the Federal blockade stretched across an arc about forty miles wide, from New Inlet, twenty-five miles south of Wilmington, down around the Cape and Frying Pan Shoals to Old Inlet, which lay just below Smithville and the mouth of the Cape Fear River.

He saw that the ship was quiet, his crew alert. Someone reported that all hatches had been tightly covered with canvas to assure that no light from the fireroom below would show and give them away. There was one remaining light left aboard, which shone on the binnacle, but it, too, had been shielded by heavy canvas. Once Derek was satisfied that the ship was dark and blended in with sea and sky, he softly called orders down the tube, and the *Pamlico*, its engines smoothly humming, began steaming toward the line of blockading cruisers.

He wished he could use the running lights for the twenty-five mile stretch of marsh-bordered water leading to the channel between Wilmington and Eagle's Island. Just inside the channel, a few yards from shore on the east, there was an ancient cypress called the Dram Tree, which marked the beginning of real danger, for once it was sited it was inevitable that they were heading straight towards the blockade. With good navigation, and luck, they would make it through again.

All eyes, Derek knew, would be straining for sight of The Mound, a hillock no higher than a tree which would show a slight gradation of color marking black shore from black sea, and would mean that they were moving to New Inlet.

They would then steam toward Confederate Point, a few miles above New Inlet. As they moved out of shallow waters, Derek stationed his leadsmen at each quarter of the ship. He could hear the men whispering measurements to each other. Ten feet. Twelve. Fifteen. He, himself, felt the pull of the waters.

They were navigating now through New Inlet, a channel that had been opened by hurricanes over a hundred years ago. Even though it had a bar of shifting sand and silt, Derek was one of the few pilots who found it easy to navigate, and it had the added advantage of being protected by the small fort of palmetto logs and railroad iron called Battery Bolles.

Derek knew that the Federals hung in as close to the shore as their drafts would permit, anchoring off the two main channel inlets of Cape Fear. Old Inlet entered the Cape Fear River at its mouth, which was guarded by Forts Holmes and Caswell. Navigationally it was the most dangerous route, and a boomerang-shaped bar known as The Lump lurked just two to five feet below the surface. One small miscalculation and the *Pamlico* would be run aground and left helpless and exposed to the fire of the Yankee cruisers, but Derek felt pride in knowing that his men placed their full trust and confidence in the fact that he could navigate them through the dangerous pass. He would never let them know that he too breathed a sigh of relief once he had succeeded.

Now they were moving cautiously through Onslow Bay. No sound was heard, and Derek could smell no telltale smoke, yet he knew with the instinct of a jungle animal that somewhere out there in that foreboding darkness, they were there, like a giant spider in a massive web, waiting . . . for a sound . . . a flicker of light . . . a single mistake that would present them with a target for their guns.

Derek had lost count of the number of times he'd run the blockade. Since the *Ariane* had been blown to bits and he'd narrowly escaped with his life, he'd stopped thinking of the war in terms of making money and coming out of it a wealthy man. Now he wanted only revenge, and since he was akin to the sea and knew all the hazards waiting beneath the ocean's murky depths, he liked the idea of making fools of the Yankees as he maneuvered the ship assigned to him through their damned web.

Tension surrounded him. He could feel it in himself and his men. It would not last much longer, but each second seemed an eternity. He tried not to think of the present. Every possible precaution had been taken, he told his pounding heart. They had succeeded before, and they would make it this time. He would think of Julie, and how sweet it was going to be to take his pleasure with her once again.

Suddenly his muscles tightened, and he gripped the railing with a grip like a steel vise. Something was not right. He could just *feel* it, dammit. His eyes darted everywhere, searching for something to tell him why he felt so anxious, why his nerves were stretched taut. Straining his ears, he listened for any sounds . . . voices . . . scrapings. Suddenly he knew. He could just feel it in his bones. Something was wrong, and a deep chill of foreboding began to wash over his body.

And then the night exploded with brilliance as a Drummond light illuminated the sky. There, less than a mile apart, two ships waited. "Full speed ahead!" He thundered the order. "We've been spotted. Make a break for open waters, fast, dammit—"

But just then both Yankee cruisers fired, and their shots landed heavily in the water nearby. Next the onshore battery of the Confederacy opened fire on the Federal ships, but they were too far out. At fifteen knots, Derek felt the *Pamlico* was crawling; yet their only chance was to hit the open waters and outrun the cruisers.

A shot whizzed by his head, hitting the edge of a large wooden crate and sending it crashing down from its moorings on the port foredeck. It hit a seaman, who smashed against the deck with an agonized cry.

And then another shot fell astern. "Four points starboard! . . ." Derek cried. The Confederate battery continued to fire, and the *Pamlico* steamed along. But the deck was a mass of confusion, with the crewmen running for cover.

Another shot screamed through the night, and this time the *Pamlico* was hit. Fire shot upward like a giant fist of crimson against the black sky.

"Abandon ship! Abandon ship!"

Derek heard the cries fill the air. He heard men shrieking as they clambered over the railings to jump into the water. They would try to swim back to shore, but he knew they would never make it. They were too far out at sea.

Another shot split the sky, this one landing so as to splinter the port side. It was all over. Derek gave the order to abandon ship, but no one was listening to him any longer, as each man fought to save his own life. Fights broke out over rafts, boards, anything that might keep a man afloat.

Derek turned his head at the sound of a blood-curdling scream and saw a man running across the crowded deck, his whole body aflame. Someone else knocked him down with one mighty swing from a rifle, and he was left to die in agony.

Derek knew they could be hit again at any second, and this time they would be sent straight into eternity. Any other time he, too, would have scrambled to jump overboard. He wasn't about to honor that age-old rubbish about a captain going down with his ship. Besides, he reasoned wryly as he made his way below, he wasn't really the damned captain anyway. The Confederacy wouldn't bestow such an honor upon him after he'd lost his ship. He was just the pilot. Although technically in command, nevertheless it wasn't *his* ship going down, and he saw no need for a heroic stand.

The only "heroics" he had in mind were saving Julie. Alone, helpless, she didn't stand a chance, and he wasn't about to leave her below to sink with the ship.

He stepped over a body, shoved someone aside with a sharp jab of his elbow. The scene was one of mass confusion and hysteria, punctuated by the screams of those already hit and wounded, who knew they were going to be left behind to die.

Smoke stung at Derek's eyes. The *Pamlico* was burning, and he had no way of knowing if there was time to make his way below before the ship was caught in the suction that would pull it beneath the surface and to the bottom of the ocean. But he had to try to make it. He had to.

Bursting through the cabin door, he could see Julie in the red glow that was coming through the porthole from the burning deck above. She was sitting on the side of the bunk, staring about, dazed. And then she lifted confused eyes and gasped, "Derek. It—it is you. . . ."

"No time to talk, Julie." He lifted her as effortlessly as though she were no more than a sack of flour, threw her over his wide shoulder, and turned back toward the door.

"Derek, what's happening?" she cried then, smelling the smoke, struggling against the rough way she was being carried. "Tell me—I have to know. . . ."

Ignoring her pleas, Derek stepped into the narrow hallway and turned toward the steps. His heart froze as he saw the flames licking at the top, knew he and Julie were trapped from that end. As he turned to go the other way, Julie also glimpsed the fire and screamed in terror.

Derek ran down the passageway toward the other ladder that led up. Just then the ship gave a sudden lurch downward, and he stumbled against the wall, struggling to remain upright.

Water began pouring through the opening above. They were sinking. His heart racing, he made a lunge for the ladder, yelling at Julie to hold on. "I've got to use both arms to get us up. You must hold tight to me. . . ."

Terrified, she looped both arms about his neck and clung to his body as he began to make the ascent.

Then a blast of water hit them, and Julie gasped and choked and tried to scream and couldn't. She realized that the ship was indeed sinking, and they were headed straight for the bottom.

Derek felt something hit the side of his head, and for a moment he struggled to remain conscious. The water would be filled with cargo that had come unleashed, every bit of it a potential barrier to their struggle to reach the surface. They were completely under water and sinking lower because the ship's suction was pulling them down. Derek could only pray that Julie would hang onto him, as he was having to use his arms to fight his way through the tumbling cargo and could not keep a grip on her.

Then he felt her arms slipping. For a split second he

reached out and shoved her arms back around him, hoping she felt the reassuring squeeze he tried to bestow to let her know that if there were any way possible, he'd get them out of this, but she had to do her part. She had to fight. God, she had to find the strength, and she was such a tiny thing. He scarcely felt her weight as she clung to him weakly.

Derek's head reached the surface of the water, and as he gulped in the sweet, fresh air, he felt Julie let go. Quickly he dropped back down, groping in the cold, dark waters. His fingers touched her long, stringy hair, and he yanked upward until the two of them were struggling to keep their heads above water.

Holding her tightly against him with one arm, he used his other to tread water, kicking his legs to move away from what was left of the burning ship. He could make out objects floating all about them, crates and soaking cotton bales which would eventually absorb water sufficiently to sink. He could see lights, knew that the Yankees would probably fire a few more shots to take care of any survivors, but they would not dare move closer in for fear of being hit by the Confederate battery on shore.

A strong wind was starting to blow. The sea was getting rough. Derek knew it was futile to try to make it to land, because the tide was moving out. He was a strong swimmer, and without Julie perhaps he could have made it, but he wasn't concerned about himself at the moment. Julie was the weaker, and without him, she would die. And while he felt a mixture of emotions, he wasn't going to try to sort out his thoughts at the moment. He would struggle to save her as well as himself, and later there would be time to try to understand why he'd suddenly felt such a burning need to keep this girl alive at the risk of losing his own life.

Something struck his shoulder hard, and he almost lost his grip on her. It was a long, flat crate, bobbing up and down sharply in the ever-roughening seas. "Julie . . ." he cried loudly above the wind. "Julie, can you hear me?" She was so still, so quiet, that he wondered if she'd lost consciousness.

She stirred, moaned, muttered something about being so very cold.

"Listen to me," he ordered in the tone he always used

with his crewmen—harsh, authoritative, with an air of finality. "I'm going to shove you up on this crate, and you hang on tight, do you understand? A storm's brewing and we've got to cling to something, or else we'll drown. Now when I shove you up, you hang on tight till I can get up there too. If you let go and I lose you again, you'll die. Do you hear me? You'll die. . . ."

"Myles . . ." she whispered, then coughed and choked as her mouth filled with the churning salt water. "Myles . . . will die. . . ."

"No, *you* will die if you don't hang on," he snapped. He fastened his strong hands around her tiny waist and lifted her up and out of the water and onto the bobbing crate. There was not time to make sure she was following his orders and gripping its sides. He had to get himself up on the wooden object before it was swept away from him in the increasingly wild current.

A wave washed completely over him, and Derek felt the flesh from his fingers being ripped away on the wooden side of the crate as he fought to hang on. Rising to the surface once again, he pulled himself up, then fell on top of Julie, pinning her beneath him.

Spread-eagling his body, Derek stretched his arms out so that his fingers were clinging tightly to each side of the crate as he lay on his stomach, face pressed against Julie's head.

"We've got to ride it out, Julie," he screamed above the howling wind. "This is one of those nor'easters that blow up so quick, but it shouldn't last long. We'll make it. . . ."

Julie had mercifully lost consciousness once again, weakened by the ordeal, her breathing labored because of the weight of the man above her, pinning her down.

Derek's fingers were growing numb, and his legs ached from the pressure he exerted to hold them pinioned on the crate. The waves tossed and rolled, and several times he thought they were going to be thrown into the water, but because of his size and strength, he was able to cling to the bucking, heaving object and ride out the storm.

His eyes were growing heavy, despite the nervous tension that coursed through his veins. Was it his imagination or were the waters really becoming calmer? The wind had died down. The sun began to rise in the east. He could dare to close his eyes for just a moment. Every muscle, every bone felt as though it were on fire. He could hang on, and still rest. . . .

"Derek, I can't breathe—"

His eyes flashed open. Julie was struggling beneath him. The sun blazed down on his bare back. Lifting his head, he saw that the ocean was calm once more, and the waves that rolled them along were not dangerous. God, he wondered, how long had he slept?

Julie twisted her body again. "Derek, move, please," she cried. "*I can't breathe.*"

He looked at the crate to gauge its size. Cautiously he moved his hands from the edge, placing his weight on his forearms as he lifted his body. "Careful," he told her. "I'm going to sit back and try to keep us balanced while you move from under me."

In a few moments they were sitting opposite each other, and he saw that she was almost naked, her dress hanging in strips. He gave her a sideways grin and nodded to her exposed breasts as he murmured, "I always wanted to be adrift with a mermaid."

Following his gaze, she gasped, folding her arms quickly across her bosom as she said tartly, "You haven't changed a bit, Derek Arnhardt. You're still an animal."

He began to laugh.

"Oh, how can you sit there and laugh?" she demanded, her arms falling away from her breasts as she realized it was futile to attempt to keep herself covered in her present predicament. Besides, the way the crate they were riding upon kept bobbing up and down on the waves, she felt more secure with her hands gripping its edges.

"We're in the middle of the ocean, sitting on a wooden box, and you can sit there and laugh about it. Would you mind telling me what happened?"

"We didn't make it through the blockade," he said, as though it were all quite simple. "The Yankees spotted us, fired, and hit the ship. It caught on fire and sank. I saved your life, in case you're interested."

"I'm not so sure you have saved it," she said doubtfully, looking around at the endless water blending into sky in every direction. "I suppose we'll either drown when this crate finally sinks, or we'll starve, or . . ."

Suddenly her voice trailed off and her eyes widened. "Derek . . ." she whispered, feeling quite foolish as she

realized that she had actually seen him for the first time
. . . actually was aware of his presence. "Derek—it *is*
you. . . ."

Her arms reached out to him so suddenly that the crate
pitched precariously, and he fought to steady the structure
at the same time that one of his arms folded her against
his chest. "Yes, misty eyes," he murmured, nuzzling her
soft, damp·hair with his lips. "It's me, and we're going
to be all right. A passing ship will see us sooner or later.
This is a rather sturdy crate, or it would've sunk during
last night's storm." But they had not yet reached the Gulf
Stream, he thought silently, so there was actually little
chance of a ship passing by.

He cupped her chin in his hand, lifting her lips for a
deep, soul-stirring kiss that left both of them shaken. Releasing her, he smiled fondly. "Misty eyes, you're beautiful. I've lain awake many a night thinking how I once held
you, and if it weren't for tipping us over, I think I'd take
you here and now."

"You wouldn't dare!" She moved away. Then, lowering
her gaze, she realized that indeed, he just *might* dare, and
she felt a stirring·in her own loins as she admitted shamefully to herself that she would enjoy knowing his body
once again.

Hoping he did not notice her trembling, she took a deep
breath and said, "Let's talk of other things to pass the
time. Tell me how you escaped when they forced you
overboard."

"I used the knife you gave me," he replied. "I had the
good sense to be as still as possible so I wouldn't draw the
sharks to me once I cut the ropes. Then, when I thought
it was safe, I swam to the Yankee ship and held onto their
anchor line. When the *Ariane* was blown up, I managed to
find a piece of the wreckage to cling to till my crew came
out to investigate the explosion. They found me."

"You make it sound so simple," she gasped, stunned.

"It may sound that way now, but at the time, I was
scared to death." He laughed softly, then said, "Let's talk
about you, Julie, and what's happened to you all these
many months. How did you come to be hiding in the hold
of my ship with a Reb deserter?"

She gestured helplessly. "I really don't know where to
begin. So much has happened, so much heartache—" her
voice broke, and she struggled to regain her composure.

Derek was a strong man, and he probably hated a weak woman, and she needed him—not only to help her survive, but to help her rescue Myles.

Derek grinned slowly. "It seems we've got all the time in the world for talk." He gestured at the endless sea that surrounded them.

And so she began, telling him everything and leaving nothing out. When she told about Virgil, how she'd been forced to submit to him, Derek gritted his teeth, black eyes flashing fire.

When she finished, she looked at him beseechingly and asked, "Do you see now why I had to find you, Derek? You're the one person who can help me get my brother out of Libby prison."

He frowned. "I'm not so sure, Julie. You're talking about breaking a man out of a place where there are hundreds of guards."

"But I've a cousin there who might help," she explained anxiously, and told him about Thomas.

Derek's eyes looked doubtful. "I don't think he'll be much help. It's dangerous, and I see no way—"

"Derek, I'll do anything you ask," she whispered in desperation. "Anything at all. You asked me to be your mistress once, and I refused. If you'll help me free Myles, then I'm yours, any way you want me. He's all I've got left, and he saved my life once, and it left him with a bad leg. I've got to do what I can to help him."

He stared at her for a long time, pulling at the tip of his mustache thoughtfully. Finally he said, "I make no bargains with you. We don't even know if we'll survive."

"But if we *do* survive—"

"You'd better take off what's left of your dress and cover your face." He wanted to change the subject. "Your skin is going to blister and swell."

"What about you?" she blinked.

He began to unfasten his trousers. "I'm going to cover myself as the need arises. If you're embarrassed after all those hours we frolicked naked, then you'll have to cope as best you can. Survival is the important thing now."

The sun beat down mercilessly, and Julie covered her face as Derek instructed. She watched as he tore his trousers into strips, moving the cloth about his body as the skin reddened.

The day wore on, and when darkness began to fall Julie

felt better, even though her stomach was knotted with hunger and her throat and lips were parched and aching for water. "Sleep," Derek whispered soothingly, brushing her hair back from her face so that the cooling evening breeze could kiss her feverish skin. "I'll stay awake in case a storm brews and the seas get rough."

As she closed her eyes, Julie wondered wearily why she always felt so protected in his presence. Surely they would survive. She just felt it in her bones, because Derek Arnhardt filled her with a sense of comfort that was unexplainable but satisfying.

"Did you hear that?"

Julie sat up, startled at the sound of Derek's excited shout. The crate tipped, and they both struggled to keep it from turning over. "Julie, did you hear it?" he repeated.

Her ears and eyes were straining, immediately alert. She could barely make out the first pink hem of dawn that touched the eastern horizon. But the only sound she heard was the gentle lapping of the water against the bobbing crate.

"It was a bird. I know damned well it was a bird." He slapped his hands angrily against his thighs. "I didn't doze off. I've been awake all night, and I know I wasn't hearing things. I heard a bird cry."

Julie yawned, rubbing her hands against her bare shoulders, grateful for the chill. Soon the sun would rise and the unbearable heat would be upon them to blister and burn them once again. "What difference does it make, Derek? How is a bird going to help us unless he happens to land and we can eat him."

"I'm hungry enough to eat one raw, that's for sure," he said. "But a bird means land is nearby, Julie."

"Oh, praise God!" Now she shared his excitement, and they sat very quietly, listening, and then they both heard it and screamed in delight.

"There!" Derek was yelling, and she could barely make out where his arm was extended, pointing. "Land. An island. I can just see it. And we're drifting toward it. Paddle, Julie. Use your hands and paddle so we don't get washed out to sea should the tide start to change. We've got about a mile to go. We can make it. I know we can. . . ."

She followed his lead, thrashing her hands wildly in the water in a rhythmic motion to match his. Slowly, steadily, the wooden crate began to move toward the island. And as the sky grew rosier and it became lighter, they could see that it was indeed a small island. And there were trees. When they came closer, Derek commented that there would probably not be food, "But God, we'll eat leaves, roots, anything. I'll wade out and catch fish with my hands if I have to. We can't just keep drifting. This is a chance, Julie. It's our chance to live. . . ."

It seemed to take forever, but then all of a sudden the crate hit a sand bar. Derek leaped over the side, and Julie could see that he was standing thigh-deep in the water. He held out his arms to her and she fell into them, laughing and crying all at once. They began to wade toward the island, but then Derek turned and clutched at the crate, saying they had to drag it with them.

"I don't know what's in the damn thing. Maybe it's something we can use."

Together they struggled to pull it along with them. Once they reached the sandy beach, Julie fell onto the sand, clutching the precious grains in her hands, laughing with the delight of a child as she watched them dribble through her fingers. "I never thought I'd touch land again," she cried. "Oh, Derek, we are going to make it. I know we are."

But he was not listening to her exuberant talk. She looked up to see him running up the beach to find what vegetation existed. "There's not a lot here," he yelled back. "But we can suck on leaves for water. We can chew bark if we have to. And I'll find dry wood and be ready to start a fire if we sight a ship."

He turned back toward her, and she watched him running naked, his body a pinnacle of proud, masculine beauty as he exuded strength in his every movement. Whisking her into his arms as easily as though she were no more than a seashell, he whirled her around and around, and they laughed together joyfully, thankful for this much good fortune, at least.

Then, slowly, he stopped turning about, setting her on her feet but still holding her close. They were naked, bodies touching, her nipples brushing against the thick, dark down on his massive chest.

His hands moved down her back to cup her firm, rounded buttocks and press her against him. Lifting her slightly so that she stood on tiptoe, his erect shaft slid between her thighs, and she sighed aloud as he touched the special place that sent sweet-hot fires dancing through her loins.

Gently he lowered her to the sand, easing his body down upon her. His mouth crushed against hers as she opened her legs to him, thrusting her buttocks upward to meet his first thrusts into the velvet recesses of her body.

"How I have dreamed of this moment, this time," he murmured, his lips barely touching hers, his tongue moving to and fro, flicking at hers to tease her into a frenzy as his manhood pushed in and out. "There's never been a woman like you, Julie. There's never been a body like yours. It's like drenching myself in scalding honey and absorbing the sweet nectar into every pore of my body. . . ."

And she received him, all of him, marveling that her tiny body could accept such a magnificently built man. Her legs wrapped around his back to hold him even closer, wanting everything he had to give. That he should find her so attractive, so desirable, was beyond her realm of understanding. Any woman would revel in his embrace, but for the moment he was hers, every glorious inch of him, and she wanted this hour, this time, to continue for all eternity . . . just as relentlessly and unendingly as the foaming breakers crashing upon the shore. . . .

She felt the crescendo building from within the confines of her belly, and Derek felt it also, and he drove even harder into her. Her lips parted in a scream of ecstasy, and he shifted his weight so that his hard, muscular shoulder was pressed against her mouth.

"Let me feel it," he commanded. "Let me feel your glory, Julie. . . ."

And her teeth sank into the firm flesh, biting harder as each wave of passion shuddered through her body, and then he was crying out loud in ecstasy as he ground mercilessly into her, driving her buttocks into the rough sand, filling her with the glory of his seed.

They lay together, neither wanting the moment to end. The closeness, the wonder of it all, was too overwhelming for either to comprehend.

At last Derek rolled to his side, still penetrating her, holding her tightly. His lips mere inches from hers, he murmured, "Love me, Julie. Love me for all time, because now that I've found you, I'll never let you go again. . . ."

And then he was gently probing at her again, and the sweet passion was returning, dimmed for Julie only by the gnawing realization that he had demanded that she love him for all time—but he had professed no vows of undying devotion . . . he was taking, not giving, and despite the ecstasy that flowed through her veins, her heart shuddered with an unfamiliar sadness.

Chapter Nineteen

TIME seemed endless. Their world consisted of the sand, the sea, the stars, the sun . . . and the joy they found in each other's arms. It was as though life had no beginning, no end; there was only the sweet bliss of endless passion.

The surf broke high, rolling over into tunnels and flashing in the sunlight as its froth crept along the shore. The sea oats blew lazily in the breeze.

Julie liked the mornings best of all, when she would rise sleepily to the red sunrise, the sea looking like molten bronze. And each night she opened her thighs to meet Derek's deep thrusts with all the strength and vigor her body had to offer, holding nothing back. They became one entity, possessing all of each other, giving, taking, belonging only to one another.

Derek had been disappointed to find that the crate contained only coffee taken aboard for the crew, but ruined by the seepage of sea water. He became adept at catching the small fish that swam in the surf close to the island. He caught some with his hands, but he also fashioned a crude spear from a piece of driftwood and a sharp conch shell. When the rains came, he and Julie would spread out the larger shells as cups, to catch the fresh water for drinking.

Together they spread palm fronds from the trees to make a crude shelter, but as always, Julie felt completely protected with Derek's strong arms about her, had a secure sense that no harm could come as long as he held her against him.

"Love me. . . ." he would command as he took her, seemingly without end.

And she obeyed, whispering the words he wanted to hear and realizing with each passing day that she meant them more and more.

"What if we're never found?" she asked him one day as they frolicked together in the turquoise waters, their skin long since bronzed by the sun. "What if we have actually died, and this is our heaven, our Garden of Eden, to live in through all eternity?"

He laughed, raising an eyebrow as he looked at her with fond amusement. "Would you really mind? You seem quite happy, misty eyes."

"I would be," she said wistfully, "if it weren't for worrying about Myles, wondering if he's even alive and still in that miserable prison. We don't even know how long we've been *here*. Maybe the war is over."

"I hope it is. There's been enough suffering on both sides."

"At least we don't suffer. I'll admit I get tired of eating fish all the time and chewing leaves and bark, but we are managing to survive. We aren't skin and bones *yet*."

His eyes raked over her, and as he led her from the foaming waters, she saw that he was aroused and knew that he wanted her again. Would he ever tire of her? She admitted secretly that she never ceased to thrill to his endless lovemaking; but then, he seemed to be a skilled, perfect lover. What woman could ask for more? But, she worried, for all she knew, he had taught her, and perhaps, after a time, he would become bored.

He lowered himself onto the sand, lying on his back, arms folded behind his head, knees bent. The weather was warm, and they did not try to cover their nakedness with palm fronds.

She stared down at him, marveling once again at his gloriously formed body. How could any man be built so perfectly?

"Sometimes I hope we're never found," he murmured huskily, reaching to pull her down beside him, "because I can't get enough of you. And if we ever do get off this blasted island, you might want to leave me, and I don't want that to happen."

"Derek, I don't want to leave you," she whispered, her

fingers dancing through the thick, dark hairs that covered his chest.

And then she lowered her head between his thighs to receive him in the way she knew would drive him into writhing, moaning ecstasy.

Yes, he had taught her this too, and she reveled in the knowledge that she could give him so much pleasure. Did he know that she had fallen in love with him, that the words he asked her to speak came truly from her heart? She prayed that it was so.

But did he return that love? He never said the words, and when he looked at her in that arrogant way at times, white teeth flashing, as though he were so confident that he had mastered her spirit, she wondered if it were all a game for him to wile away the lonely hours.

Aroused to near insanity, Derek reached down and grabbed her about the waist and slung her roughly upon her back so that he could plunge himself deeply into her. Again and again he entered her, and when at last they were both spent, they lay side by side on the warm sand, faces lifted to the azure sky.

Suddenly Julie spoke the words that had been burning within her for so long. "Derek, do you love me?"

She heard the quick intake of his breath, and he was silent for so long that she had to fight the impulse to leap to her feet and run away lest he reject her in his usually blunt manner. She could feel the tears stinging her eyes, and did not want him to see her cry.

But she forced herself to lie still and wait, praying all the while that he would speak the words she longed to hear.

"Julie . . ." He said her name in a sigh. "I've never felt this way about any woman. You mean a great deal to me. But to speak of love—"

"You demand that I speak of it!" she snapped, unable to hide her bitterness. "Every time you take me, you ask me to say that I love you."

"I want to hear the words. I like to think you mean them. But you don't. In your own way, Julie, you're using me. You enjoy what I give you, just as you take pleasure in what you give me. There's no one else for either of us right now, but when this is all over, what then? You'll expect me to help you free your brother, if he's still in that prison in Richmond."

"Yes, I suppose I do expect that," she said candidly, moving out of the circle of his arms. "But you can afford to promise me that you will help me, because we both know there's a chance we may never leave this island."

He nodded. "That's true. But let's suppose we do get off, and I help you rescue your brother. What will you want of me after that?"

"I told you that I love you, and whether you believe me or not, Derek, I mean it."

She flung herself across his chest, loving the feel of his body, the way he tensed as her fingers trailed downward to toy with the thick mat of hair about his manhood. "When Myles is free, I still want to be with you."

"As my mistress?" He gave her that arrogant smile she hated.

She jerked away once again, suddenly angry. "Would you love your mistress as you would love a wife?"

He laughed, and that angered her even more. She tried to scramble to her feet, but his hand shot out to fasten around her arm, and as always, she was helpless in his powerful grasp.

"Look, Julie, I never intend to marry any woman, no matter how beautiful she may be or how much she pleases me with her body. I've told you that I desire you more than I've ever desired any woman. I want to keep you with me always. More than that I can't and won't give. That has to be enough."

Her angry eyes flashed and sparkled with red fires in a mist of green. "And if it isn't?"

"It has to be," he said simply. "For now, we're together. If we ever get off this island and you do leave me, then it's over. You know I could never hurt you, although I'd probably want to if you left me. But if you go, then I'd just forget I ever knew your name, your face, and your beautiful, desirable body."

He released her and she scrambled to her feet, still incensed by his bluntness and mirth.

"I suppose I should try to find us something to eat," he yawned. "I can't feast on that luscious body of yours all the time, but you do wear me out, woman. I've always felt I was a better man that most when it came to satisfying a woman, but you are a challenge."

She turned and began walking up the beach toward

their palm-frond shelter. "Maybe I'll give you a rest," she said over her shoulder. "Maybe if I refuse to give you what you want every time you want it, you won't be so damned sure of yourself."

"'Now that's a fine way for a genteel southern lady to talk," he laughed, getting to his feet. "And by the way, Julie, you've sure got a cute bottom. I like the way it bounces when you walk, especially when you're mad. When I finally make you my mistress, I think I want to keep you naked. So don't expect to be dressed in fine fashions as kept women usually are."

"Damn you, Derek Arnhardt!" She whirled around to scream at him. "I'll never be your kept woman, and it'll be a damned long time before you take your pleasure with me again. I'm sick and tired of your smugness!"

Still laughing, he started walking toward the water. "I'm not worried about your threats, Julie. All I have to do is touch the right places, and you'll squirm and scratch and bite and beg for more. . . ."

She stooped and grabbed the first thing she could find, a large conch shell, and she flung it at him, but he merely chuckled as he reached out to catch it easily with one hand.

"Remember, misty eyes," he called teasingly as she quickened her steps to hurry away from him, "I can always catch anything you throw my way, and so far, I've been able to throw back even more. . . ."

I hate him, she thought furiously as she threw herself down upon the dried palm fronds beneath the little shelter. *I do hate him! I only think I love him, because he makes me say the words over and over, and we're here alone on this miserable island, and there's no one else, and I'm making myself think I love him to justify all that we have together! It can't be love! I won't let it be, because I could never, ever love such a beast!*

She struck at the sand with her tiny fist, cursing herself for letting him make her so angry. If only she could return his arrogance, his smugness . . .

"Julie!"

At first she ignored his call. Damn him, anyway, she thought. He was going to learn that she would not come running every time he beckoned.

"Julie, come quick. . . ."

There was an urgency to his tone that she had never heard before. Forgetting her anger for the moment, she rose, moving quickly to peer out of the shelter to where he stood waist-deep in the water. Had he been stung by one of those jellylike creatures that were forever washing up on the beach and that he said would burn like fire if they touched you? Or was a shark nearby? Dear God, if he'd spotted one of those terrifying fins slicing through the water, then why was he standing there staring out at the open sea, his back to her, waving his arms wildly over his head and yelling at the top of his lungs?

And then she realized what was happening. She could see it, too—so small it looked like one of the wooden carvings she'd been so fascinated to see the crusty old seamen whittle as they sat on the docks at Savannah. A ship! It really was a ship!

She broke into a run, stumbling in the sand as she made her way to the foaming surf, wading in to stand beside Derek. He was so much taller, the water was up to her bare breasts while it only reached to his waist.

"Is it a Confederate ship?" she cried, raising her arms to wave with him. "Can you tell?"

"It doesn't matter," he said excitedly, turning around to splash his way back to the beach.

She followed him, watching as he gathered the dried-out driftwood that they always kept for fires. In moments he had a blaze going that sent smoke skyward.

"They should see that," he said anxiously, staring back at the murky waters. "They aren't that far out. Can't imagine what a ship would be doing nearby. We haven't seen one before."

Suddenly he reached out and hugged her tightly against him. "Julie, I think they've seen us," he cried, and she could feel his body trembling. "Yes . . . yes, they have. I can tell. They're coming this way. We're saved, Julie! They're coming after us. . . ."

A strange emotion washed over her as she allowed herself to be lifted in his arms and swung about in jubilation. Derek did not notice that she was not smiling, did not share his enthusiasm. He finally set her back down on her feet, leaving her to run and stand at the water's edge and watch the ship's approach. Her mind was a jumble of confused thoughts. What if Yankees were approaching, and not Confederates? Would she and Derek be taken prisoner? And if it were a Rebel steamer, what then? Would Derek help her rescue Myles from the Black Hole?

She shook her head, body trembling. Dear God, she did not know what she was supposed to feel at this moment in time. Should Myles be dead, or already freed and making a life of his own, in peace, what was there left for her to return to? Here, on this quiet island, she had found solitude and love, even though the love was obviously felt only on her part. At least there had been happiness and joy, but now, with rescue in sight, the future suddenly seemed more uncertain than ever.

Suddenly, as though he finally remembered her presence, Derek turned. "Those clothes . . ." he called. "The ones we had when we arrived—get them. I know they're rags, but I don't want them to find us just standing here naked, Julie. Piece together what you can. . . ."

And then he was facing the sea once again, turning his back on her and the life they had shared together, the passion, the bliss.

Bitterly she walked to where they had tucked the remnants of clothing beneath a large rock, planning to fashion them into some kind of blanket should the weather ever turn cool. Yanking her tattered dress about her, she knotted the dangling sleeves across her breasts, cursing herself all the while. Here they were, about to be rescued —how could she be so foolish as to feel sad? It was ridiculous. Why, the world was waiting out there, a new life, and however confused and tumultuous she might find it, she would find a way to face it. There was no point in looking back now.

She carried the remains of Derek's clothing to him, and he wrapped a piece of cloth around himself large enough to conceal his privates. Then they stood side by side, the lapping water foaming about their feet as they waited in silence.

Soon they could make out a small rowboat moving steadily toward the island. Julie could feel Derek tensing beside her, knew that he was worrying over whether their rescuers would be Confederates or the enemy.

Then they were able to see the faces of the three men in the boat. Two carried rifles, which were pointed straight at them. The third man sat in the bow, eyes slitted as he studied them suspiciously. All were bearded and wore the clothes of men of the sea. There was no way to tell on which side they fought.

One of the armed men lay down his weapon and jumped into the waist-deep water, leaping up now and then to ride a breaker as he guided the boat to the shore line. The seated man continued to stare, while the other kept his gun trained upon them. Derek did not move, but Julie had begun to tremble, and she sidled closer to him so that their bodies touched. His arm went about her protectively, and despite the tension of the moment, she felt a shudder of confidence at his nearness.

The man who had been seated stood as the boat slid smoothly onto the beach. Parting tight-set lips he barked, "My name is Joseph Bosworth. I am first mate on the *Judy T.* This is Bradley Whitlock," he nodded to the man who had pulled them through the surf, then to the one holding the gun, "and this is Sherman Kiser. We are fishermen. Who might you be and why are you marooned here on this island?"

"I'm Derek Arnhardt," Derek's voice rang out, clear, steady, and if fear mingled with the blood in his veins, it was not evident in his tone. "My ship was destroyed by the Federal blockade at Wilmington some time back. We don't know how long we've been here. But whether you are friend or foe, I pray we can be grateful that you've come to rescue us."

"Arnhardt!" Joseph Bosworth's tight-set lips curved slightly into a pleased smile of recognition. "I've heard of you, sir. It's *Captain* Arnhardt, isn't it? And sometimes you are called Ironheart, because they say you rule your crew with a fist of iron and a heart to match. We heard you were lost at sea with your ship."

He stepped from the boat with an outstretched hand, and, shaking Derek's warmly, he told his men to lay down their weapons. "We have nothing to fear." To Derek he said, "Neither do you, sir. It's a pleasure indeed to have a hand in rescuing a man of your worth, believe me. We are fishermen. We take no part in the war, but we're southern blood, and that is where our loyalties lie. If my pilot hadn't gotten himself saturated on rum he smuggled aboard and fallen asleep on duty, we wouldn't have gone off course. We sail in and out of Richmond, and here we are on the other side of the Gulf Stream on an uncharted island. Now I'm glad that we did, and I won't have that man keelhauled, because it was surely a stroke of fate that we happened this way and found you."

"Thank you, sir," Derek murmured gratefully. Then, remembering Julie's presence, he nodded in her direction and made the necessary introductions.

The men exchanged uncomfortable glances, and Julie felt her cheeks flaming. It was not hard to figure out why they were so embarrassed. Shipwrecked on an island for untold months, it was obvious what had transpired between them, especially since they stood there barely clothed in shreds and remnants of material.

"We should get you on board at once." Mr. Bosworth extended his hand to Julie to lead her to the rowboat. "We'll get some good solid food into you, then we'll be on our way back to Richmond."

It was Bradley Whitlock who asked, just before shoving the boat back into the surf, if there was anything on the island they wished to take with them to the *Judy T*. Derek glanced at Julie expectantly, but she lowered her eyes and shook her head. What she had left behind, she thought painfully, could not be brought with her, for she feared that she was leaving forever any love the two of them might have shared.

Once aboard the fishing boat, they were introduced to the captain, a burly, potbellied man named Meade, with warm gray eyes and a friendly smile despite his authoritative air. He ordered food brought to them immediately, then he instructed one of his crew to bring them some clothes.

"We'll have to dress you like a man for awhile, missy," he said jovially to Julie, and she smiled slightly, grateful for anything they would give her to wear.

When they were fed and clothed, they went to the captain's cramped quarters. Julie lay her head on Derek's strong shoulder as they sat on the narrow wooden bunk, listening sleepily while he spoke with Captain Meade as the two shared a bottle of brandy.

"I just can't believe what you're telling me." Julie snapped to alertness at the loud, stunned tone of Derek's voice. "It can't be nearly winter. . . ."

"Ahh, but it is." Captain Meade smiled sympathetically.

"It seems the two of you were lost in another world, and you may wish before this dreadful war ends that you had stayed back there in your own private realm."

Derek leaned forward, eager to hear all that Meade knew about the war.

The captain packed his corncob pipe with tobacco, lit it, drew on it, exhaled, and then began to talk.

He told them about a man named John S. Mosby who, with his Confederate partisan rangers, had attacked Fairfax Court House, Virginia on the night of March eighth, only a few miles from Washington, the Union capital. "The only thing they got," he chuckled, "was the garrison commander, General Edwin Stoughton, who was asleep when they went slipping in."

But the humor left his voice as he told about how Federal cavalry under General George Stoneman had cut a swath of destruction through Virginia from April twenty-ninth to May eighth, almost to Richmond itself. "Stoneman being gone from the Army of the Potomac helped Lee win one of his biggest battles yet, though," the captain explained. "You see, late in April, General Joe Hooker headed south toward Richmond with an army that they say numbered over a quarter of a million. He marched through a mass of thick woods and dense underbrush called The Wilderness, and Stonewall Jackson hit him with a surprise flank attack at a road junction called Chancellorsville. The fighting lasted for about three days, and it went all the way from Chancellorsville ten miles eastward toward Fredericksburg. Ol' Hooker lost almost twenty thousand of his soldiers, I hear tell."

Suddenly his voice dropped, cracked, as though he were fighting for composure. In a whisper so low they had to strain to hear, Captain Meade said, "We lost Stonewall there. He was accidentally hit by one of his own men."

"Stonewall Jackson!" Derek breathed reverently. "God, what a blow to the South. . . ."

"But Lee got started on a second invasion of the North." The captain slammed his fist on his desk. "He wanted to capture an important city in the North, like Baltimore or Harrisburg, or even Washington. The papers said if he could do that, it would relieve the pressure on Vicksburg, down in Mississippi, and we might negotiate a victorious peace. Then the South was also hoping that if we could win a great victory on northern soil, England might raise its eyebrows and offer to mediate.

"Lee also wanted to get some of the fighting out of Virginia," the captain went on after pausing to draw on his pipe thoughtfully. "And the South needs supplies bad. So last June, Lee took his army and crossed the Potomac. Lincoln had replaced Hooker with a Pennsylvanian by the name of General George G. Meade."

He chuckled bitterly. "I hope to God I'm not kin to that man somewhere back along the line. I hope not a drop of Yankee blood flows in these tired old veins of mine."

Julie saw Derek smile politely, but could sense his anxiety to hear more about the war.

"Well," Captain Meade went on, "by the end of June, the Yankees were moving north from Maryland into Pennsylvania, looking for Rebs, and the Rebs had turned south to look for supplies. They came together from opposite directions and collided at a place called Gettysburg, Pennsylvania."

He shook his head sadly, stared at the crude wooden floor in desolation for a few moments, then said, "It was three days of hell, it was. Lee delivered one attack after another, but on the third day, a general named Pickett charged about fifteen thousand men across an open field, right against the center of the Yankee line. He failed, lost half his men, and the battle ended. The Yankees were credited with that one and ever since, the South's morale has been at its lowest ebb. It's like looking at the shoreline when the tide has gone out and wondering whether it's ever going to come back in. The sea returns, but will the South?"

He looked at them wonderingly, as though they might be able to give him an answer, then shook his head once more in weary sadness. "Lee retreated to Virginia. Now they say both armies are sitting on opposite sides of the Rapidan River, each one waiting for the other to make the first move. I imagine they'll hole in for the winter, though we get news of a few cavalry engagements and some skirmishes among the infantry now and then, but nothing big."

Derek sighed, closed his eyes for a moment, then spread

his large hands helplessly and said, "So you're telling me, Captain Meade, that things don't look good for the South."

"Yes, I guess I am. Like I said, morale is mighty low. The blockade is getting tighter too. One bright spot you might be interested in hearing about, though, is that the Confederates have built something they call a torpedo boat. It's a small vessel propelled by a steam engine. There's one called the *David*, and early this month it was in Charleston harbor and hit and damaged a blockading warship called the *New Ironsides*. They say she just drifts along the surface of the water and attacks enemy ships with a torpedo suspended from a long spar."

Derek said nothing.

The captain tapped his pipe into a cup on his desk, then began repacking it with fresh tobacco. Glancing sideways at Derek, he warily asked, "Don't that news get your ire up, sir? Doesn't that make you want to get back to Wilmington and start running that blasted blockade again?"

Derek was silent for a long time, and Julie finally turned her gaze upon him and saw that he had a strange look in his smoky eyes, as though he were deep in thought. Finally he murmured to no one in particular, "No, it doesn't make me want to go back to war. I'm beginning to wish we could have just stayed on that island, because it seems neither side will be satisfied until all of America is destroyed in body and in spirit."

"Aye, it's easy to see how you feel." Captain Meade nodded with understanding. "I suppose you might call the *Judy T* my own little island. I take her out and catch fish to feed my family. My crew does the same. I'm an old man, Arnhardt, too old to do anything in this infernal war except get in the way. You'll notice my crewmen are on in years as well. Oh, a few of them did go off to fight. A few got killed. The others came back without an arm or a leg. So they joined me again, just wanting to be fishermen on the sea and pretend there isn't a war. I don't feel ashamed because I don't take part in it. I can't blame anybody wanting to escape the hell of it all."

Glancing at Julie apologetically, he said, "You don't look none the worse for your stay on that island, young lady. I suppose you're wishing we'd just left you there, but then I suppose you've got family somewhere that have spent many hours grieving over you."

"I have a brother in Libby prison in Richmond," she told him calmly. "As soon as we arrive, I plan to get him out of there, using whatever means is necessary."

Derek shot her a warning look, and the Captain's bushy brows shot up in surprise, but she quietly continued in a very calm voice, explaining in complete detail why her mission was so important. "It is what I set out to do when I left my home in Savannah," she finished. "I won't rest until I know my brother is out of that dreadful place."

"Well, you've got a right to want him out if he's innocent," the captain nodded briskly, "and even if he isn't, being your brother, I can see why you'd want him freed. I've heard terrible stories about the Black Hole and the atrocities there. . . ."

Suddenly Derek got to his feet. "If you'll show us where we can bed down, Captain, we'd be grateful. We're rather tired."

Julie did not miss the way the old man's lips fought to suppress a knowing smile as he said the ship was, after all, small, and they were cramped for quarters. "I suppose since you two have shared an island for several months, you won't mind sharing a cabin for a few days."

"I can sleep with the crew," Derek snapped, eyes sparkling as he moved toward the door. "Just tell me where I can take Julie so she can retire."

The captain rose. "I suppose I'll have to let her have my cabin, Arnhardt. The men sleep in the hold on sling hammocks. I have no other cabins. I was prepared to put the two of you in here, but if you prefer—"

"I do prefer," Derek said with finality.

"Very well." Captain Meade went to the door, nodded in Julie's direction, and murmured that if he could be of further help, they should let him know.

Julie choked out a hollow-sounding thank you, and once the door was closed behind the old man, she turned to Derek with tears stinging her eyes as she whispered in anguish, "I've never been so humiliated in my life. Every man on board this ship knows what must have gone on between us while we were on that island. How can I face them? How can I face anyone?"

Giving her a look of exasperation, Derek sighed, "What difference does it make, Julie? Once we reach Richmond, you'll never see any of them again. Just be grateful that we've been rescued. Now you can try to do the same for your precious brother."

She stared at him, stunned momentarily, then gasped, "Why, Derek, you sound jealous! Can't you see how much it means to me to have Myles out of that horrible place—"

"Yes, yes, I've heard it all before," he said wearily, running his hands through his shoulder-length hair. "Look, we'll talk about all of this later. Right now I'm going to get a haircut and have a bath."

Julie bit down on her lower lip thoughtfully. It seemed so strange, after all this time, for them to no longer be alone together, to be surrounded by other people. It was almost as though their island of paradise, the closeness they'd shared, had never really existed. Derek was different somehow. She could sense the change, and she did not like the bitterness she felt over this realization.

He turned to go, but she ran to him, flinging her arms around him and pressing her face against his broad back. "Promise you won't leave me, Derek," she cried, squeezing him tightly, her body trembling. "You can't say that what we shared together meant nothing to you."

Turning, he encircled her tiny waist with his large hands, dark eyes boring into hers for long, silent moments. Then he moved one hand upward, trailing it slowly across her breasts, touching the hollow in her throat, finally cupping her face and squeezing gently, possessively, "No, I can't say that what we shared meant nothing to me." His voice was husky yet tender. "But if you want to remain with me, Julie, then you have to go where I go and follow me."

"And that means being your mistress—"

He raised one eyebrow and gave her a crooked smile. "Yes, it means being my mistress. You're beautiful, desirable, and you bring me much pleasure. I'd miss you if we had to part, but it's up to you."

Julie took a deep breath. Her heart was pounding. She did not want to lose him, and if it meant being his mistress, then so be it. But there had to be one concession on his part. "I'll go with you. I'll do anything you ask of me and be anything you want me to be. But help me free my brother. Then I will swear to you that I'm yours for as long as you want me."

He seemed to peer into the most secret recesses of her

soul. Here was a man she knew she would never be able to maneuver. To go with him, to belong to him, meant giving him not just her body, but her being, her life.

She felt desire rising within her at just his nearness, the feel of his warm breath upon her face. Love? Passion? Which did she really feel? She could not even answer the questions her own heart was demanding of her. She knew only that when he was near, holding her so closely, there was no fear, not of war or man. Derek would always keep her from harm.

Painful memories flashed before her eyes. With Derek she would be protected. Yet she knew that at that very moment he could crush the life from her body by merely lowering his fingers and tightening them about her throat. Gentle, soothing, tender, this giant of a man could also be brutal, cold, and savage. And he could move from one mood to another with a mere blink of an eye.

Suddenly he lowered his face, covering her mouth with his lips. His tongue pressed against hers, and he held her so close that the embrace was almost painful. They seemed molded into one being. He quickly stripped her of her clothes, then pulled off his own. He cupped her buttocks tightly and lifted her up against him, impaling her as he thrust himself in and out . . . again and again . . . till their bodies quivered together in ecstatic climax, their passion once more satiated . . . if only for a short while.

He lowered her so that her feet touched the floor once again, and he lifted his face from hers. "All right, Julie," he said quietly. "I'll help you try to free Myles."

"Derek, you won't regret it, I swear it," she responded joyously.

He pressed a fingertip against her lips for silence, and she saw that his eyes were cold, ominous. When he spoke, his tone was frightening. "Heed me well, Julie. You've made me a promise, and I expect you to keep it. If you attempt to use me, to manipulate me, then God help you, because I won't take that from any woman—no matter how beautiful she may be . . . or how much pleasure her body gives me. That includes you, misty eyes."

He stepped away from her, eyelids lowered as he regarded her with suspicion. "You belong to me now. We've sealed our agreement."

He left the cabin, closing the door quietly behind him, and the sound seemed to punctuate the pronouncement of his warning. Julie wrapped her arms about her naked body, unable to control the tremors that had begun to sweep her entire being.

No, she felt no fear of any man or thing when Derek held her tightly in his powerful arms . . . no fear, that is, except of Derek himself.

❧ Chapter Twenty ❧

JULIE stood silently beside Derek in the cold November wind, staring toward the large, white-walled three-story building a block away. Julie saw that the windows were barred and began counting the ones on the third floor. Fifteen. An equal number on the second floor. Only eight on the first level, with five doors at varying intervals. To the far right, a porch extended from one entrance. She assumed that would be the one they should enter to inquire if Myles was still there.

She squeezed Derek's hand as she asked, "Can we go in there now? I can ask to speak to Thomas, and—"

"Hell, no," he all but shouted, then lowered his voice as a few people walking by turned to stare curiously. "Can't you see all those guards walking around? Those aren't tree branches they're carrying. Those are guns. And if we walk toward that door, they're going to start asking questions."

"I have a right to ask to see my cousin."

She felt as though her fingers were surely going to be crushed as he squeezed her hand angrily. "I told you I'd handle this. We aren't going to just walk in there. If Myles is in there, still alive, we've got to plan his escape. That's going to take help, and it's also going to take time. I've got to get some men together who are willing to help."

"And where are you going to find them?"

"Leave it to me. But we're going to need money. Any man who joins an escape attempt at that prison, or any prison, knows he's putting his life on the line. He's not going to do that for free. He's going to have a price, and it will be high."

She was suddenly afraid. "We don't have any money! Captain Meade's wife had to give me this dress because there was no money to even buy clothes for us. And if he hadn't loaned you a bit, we'd be completely destitute."

"Trust me," he said wearily, impatiently. He gave her a tug as he turned back the way they had come, along the docks. She did not move. He sighed. "Julie, come along now. We can't arouse suspicion, and some of those guards are starting to look this way."

She was about to let him lead her away, but just then she glimpsed the face of a prisoner at one of the windows on the third floor, peering out through the bars. From where they stood, she could not make out his features, but still her heart leaped with what she knew was only foolish hope. "There's one of the prisoners," she cried, pointing. "It could be Myles, or he might know Myles—"

Then her hand flew to her mouth in horror as one of the guards spotted the prisoner, quickly pointed his rifle, and began firing. Julie screamed, and Derek quickly put his arms about her to lead her away. She was stumbling, shuddering with terror. "Dammit, you listen to me." He shook her hard, guiding her as fast as he could. "He probably didn't hit that prisoner. I've heard the guards take pot shots when one of the Yankees looks out. Sometimes they get killed, but not often. And if Myles is still alive, he's learned by now not to go looking out windows, or he *wouldn't* be alive. Do you understand what I'm saying?"

Some of the horror was passing, and being replaced by anger. "I can't believe Thomas is one of the officers there. He'd never allow such a thing to go on. He was always gentle and kind—"

"And he's a soldier now. An officer. He's all grown up and trained to be a full-fledged Yankee-killer. It's war, Julie, and people change."

She jerked out of his grasp. "I'm going back there and demand to see him. He'll tell me if Myles is still there, and then we can plan the escape. I won't rest easy till I know he's alive."

"He's alive, Julie."

She had taken a few steps in the direction of the prison but turned to stare at him incredulously.

"You heard me. Myles is alive. I had someone check that out for me the first day we arrived. It cost me a keg of rum, but I swiped that from Captain Meade," he grinned. "Now come along."

They turned from the waterfront. Light snow was beginning to fall from ominously gray skies. Julie asked where they were going but Derek just kept plodding ahead, refusing to answer her questions.

Soon it was snowing quite heavily, and they were caught up in an alabaster world. Any other time, Julie thought miserably, she would have been enthralled, but she was too lost in thought to enjoy the beauty around her. Derek noticed she was shivering as her dress and shawl grew damp. He put his arm about her, drawing her close, and she did not pull away.

Suddenly he slowed his pace. They were standing in front of a large, two-story house. "Who lives here?" Julie demanded as Derek led the way up the snow-covered walkway to the wide front porch. "Why are we stopping here?"

"I've got to leave you someplace, Julie, to make sure you don't get in trouble while I'm gone." He began to bang on one of the glass-paned doors so hard that it rattled.

"What do you mean? While you're gone where? I'm not staying here. . . ."

He ignored her and continued to knock. Then they heard the sounds of footsteps from within. The door opened, and Julie found herself staring at one of the most painted-up women she had ever seen. Her cheeks were a flaming orange, and her lips, the color of blood. Long yellow hair streamed down her back, and she wore a thin green silk wrapper that revealed she wore nothing underneath.

"Derek Arnhardt, you old son of a gun," she shrieked happily, throwing her arms around his neck. "It's been so damn long, I thought you'd died, or worse, gotten married!"

"You know me better than that, Opal." Derek dropped Julie's hand to lift the woman high in the air and whirl her around as she giggled shrilly.

Julie stared at the rich furnishings inside, the magnificent crystal chandelier which hung from the ceiling. Her mouth dropped open as she saw the paintings of naked women on the walls. The air was heavily scented with perfume.

Derek set the woman down and yanked Julie into the

house. Her head jerked around at the sound of voices from above. A man was walking down the stairway, smiling as though quite pleased with himself. Above him, leaning over the railing, there was a woman painted up as gaudily as Opal, and Julie glanced away as she saw her bare breasts hanging out of her lace wrapper.

"You're the best I've ever had, you big, old stud," the woman called to the man. "You come back to see me, you hear?" Her laughter sounded artificial to Julie's ears, but the departing man grinned broadly. He blew her a kiss and scurried out the front door.

". . . and I must go to Wilmington on business." Julie cocked her head to catch the tail end of what Derek was saying. "I want you to take good care of her while I'm gone."

Julie's emerald eyes flashed at Derek and the woman in turn, then she snapped, "You aren't leaving me here. I know what kind of place this is. It—it's a *whorehouse!*"

"Hey, you watch your mouth," Opal whirled about angrily. "I run a nice business here. You can't call none of my girls whores. They're all ladies—"

"Whores, harlots, prostitutes! It's all the same. I've no intention of staying here." She turned toward the door, but Derek caught her arm and spun her about to press her back against the wall. Placing a hand on each side of her shoulders, he pinned her in front of him, leaning forward to flash that arrogant smile she hated.

"Calm down, misty eyes," he said lazily, confidently. "Opal here, is one of the nicest madams in town. She runs a good, clean business, and she's selective of her customers. They don't get in unless they're recommended. Now she's agreed to look after you while I go to Wilmington to get the money we need. I've got some hidden there."

"I'll go with you," Julie said

"No. You'd slow me down. And I can't afford the price of a hotel room. Besides, you might get in trouble. I can't risk leaving you alone."

"I'll be fine by myself. Derek, I can't stay here, in this place." She gave Opal a cold look. "What if she sends a man to my room? Am I supposed to earn my keep?" she added icily.

Opal snorted. "Hell, who'd want you? You're green as hell. I can look at you and tell you don't know a damn thing about pleasuring a man, not the way my girls do."

Derek shifted his gaze to Opal. "She knows how to please *me*, and she belongs to me. Remember that. You get any funny notions and I'll break your neck."

Opal tossed her head as though unfazed by his threat, but Julie could see she was unnerved. "I said you didn't have to worry," she snapped, placing her hands on her hips and letting her wrapper fall open to expose her breasts. Derek didn't even glance at them, turning instead to Julie.

"She'll give you a room of your own, and that's where you'll stay till I return. I'll try to make it as fast as possible, but with this weather, I may be slowed down."

Julie looked about helplessly, floundering, not knowing whether to scream or cry. "You—you can't do this to me, Derek. You can't leave me in a place like this. God, why are you doing this to me?"

He pulled her outside onto the porch, telling Opal they would return in a few minutes. Then, ignoring the frigid weather, the snow swirling about them, Derek tried to explain to her, "You'd be stupid enough to try to get Myles out of that prison by yourself. I saw the look in your eyes when you were there, staring up at those windows. No, I can't take a chance on leaving you alone."

"I won't stay," she bristled with anger. "I'll run away, Derek—"

He laughed, which only made her even more furious. "I thought of that. Opal has guards around to keep her customers and her girls in line, so she's well equipped to make sure you stay put till I get back."

Leaning forward, he attempted to kiss her, but she jerked to one side. His lips brushed her cheek and he chuckled. "All right. Be angry with me. But when I return and all this is behind us, you'll learn not to turn away from me. I'll make you into the most loving and obedient mistress a man ever had."

"You'll die trying!" she cried, pushing at his chest, but he was holding her tightly. "I'll never let you touch me again. Never. I was a fool to think I cared. I hate you!"

"You only think you hate me, because you aren't getting your way. You've finally met a man who won't give into you merely because you happen to be quite beautiful. We have an understanding, remember? I get your brother out of prison, and you become my mistress."

"You can forget our understanding, as you call it. I don't want your help."

"Ah, but you have to have it." He reached out to squeeze her bottom, then released her. "Now I have to be on my way. Don't give Opal any trouble, or she may charge extra for your keep."

He opened the door as he spoke. Opal heard the last remark and spoke up quickly. "She won't give me no trouble. I got ways of dealing with uppity little snits like her—"

Abruptly Derek spun to face her, and Julie knew from past experience that he was infuriated to the danger point. He shook his fist in the woman's face and ground out the words, "If she's harmed in any way, I swear to God I'll kill you and anyone else who touches her. You heed me well."

Opal shrank back, retreating a few steps into the room and smiling nervously as she whispered, "Now, Derek, you know I'll do exactly as you ask. We've been friends a long time, and you know me—"

"And *you* know *me*," he retorted menacingly. "I don't make idle threats. Take care of this girl. She means a great deal to me."

Later Julie was to remember his words with pain . . . how he did not say: "I love her," but rather, "She means a great deal to me." She would remember, and ache, and hate herself for caring even that much.

❦ Chapter Twenty-one ❧

JULIE was awakened by the sound of someone fumbling with the outer locks on her door. She sat up and stared in surprise at the young girl who entered. She wore a taffeta dress of shocking pink; it dipped low in front. Her honey-gold hair was coiffed in ringlets, pulled back, and tied with a black bow. Despite the heavy make-up she wore, her heart-shaped face looked quite immature.

"Hello. My name is Garnet." She spoke in a breathless voice. "Actually, my real name is Annie, but Opal makes all her girls use fancy names. Garnet *does* sound fancy, doesn't it? Opal says her clients would rather ask for Garnet than Annie. I say they don't care as long as they get their money's worth."

She was carrying a tray, and she walked over and set it down on the bedside table. Placing her hands on her hips, she looked up and said, "Well, I see Opal fixed you up just fine. This is one of the nicer rooms, reserved for special clients.

"Hey, I saw him!" She suddenly broke into a wide grin. "That man who brought you in yesterday. He's really handsome! And what a body! I've never seen a man built so big—and proportioned just right, too. And those eyes!" She made a smacking sound. "He's a fine one, he is!

"This room's a lot bigger than mine," Garnet murmured. "I like the drapes, too. Red velvet. Pretty, aren't they? One thing about Opal. She don't run no cheap joint. That's how she gets away with charging big money from the men who come here."

She looked from the tray to where Julie sat, still staring

at her, open-mouthed now. "What's wrong? That's a steak that Opal had the cook send up. And a bottle of wine, too. Your man said you was to receive the very best. You really should eat. You've got nice teats, but you're on the skinny side. Some of the girls are jealous of how pretty you are. Me, it don't matter. Of course, I'd like to have a man like yours in *my* bed, but I ain't the jealous kind."

She took a deep breath, bosom heaving, and shook her head in exasperation. "You're a quiet thing, aren't you? You going to just sit there and stare at me? I figured you'd be grateful for some company. Hell, you been locked up in here since yesterday."

Garnet cocked her head to one side, and her voice took on a sympathetic note. "You been crying, ain't you? Didn't you know that makes wrinkles? A girl with looks like yours should try to take care of them, you know."

"You . . . you haven't given me a chance to say much," Julie whispered, her stomach rumbling as she looked at the steak and wine. "Thank you for bringing me the food, Garnet. I am hungry, and most grateful for the company."

Garnet slapped her hip and laughed raucously. "That's more like it. Opal says you're a priss, but I don't think so."

Julie pulled the tray onto her lap, then picked up a knife and fork and began cutting the meat. "What's a priss?" she wanted to know.

"Oh, you know—prissy, conceited, putting on airs. She says you think you're too good to be in a place like this. Hell, we're just working girls. Sure beats starving to death like the rest of the South. Richmond's a big place. Busy, too, it being the capital of the Confederacy and all. And, like I said, Opal runs a nice place. We get officers here. And merchants. Lots of rich men. They don't want to go looking for their loving down at those waterfront rat holes. They're afraid they'll get the pox along with their pleasure." She giggled, then added, "They know Opal's clean, too, and she keeps her girls that way."

She drew up a high-backed chair of gold brocade and sat down daintily, careful not to muss her skirt. She watched Julie eating for a few moments, then asked, "How come that man of yours is keeping you locked up? I don't know why in hell you'd want to run away from him."

"There's more to it than that," Julie told her, still a bit wary of this strange girl but grateful for the company.

"My brother is in Libby prison, and I want to get him out. Derek says he'll help me, but I don't altogether trust him anymore. And he's afraid if he doesn't keep me locked up, I'll try to get my brother out by myself. And I probably would."

"Libby prison, huh?" Garnet reached over and picked up a piece of Julie's steak with her fingers and popped it in her mouth, smacking her lips happily. "Mmmm, that's good. We don't get steak often. Opal's tight with her money when it comes to food. Says we girls have to stay slim, too.

"Libby prison," she went on thoughtfully. "That's that old warehouse they call the Black Hole. What's he doing in there? It's a Yankee prison. Is he a deserter or a traitor?"

"Neither!" Julie cried sharply, then went ahead and told her the whole story. It helped, she realized, to talk to someone, and despite the girl's brittleness, she did seem friendly. Also, in the back of her mind she was already formulating a plot for an escape of her own, and a friend just might come in handy, she reasoned.

Garnet slapped her thighs when Julie finished. "Wowee, that's some story. So your man is Derek Arnhardt, the infamous Captain Ironheart everybody's heard about, huh? And he wants to make you his mistress. Well, you could do a lot worse. I think Opal wants him, though, 'cause she don't like you."

Julie blinked. "I had that feeling. Why doesn't she?"

"I told you. She says you're a priss. And she says she don't know what he sees in you. She's like me, I guess, chomping at the bit to be his woman and wondering why you're having fits and wanting to run away. Besides, your brother's probably dead by now if he's been in that place as long as you say."

Julie's heart was wrenched painfully as she whispered, "Myles is strong, both in mind and body. If anyone can survive, he can. And Derek told me he found out that he's still there."

"So how would you go about getting him out?"

Julie told Garnet about Thomas. "I sing a little," she confided. "I'd just go there and tell my cousin to set me up to entertain the officers and guard with my singing. Then I'd find a way to get Myles out. I'd learn my way around the place, and I'd find a way. I promise you that, Garnet."

"Sounds like fun," the girl giggled. "If there was any money in it, I'd help you."

"You would?" Julie's eyebrows rose in hopeful surprise.

Garnet eyed her suspiciously, then said, "I'm just teasing. I've got a good thing going here, and I ain't going to louse it up. But don't worry. I won't tell anything you told me to anybody. Now I got to be going before Opal really gets mad."

After she left, Julie paced up and down the room restlessly. From below, she could hear the sound of music, voices, and now and then muffled giggles and laughter as Opal's girls led their clients to their rooms. It made her furious to think Derek would confine her to such a place. Just who did he think he was, anyway? She wasn't his slave!

If only she could get out, she thought with a fierceness that set her blood to boiling. He'd receive quite a shock if he returned and found her gone. She stamped her foot in disgust. All his words of devotion had merely been an act. He cared for her only because he enjoyed her body and thought her beautiful. He would never love her. Dammit, she had to get out of this place and free Myles so they could be on their way to a new life!

The windows in her room were sealed. She was on the second floor, and even if she did manage to open one of them, she would break a leg if she jumped. So she would need Garnet's help. Garnet was interested in money. She had let that be known. But Julie had nothing to pay her with, not even a piece of jewelry!

It all seemed so futile, and she worried on top of everything else what her fate would be if Derek decided not to return. Would Opal force her to become one of her girls? Things like that happened—women being kept as prostitutes against their will. Was this to be her lot in life?

The hours dragged by with painful slowness. Now and then Julie slept, only to be awakened by shrill laughter and music. Finally the house was quiet.

Garnet came the next morning, wearing a bright red wrapper and carrying a tray of eggs and a cup of coffee. "I got up early just to come visit you," she yawned, but her eyes were shining. "I guess I feel sorry for you."

"It was awful last night, " Julie admitted. "I'm so glad you came."

"It's worse on the outside. Have you heard how bad some people are suffering?" And Garnet launched into a description of conditions in the South. Some women were making fans of palmetto, paper, and goose feathers. Starch was being made by soaking wheat bran, grated corn, or sweet potatoes in water until they fermented. Then the surface was skimmed, and the remainder of the solution run through sieves and cloths.

As Julie picked at the eggs, Garnet rambled on, seemingly just as eager for company as Julie. "They make soap by mixing lye, drained from ashes, with leftover grease. 'Course, country folks been doing that all along, but the fine families are having to do it now too. And some folks are even making shoe polish by mixing soot with lard. And they use twigs to brush their teeth, chewing the twigs at the end to separate them a bit. Some even use *hog* bristles. Can you imagine?" Garnet wrinkled her nose. "And can you imagine using lard, scented with rose petals, for hair oil?"

Julie pushed the tray away, her food only half-eaten. Garnet reached for it eagerly and began to eat, talking around the food in her mouth. "Some women fix their hair with combs carved from cow horns. Isn't that disgusting? And they make hairpins from thorns."

Suddenly Julie interrupted her. "Garnet, how old are you?"

"Fifteen," she said easily, laughing at Julie's reaction. "You'd never know it to look at me, would you? I've always been big for my age, especially in the places that count." She winked.

"But how did you—"

"Wind up here?" Garnet shrugged. "I didn't want to stay on the farm. Ma cried, and Pa didn't care when I left, I was just one less mouth to feed."

Neither of them heard the door open, and did not realize Opal had entered the room till she spoke sharply. "Garnet! How many times have I told you to keep your personal life to yourself? Julie is our guest, and she doesn't want to be bothered with your mindless chattering."

"It's all right, really," Julie said quickly. "I'm grateful for the company. I'm miserable shut up here all the time."

"Are you now?" Opal's eyes began to shine. "That's a pity, because there's no telling when Derek will return. I've

known him a long time, and he's very unpredictable. I hate
to say this, but he might not even come back."

Julie jumped, startled. "I felt that way but what makes
you say that?"

Opal shrugged. "Like I said, he's unpredictable. Or
maybe *unreliable* is a bettter description. I can't tell you
how many young girls he's gone off and left, promising to
return." She smiled a bit shamefacedly. "I must admit I'm
one of them."

"Y—you?" Julie sputtered. "I—I don't believe it."

"Oh, it's true. Derek and I had quite a romance going
once, but he went away for so long I knew he wouldn't be
coming back—at least, not for anything permanent. I settled for seeing him whenever he was in town, but I learned
a dear lesson. I don't give my heart—just my love." She
looked at Garnet and the two shared a laugh while Julie
looked on, hurt as the realization of what Opal said
washed over her.

"Look, dear, we got off to a bad start." Opal sat down
beside her on the bed and put a friendly arm around her
shoulders. "Garnet can tell you I'm really not a bad sort.
Now I feel sorry for you. I know what you're going
through. But it isn't the end of the world."

Julie looked at her hopefully. "You'll let me leave?"

"Oh, I can't do that." Opal shook her head quickly. "If
Derek does come back, he'd have my head. No, I can't let
you leave, but I can give you more freedom. Suppose I
send Garnet in a little later with a pretty dress for you?
You can go downstairs and serve wine and brandy to our
clients as they arrive. You can help me be hostess."

Julie stood up, lips set angrily. "I'm not going to work
for you, Opal."

The older woman laughed once more. "Come now,
dear. Do you think I would put you to work? Why, you're
too inexperienced. My clients demand the best. But you
are lovely, and I thought you might like to mingle and get
out of your room. But it's up to you. If you would rather
stay here, then so be it."

Julie looked at her suspiciously, then decided no one
could make her go to bed with any of the men; and if she
were forced, somehow, Derek would find out . . . *if* he
came back, she thought painfully, bitterly. "All right," she
said finally. "I will do it. Anything is better than being
cooped up in this room."

Later in the day Garnet appeared with a bright satin dress of sunshine yellow. "It'll look nice with that black hair of yours," she bubbled. "I've got some yellow velvet rosettes in case you want to tie back your ringlets."

An hour later Julie was moving through the parlor, holding a tray from which she served crystal glasses filled with brandy. The men eyed her appreciatively, some with lust, but Opal hovered nearby to make sure they knew Julie was merely a hostess and not one of her girls.

The parlor began to empty as everyone disappeared upstairs. A few still lingered about, sipping their drinks. Suddenly there was a loud commotion at the door, and Opal rushed to answer the thundering knocks. With a blast of icy wind and gusts of powdery snow, three men burst loudly into the room. Obviously merry from too much to drink, two of them hugged and kissed Opal, and she seemed equally happy to greet them. It was clear to Julie that they knew each other.

Except for the third man. They all wore the uniforms of officers of some rank, and the one who hung back was tall, attractive, almost regal. But there was something about his eyes, gray and piercing, that made him seem ominous in a way Julie could not define.

"I haven't seen you boys in months," Opal was saying, her voice at once tinkling and fawning. "I thought maybe you'd found another place you liked better."

"Not us, you big hunk of sugar cane," came a cheerful response from one of the two who hugged her. "We'd never run off and leave you."

"We've been out fighting the goddamn war," the other one said. "Thank God, it's gotten so damned cold both sides seem to be holing in for the winter—save for a few diehards skirmishing now and then."

"Who's your friend?" Opal nodded to the other man. "I don't believe I've met him before. Handsome, too." Her eyes flicked over him with interest.

He bowed slightly. "Major Gordon Fox, at your service. Let me say I've heard all about you and your establishment, Miss Opal, and I must say you have a fine house. The women are rare jewels of beauty—" his eyes went to Julie, and she glanced away self-consciously.

Opal noticed his glance and hastened to explain, "She isn't one of my girls, Major. I'm sorry. And I've only got one lovely young thing left besides me. Some of the others should be down before long. We seldom entertain for the entire night, you know."

When Julie realized she was about to be left alone with Major Fox, she decided to busy herself by refilling the decanters of brandy from the big bottle in the next room. One of the other girls would be down soon she hoped, and then he would be taken care of.

She wondered why he frightened her. There was something about the way he looked at her, that first moment—his steely gaze. She was behaving childishly, and she silently admonished herself. But that did not assuage the ominous feeling that was tingling up and down her spine.

"You're spilling some of that, lovely lady."

Julie turned so quickly that she dropped the crystal glass she was holding. It hit the thick rug, but the stem broke. She started to bend to pick it up, but he was already across the room retrieving the pieces for her. "I'm sorry. I didn't mean to frighten you." He smiled warmly. "I was lonely out there and thought perhaps you and I could keep each other company."

"I—I don't really mingle with the guests," she stammered, trembling involuntarily.

He noticed, tilting his head to one side and raising an eyebrow inquisitively. "You're afraid of me. Why? Have I done something to offend you? I don't see how I could have—"

"No, no, it isn't that." She hated the way her voice was so squeaky and nervous. "I don't like being here, you see, and I'm not used to all this, and—"

"I see." He reached over to take her hand and drew her into the parlor, before the fireplace. She followed, knowing she could do nothing else except make a scene, and that would be ridiculous. After all, he hadn't really done anything that should make her react in such a fashion.

"Your hands are cold. You stay here by the fire and warm yourself. That's quite a snowstorm we're having out there. I suppose that's why my friends filled themselves with spirits, thinking they could warm their insides against the weather." He laughed, and it was a nice sound. "They'll regret it in the morning. I learned my lesson about overimbibing as a youth. I know my limitations. Every man should, you know."

"I—I suppose," she murmured, feeling foolish but not knowing what other comment to make.

He sat down at the hearth, and his scabbard scraped uncomfortably on the ground. He rose and began to unfasten it from his side. "Would it seem terribly improper for you to at least tell me your name?" he asked.

"I suppose not," she answered, then told him as she admired his uniform. The coat was gray, with gold cord curling from the elbows to blend into a wide cuff. The stand-up collar bore one star on each side, denoting his rank of major. His belt was black, edged in gold to match the double row of brass buttons down the front of his coat, each engraved with the initials of the Confederate States of America: CSA. The trousers were blue, the shade of the berries that grew in the woods near Rose Hill, and there was a gold stripe down the outside of each leg.

"You're staring at my uniform," he said.

"Oh, I'm sorry. I didn't mean . . ." She shook her head, flustered, and wished she had just stayed in her room. Then she quickly said, "May I get you a glass of wine? I'm not a very good hostess, I'm afraid."

He accepted, and when she returned, she took her place beside him, folding her arms about her knees to listen as he told her a bit about the war. She lost track of time, urging him to continue talking, asking questions now and then. Suddenly the sound of laughter from above made them turn their gaze toward the stairway. Opal was coming down with one of the two men who had come in with the major. Julie heard her call him by his name, Jarrett.

They reached the bottom step, and Opal looked at Major Fox and Julie with a secretive smile on her lips. "I hope you two got along well?"

"Yes, quite." Major Fox got to his feet. "I find Julie's company quite charming."

"Well, if you care to wait awhile longer for one of the other girls—"

"No, we'd best be getting back."

Opal turned to Jarrett. "And how long before I'll see you again?"

"Hard to say," he replied. "We never know when we can get leave. They're bringing in more and more of those Yankee bastards every day, and the guards are griping about where to put them. We're stacking them on top of each other."

"That place is terrible, I hear," Opal clucked sympathetically.

"Well, prisons usually are," he agreed.

Julie's eyes widened as she gasped, "Are you speaking of Libby prison? You're there . . . with the prisoners?" The words erupted from the depths of her anguished heart.

Jarrett laughed, but Gordon Fox was watching her in silent rumination.

"We're in no danger," Jarrett said, pulling on his woolen greatcoat. "Those Yankees know our men would just as soon shoot them as look at them—and often do."

Julie made a whimpering sound as she turned away. Gordon moved quicky to grasp her elbow. "Has something distressed you, my dear? You seem upset."

"I'm sorry." She shook her head. "I just have a headache, that's all. Excuse me."

"Of course," he nodded as she hurried up the stairs. "I will see you again."

But she did not respond as she ran as fast as she dared, blinking back tears. It all seemed so hopeless, so futile. Myles was so near . . . yet so far.

✨ Chapter Twenty-two ✨

OPAL Bordine frowned as Major Fox swung his booted feet up to prop them on the cherrywood desk. He took out a cheroot and wet it with his tongue before lighting it, ignoring the way she wrinkled her nose in distaste. He lit it, inhaled, and watched the bluish-gray smoke swirl upward.

"Major Fox," Opal exploded, "you are trying my patience. It's enough that you have come here almost every night for two weeks, drinking my brandy and taking up the time of my hostess, all without remuneration to me, but now you have the nerve to demand my time as well. Get to the point of your visit, please."

"If you wish to be paid for your brandy, I will be happy to oblige," he remarked coldly. "As for remuneration for time spent, Miss Marshal has not offered her, uh, services to me . . ." he paused to smile, then added, "nor have I requested them."

"Get to the point," she repeated.

He regarded her coolly, then said, "What I'm about to tell you is quite confidential, and should you reveal anything I say, you will be dealt with severely."

She gasped. "Are you threatening me?"

He shrugged. "Take it as you wish." He drew on the cheroot, then removed it from his lips and turned it around in his fingertips, staring at the red, glowing tip. Finally, when he was confident that Opal was sufficiently intimidated, he continued. "I am a member of the Intelligence Department of the Confederate Army. Part of my job is to ferret out what I consider suspicious situations that might be a detriment to the security of the Confederacy."

She was unnerved, and he knew it, as she asked in a shrill voice, "Well, what has that got to do with me and my establishment?"

"I consider the fact that a beautiful young woman is being boarded here, by a man you will not name, to be highly suspicious. Miss Marshal is obviously a woman of intelligence and good breeding, so why would any man want her kept *here*? For what reason?"

He lowered his feet so quickly that they hit the floor with a loud thud and Opal jumped, startled. Leaning forward, his eyes stormy, he pointed the cheroot at her as he ground out the words: "I intend to have the whole story—now!"

"I—I don't know why he left her here," Opal stammered. "I mean, he didn't give a reason, just said to make sure she didn't run away. He said he'd pay me well when he returned. I thought he'd be back before now. So did she. That's all I know."

"You know his name," he snapped. "You must also have your own opinion as to why he left her."

She began to shuffle papers on her desk nervously.

"You're wasting my time. You would save both of us a great deal of inconvenience if you would cooperate." He leaned back in his chair. "Would you care to go to my headquarters and be questioned there?"

"No, no!" She slapped her palms down on the desk. "All right. I'll tell you everything I know about him. His name is Derek Arnhardt, and he's a blockade runner. He went to Wilmington to get money. I overheard him telling Julie something about that. As for why he's afraid she'll run away, I only know what she confided to one of my girls, that her brother is in Libby prison, and Derek has gone to get money to hire men to get her brother out. He's afraid she'll try it without him, because she's so desperate.

"Please," she begged, "don't let anyone know what I've told you. Derek can be quite mean, and he would be very angry if he knew I had told you all this."

Major Fox smiled slowly. "You can be assured that our conversation will be kept confidential."

He rose, nodded a curt goodbye, and left.

He returned that evening. He watched Julie's every move, as usual. He found in her an ethereal charm, a beauty to behold with her shining black hair and shamrock eyes framed by thick lashes. She was what he wanted, all right, and while he felt she was quite vulnerable, he also had the feeling that she could be quite beguiling when properly motivated.

Julie Marshal would serve his purpose well.

Finally the room was empty except for the two of them. Julie, perplexed as to why he continued to visit nightly without engaging one of Opal's girls for a few hours of sensual pleasure and frolic, faked a yawn and murmured, "I am quite tired tonight, Major. Would you excuse me if I retired for the evening?"

Quietly he said, "We need to talk, Julie, about your brother."

Astonished, she could only stare at him.

"You heard correctly. I know all about your brother, how he's being held prisoner at Libby. Shall we go upstairs to your room where we can talk privately? Be assured I do not have other motives in mind. I just don't want to take a chance on being overheard down here."

"But—but how did you know about my brother?" she stammered, allowing him to lead her upstairs.

"I have ways of finding out what I want to know. Don't concern yourself with that. Just be assured I want to help you, if you will cooperate."

Heart pounding wildly, she sank into a chair beside the fireplace in her room. Major Fox continued to stand, but she did not trust her suddenly weak knees to support her.

"Let me begin by saying that you may trust me implicitly. Now, I want you to tell me all about your brother and about this man Derek Arnhardt."

Her brain was spinning. She was still stunned by it all. "I—I don't know if I should tell you anything," she gasped, her hand clasping her throat as she stared at him through blurry eyes. "How do I know this isn't a trick? It may jeopardize Myles's life—"

"As long as he remains in the Black Hole, his life *is* in jeopardy, my dear. Now do you want me to help you or not?"

Suspicion was a needle pricking along her spine. "Why would you want to help me?"

"I have my reasons, but I'll want something in return."

Her eyes narrowed. "And what might that be?"

"I work for the Intelligence Department of the Confederate Army. We have need of beautiful and sharp-witted women like you. If I help your brother to escape, then you will return the favor by serving your country in the manner I prescribe."

"I don't understand any of this." She was completely baffled. "And if you have influence, why can't you just process Myles's release through normal channels? He was unfairly and unjustly put there to start with—"

He waved her to silence. "I don't care why he was imprisoned. And you aren't to start asking me a lot of questions. I will tell you that in order to get him out, it must be done quite secretly and made to look like an authentic escape. We can't afford any repercussions."

Julie stared at him intently, trying to absorb all that he was saying. She was already in a quandary over his frequent visits of the past two weeks—and now this. He was also an attractive man, though she still found that something about him made her apprehensive, almost frightened.

"Another thing," he continued. "I can't tolerate any questions, because my work is justifiably secret. You either cooperate with me, or we forget the whole matter."

"And if I refuse?"

His smile was insidious. "I would hope you would not be so foolish."

She shook her head slowly. This had all come about so quickly. "I don't know. I can't give you an answer. I have to think."

"There's no time for that. All you have to do is give me your word that you will work for me, and then your concern for your brother will be over. He'll be freed."

"He might want me to go with him," Julie pointed out. "We have no family left, only each other. He might not understand my leaving him."

He raised an eyebrow. "And what was your bargain with this Arnhardt fellow? What did you promise him in exchange for helping you?" He saw her face color slightly and smiled in triumph. "I don't think you have to tell me. I think I know. What do you suppose your brother's reaction would have been to *that*?"

She had never really thought of it in that light, but now, looking at the situation, she realized Myles would never have approved of or accepted such an arrangement. There would have been trouble. Perhaps Derek realized that and had decided not to go along with the plan. Maybe that was why she had not heard from him. He might not be coming back, she realized with a pang of terror. Why, she could be forced to remain a prisoner here!

Suddenly Major Fox was kneeling before her, clasping her cold hands in his warm grip. "Julie, I need your help, and so does your brother. I'm sure you've heard of the atrocities in that place, but you couldn't know the reality, the true horror, unless you were to witness it for yourself. How can you even hesitate? Arnhardt offers you the demeaning position of a mistress. I offer you an honorable way to serve your country. And it won't be forever, just until the war ends."

He waited a moment for his words to penetrate, then continued. "I don't plan to be in Richmond much longer. I have business elsewhere. Now, if you agree, I will go right away to make the necessary arrangements. We can have your brother out of prison by this time tomorrow night."

Julie pursed her lips thoughtfully. Lord, this was happening so fast. There wasn't time to think. "Will I be able to see him, if only for a moment?" she asked in a rush. "Can I let him know where I'll be going, so he won't worry?"

He sighed, rubbing at his forehead with fingertips. "Oh, Julie, you're making this difficult for both of you. But very well. I know you're concerned and want to make sure he's well. I'll make sure you see him—but only briefly. And you won't be able to tell him where you are going.

"Besides," he pointed out, "your brother will be a hunted man. I'll see that he's taken somewhere for the remainder of the war, somewhere he'll be safe. You can arrange to meet later."

Was there another way? Dear God, she didn't know. Derek could have sent word, and he should have returned. Her first loyalty was not to him anyway, she reasoned. She had to save her brother's life. And Major Fox was right. All Derek had ever offered her was the status of being his mistress. He had never offered love.

"All right," she said finally, tremulously. "I don't see that I have any other choice except to agree to what you offer, Major Fox."

"Call me Gordon." He grinned, patting her knee before standing. "We're going to be good friends, Julie. You'll see."

He walked over to the window, and in seconds had the lock broken. "No one will notice this between now and tomorrow night. As soon as it's dark and activities begin downstairs, come up here and lock your door. Open the window and wait. One of my men will be downstairs, and he'll throw a rope up to you."

He gave the bedpost a shake. "This is sturdy enough to hold you. Tie the rope around it and work your way down. My man will be there to help."

"But what about Myles?" she demanded fearfully.

"You'll be taken to a place where you can see him for a few moments."

She closed her eyes, praying she was doing the right thing. But she had to be. It was the only way. "And then where do we go from there?"

"You go with me. It's as simple as that. You're not to worry anymore. Your brother will be free, and so will you. When the war ends, you'll be together."

The clock on the mantel chimed the midnight hour. It was the only sound in the room except for Julie's anxious breathing. She was frightened of this man, and she was now in his clutches whether she wanted to be or not. There could be no turning back.

He walked to the door and nodded curtly. "I won't let anything happen to you, Julie. Until tomorrow night, goodbye."

She spent a restless night, and when dawn came, she had fearfully decided there was one other possibility to be faced. Gordon could be lying. What if he helped her escape from Opal's only to whisk her away and keep her locked up somewhere for his own pleasure? She had seen the way he looked at her at times, eyes shining with desire. Perhaps he had no intention of getting Myles out of prison. It could be a trick, and she should prepare herself for that possibility just to be on the safe side.

She thought of Garnet. They had become close friends, and she would have to take a chance that the girl could be trusted. If anything went wrong, perhaps she could depend on Garnet to get word to the authorities.

Anxiously, she waited a few more hours before going to

Garnet's room, knowing her friend would be quite grumpy if she was awakened too early. It was almost ten when Julie finally knocked on her door, and when Garnet answered, she blinked in annoyed surprise.

"I've got to talk to you, Garnet." Julie stepped inside and locked the door behind her.

"What's so important?" she yawned, padding back to her bed to snuggle beneath the covers. "Good grief, what time is it, anyway?"

"You've got to listen carefully," Julie whispered after sitting down on the side of the bed. "Listen to everything I'm going to tell you, and remember, I'm trusting you to keep all of this confidential."

When she had finished, Garnet stared at her with wide eyes and gaping mouth.

"Well, say something," Julie prodded. "I have to know I can depend on you if something goes wrong."

"How will I know if anything does go wrong?" She looked at Julie as though she were surely out of her mind.

"If someone escapes from Libby, you'll hear about it. All of Richmond will know about it. If you don't hear anything, then come right out and ask those men who came with Major Fox if an escape attempt was made. If they say it wasn't, then go to the authorities and tell them I was kidnapped."

Garnet yawned again. "Did you ever stop and think how he might get your brother out and then make you his prisoner? The man sounds weird to me."

Julie chewed her lip nervously. "I'll figure that out later. Right now, I only want to do what I left Savannah for— and that's free my brother."

"All right. I'll keep my ears open. But for your sake, I hope it all goes well. Now how about letting me get back to sleep?" She gave Julie a weary smile. "And you'd best be getting back to your room. If Opal catches you up and about, she might get suspicious."

Back in her room, Julie could not go to bed. Instead she stood at the window and stared down at the ground, covered in a white blanket. The sun peered out from behind the clouds now and then to make the snow sparkle like thousands of tiny slivers of the finest crystal.

Staring downward, she thought about the man who would be there tonight to help her slither down a rope. It was scary, but still she had a feeling of exhilaration to think that at long last, Myles would be free.

She would not let herself think of Derek . . . and what might have been . . . had they shared love, instead of only passion.

❧ Chapter Twenty-three ❧

WHEN Julie went downstairs around noon, she found Opal, fully dressed, going over a shopping list with her cook as they stood together at the front door. "Don't forget anything, Ruth," she was saying. "I'm having this party to bring in some business. Things have been slow lately. Now, have I overlooked anything?" She touched a finger to her cheek musingly. "I sent Allen and Craig to post invitations in the necessary places. We should have a large crowd."

"A . . . party?" Julie asked fearfully, stepping up.

They ignored her. Ruth looked mad. "You're going to give me a headache, is what you're going to do," she whined, jerking her shawl about her tightly. "It's colder'n all get-out, and you send me traipsin' out to do marketing."

"You can always seek employment elsewhere if you're dissatisfied here, Ruth," Opal snapped, thrusting the list at her. "Now be on the your way. You need to get in the kitchen as soon as possible to start preparing some of the dishes I have on the menu."

Ruth stomped out of the house, a gale of frigid air rushing into the room before she closed the door. "She deliberately did that," Opal fumed, "leaving the door open. The old fool." Turning, she saw Julie. "Well, good morning."

"Did I hear you say something about a party?"

"Yes, and don't look so distressed about it. I should think you'd enjoy all the people. It must be getting terribly boring for you, what with Derek taking his time coming back." She fluttered into the dining room, with Julie right behind her. "Would you mind polishing the crystal, dear? You've nothing else to do."

Suddenly Julie knew she had to ask. "Opal, do you believe Derek is going to come back?"

The look she received was one of pity. "It's hard to say, dear. Derek always was unpredictable. I will say that he's been away longer than I thought he'd be."

"And what happens if he doesn't come back?" Her heart was pounding fearfully.

Opal's expression was quite serious, businesslike, but her voice was gentle. "I can't continue to support you indefinitely, Julie. I'm sure you know that. I'll give him a few more weeks, and then we're going to have to sit down and discuss how you'll pay me back for your room and board."

"I don't have any money," she cried defensively.

Opal's eyes flicked over her body, and she smiled. "You have more to offer than my other girls, my dear. In no time at all you would be the most sought after and the highest paid. Derek would have no one to blame but himself for leaving you on your own to get by as best as possible. And I certainly couldn't allow you to leave until your debt is paid."

"But, I couldn't—"

Opal waved a hand, dismissing her. "Please. I've no time for this conversation. There's too much to be done. Get on the crystal, please, and then the silver. I'll see that Garnet loans you a lovely dress for tonight. Who knows? It might be your debut." And with a chuckle, she hurried from the room.

Julie knew now that Major Fox's offer was her only way out. To stay meant becoming a prostitute, because with each passing day it seemed more doubtful that Derek would return. She hated him for putting her in such a position.

She took out her fury upon the crystal, and by midafternoon every glass was sparkling. Then she turned to the silver, and finally it was time to go to her room and dress. Opal had declared she wanted every girl looking her loveliest and in the parlor earlier than usual, should some of the guests arrive early.

The gown left on her bed was a bright emerald velvet with a shockingly provocative neckline. With a nagging fear of what lay ahead, Julie dressed, wondering how she could escape to her room early if there was to be a big dinner party. She would have to find a way, no matter what.

With her hair piled high in tightly ringed curls held in place by ivory combs, she could see by her reflection in the mirror that she did look nice. Chiding herself for her moment of vanity, she heard Opal summoning everyone to the parlor.

"You are without a doubt the rarest gem in my collection of precious beauties," Opal beamed as she descended the stairs. Julie said nothing, grateful when someone knocked on the door. The guests began to arrive.

Filling a tray with glasses of various kinds of spirits, Julie began moving through the ever-increasing crowd that was filling the parlor and overflowing into the dining room. Opal would be happy, for this was the largest gathering of clients she had seen in one evening. Many of the men would be forced to wait their turn with the woman of their choice, for Julie counted at least three men to each girl.

She felt strong fingers wrapping about her wrist and she glanced up, stunned to see Major Fox beaming down at her. "I'll have a sherry," he said warmly, then added, loudly enough for everyone else to hear, "Later I shall have you."

She stared at him, shocked, and he pressed his lips against her ear, pretending to kiss her as he whispered, "Smile, my dear. You've nothing to worry about. Everything is set. My being here is merely a front so that no one will ever suspect I had a part in the escape."

Hearing his words, her fears were assuaged, but she had not liked something he said. "What do you mean—later you'll have me?" she said tightly. "Everyone knows I'm not one of Opal's girls."

"Perhaps you're not available to everyone, but let them think you and I are smitten with each other. Then there won't be any suspicions, after we seemed so close, as to why you suddenly disappeared." The muscle in his jaw tightened. "Don't ever question my motives, Julie. I know what I'm doing at all times."

He mingled with the other guests, then a short time later approached her for more sherry. This time he conveyed the information that according to the schedule, her brother was to be freed within the hour. "Word will come here, to Ned Rogers and Jarrett Payne, that there's been an escape. They will have to leave immediately, and I'll go with them.

At that time, in the confusion and excitement that is sure to follow, you slip upstairs to your room. Someone will be waiting below your window to help you climb down, as I told you."

"I can't believe it's happening—"

"It is." He patted her shoulder. "Just as I promised."

Opal appeared in the dining room archway, holding a tiny silver bell which she jingled till she had everyone's attention. She announced dinner was being served, and everyone moved in her direction. Gordon made his way along with Julie, escorting her into the room.

The long table was laden with platters of roast turkey, duck, and goose. There were bowls filled with stews, gravies, sweet potatoes, and boiled eggs. Ruth waddled in wearing a greasy apron, to set a basket of steaming, hot biscuits in the middle of the table. The procession moved around, with everyone filling a plate, then finding someplace to sit and eat.

Julie was surprised that she was able to keep her hands steady as she served herself food her fluttery stomach would probably never accept. Gordon was chatting amiably with Ned Rogers, who was in line just behind him.

Ned was recounting his recent visit to General Lee's winter encampment along the banks of the Rapidan River. "You should see it, Gordon. It's like a city there: tents, huts, a sea of people. The men amuse themselves by playing in the snow like children."

"They had better enjoy themselves while they can," Gordon commented drily. "With spring, both sides will no doubt move into full-scale battles. What were you doing out there, anyway?"

Julie looked at Ned as he explained he had wanted to get away from the prison for awhile. "I get sick of seeing them carry out the bodies every day," he said wearily. "They die like flies—from dysentery, typhoid, malnutrition. I can't help but pity the poor bastards."

Julie's heart constricted with pain. Myles was there—in that horrible place. Dear God, the plan had to work. He had to be freed!

"It's a shame the prisoner exchanges broke down," Gordon commented. "Both sides are overloaded with prisoners of war."

"Nothing to be done about it except beat the Yankees and end the war," Jarrett laughed.

Julie kept her face turned away lest someone see the anguish in it. She heard Opal complaining about the war talk, saying they were supposed to be having a party.

She saw Jarrett reach out and squeeze Opal's bottom, and his plate tilted, dribbling gravy to the table as he laughed, "I'll show you a good party in a little while, baby. You just eat and get your strength up, because you're going to need it for what I've got in mind."

Frowning at the stain on the linen tablecloth, Opal went off in search of Ruth. The crowd continued to circle about the table, conversation filling the air with a noisy ring. No one heard the pounding on the front door.

Opal, returning with Ruth, paused at the sound of glass rattling. Turning, she saw the outline of someone standing on the porch, barely visible through the thin gauze curtain. "A late arrival," she smiled happily, swinging the door open with a wide grin of greeting. Then, at the sight of the grim-faced soldiers, she felt a wave of annoyance. They were not invited guests. "What do you want?" she demanded curtly.

There were six of them, and the one who seemed to be in charge removed his cap and told her it was imperative that he see Lieutenants Payne and Rogers at once.

"We're having a dinner party!" Opal snapped. "Your officers will be furious if you disturb them for some silly military business that can wait."

"Sorry, ma'am. This is important." He didn't sound sorry at all. "If you don't call them, we'll have to go in and get them."

"Oh, for heaven's sakes, all right. But you shall suffer the consequences. I can assure you they're going to be quite angry with you for disturbing them."

"Yes, ma'am," the soldier nodded politely. "I accept the responsibility."

Opal closed the door in their faces. The icy air was chilling the parlor, and she didn't want to invite them in to tramp up the carpets with their snow-caked boots. Hurrying to the dining room, she stood on tiptoe, scanning the crowd until she saw Ned Rogers. Catching his eye, she pointed to him and Jarrett, then motioned for them to come.

Still carrying their plates of food, the two men maneuvered back through the line to where she was standing.

"Soldiers!" she made a face. "I told them we were having a dinner party, but they insisted. . . ."

The two exchanged anxious looks, then sprinted for the door. They stepped outside and were gone but a moment, then ran back and demanded to know where their greatcoats and hats had been placed. Several people had wandered into the parlor and stood watching them curiously, as it was obvious they were extremely upset. But it was Major Fox who demanded to know what was going on.

"Escape at the prison," Ned told him as Ruth handed him the huge cape and his hat. "We don't know all the details, but a couple of guards were killed while on duty. Evidently the murdering bastards then slipped inside, wearing Confederate uniforms, and took a prisoner."

"Only one?" another officer asked with raised eyebrows.

"Like he said, sir," Jarrett interjected, "we don't have all the details. We've just been told to get over there at once."

"Well, I'll come along. . . ." Gordon told Ruth to get his coat also.

Someone else said he thought he should report to the prison as well.

"For, heaven's sake, you can't *all* leave because of a little old jail break," Opal exclaimed indignantly. "After all, I went to a lot of trouble for his party, and now to have this happen!"

"Oh, stop your fretting," Ned chided her gently as he hurried toward the door. "We'll make it up to you later, but we've really got to be on our way."

At least a dozen men left in all, following the soldiers into the street, and while everyone else was milling about speculating over what had happened, commenting on the excitement of an actual prison break, Julie did what Gordon had told her earlier to do. She slipped unnoticed up the stairs and into her room, locking the door behind her.

She hated to climb out of the window and slither down a rope wearing her fancy ball gown, but she was afraid there would not be time to change. She did, however, remove the cumbersome hoops. Then, grabbing the cape she had borrowed from Garnet, she rushed to the window and slid it open easily.

The wind tore at her carefully styled coiffure as she leaned out into the night chill. Snowflakes kissed her excited, feverish cheeks as she called softly, "Hello . . . is anyone down there?"

"Here!" The voice was gruff but reassuring. "I'm throwing a rope. Catch it and tie it to your bedpost as you were told."

She heard the sound of something slicing through the air, and she groped blindly but felt nothing.

Curses came from below. "Dammit, you've got to catch it, woman. We've got to get the hell out of here. . . ."

Again she missed.

"I'm sorry," she cried, the frustrated tears that streamed down her cheeks freezing upon her skin. "I can't see. . . ."

And then the rope looped upward and fell across her outstretched arm. She clutched at it frantically. "I've got it! Oh, thank God, I have it. Now wait . . . let me tie it. . . ."

Her fingers were so cold they were stiff, and her nerves were on edge, so tying the rope securely proved quite time-consuming and difficult.

"Dammit, woman, if you don't hurry, I'm going to leave you. . . ." came the irate voice from below.

She paused to call back down, "Please be patient. I'll only be another moment. . . ."

Finally she was ready. Throwing one leg over the window sill, she grasped the rope tightly with both hands. "Now what do I do?" she asked, shivering from fear now instead of from the cold wind.

"You climb down the damn thing," snapped the voice. "Unless you can fly!"

She pulled her other leg up, and she was sitting on the ledge, the rope in her hands. Twisting about so that she was facing the house, she gave herself a little push. The sudden jerk was terrifying as she felt herself hanging in mid-air, the rope burning into her flesh as she held on tightly, knowing that one slip, and she would plummet downward. And in the darkness, the stranger who waited below might not be able to see her and catch her. It was a long drop.

"Okay, I can see your outline," her rescuer whispered above the wind. "Just put one hand below the other, very slowly, and don't panic. Stay calm. . . ."

She hated to release one hand from her deathlike grip on the rope. If only she could just slide downward, but that would mean the flesh on her hands would be torn to shreds by the rope.

"Come on . . . come on. . . ."

She slid one hand down. The rope burned, and she winced with pain. It was just going to have to hurt, she thought miserably. She could not make herself let go and maneuver herself down that rope like a monkey on a vine.

She slid but a few inches before she screamed in pain and gripped the rope tightly again.

"Dammit, you can't slide down!" The man raised his voice angrily. "Now come on down. You can do it. Stop acting like a silly, helpless female!"

Now *she* was angry. Helpless, was she? Bristling with a white-hot flash of determination, she removed her left hand from the rope, clinging tightly with her right, and lowered herself at least a foot. When she moved her right hand, she lowered herself perhaps two feet. Down and down she went, and suddenly she felt hands wrapping about her ankles.

Startled by the touch, she released her grip. Her abrupt fall into the man's arms sent both of them tumbling into the deep snow.

Scrambling to his feet, the stranger yanked her to hers roughly. "My name is Leo. Just come along with me and don't ask any questions. . . ." He began trudging through the snow, and she hurried to keep up with him, listening as he muttered to himself about the stupidity of women.

After they'd gone at least several blocks, Julie's cape and dress were soaked from the heavily falling snow. "I can't go on like this much longer," she panted. "I'm weak, and I'm going to be sick—"

"It ain't that far. Hurry up. I was told to get you away from that house as quick as possible, and you took up a hell of a lot of time shimmying down that rope."

"Well, I've never done much rope-shimmying before," she retorted. "It's not the usual way I leave a house."

"It is if they won't let you out the door," he snickered.

She ignored his ungenteel attempt at humor, using her remaining energy to stumble along behind him. It was a dark, moonless night, but here and there a lantern glowed from the window of a house as they passed, and they managed to make their way along.

Finally they rounded a corner and Julie cried out with

relief as her escort shoved her toward a waiting buggy. To the driver he quipped. "Okay, she's all yours now. My part's done, and now I'm off to have a drink. Thanks to her, I sure can use one."

The driver extended his hand, pulling her up beside him. "Sorry there's no top," he said as though he really didn't care. He wore a wide-brimmed hat and a heavy poncho, so he was protected from the elements.

He popped the reins across the donkeys' rumps and the wagon began to move slowly forward, the way made difficult by the snow drifts.

"I hope we don't have far to go," Julie said with chattering teeth. "I don't believe the donkeys can make any distance in this snow."

"Oh, don't you fret about Jimmy and Bill, here. These are two of the strongest jackasses around. If anybody can get through the snow, they can. And we ain't got far to go. You just sit there and try to relax."

"Relax? When I'm soaking wet?"

"Like I said, we ain't got far to go."

To Julie it seemed hours, but finally the man was pulling the donkeys to a stop in front of a darkened house. "You're to go up there and knock on the door two times, wait a minute, and then knock three times. Need some help getting down?" He sounded as though he hoped she didn't.

"I can manage," she said, determined to do so or break an ankle trying. She did stumble, but managed to grab one of the cart wheels to steady herself. Then she went around to the front of the donkeys, struggling to lift each foot as she moved through the deeply piled snow.

There was no railing on the steps. Lowering herself to a stooping position, she groped with her hands. Taking one step at a time, she made her way up to the porch, then slowly shuffled through the thin coating of snow that had blown across the floor.

She felt for the door, took a deep breath, then knocked twice, sharply. She could hear no sound from within. Waiting the requisite moment, she pounded three more times in succession.

The door opened so quickly that, startled, she fell forward. Strong arms went about her, and she heard a familiar voice whisper, "Thank God, you made it. I was beginning to worry. We don't have much time. We've got to get Myles out of the city and to safety. The commandant of the prison is calling every available soldier in to search for him."

It was like a dream. She told herself it was real, but her heart kept screaming it could not be. It had been too long. So much pain and anguish, so many prayers. Julie clutched at his greatcoat, her words coming out in a frantic, almost hysterical, stutter. "He—he is . . . here. You did it. You . . . freed . . . my brother. . . ."

"Oh, Lord, Julie, you're soaking wet and shaking like a frightened puppy," Gordon said in a rush. "We've got to get you into something dry." He called into the darkness for someone to get him a blanket.

"Now strip out of those wet things at once. After you've seen Myles—and remember, you can only see him for a moment—we've got to be on our way out of town, too. I know a place not too many hours' ride from here where I can get you into bed and try to keep you from coming down with the fever."

"Here." Something woolen was thrust into her hands. "Now strip."

Despite the chill that was consuming her whole body, she hesitated.

"For God's sake, Julie, it's dark. No one can see you. Now hurry. Do I have to keep telling you we haven't much time?" He groped for her in the darkness to give her an impatient shake.

Her hands too numb with cold to undo the fastenings, Julie asked Gordon to help her remove her dress. His touch was warm, gentle, but not seeking. She was grateful that their relationship continued to be based strictly on business and nothing more. That was the way she wanted it, the way it had to be. And she had already made up her mind to let him be aware of that fact should the time ever come and he did happen to get any foolish notions.

When she had wrapped the thick blanket about her, Gordon said he was taking her downstairs, into the cellar, where Myles was waiting. "We have a lantern there that cannot be seen from the outside."

As he led her along, the past danced before her in the mind-boggling darkness. The old sugar mill . . . playing with Myles when they were children . . . laughing happily together as they skipped along the river bank. Neither of them dreamed in those days that such miseries lay ahead. But, she reasoned, she had come to learn that life was a mystery . . . a composite of happiness and sorrow.

There was a loud, grating squeak of ancient hinges as a door opened that Julie could not see. Then, from below, a mellow light cast shadows up the steep, narrow stairway.

Suddenly she heard a voice that answered so many prayers: "Julie . . . God, Julie . . . is it you?" Gordon tightened his hold on Julie. "We told him you were coming," he whispered quickly. "He's weak from being in that hell-hole for so long, Julie, and we didn't want him to face another shock tonight without preparing him for it. When he realized he was actually being rescued, I'm told he fainted and had to be carried out."

They had made their way down the steps, their feet finally touching the damp dirt floor. Moving into the halo of light, Julie blinked her eyes rapidly, not at the sudden brightness, but at the horrifying sight before her . . . the ghastly, grotesque creature struggling to rise from a cot. The arms feebly reaching out to her were merely bones covered with sick, yellowed skin that hung loosely.

Julie's brain was silently protesting that this could not be Myles. Her stomach lurched with nausea as she moved even closer to Gordon, seeking protection from this frightful, shuffling . . . *thing*. His hair hung long and matted, slimy as the muddy bottom of the Savannah River, and the emaciated, cadaverous body was stooped over, gnarled, twisted, as he struggled in obvious pain to reach her.

Where was Myles? Where was the man who had stood so tall and proud, with eyes that sparkled like dewdrops on a rose petal, and hair the color of golden corn? She shuddered, pressing her knotted fist against clenched teeth to suppress the scream bubbling in her throat.

The thing spoke. "Julie . . ." He was getting closer. Wave after wave of sick revulsion ripped through her body. No, this wasn't Myles. It was a stranger—and these people gathered about were playing a cruel, cruel prank. Myles could never look this way . . . never.

Jerking her head from side to side, her voice cracked with anguish. "No . . . stay away from me—" Gordon held her tighter as she sobbed, "No, this isn't my brother!"

Myles stumbled, but someone grabbed him before he toppled to the floor and held him on his feet.

"I was afraid of this," Gordon mumbled, moving quickly

to slap Julie's face sharply, attempting to bring her out of her rejecting hysteria. "Listen to me. This *is* your brother. Remember, he's been in that filthy place almost a year, and this is what they did to him. You must accept it, because we don't have much time for you to spend with him. We have to get out of Richmond at once."

The others helped Myles back to his cot, but he struggled to keep them from laying him down. "Julie . . . oh, God . . . Julie. I hate for you to see me this way. . . ." Tears were streaming down his sunken cheeks, his bony shoulders trembling, shuddering.

Suddenly she stiffened. Pulling herself away from Gordon, she took a cautious step forward. The sound of Myles's heart-shattering sobs was bringing her out of her shock. Slowly she moved toward where he sat with his face buried in his skeletal hands. He had always taken care of her. He had been the stronger one, but now . . . now it was up to her to lend him strength. Taking a deep breath, still fighting to hold back her own tears, she knelt before him. He must not find her weak now. "Myles, it is you," she whispered painfully, fiercely. "And this is what they've done to you. Oh, may God damn them to eternal hell!

"Please don't cry." She covered his hands with hers, anger making her strong. "You're going to be all right, Myles. We'll make you strong and well again. You'll see. It's behind you now, all of it."

With great effort, he raised his head, lifted his hands slowly to cup her face lovingly. "Julie . . . thank the Lord for answering my prayers. I thought I'd never see you again—"

"He's got more grit than most men!"

It was a familiar voice, speaking from the shadows, and Julie glanced sharply about. Whose voice was it? So much had happened in such a short period of time that it was difficult to order her thoughts. Then she looked back at Myles as she heard Gordon snapping that they had to be on their way.

There was something on his forehead . . . on the skin . . . there . . . beneath the shock of matted hair. Hesitantly, with shaking fingers, she reached to push the hair aside. Then she saw . . . and could not contain her scream of rage.

For there—burned into his flesh—was the letter *T*, branded upon his forehead forever.

"Why?" she shrieked with rage. "Why did they do this to you?"

Myles tried to speak, but he began to cough, his withered body convulsing. Someone moved forward with a tin of brandy, holding it to his bluish lips, urging him to sip it slowly.

"Julie, they brand a lot of the prisoners," Gordon told her impatiently. "It's also a form of punishment that both the Federals and the Confederates use on their own soldiers. They brand a *D* for deserters or a *C* for cowards. In this instance, from all I've been told, I would assume that he was marked with a *T* because he was considered a traitor to the South."

"The bastards . . ." She spat the words out venomously. "The savage, monstrous bastards!"

Gordon's voice was filled with elation as he stepped forward to clamp firm hands upon her shoulders. "That's the spirit, Julie. That's why you're going to fulfill your mission to perfection. This way you'll be getting even with them for what they did to your brother. Now we must be on our way. It will be daylight soon, and we simply must be out of the city. You aren't to worry about Myles. He's going to be taken care of. Later, when it's safe, perhaps we can arrange for you to see him again. . . ."

Her eyes filled with tears, Julie looked up at Gordon through a blur, as though she had never really seen him before. With a bewildered shake of her head, she murmured, "I can't leave him. Not now, the way he is. And what do you mean—I'll be getting even with them? I don't understand."

"We made a pact, dammit!" Gordon gave her an angry shake. "'I kept my part, at great risk to myself and others, and you are going to fulfill yours. You might as well know, Julie, I'm a Union spy. I work for the Federal army, just as you are going to do also."

"Leave me?" she heard Myles whisper as she tried to grasp all that Fox had just told her. She saw Myles's head bobbing and wagging as he struggled to remain conscious. "No, Julie, you can't leave me now."

She tried to fight her way toward him, and Gordon lost patience and brought his hand up to strike the side of her head, sending her reeling backward to the cold, damp floor. She heard a great roaring sound, and it was only through tremendous effort that she was able to hold on, to keep from slipping away to the waiting black void.

In the shadows a man clenched his fists and ground his teeth together as he fought to keep from going to her aid.

Julie heard a soldier whisper through the dizzy shroud that enveloped her, "This is a big crock of shit, Fox! It ain't going like you said it would. She's out cold, and now he's out again too."

Another angry voice reached her ears. "Ain't nothing going like you said. You was supposed to get us out of Richmond once we got this bag o' bones out of prison, so's we could hide out in the mountains till the goddamn war is over. Now we've got the two of them unconscious, and Richmond is crawling with soldiers looking for us. We'll probably all end up in front of a firing squad!"

"Nonsense. We're going ahead with our plans." Julie heard Gordon snarl and snap his fingers at one of the men. "Luther, pick the girl up and let's be on our way. Maybe it's better that it turned out like this. I had my doubts she would ever be properly persuaded to get secrets from the enemy. Now she'll either do it or this wretch here *will* die. And not in prison, either."

Then he yelled that Myles was to be taken to the hideout in the mountains and kept there until Gordon sent further orders. "Once she knows he's alive only as long as she obeys me, I doubt I'll have any more trouble with her."

Julie's head was aching fiercely from Gordon's blow. She was using every ounce of her strength to keep from slipping away, wanting to hear as much as possible so she would know what was going on, even though she was powerless to do anything about it.

She felt herself being lifted and thrown over someone's shoulder. They were moving up the steps.

They reached the upstairs hallway, and once the door to the basement clicked shut, Julie heard Gordon say to the man carrying her, "Luther, you think I can trust them to get Myles to the mountains? They're all strangers to me. I can only go by what you and Veston tell me."

"Most of them can be trusted," she heard him answer. "A few will probably desert as quick as they get out of Richmond, but there are a couple who will follow orders. I don't think you have to worry, but frankly, I'm worried about us getting out of town without being spotted."

"We'll be careful," Gordon replied.

"There's a new man down there I don't know nothing about," the man called Luther said, tightening his grip on Julie. "He insisted on coming along. He heard about the escape plan and threatened to blow the whistle unless he was included. Said he wanted out of that place."

"No matter," Gordon snapped. "Let's be on our way."

The sound of the squeaking door caused Myles to stir slightly. "Julie . . ." he whispered weakly, "don't leave me . . . please."

"Let's go!" a man cried, then pointed to another who had moved out of the shadows. "You! Carry him upstairs. You insisted on coming along, so you might as well make yourself useful."

The others hurried up the steps, leaving the soldier in gray behind with Myles. Bending, he clasped the bony arms and whispered hoarsely, "Myles, listen to me. We've got to get out of here. We've got to get you out of Richmond."

Myles's eyes opened, squinting in the lantern's glow. His face turned ashen as recognition rippled through him. "You! Oh, God, how—"

"No, don't say it!" A finger was pressed against Myles's trembling lips as the man rushed on. "Don't let on you know me. They'd kill me for sure. Just listen carefully. When I heard about the escape plan, realized it was you they were going to break out, I knew Julie had to be behind it somehow. I insisted on coming along, and I'm going to stick by you and see that no harm comes to you."

"I never would have let them take Julie," he went on miserably, "but I was outnumbered. If I'd tried to stop them, we might have all been killed. So this is the only way. Just pretend you don't know me, and once you're strong, we'll get away and find her. I swear it."

He gave Myles a shake. "Do you understand all that I'm saying? Will you pretend you don't know me and keep your mouth shut?"

"Hey!" An impatient voice boomed from above. "You going to take all night? Lift that bag o' bones and let's get the hell out of here!"

"I'm coming!"

"Well, get the lead out, Carrigan! You're the one who insisted on coming along!"

"Yes, yes," he nodded feebly. "I can do it."

Yes, Lieutenant Thomas Carrigan thought silently, *I did insist on coming, and by God, you bastards will rue the day you brought me!*

He lifted Myles in his arms, shocked that the man felt as light as a child. "Let's go, cousin," he whispered tremulously. "We've a long road ahead, but we'll make it . . . together."

❦ Chapter Twenty-four ❧

ICE pelted the hotel window as Julie stared down at the silent, shadowy Washington streets. Running trembling hands up and down her arms, she knew she should do something about making a fire in the grate, but despite the chill, she could not move. She was overwhelmed by all that had taken place in the past three days. Gordon had insisted they keep moving north, despite the terrible weather, saying he would feel safe only when they crossed Union lines. She questioned him constantly about what he planned to do with her, but received no answer.

He was furious with her because she wanted to change her mind, but couldn't he understand why she didn't want to leave Myles after she saw his condition, saw how close to death he really was? How could she have known what her reaction would be when she saw him? She had no idea he would be so frail . . . so emaciated.

She had offered Gordon the family heirlooms, safely buried back in Savannah, if only he would reunite her with Myles and let her go. And he laughed at her! Then she tried talking to the two men who accompanied them; Luther, who despite his brawny, brash exterior seemed to have an underlying gentle quality; and Veston, who frightened her with his filthy talk and eyes that seem to undress her. But neither would tell her anything, not where Myles was being taken, or where she was being forced to go. She knew only that she was in Washington, and Gordon intended for her to work for the Yankees.

God, she shuddered at the thought. At the time she had

agreed to go with him, she'd been desperate. Now she could look back and see how foolish she had been. Myles was still a captive, as far as she knew.

She whirled at the sound of her door being unlocked, and her heart sank at the sight of Gordon. She would have preferred seeing Luther, who had brought food to her since their arrival two days earlier. He, at least, could be quite pleasant.

Gordon bowed slightly, giving her an arrogant smile. "My darling, you look stunning tonight."

She knew he was only being nasty. Her hair was brushed down, long and straight, and she wore only a woolen robe that Luther had procured for her from one of the hotel maids. It looked frightful, and so did she, but she certainly didn't care.

Turning back to the window, she did not acknowledge his remark.

"We're really going to have to do something about your wardrobe," he commented, walking to the fireplace to throw more logs onto the dying flames. "We can't take you back to Richmond looking so frowsy. What man would want you? And remember, we're after important men—officers of high rank."

"What makes you think I'm going back to Richmond and do your dirty work?" she snapped, still staring at the sleet glazing the window. "I'm not budging from this room till I know where you've taken Myles. And I've no intention of becoming a spy for you. I was vulnerable when we made our bargain, and you were well aware of that fact. You took advantage of me."

"Oh, did I now?" He sounded amused. "Really, Julie, you can be so childish at times, despite the fact that you are a devastatingly beautiful woman. You knew what you were doing when you made your promise to me, and you should know by now that I have every intention of holding you to your word. Why do you want to cause everyone an inconvenience by being so stubborn?"

"You wait a minute!" she shouted angrily, turning to face him. "You never said anything about being a damn Yankee till *after* you'd gotten Myles out of prison. And I never said anything about working for the Federal government. You seem to forget I'm a southerner, sir, and proud of it, and I'll never lift a finger against the Confederacy."

"Now, then!" He got to his feet, satisfied that the fire was going well. "I think it is time that we discussed the arrangements."

"You may discuss anything you want, but my mind is made up. I want to be taken to my brother." She turned back to the window.

He went on as though she had not spoken. "Tomorrow we shall have you fitted with a wardrobe suitable for a lovely, talented young lady who will be traveling about entertaining the poor Rebel soldiers with her sweet voice. Once that is done, you and Luther and Veston will start on your little tour.

"Luther is quite a gifted guitarist," he went on, moving to stand directly behind her but making no move to touch her. "He will accompany you when you sing. Veston will more or less serve as your driver, but he will be the one who will relay the information to me that you get out of your men friends."

"Men friends!" She spat out the words, whirling about to face him with glaring eyes. "Do you really think I'm going to be your—your *whore?*"

He raised an eyebrow and chuckled, "Now, Julie, don't be so dramatic. Have I asked you to be my whore? I explained everything to you, how you will be taught to drug the men you take to your bed. If you don't want to make love to them, you don't have to. You can get the information you need, they will fall asleep, and the next morning you can tell them what wonderful lovers they were. Everyone will be satisfied.

"Believe me," he went on, "I have several young ladies working for me, and they are quite satisfied with their situations."

"Well, how your other 'young ladies' feel is of no concern to me," she blazed, "because I have no intention of going along with your filthy scheme. The very first chance I get, I intend to expose you for what you are—"

Suddenly he reached out to clamp strong hands upon her shoulders, giving her a backward shove that sent her reeling onto the bed. Stunned, she could only stare at him in terror as he unleashed his fury. "You little bitch! You'll do whatever I tell you to do, and you'll keep your goddamned mouth shut, because the first time you open it when you aren't told to, that half-dead brother of yours will be put in his grave. We made a bargain. I kept my end of it, and you'll do the same with yours. Now I don't intend to listen to any more from you, is that understood?"

When she did not—could not—answer, he reached out and clasped the front of her robe, pulled her inches from the bed, and whispered harshly, "I asked you a question, dammit, and you're going to learn to obey me. Do you understand?"

Her whisper was barely audible, hissed between angrily clenched teeth. "Yes, I quite understand you, you bastard!"

The play of a smile was on his lips as he released Julie, moved to an erect position, and stared down at her with half-closed lids. "I think," he murmured, starting to unbutton his shirt, "that it's time you learned a lesson, my pretty lady. I'm going to teach you the only thing a woman is really good for, and you'll most likely beg for more and more. I like to hear my women plead for it. . . ."

"You're out of your filthy mind!" She was on her feet and screaming, running for the door to beat upon it with both fists, not caring who heard.

He was right behind her, tearing at her robe, yelling at her to be quiet. "I'll make it rough for you . . . you'll make me hurt you—"

The door opened so quickly that it struck Julie across her face, and she fell backwards onto the floor. Through a haze of pain, she saw Luther rushing in, gun drawn. "What the hell is going on—" and then he saw Julie and reached down to lift her into his arms. "Are you hurt?" he demanded, then whipped about to face Gordon furiously. "What did you do to her?"

"Stay out of this!" Gordon snarled.

"The hell I will!"

"You seem to forget I'm your commanding officer—"

"And you seem to forget I don't give a shit. I said I'd go along with using her as a spy, but dammit, that didn't include you treating her like she was your woman and using her like you would a whore."

Gordon was livid with rage. "Luther, I'm not going to put up with this."

"Then you'd better find somebody else to play your goddamn guitar, because I'm not having any part of it." His anger was equally fired.

Gordon took a deep breath, then let it out slowly as he

tried to get hold of himself. "Very well," he said tightly. "You win. For now. But sooner or later, I'll get what I want."

"Not while I'm around, you won't." Luther was struggling to keep from smashing his fist into Gordon's face. Fox might be his commanding officer, but Luther'd never liked the damn bastard.

"That," Gordon smiled, "can be taken care of, Luther. I can have you transferred elsewhere."

"You won't, because you need me."

"In that case, our day will come, and we'll settle our differences then." He buttoned his shirt, then walked out and slammed the door behind him.

Luther turned to Julie with a gentle expression on his face. "Are you sure you're all right?" he asked softly.

She nodded shakily, still frightened. "Thank you, Luther. If you hadn't come when you did . . ." She shuddered to think of what would have happened.

"I was close by, figuring he'd try something." He reached inside his coat and brought out a bottle. "Here. Drink this. You look like you could use it. It'll make you relax."

She tipped it to her lips, drank, then coughed as the liquid burned in her throat. Luther walked over and sat down next to the fireplace. "Maybe you can get some sleep if you drink enough of that. I'll sit here with you, if it'll make you feel better. And don't worry. I'm not going to touch you."

Julie went to her bed and sat down uneasily. She found him handsome, in a rugged, coarse sort of way. His hair was a cross between red and blond, and his eyes were deep blue. But there were lines in his face that made him appear older than she guessed him to be. It was obvious he'd led a rough-and-tumble kind of life, and she found it strange that he could be so gentle with her.

"I'm a soldier, too, Julie," he spoke quietly. "Maybe not like the others, because I'm considered part of the secret service, like Fox. But he is my commanding officer, and I take orders from him. I was pretending to be a Reb, and that's how I got assigned to Libby, like Fox wanted."

"Yet you stood up to him just now," she murmured, awed.

He grinned, and suddenly he didn't look so rough anymore. "Yeah—well, I do that now and then, and he really hates my guts for it. I figure sooner or later along the line we're going to have one hell of a fight. I'll be ready for it. He's a sharp one, though."

"He's vile and vicious, and he still holds my brother prisoner," she cried, blinking back tears.

Luther gestured helplessly. "That's the way it is, honey. This is war. I hate it as much as you do, but—" He paused to take a breath, then murmured, "Look, you're upset, and you've got a right to be. Why don't you just drink some more of that stuff and maybe you'll go to sleep. You'll feel better in the morning."

She shook her head but took another swallow. She didn't want to sleep. She wanted to talk. "He said he'd have Myles killed if I don't do as he says."

"He probably will. It won't be so bad if you do what he wants. I'll be around to try and make things easy."

Julie continued to sip from the bottle, and soon her voice was slurring, eyelids growing heavy. As the bottle slipped from her fingers, Luther reached to take it away before it fell to the floor. "I'm not going to touch you, Julie," he said with tenderness as he laid her down and pulled a blanket up to tuck beneath her chin. "I'm going to sit here next to you and make sure nobody bothers you— this night, at least."

She groped for his hand gratefully, and he squeezed her tiny fingers as she looked up at him once more to smile and whisper, "Thank you, Luther . . . thank you for being my friend."

He sat there for a long time, staring down at her. Dammit, he'd never let himself go soft for any woman before. He'd had his share, but he couldn't remember ever feeling quite this way. Hell, he felt sorry for her. He wanted to yank those covers off and strip her naked, and Lord, he knew it would be good. But something was stopping him. Pity. Dammit, he'd never felt pity for anybody or anything, so why in hell was he starting now, in the middle of a goddamn war? Maybe it was because she wasn't like the others. They didn't have to be coaxed into doing their job for Fox. Some of them even went ahead and slept with the men they lured to their beds, even after they drugged them and got what information they needed out of them. They seemed to enjoy it.

But this one, he knew, would never submit willingly.

She might be tiny and delicate, and maybe physically she couldn't fight back, but she'd never give in. She'd fight with every ounce of strength she had in her.

She stirred, moaned, whispered a name he could not make out. He leaned forward, wanting to hear, but there was a sharp rap on the door and then the sound of Veston's belligerent voice. Luther didn't answer. He kept staring at Julie, feeling the pounding of his heart and cursing himself for the emotions that were starting to smolder within, despite his determination that he wouldn't let himself feel anything for her.

"You gonna open this door or you want me to bust it down?"

Luther's head jerked up. Slowly he got to his feet and walked to the door. As soon as his hand fastened on the knob and the click of the lock could be heard, Veston was pushing his way into the room. He looked at Julie, then grinned nastily. "Already finished, huh? Well, it's my turn now."

Luther quickly positioned himself between Veston and Julie's bed. Grimly he pronounced, "You aren't going to touch her."

"Are you kidding me?" Veston's eyebrows were raised in surprise above eyes glimmering with desire. "We always break in the good-lookin' ones. What'd you do to her, anyway? How come she's asleep?" He threw back his head and laughed tauntingly. "Puttin' your women to sleep these days, eh, Luther?"

"I said you are not going to touch her."

"Hey—" he drawled, stiffening. "You *aren't* kidding, are you? What the hell's going on?"

"I gave her some whiskey to make her relax so she'd fall asleep."

Veston twisted his mouth thoughtfully, then took a step forward. "I'm going to have me some—"

Luther reached quickly for the knife he always carried. The blade glimmered and sparkled in the glow from the fire in the grate, but its radiance was dim compared to the heat glowering in his eyes as he warned, "I'm not letting you near her, so get the hell out of here!"

Veston looked from the knife to Luther's eyes. "Fox is gonna hear about this."

"That's fine. I've already had a run-in with him about her."

"He'll kill you."

"No he won't. He needs me." Luther sounded quite confident. "You see, I'm going to keep a watch over her. I'm going to try to keep as much misery from touching her as I can. That's the least I can do. She isn't like the others, and that's why you and Fox can't have her."

Veston stared at him, stunned for a moment, and then he laughed. "Well, I'll be danged. Am I hearing right? You, of all people—one of the biggest, hell-raisin' fuckers I ever messed around with, standing here tellin' me you're going to watch over that fine piece of woman flesh like she was your very own—"

Luther could have told him that he did indeed wish she were his own. But he knew he'd said enough. The point had been made. There would be a reckoning with Fox later, and he'd face that when the time came. "I think," he took a deep breath and let it out slowly, "that you'd better just get the hell on out of here."

"Sure," Veston snorted, moving toward the door. "Ain't no woman worth fightin' for, but you sure beat everything I ever seen."

When Veston had gone, Luther put his knife away and sat back down. Julie slept deeply for awhile, and then she would twist from side to side, crying out as though reliving some horrible nightmare. He would reach out and stroke her face or smooth her silky black hair back from her forehead as he spoke to her in gentle, soothing tones. He would tell her she was safe, that he was there and would watch over her. After awhile, she would drift into peaceful slumber once again.

He was still sitting there when dawn tried to break through the thick snow clouds and light struggled to creep into the room. He had not once dozed, wanting to be alert should Julie cry out in terror again. Fox had not returned, and Luther was relieved. Another confrontation might awaken her, and he knew she needed to sleep as long as possible. The road ahead was not going to be easy for her.

"You're still here. . . ."

He glanced up to see that she was awake and staring at him intently.

"Yeah, I wanted to make sure you slept all right," he told her. "Veston came, but I ran him off. You had a restless night. I wanted to help if I could."

"Why?" She sat up, unaware that her robe had fallen open, exposing her magnificently sculptured breasts. He saw and sucked in his breath. Julie looked down and gasped and yanked the garment closed. Her eyes grew suspicious, wary. "Why did you stay? What do you want of me?"

He shrugged. "I know you don't trust me. It's something I can't explain. There's just something about you that makes me feel you need protecting. I don't know how much I can do for you, but I aim to hang around and do my damndest." He gave her a lopsided grin which he hoped put her at ease.

She lifted her chin a little. Despite his apparent attempt at friendship, and the way he had saved her from Gordon Fox the night before, he was still one of "them." Her voice was cold. "I can take care of myself."

"No, hell, you can't." He spoke gruffly for the first time. "Fox is going to send you around entertaining Reb troops, you know, and it's going to be dangerous. You need somebody around to look out for you. I aim to be that somebody."

"If you truly want to help me and my friend, you'll help me find my brother so we can escape all this madness. You won't let Gordon go on with his mad scheme."

"Oh, I can't help you there," he said. Gently, he hastened to explain. "I told you, Julie, I'm a soldier. I've got a job to do. I'm going to travel with you and play the guitar while you sing. I aim to be your bodyguard, and God knows, you're going to need one. But don't ask me to help you escape. I'm in this war because I believe in the northern cause, and I'll kill a Reb as quick as I'll mash the life out of a toad. But as much as it's within my power, I'll keep you from getting hurt. And that's all I can offer you," he finished with a sigh.

There were a few moments of silence, and then Luther spoke the words that seemed to be smoldering within him. "I'm probably making a fool of myself, but I'm going to say it, Julie. You shake me up. I wanted you something fierce last night, and I'd move quicker'n a scalded dog if you asked me to climb under them covers with you right now. But I'll never touch you 'less you want me to. I promise. Just let me be your friend, 'cause you're going to need one."

Shivering not only from the chill of the room, Julie

wrapped the covers tightly about her; then trailing them behind her, she went to stand in front of the fireplace.

"I'll go get some more wood," Luther said quickly, noticing how she was shaking. "I'll bring you something to eat, too. I'll get the hotel cook to whip you up some hoecakes and bacon. You need something that'll stick to your ribs. The major's going to take you shopping today, get you fitted for some fine clothes, and you'll be out running around in all that snow."

"Promise me one thing, Luther," she interrupted, whipping about to face him, no longer trembling, for her bones had stiffened with the determination and fortitude that she knew instinctively she must gather if she were to survive. "Promise me that you will do everything in your power to see that my brother lives. I can pledge nothing in return, but you say you want to be my friend. I want to believe you, and if you mean what you say, then make this one promise to me."

He sucked in his cheeks, then let out his breath in a long whoosh. She was asking a lot, and besides, he wasn't about to tell her how he'd had his doubts all along that the bunch that left Richmond would stick together and take Myles to the hide-out. They had probably already shot him or left him to die, and then taken off. If she hadn't made such a scene there at the last, Fox might have made sure her brother would be protected, but he'd gotten mad and didn't give a damn. Besides that, rumor had it that the war was fixing to bust loose like all hell, and Fox had plenty of other worries—one of which was to get Julie working as quickly as possible.

Finally, after giving her a long, searching look, he nodded his head slowly. Better to lie, he reasoned, than cause her more pain. "I'll do my best, Julie."

Just then the door opened, and Gordon Fox walked in without bothering to knock, eyes narrowed and lips set grimly. "Well, what's going on in here?" he demanded.

"Julie had a restless night," Luther said tightly. "I sat with her."

"Like a mother hen." Gordon laughed sharply, then snapped his fingers in Julie's direction and told her to get dressed. "Luther will bring you some food. Then we'll be on our way to get you outfitted properly. We're going to be leaving in a few days."

There was a dressing screen in one corner of the room, and Julie stepped behind it and reached for the dress she'd worn from Richmond. It had been washed by a hotel maid, and she thought absently that it did not look too much the worse for wear.

"I've decided we won't go to Richmond," she heard Gordon tell Luther. "It would be too dangerous there. I think we can pick up valuable information around Wilmington. After all, that's the last real stronghold of the blockade. You should find many busy pilots and ship captains there. Set Julie up in one of the saloons along the waterfront and establish her as a lady of talent. Then we can start moving through the fields, visiting camps.

"I'll be talking with my commanders," he went on. "When we leave Washington, we'll have a definite plan of action. Things are truly going to be moving into high gear. From all reports, President Lincoln wants to do everything possible to bring the war to an end. He's started by naming Ulysses Simpson Grant supreme army commander, and Grant is making no bones about his plans. Attack. He says he wants to strangle the Confederacy, and he's going to order Federal forces to attack simultaneously at all points to apply constant pressure on the South. And the South is weakening. There's no doubt about that. Grant says they can't withstand a continual onslaught, which is what he is about to set in motion."

"A lot of men are going to die," Julie heard Luther murmur, and she was surprised to hear the sadness ringing in his voice.

"Be glad you probably won't be one of them," came Gordon's snappish reply. "All you have to do is play a goddamn guitar, not pick up a rifle and march into battle. You should be grateful that I chose you for this assignment."

Luther allowed as to how he was appreciative, but added, "It just seems a waste. All the killing. It's been going on three years now, and I don't see any end."

"Well, there will be an end, and people like me will help bring it to a close. Wars aren't won merely by men shooting at each other, Luther. It takes brains and strategy, like using spies to find out where the enemy will attack next, where their weak points lie."

Julie heard the door open. "But I shouldn't have to waste my time telling you all this. Come along. I'm sure

Julie must be famished. . . ." His voice trailed off as the two stepped into the hallway, closing the door behind them.

Julie was grateful to be alone with her thoughts. What lay ahead, she did not know, and she ran cold fingertips up and down her arms. Her lips trembled. No, she told herself fiercely, she was not going to cry. She had to be strong—stronger than ever before.

She thought of the past. Warm, sunny days on that isolated beach with Derek . . . strong arms about her . . . hot, seeking kisses that always led to fulfillment from his satiating penetration to the very depths of her soul. A quiver of warmth moved through her as she remembered the way he had possessed her, carrying her along on a wave of passion that made her writhe and beg and plead for him to go on and on . . . which he did . . . till she lay spent and exhausted beneath him.

Derek.

Once she had hated him.

Once she had loved him.

What she truly felt in her heart, she did not know. She was certain of but one thing. She wished she had stayed in Richmond and Derek had returned, and she could be folded in his arms and held tightly against his chest.

For on that snowy day in Washington, in March of 1863, Julie Marshal had never felt more alone and vulnerable. And her heart grieved with the knowledge that probably never again would it pound with thundering ecstacy as she was held tightly against that giant of a man . . . Derek Arnhardt. . . .

🌑 Chapter Twenty-five 🌑

THE ride had been extremely difficult, and several times Thomas feared that Myles had died. He had positioned Myles directly behind him on the saddle, on the horse's rump, lacing his cousin against his back with a rope. Every so often he would stop, despite the protests of the others, and maneuver himself to press a hand against the frail chest to see if Myles's heart was still beating.

"Hell, throw the bastard in the snow and be rid of him," one of the men yelled only a day after they slipped out of Richmond. "We ain't never gonna hear from Fox nohow. Who gives a shit? He's just dead weight."

Thomas knew the man who spoke only by the name of Satch, and that he was from somewhere up in Pennsylvania. He had never laid eyes on him, or the others who aided in the escape, until that night when he left Libby Prison with Myles. Thomas found Satch to be a surly sort, mean, ugly, always spoiling for a fight, constantly badgering everyone around him. And if Satch insisted on discarding Myles, Thomas knew he would have quite a scrap on his hands.

"We have our orders, and I intend to follow them," Thomas answered quietly, hoping his voice relayed the underlying message that he was not afraid of any challenge.

"He's gonna die anyway," came Satch's snarling reply. "And he's holding us back. It's hard enough trying to get these goddamned horses through this blasted snow, without you stopping every few feet to see if the son of a bitch is still breathing."

"Well, he is still breathing, and as long as he's alive, I'm going to do everything I can to keep him that way."

That night, when they were all huddled around a small fire hidden among some rocks and snow-laden trees, Thomas gave his portion of the rations to Myles. He had to forcefully spoon the gruel between Myles's thin blue lips, coaxing him to swallow.

Suddenly he became aware that all eyes were upon him, and he turned to see Satch's mouth twisted into an evil grimace and his eyes narrowed into suspicious slits. "What's he to you, anyway, Carrigan? The rest of us don't give a shit if the bag o' bones dies, but you're sittin' there feedin' him right out of your own belly. You one of them funny ones what likes men?"

Thomas fought for self-control. Now was not the time for the reckoning that was sure to come. He was counting on some of the men slipping off as they moved along, until their number was so narrowed down that he and Myles would have a fighting chance. There were too many to stand up against now.

"You've got a sick sense of humor." Thomas forced a laugh. "I'm just following orders, Satch, like I said. Besides, I was a guard in that prison, remember? And I saw the way this poor bastard was treated. Seemed like every guard there, and even some of the prisoners, were doing their best to see him dead. I grew to admire him because of the way he struggled to survive. Now that he's been given a second chance, I'm not wanting to take it away from him."

"Hell, you shoulda been one of the ones wantin' him dead," one of the other men spoke up. Thomas knew him only as Kelso. "You're a southerner, ain't you?" Kelso went on. "You saw that *T* branded on his head, and you know he was a traitor to you Rebs. So how come you give a shit whether he lives or not? Don't make sense to me."

Thomas turned burning eyes first upon Kelso, then on Satch, and all but snarled his reply: "I'm not asking any of you to help me. I'm not asking you to share your food. So why don't you just mind your own business and let me follow orders? What the rest of you do is your affair. Leave me be."

"Well, well, I do believe our Johnny Reb is a man's man." Satch threw his head back and laughed. "He likes the old bag o' bones. Maybe they was good friends back in that prison. Maybe he's tryin' to fatten him up so they can be married. . . ."

The others guffawed and cackled, and Thomas's hand trembled as he spooned more gruel into Myles's mouth. Despite his cousin's weakened condition, he could see the slight sparkle of anger in the watery, hollow eyes. It was a good sign. It meant that there was spirit left beneath the waxy, papery skin . . . spirit that would grow and become strong and help him to *live*, by God.

Thomas's back was to the others as he squatted before Myles. Lowering his voice to a barely audible whisper, he told Myles to pretend he had heard nothing. "Don't let them know that you might be starting to regain your strength. We are outnumbered, and now isn't the time for any confrontation."

To the others he tossed the words over his shoulder, "You all go on and have your fun. When we see Major Fox again, just be sure to let him know that *I'm* the one who kept this man alive, the way he wanted."

The other men finally tired of making their taunts when they realized that Thomas was not going to be goaded into a fight. So they turned to talk of other things: the war, the wretched weather, how much further they had to travel. Thomas put a blanket over Myles after making him a bed of dry pine straw, which he had difficulty in finding. Only after digging beneath three feet of snow and several more layers of wet straw did he find any that was dry. By that time the others were drinking and talking about tawdry women they'd known in the past, and they were ignoring him.

Then Thomas made his own bed nearby, shivering in the freezing night air and praying he did not come down with the fever. If he died, then Myles was surely doomed also.

The next morning he awakened to hear Satch cursing because two of the men had slipped away during the night. "The yellow-bellied bastards!" he roared. ". . . took half our supplies, and there ain't no telling how much further we got to go with the weather like it is. Look at them clouds. It's gonna snow again today for sure."

The others exchanged uneasy glances, probably, Thomas figured, thinking about the time when they too would slip away. They were tired of the war, the fighting, wanting only to run away and hide until it was over.

". . . wish I'd heard 'em," Satch went on, his face red

with anger. He smashed his fist into a tree, bloodying his knuckles and causing a thick shower of snow to fall from the stark branches above. "They was the ones with the popskull, and that's why they kept pushing it at us, wantin' us to get drunk and sleep dead to the world so they could creep out. If I'd heard 'em, I'd have put a ball in their yellow backs for sure."

Suddenly he whipped around to glare at Thomas, who was standing silently watching and listening. "How come *you* didn't hear 'em, Carrigan? You wa'n't drinkin' nothin' last night. . . ."

"I slept further away from you all, and I didn't hear anything that went on," Thomas answered slowly, evenly. "I was also burrowed beneath my blankets, trying to keep from freezing. The wind was up and howling, too, drowning out any sounds.

"What difference does it make?" he went on as though he were not at all concerned. "We'll pass a farmhouse sooner or later and forage for some food. Two less among us doesn't make any difference."

"We're wasting food on him!" Satch pointed a finger at Myles, who was struggling to stand, legs trembling.

"He'll share my rations." Thomas met Satch's stormy eyes without a trace of fear. "And I don't want to hear any more talk about him being dead weight. I'll look after him. You just lead us to wherever it is we're going."

As each day passed, Myles gradually grew stronger, and he and Thomas were able to talk about their predicament when the others could not hear.

"We're going to get out of this," Thomas said fiercely, more than once. "For now, we've got to play along with them, but when we get our chance, we'll take it. Then we'll find Julie, by God."

Mules wanted to know how Julie came to be in Richmond, and Thomas could only tell him what he had overheard the night of the escape, how some sort of bargain had been made between her and the secret-service man called Fox. Thomas had also managed to pick up bits and pieces of information as to how Fox had met her from the others' conversation.

"You mean she was staying in a bawdy house?" Myles yelped, and Thomas had to shush him before the others heard.

"I don't think it was that way," he explained. "There

was a fellow named Arnhardt involved somehow. He left her there while he went to Wilmington for men, and for money to pay them to get you out of prison. He didn't come back, and she got tired of waiting."

"I remember Julie telling me something about a man named Arnhardt," Myles said thoughtfully, then his eyes flashed fire. "I remember now. He's the one that kidnapped her from Bermuda. Why in the hell was she with him in Richmond? Why did she go to him for help?"

"I don't know." Thomas shook his head. "We'll just have to find out."

"Damn right," Myles fumed. "I want to know the whole story."

They traveled northwest along the James River from Richmond, stopping along the way to beg or steal chickens, potatoes, hams, anything to eat from the farmhouses they passed. At the end of two weeks, they were deep into the mountains, and only four of them remained—Thomas, Myles, Satch, and Kelso. All the others had deserted.

Myles was still weak, but Thomas felt certain now that he would fully recover. All they had to do was wait for the right time to make their move, and he hoped it came before they reached their destination. There was a possibility that others would be at the hide-out increasing the odds against their escape.

One night as they sat around a fire drinking coffee made from boiled peanuts, Thomas casually asked Satch just how much further they had to go. "Seems like we've been on the road for months."

"Tomorrow or the next day," Satch yawned, scratching at his long, matted hair and pulling out a nit, which he tossed into the fire. "I've started seeing a few signs along the way that show me we're getting close."

"Signs? You mean we're following a trail in this wilderness?"

Satch laughed. "You don't think I'm just wandering around, do you? I thought you knew we got a hide-out up here, a regular nest of men wanting to stay out of the fighting. They left a few markers along the way, notched trees, stuff like that."

"Then why did the others desert us?" Thomas persisted. "If you have a hide-out, and they knew they wouldn't be called back to the war—"

"Well, we're still in the war, in a way. We do what Fox tells us to do. He needs a place to hide somebody out, we've got it ready for him. Sometimes we bring prisoners up here and torture 'em into telling us what we want to know. You'll find a few skeletons once the snow thaws, I guarantee you. Some of 'em wouldn't talk, so we just slit their throats."

Kelso guffawed, and Thomas exchanged a nauseated glance with Myles.

"I reckon the others just wanted to run back home," Satch went on. "Or maybe they was afraid Fox would call us all back to the lines. Who gives a shit? We're almost there. And it wouldn't have taken near as long if it hadn't been for the damn snow. Shouldn't be too long till the spring thaw, though. I'd say we're well into March now. Few more weeks, and things'll go to melting."

Satch went to search for dry firewood, which Thomas knew would be no easy chore. Kelso shuffled through the snow to where the horses were tied to see if he could find a bottle of popskull that they might have forgotten about.

As soon as they were out of hearing range, Thomas turned frantically to Myles. "We've got to do it tonight. We've got to get away, or this time tomorrow we might be in a whole nest of Yankees and Reb deserters. Who knows? They might kill us. We've got to do it tonight, Myles. Are you up to it?"

Myles looked at him for a long time without speaking. His eyes were still sunken into his head and had deep circles beneath them. The veins were still visible beneath the yellowed skin, and his fingers had lost none of their skeletal appearance. Finally he took a deep breath, his shrunken chest heaving. "I suppose we have no choice, do we? Do you think we can find the way back?"

"We'll look for the same signs that Satch found to lead us this far. Once we make it to the James River, we'll just follow it back to Richmond—"

"We can't go there!" Myles cried, stunned. "They'll put both of us in jail. I'm an escaped prisoner, remember? And you helped me, so they'll be looking for you too. It isn't safe in Richmond."

He shook his head wearily, eyes sparkling with tears of frustration. "Thomas, I appreciate all you've done to help me. I swear I do, and I'll never be able to repay you, but there's no way out. We have to face it. There's nothing to do but take our chances with Satch and the men who'll be waiting at the hide-out."

"Which is no chance at all!" Thomas scoffed sardonically. "What the hell's the matter with you, Myles? What happened to the man I was proud to call my friend? Maybe they *did* beat you down in the goddamned prison, and you're nothing but a coward . . . all your fight and spunk gone. Maybe you never had a backbone after all."

His nostrils flared, chest heaving with anger as he raged on. "And what about Julie? Have you forgotten about her? She was willing to risk her life to save yours, but now there's no telling what kind of danger she's in. Aren't you willing to make an effort to try and save her, after all she did for you?"

Myles looked at him, stunned, and then he said in a croaky voice filled with shame, "All right. I guess I was starting to give up, but I owe it to both you and Julie to fight back. Just tell me what you want me to do."

So Thomas quickly outlined the plan that been churning about in his mind for the past few days. When Satch and Kelso fell asleep, he and Myles would just slip away into the night, as the others had done. "It's beginning to snow again. Our tracks will be covered. They won't come looking for us anyway. We'll head straight south, find our way into North Carolina and on to Wilmington. We should be safe there. If anyone does ask questions, we'll just say we're on leave, that you've been ill. Anyone will look at you and see that's no lie."

At the sounds of footsteps crunching in the snow, they fell silent, huddling near the warmth of the fire as though too weary for conversation.

It was Kelso, and he had found his bottle of popskull. He grudgingly offered them a drink, which they declined. "My stomach's knotting from hunger," Myles said. "It would make me sicker."

Thomas mumbled that he wasn't feeling well. "I may be coming down with the fever. I'm going to try to get some sleep."

Kelso looked at Myles and sneered, "We shoulda got rid of you a long time ago." Then he threw a sarcastic glance in Thomas's direction. "As for you, Johnny Reb, you ain't much better than he is. Why don't you both curl up and die?"

"Aw, lay off of 'em," Satch bellowed, returning with an armload of scraggly branches he'd managed to find beneath some rocks. "We ain't got much further to go. Fox will be glad we got the job done, just the two of us, after the others turned into such yellow bellies."

Thomas and Myles moved back from the fire, as they did every night. Even though it was bone chilling to huddle beneath their thin blankets, away from the warmth, they had long since reasoned it was better than being around the two men they found so despicable.

Myles dozed off right away, weary as always from the day's ride. Thomas only pretended to sleep, alert to any sounds from Satch and Kelso. As usual, their talk turned to women. Finally, their voices became slurred as they got drunk and sleepy. The fire was slowly dying, and they made no attempt to keep it going.

He could hear the sound of gentle hisses, knew snowflakes were falling to hasten the fire's death. Then the dampness began to seep through his blanket. Ordinarily he would have moved and attempted to find some sort of shelter beneath a bush or a rock, but he dared not move till he was sure the other two were asleep.

A half hour passed. Then, cautiously, Thomas pushed the cover back from over his head and looked over to where Satch and Kelso had been sitting. Faint smoke crept skyward from the smoldering ashes, and the two men were slumped together, blankets pulled about them as they slept deeply. Trying not to make a sound, Thomas reached out and shook Myles. He did not respond, so Thomas crawled closer, grasping his shoulders to jerk him harder, "It's time," he whispered quickly. "Quiet, now."

Myles was instantly awake. "Are you sure?" he asked anxiously.

"They're as dead as the fire. I listened to them for hours, getting good and soused. You stay put while I get the horses. It's starting to snow harder, and it's going to be rough going. We may have to walk and lead the horses, and you're going to need what strength you can muster."

"Thomas, I can make it," Myles said, hurt at being reminded of his weakened state.

Thomas gave his cousin's bony shoulder a reassuring squeeze. "I know you can. We *both* can. We're Georgians, remember? And nothing can lick us!"

Myles could not see the smile in the darkness, but he

knew it was there just the same and he returned it, feeling strength he had not known for a long time flowing in his veins.

Slowly, stealthily, Thomas stood up. His original plan had been to just take two horses and steal away into the night, but now he decided he had better make sure they weren't followed. Walking to the dead fire, he reached down and picked up a partially charred log that was still very heavy. With quick, chopping blows, he hit Satch, then Kelso. They made no sound as they slipped further down into the snow.

Myles heard and quickly asked, "Did you kill them?"

"No," came the reply. "I just want to make sure they don't come after us—for awhile, anyway. And I doubt they'll give chase on foot."

Once the horses were saddled, and the few remaining supplies packed, Thomas said there was no way they could ride out. "Our weight would just push the horses down deeper in the snow. I don't even know which direction we're headed. I can't see the stars with the storm overhead. We'll just have to keep plodding along till it gets light. Can you make it?"

"I can make it," Myles answered solemnly.

"Then let's move out. If you start to stumble, or you fall, for God's sake make some kind of sound so I'll stop for you. We've got a long way to go, and it's going to be rough. . . ."

His voice shook with emotion. The task that lay ahead was formidable. There was a good chance they would not survive the elements, but they had to try. By God, they had to try, he thought with a fierceness that made him tremble.

And it was Myles's hand upon his shoulder that gave him strength, as Thomas heard him say confidently: "It's like you said, cousin. We'll make it. We're Georgians. Nothing can lick *us*."

Together they began to push their way through the ever-deepening snow.

🐚 Chapter Twenty-six 🐚

LUTHER Saxton sat on the ground outside the covered wagon. Absently he fingered the strings of the guitar he held on his lap, then stared down at it, remembering the pride he had felt when he bought the instrument. It was newer, nicer, than the one he'd taught himself to play on. And until the war broke out, music had been his life . . . but, like thousands of others, his world had been turned upside down.

He struck a chord dejectedly, sensed rather than heard the bitter quality of the tone. He touched the tuning pegs to bring the strings to their proper pitches.

Suddenly Julie poked her head out from between the canvas flaps at the end of the wagon. In the glow of the campfire, he could see that ever-present sadness reflected in her now lackluster green eyes. "Luther, I'm dressed now. You may come in," she called flatly, emotionlessly.

Slowly he got up and walked toward the wagon, carrying his precious guitar with him. He wasn't about to leave such a prize just lying around the rebel camp. It would be stolen for sure.

He climbed inside. Julie was wearing a dress of blue silk, soft, flowing, with no hoops. The neckline dipped low, something Major Fox had insisted upon in each garment he bought for her, wanting her lovely breasts exposed as much as possible. As she self-consciously pulled a woven shawl tighter about her shoulders, draping it across her bosom, Luther said regretfully, "You know Veston is going to have something to say if you go out there like that, Julie. I'm sorry, but you know—"

She bit her lip and nodded as she took a deep breath of resignation. "I know. I'm quite aware of my duties. I'm to look as provocative as possible, and I'm to seek out men of rank and importance and entice them to my bed. Haven't I performed well on three occasions now?"

"Yeah. Even though Fox sent back word that the information you got was worthless, you still did what you were told to do."

Impulsively she reached out to clasp his hand. He could feel her body trembling, and he wondered if she knew just what her touch did to him . . . how a rage swept through him as he fought to keep from crushing her in his arms.

Dammit, he loved her. There was no denying the fact that he loved her more than he ever thought it possible to love a woman. And it wasn't just her beauty, though Lord knew she was a sight to behold. It was her gentleness, her inner strength that somehow seemed to shine through, despite the misery of her life.

He wondered what her reaction would be if she knew of his feelings. He dared not speak what was in his heart, not yet, but when this blasted war was over . . .

"Luther," she whispered, a sad smile on her perfect lips. "I've told you before, but I feel I must keep saying it. If it weren't for you, I don't think I could make it. I mean, those times were horrible, those men pawing my body as I teased them into telling me those things—" She shuddered with revulsion, struggling for composure and blinking back tears, her long, silky lashes fluttering. "But you were there at the last, to make sure they were properly drugged, and I didn't have to actually—you know . . ."

Yes, he knew. "I'm not going to let it happen, Julie." His voice was husky, and he wanted desperately to kiss those precious lips. "I aim to protect you with my life, if need be."

Her eyes searched his quizzically. "But why? Why do you devote yourself to me so? You're such a friend. And you know that despite what the Confederates did to my brother, my heart is still with the South. It's killing me to know I'm betraying my own people. I'm the one who should be branded a traitor, not Myles. But you're different. You're a Yankee, and you want to see southern blood spilled . . . for the North to triumph in this war. Yet you befriend me, knowing how I feel."

The words were locked in his throat, but he knew that

no matter how hard he tried, they were going to spill
forth. He wasn't going to be able to hold them in much
longer. He had to tell her what he'd kept inside—that he
loved her . . . and his love was the reason for his unfailing
devotion.

But at that precise moment, without warning, Veston
pushed himself up into the wagon. He took one look at
Julie and snapped, "You ain't wearing that goddamn shawl.
Get it off, and let's go. They're waitin' on you out there."

Her chin lifted in familiar defiance. "It's chilly out. How
can I sing if I'm trembling with cold?"

He took a step forward, pointing a finger. "Look, you
ain't going out there lookin' like a pious preacher's wife
straight from a church sing. You're supposed to make the
soldiers happy, show 'em those teats of yours, and—"

"Veston, shut up!" Luther's hands clenched about the
neck of his guitar. It was a precious instrument, and he
was fighting to keep from bringing it crashing down on his
partner's head. "There's no call for you to talk to her like
that, and I won't have it!"

"You won't have it!" Veston mimicked, sneering. "Fox
was goddamn stupid to let you tag along. If I could play a
guitar, you wouldn't even be here. It's plain as apple
dumplin's that you're hot for her, and—"

Luther stepped closer. "I'm warning you for the last
time."

He was not built as big as Veston, but there was something about his voice or expression that proved ominous,
for the man stepped back, still sneering but retreating from
open confrontation. "Okay, okay, I ain't gonna fight you.
It'd blow the whole job we're supposed to be doing. We
both know the war is bustin' wide open, and we never
know when she might learn something that could prove
mighty damned important."

Veston directed himself to Julie. "There's a major out
there, and I've had my eye on him all afternoon. I saw him
in a field tent with a colonel and some other high-ranking
officers. They were bound to have been talking important
doings, 'cause they had sentries posted outside and
wouldn't let nobody come within fifty feet of that tent.

"I heard this major tell somebody he sure was lookin'
forward to hearing you sing tonight, 'cause he'd seen you
and thought you was a fine-lookin' piece o' womanflesh."

Luther ached as he saw how miserable Julie looked.

"When you finish singin'," Veston went on, "you come back here and undress with the lantern still burning. Let him get an eyeful of your silhouette, and he'll break his neck gettin' here. You let him know before you finish singing that you're interested in him. You know what I'm talkin' about—give him the eye. Smile. Flirt a bit with him."

He turned to Luther. "We'll do like always—keep a watch till she gives the signal he's sleepin' like a baby. Then you come find out what she got out of him, and if I figure it's something Major Fox would want to know, I'll head out and find him.

"All you gotta do," he grinned as he turned back to Julie, "is give him some secret come-ons, and we'll have him set up in no time flat."

"I'm sure you will," she nodded miserably. "Just like the ones before him, just like the one that will come tomorrow night, and the night after that, and—"

His hand snaked out to grasp her tiny waist and jerk her roughly against his chest. "Listen to me, you little bitch! You'll do as you're told, or that no-good brother of yours will die in agony!"

Luther forgot all about his beloved guitar as it fell to the floor of the wagon with a loud thud. He sprang forward, reaching swiftly to slide his knife easily from its hiding place in his boot. Its blade glittered ominously in the lantern's glow. Pressing the edge of it against Veston's throat, he growled, "Get your goddamn hands off her, or I'll kill you!"

Veston released her at once. She stumbled, and Luther shot out one hand to steady her, still keeping the blade pressed against Veston's flesh with the other. After a few seconds, during which he glared with hatred and venom at Veston, he pulled the knife away.

Only after he had retreated from the wagon, out of striking distance of his foe, did Veston threaten, "I'm gonna see Fox about you, Saxton. You and her got something goin', and that's why you act like such a goddamn fool over her. When he hears, you'll find yourself back on the battlefield—*if* he don't blow your brains out! You won't be plinkin' that guitar and makin' time with her no more, you can be sure of that!" He disappeared into the darkness.

"Thank you, Luther," Julie whispered tremulously. "I

don't know why you've taken it upon yourself to watch over me, but I'm grateful."

"Julie, it's because I—" Once again he had been about to proclaim the love he felt with every beat of his heart, but just then, as though fate were stepping in to prevent such a pronouncement, the drawling voice of a Confederate soldier came to them from beyond the canvas flaps, calling out that everyone was waiting for Julie.

With a sigh, she dropped the shawl from her shoulders, exposing her bosom all the way down to where the rosy pink shadows of her nipples began. "I suppose we must go now," she whispered. "You're not only my friend, Luther, but you're also an excellent accompanist. Hearing you play gives me the strength to find my voice at times when I'm sure I can't sing a note."

She slipped her tiny hand in his, and once again his heart began to pound, inflamed, thundering with emotion. God, how he loved her!

He stepped from the wagon, then propped his guitar against a wheel as he reached to clasp her about her waist and help her to the ground, reveling in the few seconds he could actually hold her, touch her. And he slipped a protective arm about her waist as they moved through the darkness toward the burning campfires, where the soldiers were gathered and waiting.

They took their places. Julie stood on a makeshift platform, and Luther sat at her feet. A ripple went through the troops as the men ogled Julie's beauty, her body, and it was with trembling fingers that Luther touched the strings of the guitar.

He knew Julie liked to begin her performance with the song favored by all the men, "Dixie." She would encourage them to join her, which they always did, thus establishing a good atmosphere. Then she liked to sing another favorite of theirs, "When This Cruel War Is Over," before going into the soft, romantic "Annie Laurie."

By the time she sang "Juanita," which was usually her last song, the major had moved forward to stand at the front of the group, and Veston had long ago signaled to Julie that he was the one she should direct herself to. She had done so, and he was gazing up at her with eyes that were openly shining with lust.

Luther fought for control. Now was not the time to act. But soon he knew he would have to take her away from all this, for he was losing patience, could not stand to see her endure such anguish and degradation.

As always, the soldiers grumbled because the night's entertainment was over. Veston nodded to Luther, signaling it was time for them to pretend to bed down. They walked away together, but Luther glanced back to see that Julie was talking with Major Anders, smiling, flirting, doing what she had been instructed, and he knew it would not be long before she was leading him toward the wagon, inviting him to drink from the bottle that had already been laced with the drug that would make his tongue loose before it eventually put him to sleep.

And when he awoke, Julie would tell him what a wonderful lover he had been . . . and with her lying naked beside him, he would believe her . . . as the others had. And even though Luther knew that the Reb officer would not have actually possessed her body, it made him want to spit blood to know that the major would hold her warm, bare flesh in his arms, touch it with his hands, his lips, before finally passing into unconsciousness.

Veston settled down beneath a sprawling oak tree, jerking his blanket about him. "Look, Luther," he started, "I'm sorry about what happened before. Ain't no need for me and you to be at each other's throats all the time over that woman. We got a war goin' on with the Rebs, not each other. If you're laying her, that's okay by me, even though I'd like to have a bit myself. . . ."

"Veston . . ." Luther snarled, warning him he was going too far again.

"Okay, friend, okay!" came his quick, snappy reply. "I ain't gonna say nothin' else. But just try to keep your head on your shoulders till this war is over, and then you can do what you want with her, understand? 'Cause if you don't, then I ain't got no choice but to tell Fox, and he'll have you sent back into the field, and I don't think you want that."

Luther knew it was no idle threat, and even though he was not afraid of being in actual battle, he did not like the idea of being forced to leave Julie in Veston's hands. He promised himself that before he let that happen, he would take her and run.

"I'm not going to have her mistreated," he said, propping himself against a tree, prepared to keep a close vigil on the wagon. "The sooner you realize that, the better off we'll all be."

Veston grunted as he curled up on the ground. "Ain't no need for me to tell you to keep an eye out. I know you're gonna be watchin' that wagon like a vulture flyin' over a battlefield. When she gets anything outta him, just let me know so's I can ride out of here and find Fox."

Yes, he would be watching, Luther thought fiercely. He was not about to let Julie be harmed. He could see her in the dim glow of the lantern as the major helped her into the wagon. He had let her know he wanted her, and she was not being coy about being receptive to his intentions.

Luther saw their outline as they embraced, and he squeezed his eyes shut, turning his face upward as a painful shudder went through his body. Long seconds passed before he could open his gaze to the sky, so like a giant black hand covering the entire world in a veil of infinity . . . and endless grief.

Moments crept by with agonizing slowness. Luther tried to calculate exactly how long it would be before the drink took its effect on Major Anders. He prayed that Julie would work fast, coax him, tease him into confiding his future "plans" as though her very existence depended upon his. Luther ground his teeth together as he conjured an image of what she would be doing with her body all the while, driving the major insane with desire.

And all because of her brother!

He slammed his fist into the ground. Veston stirred in his sleep.

Her brother might be dead by now. But Julie did not know that. She would not risk his life, not when she'd been through so much already to save him. If there was one chance in a million that her actions would keep him alive, Luther knew that she would take it. He only hoped the bastard was worth it, then chided himself for thinking such thoughts. He had to be a hell of a man to warrant such love and devotion from his sister. He wished he were as worthy.

Suddenly his head jerked up. Something was wrong. He could sense it. The lantern was out in the wagon, and he could see nothing in the pitch dark. Silently, stealthily, he rose from the ground and began to move through the night in the direction where the wagon had been tied and the horses tethered.

He tried to judge how many steps it would take to reach the wagon but realized, with a stab of worry, that he had no idea. Hell, he didn't want to bump into the damn thing, make a racket, rouse the whole camp, and have to answer questions as to why he was poking about in the dead of night, especially around the wagon.

And then he heard them—Julie's voice, soft and tender, coaxing, pleading. "You know you want something to drink," she was cooing. "It'll relax you. . . ."

"No, my darling, I don't need anything to make me relax," came the southern drawl of the Reb officer. "I want to remember every second of this night, this time with you. When I saw you, my heart turned over, and I knew I had to have you, if only for a little while."

"But one drink won't hurt. Please, have one with me."

No, Julie, no. Luther cursed silently, clenching his fists at his sides. *Don't drink that shit!* Yet he knew she would, if necessary, but then she would pass out also, and how could she get information and then pass it along to Veston? Oh, damn, he knew this was going to be a hell of a night.

". . . if you insist," the officer murmured. Then his laugh, deep, throaty. "Yours spilled on your breasts . . . those beautiful, luscious breasts. Here, we can't let the delicacy of either go to waste."

And then he heard them—the sounds that tore into the depths of his soul—moans and sighs of satisfaction, and he could see in his mind's eye what that bastard was doing to Julie's breasts with his hungry, eager lips.

"Now drink from the bottle," Julie giggled, and Luther knew it was forced, just as the slur in her voice was faked.

"I live such a hectic life," Julie was saying. "You can't imagine what it's like, traveling from camp to camp, dodging those dreadful Yankees."

"But it's an admirable, honorable thing you do, my sweet. And you do have a lovely voice. My men enjoyed you, but not nearly as much as I intend to before this night ends."

"Oh, I pray it never ends," came Julie's voice once more, sounding quite sincere. "I—I do like you. We move from here to Richmond, I suppose. The fighting is getting so intense. Perhaps I will see you then."

"I doubt it." His voice sounded strained, and the wagon

shook a bit. Luther knew the officer was taking off his boots, his trousers, getting comfortable.

God, he prayed the opium would work quickly.

He could almost see Julie's petulant expression as he heard her say, "Then when will I see you again? If you don't mind my saying so, sir, a lady does not like to feel that she is only to have one night of pleasuring a man that takes her fancy as you have taken mine."

"Ah, put your hand there, that's right. . . ." The major sighed, then said, "I can understand your lament, Julie, and I truly feel the same way. But the war is picking up, what with the spring thaw. We aren't planning to move anywhere for the moment. Our defenses spread from northwestern Georgia all along the eastern edge of the mountains into Winchester, Virginia. Then we have armies along the southeast across Virginia and on through Fredricksburg and Richmond. We hear Grant and Sherman could head for Richmond anytime, and my men stand ready to move there if we are needed."

Luther's ears perked up at hearing the approximate location of the Confederate defenses, but he doubted that this was something Fox did not already know. Still, he could not take a chance on his not receiving the information. He would have to awaken Veston and send him on the way with the news. Luther would take Julie to another camp to see what they could learn there.

It was silent inside the wagon, but he could hear movements, knew that the officer was fondling Julie's body. Then he heard her coaxing him to drink again, and when he spoke once more, slurring words of desire and intent, Luther knew the opium was doing its job.

Hang on, Julie, he thought fiercely. Hang on. It shouldn't take much longer.

"Oh, I know you're going to be so good, but don't rush things."

Julie sounded nervous. He knew that she was worried that her lover would not pass out before he actually ravished her. Luther wished he could leap inside and drag that son of a bitch away from her and beat him to a pulp.

But he could do nothing but wait, his heart pounding so loudly he feared the whole camp could hear the thundering sound.

And then there was the longest silence of all. This was

it, he knew. Either the drink was taking effect or Julie had been forced to give in to the major.

Finally, when he felt he could endure the torturous waiting no longer, he heard Julie's feeble cry, hardly more than a whisper, as she called out his name.

He scrambled quickly into the wagon, trying to remember in his haste that he must be quiet at all costs, lest she have summoned him too soon.

"Yes, Julie, I'm here," he answered her softly. "Is he out?"

"I think so." She sounded near tears. "He hasn't moved in quite awhile."

And then, though he hated to do so, he knew he had to ask the question that was burning through his body. "Julie, did he—"

Her answer was quick, sharp. "No. Thank God, he passed out just in time. Were you outside? Did you hear what he said? That's all I could get out of him. They're just waiting for word from Richmond before moving—"

"I heard. Now I've got to wake Veston and get him on his way." He started to leave the wagon, then hesitated. "Julie, will you be all right? I know when dawn comes, it must be even harder for you."

"To lie here naked in the arms of a man, feeling like a whore—yes, it's agony, Luther, but I've done it before. I suppose I will do it many times over before this hellish war ends. But don't you fret about me. Just do your job, and please, please, be here as early as possible to make noise as you hitch the wagon so he'll awaken and we can be on our way."

His voice was gruff as he tried to hide the pain inside him. "Don't worry, Julie. I promised you I'd look out for you, and I will. If he wakes up, I'll be close by if you need me."

He knew she was crying. "Thank you, Luther. Sweet God, I don't know what I'd do without you."

Nor I without you, precious Julie, his heart cried in anguish. And as he ran through the night, stumbling, groping, he realized he was blinking back tears of his own.

Finally reaching Veston, he roused him and hurriedly whispered what Julie had learned from Major Anders. He could not see the other's face, but he knew by the deep silence that Veston was thinking, pondering whether the information was of any value. Finally he made movements to get up, grumbling, "Okay, I'll just have to go find the major and let him decide whether it's valuable stuff or not. It's not up to me to make the decision."

They moved quietly to the far edge of the camp, where their horses were tethered. Once Veston had saddled his mount, he instructed Luther to do as they had planned earlier. "Move north. Toward Richmond. I'll find you along the way."

Annoyed, Luther replied, "How in the hell am I supposed to know when to stop again? Am I to just keep on riding—"

Veston snarled, "Just do as you're told. I've thought it over. I'm going to have a talk with Fox about you. So just keep on riding, and don't stop."

His horse moved forward slowly, and Luther knew Veston would be a long distance from the camp before he spurred his mount to a faster gait, lest he be heard by the sentries. He was taking a chance on being shot, but he was good at being covert. That was why he'd been picked for this job.

Luther returned to the wagon to make sure Julie was all right. She had snuggled down next to the sleeping officer and whispered to Luther that there was nothing to be concerned about. "I just want us to leave here at the first break of dawn," she added with an anxious note in her voice.

"Don't worry. When you hear me outside, messing with the horses and hitching them to the wagon, you wake him up and tell him we've got to hit the road and he'd better get back to his tent before he's missed."

"Yes," she said tightly. "And I should tell him what a wonderful lover he was."

He could only agree with her, though it grieved him to do so. "You've come this far. Finish your performance. Now try to get some sleep, and remember, I'll be close by."

He took his place nearby but did not sleep. Instead he cradled his beloved guitar, wishing it were Julie in his arms instead. His eyes burned from staring toward the east, waiting for the first pink rays of dawn to caress the sky.

At last it was time. Springing to his feet, Luther ran to

untether the horses and lead them to the front of the wagon, making just enough noise to wake Julie, though he doubted she had even slept.

He felt a wave of relief when he heard the stirrings inside the wagon. He could hear the soft murmur of voices, knew she would be telling the major how wonderful it had been, how she hated to move on but had no choice and perhaps one day they would meet again.

Then he could make out the figure of a man climbing out of the wagon. He stumbled a bit, and he was rubbing his head as though it hurt. ". . . hate to say it, pretty lady, but I don't remember much about last night . . ." Luther heard him tell her.

"I have memories to last a lifetime," she said, leaning out to kiss him lightly. "Do take care of yourself. I'll be dreaming of the time when we meet again."

Then the officer was lurching off down the hill toward his own tent, no doubt to fall into his blankets and finish sleeping off the effects of the opium-laced whiskey.

By the time Luther was ready, Julie had hastily dressed, wrapping a blanket about her shoulders to fend off the chill of the early morning air. She climbed up to sit beside him on the wooden driver's bench. "Do you want anything to eat?" he asked, suddenly remembering that in their haste to be on their way, he had not considered that she might be hungry.

She shook her head. "I don't feel very well. I didn't sleep at all. Where are we heading, anyway?"

He told her Veston had said they were to ride north, that he would meet them somewhere along the way. "It'll probably be sometime tomorrow before we run into him. I don't plan to just keep on moving, though. We're both tired. I'm going to find someplace I figure is safe, and then we'll just camp out and wait for him to find us."

"What if we run into Yankees?" she asked fearfully.

"Not likely. We're smack dab in the middle of the Rebel forces. They won't ask any questions. All we've got to do is tell them we travel about to entertain the soldiers. You may have to sing a song or two, but I think you can handle that." It was light enough that she could see the comforting smile he flashed in her direction.

They had not gone far when her head began to nod. Luther noticed and told her to climb into the wagon and try to sleep. "Don't worry. I've got my gun handy, and if there are any problems, I'll let you know."

She protested. "But you didn't sleep either. I wanted to try to help you stay awake."

He laughed, pleased at her concern. "That's nice of you, but you aren't much company with your head flopping all around your neck like a chicken that's just been axed. Now you get on back there. Then if we do have to sing for our supper, you'll feel more obliging."

With a sleepy smile of gratitude, she climbed back into the wagon. He could hear her stirring about, then all was still. He knew she was resting at last.

A few times during the morning, Confederate sentries along the way flagged him down. He knew how to handle the situation, explaining that they were a traveling troupe bound to entertain the brave and valiant men of the South.

But one burly sergeant he encountered scowled and asked suspiciously, "Yeah? How come you ain't in uniform if you're so damned concerned about the southern cause?"

Luther was ready for that too. Tapping his right leg, he said, "Got a ball at Gettysburg. Can't hardly stand on it at times. The doctors say there's nothing they can do. I'd only be in the way if I took up a gun, so I took up my guitar instead. I figured that's doing my part better than sittin' on the porch back home in Alabama." He tried to make his voice drawl with a southern accent.

The sergeant was satisfied. Apologizing, he waved him on after commending him for his true and honorable spirit. Luther gave him a snappy salute, laughing inside all the while.

✺ Chapter Twenty-seven ✺

ABOUT midday Julie came out to sit beside him once again. They were near a rushing stream, so Luther reined in the horses, saying they both needed to stretch their legs a bit. He wandered away into the woods, staying close enough for her to call should she need him, but giving her adequate privacy to bathe and tend to her personal needs.

Later he found fixings for gruel and hoe cakes, and he built a small fire. After they had eaten, he said they were just going to stay put. "Veston will find us. This is the main road to Richmond, and that's the way he told me to travel."

Julie allowed as to how that suited her fine, especially since she would not have to perform for the night. "It gives me a bit of reprieve, doesn't it?"

He looked into her eyes, wondering if their lovely green depths had ever sparkled with happiness or whether they had always been shadowed by pain. How he wished *he* could make them shine. But now wasn't the time, he thought, gritting his teeth and turning to the task of rubbing the horses down and making sure they were tethered near grass and water. Later, he promised himself, later . . . when this was all behind them . . . then he could tell her what was in his heart.

They sat at the edge of the stream, enjoying the warmth of the late March sunshine. They talked of the war, how they both prayed it would soon end. Then they turned to nonsensical things, like how they wished it were warm enough to go wading.

"Back in Savannah, I loved to play in the water," Julie lamented. "Myles taught me to swim, and our cousin, Thomas Carrigan, would go with us. He's in the army now.

"In fact," she rambled on, "he was at Libby Prison the last I heard. I wonder if he was there when you all rescued Myles. . . ." Her voice trailed off, as she was shocked to see the strange expression on Luther's face.

"Did I say something wrong?" she wanted to know at once. "I was just talking about my childhood days—"

"Carrigan." He spoke sharply, something ringing a warning bell deep within him. "Did you say your cousin's name was Carrigan?"

She nodded, watching him, puzzled. "Yes. Thomas Carrigan. He was at Libby Prison. At least that's what his mother told me when she went to my mother's funeral. But why are you looking at me like that? I don't understand—"

"No reason." He reached over quickly to pat her hand. She was frightened, and he didn't want that. "It's nothing. I guess I'm just tired."

She stared at him for a moment longer, then began talking of other things, how she worried about leaving Sara and Lionel behind in Wilmington and prayed they had continued safely onto Pennsylvania. They would have been worried terribly when she did not return, she said.

But Luther was not listening. He was remembering the night they went to Libby to break out Myles Marshal. They had encountered the Confederate soldier who said he'd been waiting for just such a chance so he could desert his post and get out of the war's misery. He wanted only to hide out till the fighting was over, he assured them.

At the time, Luther recalled they'd had no choice but to take him along. It was apparent the soldier knew about the planned escape and had stationed himself in a position where he would be right in the middle of it all. He could have sounded an alarm that would have blown the whole scheme, but he hadn't. Instead he begged to go along, or rather *demanded* that he be allowed to participate. There had been no time to argue, and it was quickly agreed that he could be a part of things.

And Luther remembered the soldier's name now: *Thomas Carrigan.*

Julie saw the tremor go through him. "Are you cold?"

she asked at once. "I do hope you aren't coming down with the fever. You drive yourself so, Luther. You never get enough rest. I wish you would let me help you in some way."

He looked at her lovely face, the way her silky black hair fell in soft ringlets, dark lashes framing beautiful eyes, her brows knit together with concern for him. "I'm fine," he said quietly, wishing for the hundredth, no, the *thousandth*, time that he could fold her into his arms.

And he also wished he could tell her that she had no cause to worry about her brother, not now that he knew her cousin was with him. But he could not tell her that, any more than he could confess his love for her. He had to keep silent, not only because of his loyalty to the North, but because he feared she would leave, and he would never see her again.

Daylight was turning to dusk. Luther knew it was time to be thinking about bedding down for the night. It would be his first experience sleeping so close to her without Veston around, and he was starting to feel edgy about it. Could he keep his emotions in check? Dear Lord, he wanted her with everything in him that made him a man, and just thinking about it made his manhood swell. He kept turning away so she would not see it. He couldn't do a fool thing like make an advance toward her. Hell, she'd never believe it was because he loved her and wanted to consummate that love the only way he knew how. No, she would think that was all he wanted from her, because he regarded her in as low a light as Veston and Fox. He'd die rather than have her believe such a thing.

So it was with a feeling of relief that he heard horses approaching. Perhaps Reb soldiers were coming to camp nearby, and his temptation would lessen.

But he frowned as he recognized Veston's brown stallion galloping toward them, and he felt a sinking sensation when he realized Fox was with him. When they got closer, he could make out the grim, set expressions on their faces. He sensed trouble.

"Oh, no, not both of them," Julie cried, her hand moving to her throat as she took a step backwards. "I can't bear being around the two of them—"

Luther fleetingly wondered why she always retreated alone when she was frightened, never coming toward him.

He had tried to let her know he was there should she need him . . . but she always retreated within herself.

Then he thought of the times he had heard her cry out in her sleep—one word . . . one name . . . *Derek*. He wondered if that was the only man in whose arms she could find solace from the world that had treated her so cruelly.

But there was no more time for wondering about anything except the moment at hand, because Fox and Waters were reining in their horses and dismounting. "That information you got last night was worthless," Fox snapped at Julie immediately. "Everyone has a good idea of where the damn Rebs are encamped. You haven't been of any use to me on the road. I've decided you're coming to Richmond."

Her eyes widened, and she retreated even further. "But why? What will you do with me there?"

"Set you up in a bawdy house, what else?" he smirked. "Maybe there you can be of some use to me. I've coddled you long enough. No more spiked drinks. You're going to really work for the Union now, whether you like it or not."

Wildly she shook her head. "I can't! I won't!"

"Oh, yes, you will," he said absently, then turned to Luther, "As for you, Veston tells me you're becoming quite a troublemaker. I'm going to be watching you, and if you don't straighten up, you'll find yourself back on the battlefield."

Luther stood his ground, brown eyes flashing as he replied snappily, "I'm not making any trouble. I'm just trying to protect Julie as much as possible from the hell you're putting her through. She doesn't deserve it—"

"That's not for you to say! I'm your commanding officer, and you'll follow orders. I can have Veston shoot you down this very second, if I give the word."

Luther shot a glance at Veston. Sure enough, the man had his gun trained right on him, a sneering grin on his face.

"You're a good soldier, or I wouldn't put up with you," Fox said. "Just don't let your heart rule your head. This is war, and none of us like it, but we've got to do the best we can."

A nerve twitched in Luther's jaw as he looked from the

pointed gun to Fox's triumphant face. He knew Veston would kill him without so much as batting an eye. Luther was treading on dangerous ground, and while he would give his life for Julie without hesitation, she would be at the mercy of these scoundrels if he were in his grave. He'd be of no use to her dead. "All right," he said finally, hating the way Fox's eyes gleamed at his concession. "I'll go along with you, but nobody touches her. I intend to see that anybody you send to her is drugged. *I* haven't touched her that way, no matter what either of you think," he added.

Fox shrugged, exchanged a look of amusement with Veston. "Makes no difference to me whether you've bedded her or not. Now we've got to be on our way. We're apt to arouse suspicion standing by the roadside this way."

Suddenly Julie rushed forward. "I'm not going anywhere with you," she cried. "Not till you take me to Myles and let me see for myself that he's all right. I have to know. . . ." She was fighting tears, fighting to keep the man she despised from knowing he could reduce her to complete humility.

Fox looked at her, the play of a smile on his lips. "Well, now, Julie, I don't have any intention of doing that, and you're in no position to bargain. You will do as you are told."

She stamped her foot, fists clenched as she yelled, "But why won't you let me see Myles? Why won't you let me see for myself that he's all right?"

"Because—" Fox bellowed, eyes bulging with such anger and fury that even Luther retreated a few steps, "your brother is dead! But you're still working for me, and I—"

"Dead!" The word was a heart-shattering moan as her face contorted in agony. "No . . . you're lying . . . he can't be . . . oh, God, he can't be—" Lifting her skirts, she turned and ran toward the stream to fling herself upon the mossy bank, her body shuddering with sobs of grief that penetrated to the very core of her soul.

"It isn't my fault," he called after her, still defiant and belligerent. "Blame the goddamn Rebels. He was too far gone when we rescued him. Be glad you have a chance to avenge his death!"

Luther turned to go after her to give her what comfort he could, for his heart was grieved at the sight of her lying there, her world crumbled and crushed about her. But Fox reached out and wrapped steely fingers about his arm, yanking him back. "Let her go," he whispered harshly. "She's got to get it out of her. She needs to be alone right now."

"Did you have to tell her like that?" Luther said hoarsely. "Did you have to be so goddamn blunt about it?" He did not care at the moment how deeply he angered his commanding officer.

Fox pursed his lips, nodding thoughtfully. "Yes. It was the only way. She must go with me to Richmond, and I want her to be a good spy for the North. She is by far the most beautiful woman I have working for me, and if she cared for her brother the way she seems to have, this will make her my most devoted worker. She should hate the Rebels for what they did."

"How long have you known?" Luther demanded. "How long have you let her go on thinking she was doing all this to keep her brother alive?" Once more he was fighting for control, wanting to throw himself upon this bastard and choke the life from him. But Veston still had a gun pointed at him, he knew, so he was helpless.

"I just found out a few days ago." Fox spoke gently, as though sympathizing with his concern. "I finally received a message from the mountain hide-out. Kelso and Satch showed up . . . alone. Everyone else had deserted. They said Marshal died. He was too weak to make the trip. I was afraid of that."

Something did not add up, and Luther stood silently, listening to Julie's heart-wrenching sobs. Finally he knew he had to ask: "What about that Reb soldier who deserted his post at Libby to go with us? I think his name was Carrigan." He tried to keep his voice even, not wanting to arouse suspicion.

"The message I received was that everyone deserted except Satch and Kelso. I'm not surprised. But why do you ask about this fellow Carrigan?"

"No reason," Luther lied, turning away. "I think I'll get the horses hitched up. We can't just let Julie lay there on the ground and cry all night, can we?"

Fox's voice filtered through Luther's roaring brain as he moved toward the horses. "I'll get more use out of her than I ever anticipated. When she gets over her shock and grief, she's going to be the most cunning spy in Richmond.

Heaven help the Rebs who fall into her web." He and Veston shared laughter, but Luther kept his back turned. He did not want to give his thoughts away, and he knew without a doubt that Carrigan would never have deserted unless Myles died first, and Luther had the feeling that Carrigan had done everything in his power to keep his cousin alive. If Myles and Carrigan had escaped, Kelso and Satch wouldn't have been stupid enough to admit they'd let such a thing happen.

Luther's eyes went to Julie, still huddled on the bank, sobs ripping through her body. He could not tell her of his thoughts, either, because he had no real basis for his belief that maybe, just maybe, her beloved brother was still alive . . . along with their cousin.

For the moment, he would do everything in his power to keep her from suffering any more than absolutely necessary—and that was all he could do. A feeling deep in his gut told him he had a formidable task before him.

🐚 Chapter Twenty-eight 🐚

D EREK sat at the splintery wood table in the shadows of one of Wilmington's crudest waterfront saloons. His head nodded slightly from too much to drink, too little sleep. He had sat back and watched two brawls. In one, a seaman had gotten his throat slit from ear to ear. No one had bothered to sop up the thick pools of blood where his body lay for perhaps an hour before it was finally dragged outside.

How long had he been there? Hell, he didn't know. Didn't care, for that matter. He was tired. He wanted to be left alone. The last whore that had wagged her tail at him had been chased off by a string of obscenities, so the word had spread. No one was bothering him, and that was just the way he wanted it.

The bottle of rum before him was empty. Derek shouted into the din of arguing voices and laughter in the direction of the bartender, but the man did not look up. Derek picked up his bottle and sent it sailing through the air, and when it crashed against the wall, the bartender got his message. He came hurrying over with another bottle, reaching out to set it on the table, straining, not wanting to get too close, then backed away quickly.

Derek pulled out the cork and lifted the bottle to his lips, laughing. Everything was getting blurry. No matter. Nothing mattered. Not anymore.

He looked back over the past months and wondered drunkenly why he was even alive. Returning to Richmond to find Julie had taken off without him had been quite a blow. Then, when he learned her brother had been broken out of the Black Hole, it hadn't taken much to figure out what happened. She had guile, and she obviously knew how to wrap men around her dainty little finger and make them dance to her tune. Took off with a Confederate major, that's what he'd managed to get out of Opal.

He stared down into the amber liquid of the bottle. It wasn't amber at all. It was green . . . green like the murky depths of the ocean . . . green like those damned eyes that turned his heart inside out, and he hated admitting it . . . green . . . Julie's beautiful green eyes. His head lolled foward, and he felt sick.

Her body. God, how he'd loved possessing her, touching every inch of that smooth silky skin with his tongue and lips. Perfection. Beauty. Charm. She had it all, and he'd been a fool to let her get under his skin. But no more!

His sharp laugh caused the two men sitting at a nearby table to look at him curiously, but a sharp glare from Derek's glittering black eyes made them return to their own affairs. No one wanted a quarrel with him this night. Hell, no. Pity the poor fool who dared cross his path.

If he hadn't gotten involved in the attempt to rout the Yankees from New Bern, North Carolina, maybe he would have gotten back to Richmond in time. But he was first of all, he reminded himself as he had done then, a seaman. He had been summoned by Commander John Taylor Wood himself, an aide to President Davis, and told about the plan.

General Lee had written President Davis early in January that it was time for an attempt to be made to capture the enemy's forces at New Bern, that it had to be done. There were a lot of provisions and supplies there that were needed by the Confederate Army, and Lee also wanted that part of the country to be accessible. It had been under Yankee control too long, he said.

Commander Wood told Derek about how the President approved of Lee's plan and suggested he take command of the operation himself, but Lee was hesitant about it and said he thought Robert F. Hoke of North Carolina was the man for the job. Davis didn't think so. Hoke was only a brigadier general, and he felt an officer of higher rank was needed to take on such a big campaign. So Major General George E. Pickett was selected, and then President Davis chose his own aide, Commander Wood, to command the cooperating naval force.

And Wood had called in Derek when he heard he was in Wilmington, and asked him to go along. Derek could not find it in himself to refuse, and he also figured the whole operation wouldn't delay his return to Richmond by more than a few days; at the most, a week.

Derek took another drink from the bottle. It was so clear to him now, that morning of January thirtieth, when about thirteen thousand men and seven navy cutters were concentrated in Kingston, moving in the direction of New Bern. General S. M. Barton, commanding one of the divisions, was directed to cross the Trent River near Trenton, moving along the south side to Brice's Creek below New Bern. After crossing the creek, he was to take the forts along the Neuse River and go into New Bern by way of the railroad bridge.

Colonel James Dearing's cavalry was given the task of capturing Fort Anderson, situated north of New Bern. General Pickett, with Hoke's brigade and the remainder of the force, planned to advance from the west along the Dover Road. The simultaneous attack by all three columns on the defenses of New Bern was planned for that Monday morning, February first, 1864.

Commander Wood had been ordered to engage the gunboats at New Bern, then to cooperate with the land forces in their attack on the city.

So, carrying out the plan, General Pickett drove in the Federal outpost at Batchelder's Creek. Then, after crossing the stream about ten miles west of the target city, he moved his command to within a mile of it and stopped to wait for the sound of General Barton's guns from the other side of the Trent River.

And he had waited all day in vain, Derek recalled sadly, because on Tuesday, General Barton sent word that the works at Brice's Creek were too strong to attack, that he'd made no advance and did not intend to.

Then Colonel Dearing, who was supposed to capture Fort Anderson, reported he had found the Federal fortifications on his front much too powerful to storm.

So, faced with the certain failure of two of his columns, General Pickett withdrew his forces and his plan to attack New Bern.

At least, Derek smiled with satisfaction, Commander Wood's naval operations had not been a complete loss. In fact, he felt mighty damn proud to have been hand-picked by this daring officer to take part in his venturesome plan. They had dropped down the Neuse River from Kingston and slipped on board the Federal steamer *Underwriter*, which was anchored at New Bern.

Oh, it had been a bitter hand-to-hand fight with the ship's crew, all right. Derek lost count of the number of men he personally sent to their graves, and he himself had taken a knife's blade in his lower ribs, which still pained him. And the patch he wore over his right eye was the result of the blow from a gun butt. A doctor had told him to wear the patch to rest the eye, for he had received a serious injury there. In time, he had been told, it would, he hoped, heal.

But they had won the battle, by God, and they were making preparations to move the *Underwriter* when they realized there wasn't enough steam in the boilers to get underway. Things were complicated by harassing fire from a nearby fort, so Commander Wood said there was nothing to do but burn their "prize" and head for home. Which they had done. Even though the captured ship had to be destroyed, the fact that it *was* captured had been the only good thing to come out of the ill-fated expedition.

By the time Derek got his affairs in order, rounded up the men and money he needed, and returned to Richmond, Julie was gone.

Commander Wood had tried to talk him into going back to the sea, but for some reason he could not explain, even to himself, Derek did not want to take on a ship again. He did not want to attempt to run the Federal blockade any longer.

And he hated himself for the strange feelings that flowed through his body. Dammit, the blasted war was exploding, and he was needed, and he believed in the southern cause. So why was he turning into a sot? Each night he tried to find the answer to his misery in the amber liquid of the bottle, but his days were wretched, for he was filled with self-loathing and contempt.

Derek's fingers gripped the bottle, and had he not felt the contents sloshing in it and realized foggily that he would be wasting over half his rum, he would have sent it, too, smashing against the wall in frustration.

He felt the two men staring at him again. And he didn't like it. He was bigger and stronger than most men, and he shied away from fighting, proud of the fact that his ominous figure usually caused a would-be rowdy to back away. But now he was drunk, and those two had been sneaking glances in his direction all evening.

He'd had enough.

Suddenly he jerked his head up to look at them and snarled, "What the hell do you sons of bitches think you're looking at? I don't like to be stared at. Now get the hell out of here!"

He had decided beforehand that if they did not immediately run for their lives, he would be bullish enough to start a brawl. Hell, he felt like hitting somebody, something, *any*thing . . . to get the gnawing feeling out of his gut.

But surprisingly, the skinny one, who looked as though he had been to hell and back, gazed at him with sad yet hopeful eyes and politely asked, "Are you Captain Arnhardt?"

Derek blinked, jerked his head back as he tried to focus his eyes. "Who the hell wants to know?"

"May we speak with you, sir?" the other man asked.

Derek's head bobbed as he looked him over. Even though the stranger was smaller than he was, Derek figured he looked healthy enough to give a good account of himself if all this came to a fight. The confusing part, Derek thought, was why they were pussyfooting around with all the soft talk.

"What do you want to talk to me for?" Derek demanded. "I told you—I'm sick of your staring. Get the hell out of here before I bust your heads—both of you. . . ."

The two of them got to their feet and came toward him.

Well, Derek took a deep breath, this was it. It'd been a long time since he'd been in a barroom brawl, but maybe he needed this to let off a little steam. Maybe it would make him feel better.

"It's about Julie Marshal."

A gray mist settled about him. He shook himself. This wasn't the way it was supposed to be. About now, chairs should be flying through the air and fists smashing against flesh. So why the hell wasn't it happening that way?

He was dimly aware that the two men were sitting down at his table. He tried to focus his eyes but the misty fog was still there, and through it drifted the voice of the skinny man. "Julie is my sister, Captain Arnhardt. My name is Myles Marshal."

With great effort, Derek forced his vision to clear, his brain to stop spinning. Leaning forward, he stared into the young man's face, searching for Julie in it.

"We don't look alike," he laughed nervously. "I mean, of course we aren't *identical* twins, but we *are* twins, and I assure you I'm telling the truth."

"I'm Thomas Carrigan, a cousin." The other one spoke, and Derek's eyes moved to him. "We've been looking for you for weeks, and thank God we've found you."

Derek looked back at Myles, cursing himself because the fog was settling about him again. He wanted his head clear so he could find out what the devil this was all about. "Julie got you out?" he asked, his words slurred.

"Yes. But now she's in trouble. . . ."

That was the last Derek heard before his head hit the table with a jerking thud. The hammer of drink had finally hit.

When he awoke, he was in a strange room, lying in an unfamiliar bed. He wondered dizzily which woman he had gone home with. There had been the redhead with the small teats, and the yellow-haired one with the big teats. He had liked them both, and he'd had them both in the past, but it had not been his intent to lay with a woman last night.

And then he saw them.

They were sitting at a table by the window, watching him intently. Slowly, it was coming back. His mouth felt like it was packed with cotton, and his stomach rumbled precariously. He felt as if he were going to be sick.

"Coffee." The skinny one walked toward him, carrying a steaming tin cup in his bony hand. "We figured it was about time for you to wake up. That was some drunk you tied on. You were pretty far gone when we arrived, and we weren't sure how to approach you."

The other one grinned wryly. "We were warned it's best to leave you alone these days. Maybe now we can talk if you feel up to it."

Derek propped himself up on one elbow and took the coffee gratefully. It was hot, but it felt good sliding down into his empty stomach. Maybe he would live after all, he decided. A few more sips, and he was able to say, "All right. I'm listening."

They took turns telling the story of Julie's plight. Myles finished by saying, "We've got to find her and help her, and you're the only person we knew to come to. We know she was with you last."

"Yes," Thomas added quickly. "I was able to pick up the information from Major Fox's men that you had left her in a bawdy house in Richmond, and she got tired of waiting."

"That's Julie," Myles grinned fondly. "She always was impatient."

Derek ran his fingers through his beard thoughtfully. So! Julie had gotten herself into a peck of trouble—all because she was so goddamned headstrong and stubborn she couldn't let him take charge. No, she had to go tearing off with a bunch of Yankees. "She can take care of herself," he said finally. "You're free now, Marshal. Go back to Savannah and don't worry about your sister. I'm sure she'll do just fine."

Myles could only stare at him in disbelief, but Thomas was leaping to his feet to yell furiously: "How can you say such a thing, Arnhardt? We just got through telling you she's with that Yankee, and he's using her, because she thinks Myles is being held prisoner by *his* men now. He'll never tell her Myles got away."

"That's her problem." Derek sat up, looked about for his boots, found them, and began struggling into them. "You see," he continued slowly, "I struck a bargain with her, and there were a few conditions—such as that she was not to leave me. So she can get herself out of whatever predicament she's gotten herself into."

"And," he added, eyes glittering as a nasty mood suddenly swept through him, "while she would have everyone believe she's suffering, I rather imagine she's enjoying being a martyr."

Myles struggled to leap for him, but Thomas had sensed the explosion coming and was there to hold him back. Myles was no match for such a tower of a man.

"You worthless son of a bitch!" Myles yelped as Thomas held him. "You goddamn miserable son of a dog! How can you speak of my sister that way? I should've known better than expect you to help us. You used her, didn't you? Like all the others . . ."

Thomas was having a hard time restraining his cousin, and he was surprised to realize Myles had such strength, for he still looked wasted and weak. "This isn't getting us anywhere." He spoke harshly. "Just calm down, Myles. Let's get out of here. We'll find her on our own."

"You made love to her!" Myles screamed at Derek, who just sat there looking at him, expressionless. "Admit it! You're like the rest, wanting only one thing. Those bastards I killed tried to rape her, and that's why I killed them. And I never wanted this stinking war. This goddamn brand on my forehead isn't justifiable. I'm no traitor to the South. I-just-didn't-want-the-goddamn-war! Can you understand me? And neither did Julie! But we were pulled into it. And everything she did, everything, was because of me! Now look at me! I'm just a shadow of a man, and I can't help her. I can't save her. I can't even beat you to a pulp for saying such things about her—"

He collapsed in Thomas's arms, sobbing brokenly as he was helped back to his chair.

For a few moments there was no sound in the room except for Myles's weeping. Then Thomas turned to Derek and said, "Everything he said was true." And he fell silent.

Myles stopped crying and stared out the window, feeling humiliated because he had lost control of himself.

Derek finished dressing, then looked at the two of them and spoke with quiet determination. "Gentlemen, I have listened to you but I've got my own opinions in the matter. You do what you want about Julie, but as for me, I intend to get back into this damn war with both feet. I'm going to fight for the South as long as there's hope. When there is none, then I pray to God I never again spill another drop of human blood."

He turned toward the door, but Thomas was right behind him. "What do you intend to do? Are you going to run the blockade again? Are you saying you won't help us find Julie?"

Derek sucked in his breath, his huge chest expanding to stretch his shirt tautly. "I said I intend to get back into the war. In my own way. As for Julie, I think she can take care of herself. Right now there's more to be done than galloping off to try and rescue her, however noble an act you feel it would be."

He started to move once more, but Thomas clutched at

his shoulder. "But you didn't answer me. What exactly do you intend to do?"

Derek eyed him warily. "I'm going to fight the war *my* way. You're welcome to come, both of you, if you like." Then he opened the door and stepped into the hallway, closing the door behind him.

Thomas turned to Myles. "What do you want to do?" He waved his arms in the air. "Do you think we should go with him?"

Myles shrugged helplessly. "We can keep trying to persuade him to go after Julie. But one thing is for certain: he's going to fight the blasted Yankees, and it's high time I did too. I say let's go with him."

They began to gather their things hurriedly, anxious to catch up with Derek.

Outside in the hallway, Derek leaned against the faded papered wall, pulled out a long, thin cheroot, and lit it as he waited. They would be along. He had no doubt of it. And maybe somewhere along the way, they would encounter Julie. But for the moment, he needed time to find out just what that gnawing in his gut really meant—whether he wanted to satiate the yearning—but most of all . . . he was ready to make some Yankees pay for a hell of a lot of misery.

And yes, a tiny voice whispered deep within the giant of a man, he wanted to make them pay for what they'd done to Julie as well.

❧ Chapter Twenty-nine ❧

JULIE had lost all concept of time. The days couldn't really be distinguished one from the other, and they would finally blend into weeks which blurred in her memory.

Gordon had placed her in one of Richmond's most fashionable hotels. She could not complain about the comfort provided by her surroundings, though it did not matter.

Luther took her out for walks in the refreshing spring air, and he was constantly harping that she was growing too thin, nagging her to eat more. Bless him, she thought fondly; she knew she could not have endured her existence without him. He continued to make sure that the amorous Confederates she encountered were properly drugged, sparing her the ultimate anguish of their total violation of her body.

He was in love with her. She had sensed it long ago. And he had tried to tell her of his feelings many times but then held back. She was thankful he had not actually spoken the words. Though he was a dear, treasured friend, and she knew her life would truly be an insufferable hell if he were not ever present as a buffer, she did not want to think about love.

Love. Did such an emotion actually exist? she wondered bitterly. Of course, she had loved Myles and would forever mourn him. And maybe she had cared for Thomas once, before her venomous feelings for his mother had obliterated any possibility of their getting together. God, that seemed centuries ago. Had there ever been sunshine and warm, wind-swept skies, laughter and happiness and joy?

Perhaps, she reflected gloomily, she had known those things . . . in another life.

Thoughts of Derek kissed her mind. To be held tightly in his arms, to burrow her face against his shoulder—oh, it was to experience an overwhelming security that no other man could ever create. Yes, he infuriated her with his arrogance, but he could also make her bloom like a spring rose. His power over her had left her drunk with wonder. Now she wondered once more how her life would have been different had he kept his promise to return. But he had told her over and over that his love was the sea, and no woman would ever anchor his heart. Perhaps he had been completely honest and she was no more to him than a momentary desire which, once satiated, returned him to his life as the tide flowed into the endless horizon.

A sudden rap on her door brought her out of reverie. It was midday, but she still wore her satin dressing gown. Pulling the lace collar closer about her throat, she called out fearfully, "Yes? Who's there?"

"It's Luther, Julie," came the warm, husky voice, and she hurried to let him in.

He was holding a silver tray in his hands. "I thought you might be hungry. I let you sleep later than usual. Last night was rough, wasn't it?"

She frowned and turned away, not wanting to remember. The officer had not wanted to drink, and it had taken a good bit of coaxing to finally persuade him. During that time, he had fondled her naked body, and several times she feared he would go ahead and ravish her. A shudder went through her. Luther saw it and reached out to pat her back lightly. "It's all right, Julie. Just remember I'm in the next room, and if you ever need me, all you've got to do is tap on the wall."

Her laugh was bitter, caustic. "And if I did, and you came running in to defend my so-called honor, it would expose Major Fox's whole set-up, wouldn't it? We'd probably both be killed, he'd be so furious. No." She shook her head with finality. "I just have to keep on praying that I can get them to drink, drug them, keep on playing games. . . . dangerous games, I fear."

He set the tray on the bed. She stared at the coffee, the plate of eggs and oatmeal, then said she wasn't hungry. "Come on now." He tried to make his voice bright. "We can't have you getting sick. It's my job to take care of you, and Fox would just love an excuse to send me elsewhere and keep you himself."

"I know," she sighed, sitting down and starting to pick at the eggs. "For both of us, I'll try. I don't want you sent into battle, and I certainly don't want to be left alone with Gordon and Veston. We both know you're the only reason they leave me alone. Even though Gordon is your commanding officer, you've made it quite clear you would never stand for him . . ." Her voice trailed off as she lifted her eyes and saw the strange expression on his face. She lay down her fork, suddenly apprehensive as she asked, "Luther, why are you looking at me like that?"

He bit the inside of his cheek, folded his hands backwards to crack his knuckles nervously, glanced up at the ceiling, then finally looked her straight in the eye and said: "I want to get you out of all this. I want to take you and leave."

She began to tremble with . . . what? Fear? Hope? When she could find her voice, she whispered, "Are you sure? Are you positive you want to take such a risk? They'd kill us if they caught us."

"I'm sure," he nodded firmly, "but I just haven't figured out when or how." He sucked in his breath and averted his gaze from those luscious breasts peeking through the sheer lace bodice of her gown. He hurried on, "I just wanted to find out if you'd go with me. I mean, last night, lying there in my bed, right next door, knowing what that son of a bitch was in here doing to you . . . dammit, Julie, I couldn't stand it. I almost came bustin' in here, but I held back, not sure how you felt—"

"You mean about escaping?" She blinked, bewildered. "Surely you know I hate my life, Luther. I don't know what waits for me out there, but anything is better than this."

"Even . . ." he caught his breath, then plunged onward, "even being my woman?"

"Your—your *woman?*" she gasped, her mind dancing in circles as it tried to comprehend what he was saying.

"Yes, my woman, dammit!" He lunged toward her, knocking the tray aside, and pushed her roughly back onto the bed. With eager hands he jerked her gown open, burrowing his face between her breasts as he groaned, "Surely to God you've known how I've loved you all this time . . .

wanted you. I've tried to fight it, but I can't, not any-more. . . ."

She pushed at his shoulders, begging him to stop, but he kissed each nipple, then lifted his mouth to cover hers, silencing her cries of protest. Parting her thighs with his knee, his eager fingers darted between her legs and began to gently caress her. Raising his head slightly, he whispered, "I'll be good to you. I'll never hurt you. I swear it. I'll make it wonderful for both of us. Just let me love you, Julie. Let me do what I've been aching to do since the first time I laid eyes on you."

He began to kiss her again, devouring her mouth with his tongue as her brain screamed silently to her body that it was not to yield to the flames of desire that were being ignited. But her body was not obeying her command. They had shared too much together. He had been so gentle and tender, the way he was being now, despite his passion. And God forgive her, even though she did not love him, she wanted what she knew he was about to give her!

He did not take her right away, for he wanted to be a skillful lover, to satisfy her completely. He moved his hand to caress her nipples, gently, firmly, and even the slight twinge of pain was delicious. He maneuvered his body so that his swollen organ pressed against her, letting her know what he had to offer, and what she had to admit in all honesty she wanted to receive.

"Tell me to love you," he commanded when she was but a whimpering mass of desire beneath him. "Tell me to take you, as hard as I can, as long as I can, anytime I want. Tell me you're my woman, even if you don't love me. Tell me you're mine, and I swear to God, I'll get you out of all this and do my damndest to make those beautiful eyes of yours shine with happiness once again."

"But I don't love you, Luther," she cried, her body writhing beneath him. "I won't lie to you—"

"You don't have to lie when you tell me you want me. I can feel it. I can see it in those goddamn green eyes. You want me. Let me worry about making you love me. I know I can if you'll give me the chance. I'll never let anyone or anything hurt you, ever again. . . ."

His lips covered hers, and his hands moved over her feverish skin, making her moan with the desire he knew she was fighting against.

It took only seconds for him to release himself from his trousers, and then he was entering her, gently at first, then conveying all the hunger that had been stored for so very long. Her buttocks moved beneath him, and he slid his fingers under them to cup her and hold her tightly against him as he plunged again and again.

Julie's nails clawed at his back as she felt her insides quiver with the first shadow of release. And then it was upon her, that all-consuming wave of pleasure that made her teeth sink into her lower lip and taste blood as she suppressed the scream of joy that reverberated from the very depths of her soul.

And he continued, pushing in and out until he took her to the pinnacle of pleasure again and again. Only when she lay beneath him spent and exhausted, did he allow himself to revel in his own sweet, hungry release.

He lay with his head against her chest, and Julie absently fondled his soft, silky blond hair. She felt guilty only because she did not love him, could not return the deep feelings she knew, without a doubt, that he had for her.

She asked herself whether she could ever return his love, but her heart refused to answer. There was only one thing of which she could be certain: she would never hurt him. He was going to take her away from this decadent existence, and she would do her best to make him happy.

Happy. The word played in her mind like musical notes. She no longer asked to be happy, only that she not be *un*happy. That dream was gone forever, that dream of bliss . . . like Myles, and Derek . . . and Rose Hill. And Luther would see to it that she was, at least, not sad. He was good and kind and gentle, and they shared a love for music, and he cared for her, and dear Lord, it was a start, a beginning.

Then why, she asked her swirling inner being, did she still hold such a deep sense of despair after such rationalizing? Again, there was no answer.

Neither of them heard the gentle scrape of the key turning in the lock and were not aware of Gordon Fox's presence till he chuckled, "Well, how touching! Of course, I knew all along this was why you were so protective of our little jewel, Luther."

Luther swore as he moved away, quickly jerking the

covers up to hide Julie's nakedness before straightening his own clothing.

Embarrassed, Julie turned her face to the wall, not wanting to face the major's glittering eyes.

"You get your kicks spying on people, do you?" Luther snapped angrily as he tucked his shirt into his pants.

"Oh, don't be a fool," Gordon sniffed. "I've allowed you to drug the Rebs to keep them from having their way with her, haven't I? I think I've been very damned cooperative, so the two of you can return the favor tonight."

Luther gritted his teeth and turned away toward the window to stare down at the streets of Richmond. "What's so blasted special about tonight?" he snapped.

"We have a different situation." Gordon sat down near the bed, crossed his knees, and smiled as Julie looked at him. She pulled the coverlet even tighter about her neck, hoping the glare she gave him mirrored her deep hatred and contempt.

He continued to smile, and directed himself to her. "You won't be prying information out of anyone tonight, my sweet. You will be merely setting a trap."

Luther swung around quickly. "What kind of trap?" he demanded suspiciously.

The major's gaze remained riveted upon Julie as he asked, "Have you ever heard of the Gray Devil, Luther?"

"Yeah, I guess everybody has," he said tightly, curiously. "He's the crazy son of a bitch that dresses up like a Federal cavalryman, him and his men, and they ride right into our lines and massacre right and left. He's becoming a living legend."

"After tonight, he will be," Gordon chuckled. "But not a *living* legend. He'll be quite dead."

Suddenly Luther moved to stand beside him and exclaim, "You mean he's here, in Richmond? How can you be certain?"

Fox raised an eyebrow and gave him a contemptuous look. "It's my business to find out these things, Luther. Yes, he's here in Richmond. One of my most reliable sources informed me where he's hanging out, and that is where you will go tonight and take Julie. I've arranged for her to sing at the little saloon, and I'm having a very special dress sent up for her to wear. Our friend the Gray Devil will be quite taken with her. You will let him know she's available, for a price. Once he arrives here, in this room, and Julie gets him in a vulnerable position, he will be . . . let us say . . . disposed of."

"You're talking about me setting up a man for murder?" Julie cried, shaking her head from side to side. "I've done many things, but never this. You can't ask me to."

"Oh, you'll do it," Fox said confidently, looking almost bored over her outburst. "And don't act so virtuous. When you pass along information you wheedle and coax out of your lovers, how do you know you're not passing a death sentence on hundreds of Rebel soliders?"

She paled. "You—you've told me I've never really given you anything of great importance. I couldn't have caused anyone's death."

Gordon waved his hand in a gesture of intolerance. "It's of no consequence. You'll do as you're told, Julie, or I'll sell you into some bawdy house, where you'll wish you were dead within a week. So don't argue with me. I've no time for it."

She saw Luther's eyes flash, but felt relieved that he was controlling himself, not leaping to her defense. He would not let this terrible thing happen to her. She could just feel it in her heart.

She watched as he sat down on the side of her bed, knew he was inwardly fighting for composure as he kept his voice even to ask of Gordon: "What are your plans once we get him to the room?"

"Quite simple, really. As I said, Julie gets him into her arms, gets him very occupied, and then you and Veston come in. I don't want any noise. Use your knife. It will be messy, but we can handle that easier than we can the sound of gunfire."

Julie thought she was going to be sick. She pressed the back of her hand against her mouth.

"And then what do we do with the body?" Luther wanted to know. "How do we get it out?"

"There's a door at the end of the hall. We'll wait until everyone is asleep and things are quiet. Then you can take him outside, dump him in an alley. That is no major undertaking. The thing you must concentrate upon is getting him interested in Julie and arranging for him to come here." He flicked his tongue across his lips as his eyes raked over her. "I don't foresee any problem. What man in his right mind could resist such a beauty? *I* certainly would leap at the opportunity."

"You won't get an opportunity—" Luther snarled.

"Oh, calm down; I gave her to you, didn't I? Now, then!" He slapped his knees, stood up. "I'll be on my way. Don't either of you make any mistakes tonight." He paused at the door to flash a grim look at each of them in turn. "This is important. Generals Grant and Sherman are on the move, heading south. Sherman is reported to be heading toward Atlanta with over a hundred thousand men. Grant is bringing the Army of the Potomac in a drive here to Richmond. We've enough to worry about, what with that devil Nathan Bedford Forrest and his band of Rebel horsemen wreaking havoc, without this Gray Devil masquerading and slaughtering our men. He must be disposed of *tonight!*" With a curt nod, he left them.

"I can't do it." Julie burst into tears of frustration and bitterness. "I can't deliberately lead a man to his death."

Luther made no move to comfort her. Instead he snapped, "You've got to. This is important to Fox. If we don't follow his orders, he'll take revenge against both of us. I'll be sent to the front, and he'll carry out his threat to you. But once tonight is over, I'll get you out of all this. I swear it. Don't fail me, Julie, not tonight, for God's sake."

She stared at him and could not help laughing sarcastically. "Did I hear you correctly? For *God's* sake? For *God's* sake you want me to lead a man to his death?"

He placed his hands on her trembling shoulders, eyes boring into hers. "Yes, I want you to do this. After all, I am a Union soldier. I don't like the idea of this man being in our grasp and not taking advantage of the opportunity to do away with him. He and his men have taken many lives and shed much blood. After tonight I'll be a deserter, but this one last thing, I intend to see through. You've got to help me."

"I'm not sure if I can," she remarked stiffly, turning her face away.

"You can and you will." He gave her a gentle shake. "It's the only way. When it's done, we'll leave. Tonight. Just try to think of it as the last horrible act you'll have to perform. Then the memories can truly start fading into the past."

They looked at each other. Luther cupped her chin in

his hand, kissed the tip of her nose, and smiled. "I'll send up hot water for your bath. Fox is getting something fancy for you to wear. You'll need to look your most enticing, so maybe you should try to take a nap."

He left her then, but she did not sleep. When the hot water arrived and was poured into the deep porcelain tub behind the tapestried dressing screen, she slipped into it quickly, closed her eyes, and prayed for the strength to get through these final hours.

Yankee or Rebel, she reasoned, this man called the Gray Devil had murdered many. The Yankees had been caught off guard, thinking he was one of them. True, the Yankees probably did the same thing to the Rebels when given the opportunity. Such were the brutalities of war. But if by setting up this man to be killed, lives on either side would be saved, then perhaps she could rationalize that what she was doing was not an unpardonable sin with which she would not be able to live in the future.

The sound of the door opening and closing made her sit up straight, startled and alert. She recognized Gordon's voice as he called out for her to hurry with her bath. "I want you to see your dress," he cried jubilantly. "You'll have every man in the room smoldering with desire."

Splashing the suds from her body, she wrapped herself in a thick towel and stepped from the tub, not wanting to be so vulnerable with him in the same room. So far Luther had managed to protect her from both Gordon and Veston, but she was not taking any chances, especially when she didn't know where Luther was at the moment. Besides, she doubted either of the two were trembling in their boots for fear of his wrath.

When she had put on her dressing robe, this one thick and not at all revealing, Julie stepped from behind the screen. Gordon was standing next to the bed, and he held up a dress to her, a triumphant expression on his face.

Julie was horrified. She took one look at the gaudy, revealing dress and turned away, repelled. "I can't wear it. I won't wear it. It—it's awful. . . ."

"Oh, stop behaving like a child," he snapped, walking over to grip her arm and jerk her toward the bed. "Look at it. It's stunning. I had it especially made."

He held it up once again, and Julie stared at it, her cheeks flaming as she pictured herself actually wearing it. The skirt was made of satin and sequins, but the bodice, if it could even be called a bodice, was created of nothing but bright yellow feathers. And she knew from the way the feather tips curled up and around that they were meant to entwine her nipples, leaving the top of her breasts exposed for all to see.

Then Gordon gave the skirt a flip, showing her how it would open in the middle when she walked about on the stage, exposing her legs. "The men will go wild," he said happily. "And when our Gray Devil sees you, he'll have to have you. It's going to work perfectly."

He lay the dress down carefully, then said, "I'm sending someone up to do your hair. I think tiny yellow feathers to match the gown, entwined in a cascade of curls, will give an added effect, one of elegance. You're going to be a real charmer tonight, Julie."

Silently Julie endured the preparation of her hair, and when she saw herself completely dressed, her pink nipples peeking through the curling feathers, she told herself that it was for the last time. Tonight she could endure anything. She had to.

When Luther saw her, his eyes flashed fire and he clenched and unclenched his fists. "It's terrible, isn't it?" Julie looked at him somberly. "I feel like a whore. I *look* like a whore. And tonight I suppose I *am* a whore. So be it. When the sun rises, we'll be free, won't we?"

"You're damn right," he retorted sharply. "We'll make it. I promise. Now put a shawl around yourself for the ride to the saloon. I can't stand seeing you that way."

Veston was leaning against the hitching post as they stepped outside the hotel. "I heard about that fancy dress," he grinned, picking at his teeth with his knife. "How about giving me a little peek?"

"Go to hell!" Luther growled, grabbing Julie's arm and helping her into the waiting carriage. Veston kept on grinning as Luther popped the reins across the horses' rumps. The carriage began jouncing along down the street.

"What will you do about him?" Julie wanted to know. "How can we get away without him finding out about it and trying to stop us?"

"I thought about that. When we dump the Reb's body, I'm going to bust Veston over the head and leave him lying there. When it's all over, you pretend to be hysterical. Scream at Fox and tell him you want to be alone, for him to get the hell out. He won't suspect anything. Then

I'll high-tail it back to the hotel when I figure it's safe and slip you out. We'll put plenty of distance between us and him before he ever misses us." He reached over and hugged her against him. "Don't worry. A few more hours, and it'll all be over. For both of us."

She prayed that it was so. Oh, God, she prayed so.

They arrived at the saloon, and Luther ushered her in through the back way. They discussed what songs she would sing, and he explained how, when she returned backstage to catch her breath and take some refreshment, he would seek out the man with the patch over his eye. "That's the way Fox said I'd know him. That and the fact that he'll probably be about the biggest man in the place."

Julie felt cold with dread. "If it must be done, why can't you and Veston just *do* it? Why must I be involved?"

"There's no other way. From what Fox told me, the Gray Devil stays with his men, and there's no way we'd ever be able to lure him away from them for an ambush. And we sure as hell can't take the whole lot of them on."

He ushered her into a small, cluttered room. "This is the only way to do it, for you to set him up for the kill. I'll go set things up on the stage, and I'll let you know when we're ready. Just sing, Julie, and look beautiful. That's all you have to do. I'll take care of the details. Try not to think about it."

Kissing her forehead, he smiled stiffly. "Think about tomorrow instead, and remember that I love you and I'm going to do my damndest to make you happy."

He left her, and she stood in the little room and told herself over and over that it would soon be in the past. All of it. Luther would take her away from the war and its madness. And maybe she could never really love him the way a woman should love her man, but she would be true to him, and do her best to make *him* happy. She would not let herself think about strong shoulders, a massive, rock-hard chest covered with dark, curly hair through which her fingers loved to dance. Nor would she dwell on thoughts of eyes as dark as the blackest storm, or lips soft and sensuous, teasing her into a wild desire that only *he* knew how to satisfy. No, she could not let herself think about Derek. Not ever.

A tear slipped down her cheek, and she knew she was only lying to herself, because with her dying breath she would still remember him and wonder what might have been.

Maybe he did love me, she whispered aloud in the empty room. *Perhaps it was only for a day . . . or maybe even just a night . . . but the dreams of what could be . . . what was . . . and what might have been . . . these will last. No one can take them from me.*

"Julie, it's time."

She turned to face Luther, brushed at her eyes with the back of her hand. He gestured at the shawl she still wore. "I'm sorry." She let it slip away, heard him cursing beneath his breath, then his voice cracked, "Let's be done with it."

She followed him out of the room. When she stepped into the lights, her legs exposed, the feathers curling provocatively around her nipples, the screams and applause of the men was deafening, drowning out the roaring that had begun from deep within her.

"It's all right, Julie." The soft voice came to her despite the wall-shaking din about her. She looked down into Luther's tender brown eyes, saw his smile, the reassurance he was trying to convey. He held his beloved guitar, his fingers strumming a chord. "It's all right. I'm here, Julie, always. . . ."

And she closed her eyes and began to sing.

Luther was there. He always would be. He was not the man she loved, but she was grateful for his presence, tonight of all nights.

✋ Chapter Thirty ✋

"I"T'S all set. He's almost foaming at the mouth like a mad dog." Luther sounded nervous as they left the saloon by the back door.

He led Julie to the waiting carriage. "All we've got to do is get you back to the hotel and into your room. He kept his eye on you all evening. When I eased up beside him and said I could fix him up with you for a certain price, he took the bait."

Julie felt as though a shield of ice had completely consumed her body, holding her rigid with the fear of what was to come. She could not speak.

"It's going to be over quick." He gave her a sideways glance of concern as he snapped the reins and started the horses moving. "When it happens, just close your eyes. And keep them closed till you hear the door shut and we've got the body out of the room. It might be messy, but—"

"Stop it!" she screamed suddenly, the sound ripped from her heart. "Stop talking about it, Luther. Just do it. But for God's sake, quit telling me how it's going to be."

And once she began talking, she could not stop. "I don't even know what the man looks like. It was dark in there, except for the lights shining on me. I couldn't see anyone. And I'm glad. Do you hear me? I'm glad. And I want my room in total darkness. I don't want to see him. I never want to see his face, because if I do, it will haunt me the rest of my life."

She dissolved into tears, and Luther snapped angrily, "Stop it, Julie. You can't be all wilted from crying. He's liable to suspect something. Now pull yourself together.

You're going to have to talk to him . . . get things going—"

"No lights!" She jerked her head firmly from side to side. "I don't want to look at him."

"All right, goddammit, no lights!" He flicked the reins harder, made the horses move faster through the night.

After a few moments of tense silence, he spoke with tenderness. "I'm sorry. I know what you must be going through, but you've got to believe me when I say it's going to be over quickly, and it has to be done. This man has got to be destroyed. It's the last act I will perform for the Union before I desert."

He sounded sad, defeated, and she was touched. "You really believe in it, don't you? The northern cause. And you would not be deserting if it weren't for wanting to take me away from the life I'm being forced to live. You'd stay and see the war out to the end if it weren't for me, wouldn't you?" She searched his face anxiously in the shadows.

He sighed, obviously pained. "Yeah, I guess I would. But I love you, girl, and my feelings for you are much deeper than what I feel for the Union. I've made my choice, but I've got to do this one last thing. Maybe by helping destroy the Gray Devil, I can live with myself."

"I shot a deserter once," he went on hesitantly, as thought dreading to tell about it. "It was back in 'sixty-one, the first battle of Bull Run in July. A young kid, maybe fifteen or sixteen years old, got scared when the shooting started. He turned tail and ran. A friend of mine tried to stop him and stepped in the way of a ball coming from the Rebs that would've hit that damn coward. When I saw my friend die because of that kid, I just aimed and fired and shot him right in the back."

He shuddered. "I've hated deserters ever since. And now I'm going to be one." He shook his head dejectedly.

"You can always help me escape and then come back," Julie murmured, realizing for the first time just what a fierce loyalty he felt toward his government.

He patted her knee awkwardly. "You seem to forget I'm in love with you, pretty lady, and I want you something awful. I've got to have you. I guess I just wanted you to know that you aren't the only one doing a lot of soul-searching this night. We both have our crosses to bear, don't we?"

Julie pulled her shawl more tightly about her. "Yes, we

do, but when the sun rises tomorrow, it will be not only on a new day, but a new life as well."

"That's the way to feel." He tried to sound jovial. "Now, then. Let's stop this kind of talk. The next few hours are going to be tough, but then it's all behind us."

They rode the rest of the way in silence. Luther turned the carriage over to the boy from the livery stable and led Julie up to her room. "Remember," he said as he left, his lips brushing hers lightly, "you don't have to do anything but entice him and make him think you're all his for the rest of the night. Leave the rest to me and Veston."

She walked toward the lantern which was burning on the bedside table and he whispered, "It's going to make it harder for us if we can't see what we're doing. We're going to have to yank him out of bed before we can knife him, to make sure we don't hit you instead."

"Then so be it." She turned the lantern down until the room was plunged into darkness. "I'll take my chances. I refuse to look into that man's eyes."

The sound of the door opening and closing told her that she was alone.

Walking to the bed to sit down, she wondered how long it would be till the Gray Devil arrived. Then she decided to take off the ridiculous feathered dress. She would wait for him in her dressing gown. That way, she reasoned, she could get things started so it would all be over quickly.

Her fingers shook as she fumbled with the fastenings on the dress. There was a faint light coming through the window from the street below. She wished for an instant that she had the nerve to just leap from that window and end it all. Dear God, to think she was actually helping a cold-blooded murder take place! It was more than she could bear, and the taste of blood filled her mouth as she bit down on her lip to keep from bursting into tears.

The soft, almost hesitant, tap on the door made her jump, startled. She could not answer. The tapping was repeated, and this time the sound came from her throat in a squeaky croak as she called, "Come in, please. . . ."

She turned her back, not wanting to see even his silhouette as he entered. She heard the door open and close softly, the sound of footsteps moving cautiously across the room as he groped for her.

"I'm here," she whispered. "On the bed. Here—"

She felt his weight as he sat down upon the mattress. For a moment he made no move. Then she felt strong, seeking hands touch her hips sliding slowly upward to clasp her breasts possessively. Such big hands . . . such strength, she thought absently, praying once more that it would all be over quickly . . . that this faceless, nameless man would become just another memory to obliterate from her life.

And then he spoke. And it was as though the seas had parted, and the dead were walking out from their sandy, murky bottom, their bodies dripping with clinging weeds and flotsam, bringing back the past, so long ago that it was thought to have been buried forever.

"At last we meet again, misty eyes."

"No—" the sound was a whimper. She tried to shrink away, but his hands upon her breasts kept her pinioned beneath him. "No . . . no . . . dear God, no—" She writhed and twisted, sure that this was not real. It could not really be happening.

His thumbs and forefingers pinched at her nipples painfully, as though he wanted to hurt her deliberately. "I should have known someone as devious and beguiling as you would find a way to survive the ravages of war, Julie, but this did come as a surprise."

"Derek! God, no, Derek. Anyone but you!" she cried, trying to claw her way out of the invisible net that had fallen over her, holding her imprisoned. "Please, no!"

"Embarrassed?" He laughed mockingly. "There's really no need to be. Just think of me as another customer. I paid a high price for your favors, and I intend to enjoy myself."

He moved away abruptly. "I want to look at you. I always did take special delight in seeing your body when we made love."

She had no time to protest as he quickly ignited the lamp and the room was bathed in an orange glow. She could see him—the beautiful bulk of him—but then she saw the patch over one eye and she was trying to gain control of her swirling, muddled brain to tell him what was happening. But it was as though she was having some kind of seizure and could not speak. No words could be forced from her twisting, jerking lips.

He bent over her once again, just as the door opened

with a loud crash. Derek whirled around, instantly alert, but froze as he faced the two men who stepped quickly inside. One held a gun, the other, a knife.

"No!" Julie screamed shrilly. "Luther, no! It's Derek! It's Derek. You can't—"

Luther's brown eyes rolled wildly as the realization of what she said washed over him. Derek. The name she had whimpered so many nights in her sleep. The man who he'd felt all along she would love forever. Derek Arnhardt— Ironheart—the Gray Devil.

"Cut him!" Veston snapped nervously. "Quick. We don't want no noise, but I'll shoot if I have to."

Stricken, bewildered, Derek's eyes turned to Julie. "A trap! You set me up—"

"I didn't know," she babbled, terrified. "Dear God, Derek. You must believe me. I didn't know it was you they were after."

Veston gave Luther a nudge, snarling, "Get it over with, dammit, and be quick. Don't make me have to shoot him. It's too risky."

Derek stood with legs apart, fists clenched, ready for the man with the knife to advance.

Suddenly Julie was upon her knees on the bed, arms outstretched toward Luther as she pleaded, tears streaming down her cheeks, "Please, Luther, don't do it. You can't. Just let him go, please—"

Veston pointed his gun at her as he hissed, "Get out of the way, damn you, or you'll get yours too!"

Without warning, Luther whipped about and sent his knife plunging into Veston's chest. Derek started forward, but Julie had leaped to her feet, blocking his path. He gave her a shove that quickly sent her sprawling to the floor at the same second that Gordon Fox burst through the doorway, gun in hand.

Derek froze, facing the weapon which was pointed straight at him.

"What the hell is going on?" Gordon looked down at Veston's body in horror. "Goddammit, Luther, what have you done?"

With surprising calmness, Luther replied tonelessly, "He was going to shoot Julie. You know I couldn't let that happen."

Gordon looked baffled, and his gun hand wavered ever so slightly. Derek leaped for him. Instantly Luther was moving also. The three men came together with almost maniacal screams.

The gun exploded.

Julie fought to cling to her sanity as she saw the three melding together. One slumped to the floor. There was a flash of steel as a knife hit its target. Another fell.

Then she saw it was Derek who was left standing, and he was holding Luther's bloodied knife. He knelt quickly, lifting Luther's head in his arms as she crawled forward, the world becoming a mist about her.

"Why did you do it?" Derek demanded of the dying man, his voice hoarse and face stricken. "You saved my life when you came here to take it. Why? Why?" With anguish, he stared down at the glazed brown eyes.

Luther's whispered words were barely audible as he choked through quivering lips, "For Julie . . . just love her . . . as I did. . . ."

His head slumped to the side, eyes staring blankly. The caring, tender expression had been replaced forever by the empty stare of the dead.

Derek laid his head gently down, then turned to Julie and snapped, "We're getting out of here. The noise is sure to bring people running." He lifted her easily into his arms, carried her out of the room down the hallway. Leaving through a door at the end of the corridor, he hurried down narrow steps, moving into the shadows of the night.

She was sobbing quietly, head against his chest. She was drifting between two worlds: one of stark reality, filled with horror, and one that coaxed her into oblivion. She did not know where he was taking her or why, for suddenly it seemed as though she were not really alive at all, merely caught in an eternal limbo of pain and confusion.

He set her on her feet. They were in a narrow alley between two buildings, and a dim light from the street cast shadows over them. She saw the way he was looking at her with eyes of thunder.

His right hand wrapped coldly about her neck as he pressed her against the side of a building. For long moments he just stared at her, and she could feel his hatred. Then he ground out the words: "I don't know what that was all about, but I wish to God I'd never laid eyes on you. What have I ever done to you that you'd want me dead? You set me up. Dammit to hell, Julie, just what kind of conniving, cold-hearted bitch are you?"

He rushed on, giving her no chance to speak. "That man back there, the one who gave his life for me, who was he? He was supposed to kill me, yet he saved my life because at the last minute you begged him to. What was the reason behind that? Did you suddenly decide that you couldn't add murder to your list of sins? Well, you did a good job on him . . . twisted his heart around your finger till he was prepared to die for you. And you murdered him the same as if you'd pulled the trigger yourself!"

"Listen to me, please—" She struggled as his fingers tightened about her throat, making it difficult to get the words out. "Derek, I never knew it was you. I swear. They told me they were after the Gray Devil. That's *all* I was told. And Luther knew I was being held against my will, and he loved me. We were running away after tonight—"

He gave her head a shake, banging her painfully against the wall. "None of it makes any sense. You're a conniving little slut, and you're the one who should be dead. Hell, I could've overlooked it if you'd just turned to being a prostitute, if that's what it took to survive this goddamn war to keep from starving. I could have accepted it, but to work for the Yankees? To help kill your own people? How could you do it?"

He slapped her then, hard, and his voice spun through blurring lights and spinning stabs of pain: "Damn you to hell, woman! I ought to break your neck and end your worthless life to save other men from your devilish tricks."

"Then do it!" she screamed, suddenly boiling in a sizzling, rebellious rage. "Go on and kill me. What have I got to live for now, anyway? Everyone who ever loved me is dead. I never loved Luther, but he loved me, and he died because he knew it was *you* I'd always wanted. But now I hate you as I hated Gordon Fox and all the others who used me. So kill me! You'll be doing me a favor!"

He squinted as he stared down at her in the shadows. She did not flinch as his fingers moved about her throat once again. "Yes, I would be doing you a favor." He spoke in that quiet, dread tone she had heard him use so many times to intimidate his crewmen into trembling shreds of manhood. "But I don't want to do you any favors. You're going to suffer for what you've done. You're going to have to face the one person who believed in you."

He grabbed her arm and started jerking her along in the alley. "What are you talking about?" she cried, falling to her knees. He kept dragging her as she screamed, "Stop it! You're hurting me, Derek! Have you lost your mind? There's no one left for me. Just kill me and be done with it. . . ." She dissolved into tears once more, hating herself for being so weak.

He stopped to lift her in his arms as she beat at him with her fists in protest; but when he spoke, her arms fell limply at her sides as she stared at him in shock. "I'm taking you to Myles. I'm going to tell him how I found you, what you've become. When he hears the truth, that will be more punishment than any I could give you."

"Myles is dead! I know he's dead. He died months ago. Gordon Fox told me—"

"No, he's not dead, but he'll wish he was when I dump you at his feet and tell him what a slut his sister is."

"This is a trick. You're only trying to hurt me, torture me. . . ."

He ignored her and kept striding purposefully on, holding her so tightly in his arms that she found it painful.

"Derek!"

Julie froze at the sound of the voice from the grave.

"Derek, what in hell? Oh, God, you've found her—"

"Yeah, I found her." Derek all but threw her at his feet, not caring how hard her body landed upon the ground. "Here's your precious sister you've been searching for all this time. And I want to tell you where I found her."

But Myles was not listening. He was on his knees, cradling Julie in his arms, rocking her to and fro and sobbing with joy as she clung to him.

Then she heard another familiar voice and realized with shock that it was Thomas speaking. And he was calm, not at all upset or disturbed, as he said, "*I'm* listening to you, Derek. Where did you find her? You didn't tell us where you were going tonight. We didn't know you were out looking for her."

"It was something I had to do myself." He stared down at Julie and Myles embracing each other on the floor of the livery stable. "I heard about the beautiful woman with the sweet voice who could be had for a price. Tonight I was set up to be with her, to share her bed. She's not only a prostitute—she's a goddamn spy for the Yankees. And she had me set up to be murdered."

"She was held against her will!" Myles said tensely. "We told you that's why we had to find her."

"She was going to have me killed!" Derek cried in outrage. "There are three men back there in that hotel room dead instead of me, and one of them saved my life because he loved her so damned much he thought that's the way she wanted it. Hell, he was crazy! She's not worth living for, much less *dying* for!"

Turning, he slammed his fist into a post so hard that it bled. "She's all yours!" he cried. "They didn't kill me tonight, but the Gray Devil is dead just the same. I'm getting the hell out of this stinking war. I've had enough of the killing, the suffering, all of it!"

"They say it's over for the South anyway," Thomas said quietly. "I've heard Sherman is headed for Atlanta, on a march to the sea and Savannah."

Derek walked swiftly to a stall, roughly threw a saddle on a horse, and then led him out. When he was mounted, he stared down at them. "I found her for you, Myles," he said. "But God help each of you, because it would've been better if I hadn't. From what I've seen, she wasn't worth finding."

And he rode past them, the horse's hoofbeats echoing in the stillness of the night.

Myles continued to hold Julie, rocking her gently in his arms, trying to soothe her. Thomas watched in silence for several moments, then went and saddled his horse. When he was done, he murmured, "I think it's time you two went home, Myles. Take Julie and get her out of all this."

Myles nodded, staring up at his cousin with sad eyes. "And what about you?" he asked. "Where will you go?"

"I don't know. Maybe back to the regular army, if they'll have me. I'll see the war out to the end. Maybe the South is dying, but I'll die with it, if need be. Right now, I just need time to think about all that has happened."

Julie lifted her face from Myles's shoulder. "You must believe me, Thomas. They held me against my will. And Luther made sure none of the men brought to me ever actually . . ." She paused to swallow, shuddering with the memories. "He made sure they were drugged—"

"I understand." He gave her a sad little smile. "It's over, Julie. Try not to think about it. God be with you both."

He rode away, and Myles held her tighter and swore, "We're going to make it, together. We'll head west. Lots of southerners are leaving, running to escape the Yankees.

For now, let's just give thanks we've found each other, because we're all we've got."

The ashes of her life floated about her. Myles understood. He always had. Together they would make a new life.

But inside, she knew a part of her had died. She had found Derek, only to lose him, all in one night. And at long last, she knew that he was the only man she could ever truly love. But that love was not to be.

And there was another memory to haunt her . . . a deep love she had been unable to return. Tender, warm brown eyes crying in the rain, his life given for the love he had known she always yearned for, even if only in vain.

I'm sorry, Luther, her heart cried with anguish, *so very, very sorry.*

She closed her eyes, praying to God to forgive her transgressions and hear her plea—that one day, in the hereafter, she would once again see those brown eyes, and they would not be crying in the rain, but smiling with the knowledge that he had given his life for his love.

Somehow she felt God heard, and Luther heard, and so he had not died in vain after all.

For this much, amidst the ruins of her life, she was grateful.

❧ Chapter Thirty-one ❧

HAND in hand, they stood together before the once-proud mansion.

"It's like a giant tombstone, crumbling and cracked and about to fall any moment to the grave over which it towers," Julie whispered in pain. "I never knew it would be like this."

"Look at the rose bushes." Myles pointed around them. "It's hard to believe they ever grew in regal beauty, showering our world with their sweetness. They look like scrubby weeds."

"It's still our home."

"*Was* our home," he corrected her. "The Yankees will burn it to the ground when they come. All I want is for us to dig up the things you and Sara and Lionel buried and then get out of here."

She nodded, saddened at the mention of the two people she had lost along the way. They had not stopped in Wilmington to search for them, both agreeing that too much time had passed. The old Negroes would have found a home somewhere. She and Myles had to keep moving, get to Savannah quickly, then be on their way.

"I'll go look in the barn and see if I can find a shovel." Myles started to walk away. "Everything looks as though it's been stripped clean, and there may not be any tools left."

"I want to walk through the house." Julie began climbing the steps. "I want one last look."

"I'll go with you," he said somberly.

Wordlessly they moved through the once great rooms,

wincing at the absence of the expensive tapestries, paintings, furniture. The house was completely bare. Even the windows had been stripped of draperies.

"I'd like to know what happened to everything," Myles remarked as they left the house and moved toward the barn. "Virgil probably sold off everything he could before he went back to England, and I've an idea that's where he headed as quick as he could. But it's no matter. We can't take much with us anyway. Only bare necessities."

After much searching, they found an old pitchfork in a hayloft. Then they made their way through the brambles and weeds to the cemetery. "When we dig up everything, I'll go into town and sell them for whatever price I can get. Then we'll head for Brunswick. That wagon train we heard about is due to leave within the week, and we don't have much time."

Julie pointed out the spot where the jewelry and silver had been buried. Myles nodded, then walked to their mother's grave and stood with head reverently bowed for a moment. Julie followed him, slipping her hand into his as she let the tears flow.

Myles began to dig, and in a few moments called triumphantly, "It's here! Thank God! There's enough here to get us all the way to California. We're going to make it."

She watched him scratching at the ground with the pitchfork, then stooped to help him retrieve each piece of buried treasure. When she was sure they had found it all, Myles said he would leave immediately for Savannah.

"Are you sure it's safe?" she asked fearfully. "Someone might see you."

"Who would care now? Everyone is preparing to run from the Yankees. No one is thinking about you or me. Now you go back to the house and stay there. I'll try to get back as quickly as I can."

"Promise me you'll be careful." She gave him a hug.

He placed his fingertips on her cheeks and flashed what he hoped was a reassuring smile. "All our worries are behind us. I'm going to buy a wagon, a team of horses, supplies. We're young, healthy, and by God, we've got plenty to be thankful for. Now how about letting me see some sparkle in those eyes before I go?"

She tried, but she knew he was not fooled. They both realized it would be a long time, if ever, before she found peace and true happiness. He had told her how she called out Derek's name in her sleep and wept over Luther's death. And he had promised to heal her wounds. She wanted to believe, to hold onto what he was saying, but she knew nothing could ever remove the deep scars upon her heart.

Myles pulled a thatch of hair down over his forehead. "I've got to keep this damn brand hidden," he sighed with bitterness. "That's all I need, for someone to spot it."

"Perhaps when we get out West we'll find some way to have it removed," she offered.

"I'm not going to wait that long. I'll burn myself, or something. I'll do anything to remove it."

Gathering everything they had retrieved, they took the treasure over to the two weary horses they'd ridden on their journey from Richmond. "I won't get a trade on these old slackers," Myles said, patting the rump of the horse that bore the bags of silver and jewelry. "They're worn out. I'll do the best I can, though. Now you get along back to the house and wait for my return. I intend to do some serious bargaining and get as much as possible for each piece."

After he had gone, Julie wandered through the house once again. It was hard to envision the gala balls and parties that had taken place there so long ago. Even more difficult was to recall herself as a child growing up within the high-ceilinged rooms. This was but a shell of a house, already dead and merely waiting to be buried.

Her stomach rumbled with hunger. She thought of the root cellar out back, where Sara had stored vegetables so long ago. In the gathering dusk she hurried there, but just as she had feared, everything had long ago rotted and was unfit for eating.

No matter, she thought with determination, climbing back up the ladder. Myles would bring food when he returned. She could stand the gnawing hunger cramps. She felt she could face just about anything these days.

Smoothing the skirt of the baggy dress she wore, she recalled how guilty she had felt when Myles stole it off the fence behind some woman's house outside Richmond. But there had been no choice. The night Derek had carried her from the hotel, she was wearing only a dressing gown, and she certainly could not go traveling about in that. And Myles had no money with which to buy clothing for her.

She stared toward the silent, empty servants' cabins as

she walked by them. Where had all those people gone? She hoped they had found some kind of happiness, that Virgil had not made life miserable for them while they were there.

Virgil. The thought of him made her feel sick. He had to have been the one to strip the house so completely. She only hoped he had returned to England and was gone from her life forever.

The night was warm and she walked about the grounds, feeling pain at seeing the unkempt gardens. It would be a relief to leave, and she was glad when darkness finally came so she would not have to witness the decay any longer.

She went upstairs to what had once been her room and lay down in a corner of the hardwood floor, trying not to hear the noises of the night, the way the wind howled through the pecan and magnolia trees to push her further into loneliness.

Finally she drifted away to sleep, only to be awakened by the sound of footsteps creaking up the stairway. Joyfully she jumped up, calling, "Myles, thank God, you're back. . . ."

Hurrying from the room, she was washed over with relief. Now they could be on their way by morning, sooner than they had dared hope.

"How were you able to sell everything so quickly?" she called, laughing with joy. "And what time is it? I hope you brought food. I'm famished."

There was no answer.

An icy finger punctured her heart. She froze where she stood. The footsteps were coming down the hall. When it was too late to run and hide, she realized with terror that it was not Myles approaching. But who? A stranger? And what was she to do? She had nothing with which to defend herself. She was helpless!

"I thought I'd find you here, Julie."

She backed away, turning about blindly in the darkness as her brain screamed in rejection. It couldn't be! Terror such as she had never known gripped every inch of her body. Her legs became wooden, immobile. It was like trying to run through a nightmare, fighting through a thick fog, with the wind in her lungs being sucked out by some unseen monster.

"I saw your dear brother in town. It was no accident.

You see, I knew you would one day return. I stripped the house. Sold everything. Even the slaves and the mules and the chickens and the hogs. I got everything I could from this miserable place, so it wouldn't be here for the Yankees. And they *are* coming, you know. Atlanta is in flames."

The voice was smugly confident. It was coming closer as Julie clawed blindly to free herself from the invisible web that held her prisoner.

"I admit I had almost given up hope. It has been a long time. But I had nothing except time on my hands, so I waited. You cut me badly that day, my lovely lady. I almost bled to death. But I lived, vowing to have my revenge. Now it's upon me, the moment I've been waiting for."

She reached the end of the hall, her back to the window. She fought to slide it open, knowing she would leap out, not caring that death awaited her. The grave would be a sweet release from the torment bearing down upon her.

"You're mine now," he chuckled. "I'll have you over and over and over. When Myles returns, I'll be waiting to kill him. No one will ever know or care, because I'm going to take you away to a secret place I've found. Then I will have my fill of you, and when I'm done, I will take great pleasure in disfiguring that beautiful face of yours so you will never again beguile any man."

With an anguished scream, Julie tugged at the window once more. In desperation, she was about to smash the glass with her bare hands. But he was upon her, dragging her away, throwing her to the floor.

"I've lived for this moment," he panted, ripping at her clothes, slapping her hands away as she tried to fight him. "I want you naked. I want to touch you all over. And you're going to touch me. You're going to do anything I tell you to do, because the day you displease me is the day I start cutting your face. Now spread your thighs to me and thrust those luscious breasts forward so my lips can drink their fill. Then I will empty myself into you till you scream for mercy. . . ."

She lashed out hysterically, striking him on the side of his face. Enraged, he struck back with his fist. The blow was hard, stunning. She felt herself slipping away, powerless and helpless beneath him.

Quickly he ripped her dress away. His hands seemed to

consume her body, probing, pinching, squeezing, and all the while he was screaming how she was his, how he had waited, and now she would pay for all she had done to him.

She felt the sharp stab as he entered her roughly. Again and again he plunged into her, making her bare buttocks grind against the floor. Bruised and battered, she could do nothing but lie there as he ravished her mercilessly.

When at last he was finished, the pain consumed her, and she drifted away. "I'm not through with you!" he screamed at her from the other side of that black void. "Do you hear me? Do what I taught you to do so well. Make me ready again. You're going to wish you'd never been born. . . ."

When she did not move, he grabbed her shoulders and began jerking her up and down, her head hitting the floor repeatedly. There was nothing left but emptiness, and she gave thanks that at last her prayer was answered, for she was truly dying.

But her prayer was not heard. Death did not take her away. Her eyes opened to the pale, faint twinges of dawn filtering through the dirty window. Beside her Virgil lay naked, sleeping, his arm across her possessively.

It all came flooding back, and she moved, trying to scramble to her feet and escape, but he was awake instantly, rolling over to pin her beneath him, laughing down at her in lascivious triumph. "Yes, it's real, my pretty," he taunted. "You and me, together, for as long as you please me and obey me. Now isn't this a lovely way to start a new day?"

His hand darted between her legs, and she could not help gagging. The movement startled him momentarily, just long enough for her to react and bring her knee crashing up quickly into his groin. With a scream of agony, he clutched himself and rolled sideways, and she struggled to her feet and started running down the hall.

Cursing, he began to make his way behind her. "If you don't stop, I'll make you suffer the agonies of the damned!" he shouted. "I'm warning you, Julie—"

She reached the top step and started down, but in her haste she tripped and tumbled head over heels, finally lying helplessly at the bottom, her body aching painfully as Virgil descended behind her.

Jerking her to her feet, he slapped her once . . . twice . . .

three times . . . until her ears were ringing wildly. "Now on your knees, wench!" he commanded. "I'm going to take you like the bitch you are, and when I'm done, I'm going to tie you up and gag you so I won't have to worry about your sounding an alarm when Myles gets here. I'll take care of him quickly enough."

He threw her to her knees as she shrieked angrily, "Myles will kill you for this, you bastard! I wish I'd killed you myself—"

He beat at her backside, yelling for her to be still or he would only hurt her more.

"What in hell . . ."

Rainbow lights of hope flashed before Julie's eyes as she looked up to see Myles standing in the doorway. His arms were loaded with packages which went flying in all directions as he sprang forward, eyes blood-red with fury. The snarl of an attacking, crazed beast came from his curled lips.

Virgil was caught off guard, helpless as Myles fell on top of him. Julie rolled to one side, terror wrapping itself about her as she watched her brother's fingers close around Virgil's throat, choking the life from the man who had caused her so much anguish and indignity.

It was over. Myles towered over him, his breath coming in painful, rasping wheezes. He stared down, flexing his fingers together as he cried: "I killed a man with my bare hands, but God forgive me, I'd do it again!"

Julie crawled toward him and wrapped her arms about his knees. He lifted her up and held her tightly against him. "It's going to be all right," he said, trying to soothe her. "I ran into an old friend in a waterfront bar, someone I could trust. He told me he'd seen Virgil, that he was still about. I got worried he might show up here, so I came back. And thank God I did."

He kept talking, sensing that his voice was her only link for the moment with reality, for the look of stark terror in her eyes was frightening. He lifted her in his arms and carried her upstairs, found the shreds of her dress, and told her how they would buy her more clothes in town.

Slowly she came out of her stupor. "What . . . what do we do with his body?" she asked, a wave of nausea passing over her.

"We'll bury him in the woods. No one will know or care.

I doubt he'll even be missed. Do you feel like helping me? Two of us can get it done quicker, and we can be on our way."

She didn't feel like helping, but knew time was important. Myles gave her some of the corn dodgers he'd brought, and she gulped them down quickly. Then together they went into the woods and Myles dug a grave with the pitchfork.

"It isn't deep, but it will do," he said finally. "No one will be coming here except Yankees, anyway."

Returning to the house, the two struggled with Virgil's body. Myles fastened his hands under his arms, while Julie lifted his feet. They carried him out to the grave and dumped him into it unceremoniously.

"How I wish we had done that long ago," Myles said when the last clod of dirt was packed down. "We would all have been spared so much misery. Now the worms can have him." He took her hand to lead her away, and she did not look back.

They had no problem locating the spot where the wagon train was forming when they reached Brunswick. The town was teeming with people almost hysterical in their frenzy to escape the advancing Yankees. And it did not matter to anyone that their coastal town was well to the south of Sherman's eventual target of Savannah. They knew only that they'd had enough of war, the suffering and anguish. There was one common bond among all: head west, escape, make a new life.

In Brunswick, one day blended into the next, and Julie complained to Myles that she wanted to be on her way.

"We're waiting for other families to arrive," he explained. "We've a long way to go, and there is safety in numbers. When the time is right, we'll leave. Just don't you fret."

Don't fret, she reflected caustically. How could she just blot everything out of her mind? She still thought of Derek —for instance, when she stared at the smoldering black-red embers of a campfire, so like his eyes when he was angry. And then the fire's glow changed to deep warmth, the way he gazed at her with hunger and desire.

She could not escape him in her dreams, when his face would appear to haunt her, the harshly handsome lines that could soften her to fresh-churned butter when he smiled.

What was he doing now? she wondered. Did he ever think about her, dream of what might have been?

If only there had been time to explain, perhaps he would have understood. But he had been too angry, and it was over, forever.

She wondered, too, what would have happened had she accepted his offer so long ago to become his mistress. Perhaps in time he would have found he did love her. But that was foolish. Derek loved no woman.

She tried to busy herself around the camp, which was growing, with more people arriving each day. It amused her when young Teresa Davis began to flirt with Myles. Then she realized he was flirting back, and appeared to be quite taken with the lovely, fair-haired girl.

"I think romance might blossom on our trip west," she teased him one night when he said he was taking Teresa for a walk. "Who knows? By the time we reach our destination, I may have a sister-in-law."

"And I'll probably have a brother-in-law," he bantered right back. "I've seen the way all the eligible men look at you. If you'd warm to them, you'd have them swarming after you."

A cold wave swept over her instantly, and her reply was sharper than she intended. "I don't want them swarming. I don't want any man around me . . . ever again."

"Now you're being silly," he admonished her. "You're still hurt and angry by all that's happened, but you've got to make yourself forget, Julie, like I'm doing. Think about tomorrow and stop brooding about yesterday. Sometimes I think you're only feeling sorry for yourself."

"*Sorry for myself?*" she sputtered. "Myles, how can you say such a thing . . ." and her voice trailed off. She was ashamed as she saw the amused twinkle in his eyes. He was right. She *was* shrouding herself in self-pity, and it was wrong to do so. She had to open her heart, her eyes, to the new life, the new world.

"Just give me time, Myles," she murmured. "I need time."

He hugged her. "You'll have lots of that. It's a long journey ahead. All we're waiting for now is for our wagon master to arrive, and then we'll be heading out. And none too soon. We just heard that Sherman is on the move again, heading straight for Savannah and leaving a trail of destruction behind him."

It was but a few days later that Myles excitedly announced, "We're leaving at dawn. We've been told to get the wagons lined up and be ready to move out first thing in the morning. We're leaving tomorrow, Julie! We're going to our new home!"

There was much jubilation in the camp that night. The men played their fiddles and banjos and guitars. The women sang, and a few danced. The children played and screamed with delight, and everyone was overcome with the happy knowledge that for them, the war was truly over.

Julie looked about at the men. Some were amputees. There were others without eyes, or with part of their faces gone. She stared at the hollow-eyed women who tried to look happy over the new life they had been promised, their now-fatherless children gathered around them. These were the wives whose husbands would not be coming home, for they were buried in some far-off cemetery or left to rot on a distant battlefield.

They were not running from the war, Julie realized. Not any of them. They only thought they could leave it behind. It would be with each of them forever, a part of their lives they could never deny. And it would be handed down to their children, and their children's children, and on through the generations and for years and years to come. That was the way it should be, she surmised. No one should ever forget the tragedy of the bloody, cruel war between the states.

They were up before dawn, the skies still blue-black as people began moving about, hitching horses to their wagons, brewing one last pot of coffee, eating one last bowl of gruel before starting the journey. The air was alive with the same thunder-charged emotion of a lightning-streaked rainstorm. Only there was no rain, just smiling faces and shining eyes. Next the sky turned a pale pink, then a soft rose, and when the first golden sparkle of the sun touched the horizon, people screamed with jubilation. A new day. A new life. They would soon be on their way.

"He's here!" someone cried. "The wagon master! He's telling everyone to get ready to move out."

"Julie, can you believe it?" Myles yelled happily as he leaped up to the wood-plank seat beside her, taking the horses' reins in his gloved hands. "It's really happening! We're on our way!"

She felt happy for him, for everyone else, but could not help wondering if for her, the future would bring any joy.

Then came the sound of thundering hoofbeats, drowning out all other sounds. Someone shouted: "It's him . . . the wagon master . . . he's coming this way . . . we'll be leaving soon. . . ."

Julie folded her hands in her lap and stared down, wishing she could share the happiness that seemed to be igniting all about her. She hoped she would not dim the pleasure for Myles. Bless him, he had suffered terribly also, but he did seem to be coming out of it all, much better than she. But then, he had Teresa, and it was obvious romance was blossoming for them. And she was thankful, for both of them.

Beside her Myles sucked in his breath, gasping, but she was too absorbed in her own reverie of the moment to take notice . . . till she heard him gasp: "My God! I can't believe it!"

Only then did she lift her eyes. Then she was gripping the edge of the plank seat, squeezing it and pressing down, as though to do so was to hold on tightly to her sanity.

Derek sat upon a golden Palomino, black eyes shining in the first mists of dawn as he gazed down at her. He held the leather reins loosely as he cocked his head to one side, a slight, mocking smile on his handsome face as he murmured quietly, "So we meet again, misty eyes."

She could not speak. She could not believe it was real.

"Derek, you old son of a gun!" Myles was standing up, reaching across Julie to shake his hand. "What in hell is going on? How can you be here? I don't understand—"

Derek continued to smile as he raised his right arm in a signal. Another horse came pounding forward from beyond the wagon in front of them. It was Thomas, laughing as he told them he was their "assistant" wagon master, and he and Myles embraced.

But Julie could only stare into Derek's smoldering black eyes, a hundred questions bubbling in her heart. She could not speak. Her body began to tremble.

"I told you once," Derek murmured softly, "that when I had mastered the winds and the tides, I would come for you and conquer your love. That time is now."

He reached out to lift her in his arms and placed her on the saddle in front of him. Holding her tightly, he spurred his horse forward.

The sun made its final lunge from the horizon to kiss the watermelon sky of a new day and a new life, for all of them.

*She was all things
to two men.*

**LOVE
AND
WAR**

PATRICIA
HAGAN

*Across a landscape consumed by the scorching
emotions of Civil War, comes an epic
tale of love and conflict, desire and hate,
of beautiful, rebellious Katherine Wright
who was abducted, ravished, and torn
between two men:*

*Nathan Collins, the Rebel,
who dreamed of making Katherine his wife,
but would never accept her craving
for a life of her own.*

*Travis Coltrane, the Yankee,
who made her wild with fury one moment,
and delirious with passion the next.*

*Two loyalties. Two loves.
One triumphant saga that rips across
war-torn lands and the embattled terrains
of the heart!*

Avon 47704 $2.50 LW 10/79